D1602934

STORIES
OF WOMEN

ANTON CHEKHOV

STORIES OF WOMEN

Includes 12 Stories Never Before Translated into English

An Original Translation by Paula P. Ross

Prometheus Books
59 John Glenn Drive
Amherst, New York 14228-2197

Published 1994 by Prometheus Books

98 97 96 95 94   5 4 3 2 1

Library of Congress Cataloging-in-Publication Data

Chekhov, Anton Pavlovich, 1860–1904.
    [Short stories. English. Selections]
    Stories of women / Anton Chekhov : an original translation by Paula
P. Ross
        p.   cm.
    ISBN 0-87975-893-7 (cloth · alk. paper) —
ISBN 0-87975-901-1 (pbk. : alk. paper)
    1. Women—Fiction. 2. Chekhov, Anton Pavlovich, 1860–1904—
Translations into English. I. Ross, Paula P., 1921–   . II. Title.
PG3456.A13R67   1994
891.73′3—dc20   94-6501
                                                                CIP

Printed in the United States of America on acid-free paper.

For my daughters, daughters-in-law, and granddaughters

"A chicken is not a bird; and a woman is not a man."

—old Russian saying

ANTON PAVLOVICH CHEKHOV was born on January 17, 1860, in Taganrog, a port on the Sea of Azov. His father, a small shopkeeper, had been born a serf, but his grandfather had saved enough money to buy freedom for himself and his sons.

Chekhov had four brothers and one sister, and their needs were a primary concern for him during his entire life. The family lived in a miserable neighborhood and their one-story house had a shop in the front and a tavern in the basement. The tyrannical father did not spare the boys in any way, and Anton was an often-flogged little garbage man and bartender.

In a letter to one of his brothers, Chekhov later wrote:

> I beg you to remember that despotism and lies destroyed your mother's youth. Despotism and lies have spoiled our youth to such a degree that it is loathsome and terrible to recall it. Remember the fear and revulsion we felt every time Father threw his indignant and furious tantrums at the dinner table because the soup was too salty, reviling and insulting our mother as if she were a dim-witted imbecile.

At age sixteen, Chekhov was left to fend for himself when his father moved the family to Moscow in order to escape debtor's prison. Anton remained in Taganrog where he was in school on a scholarship. Away from his father, his true nature blossomed and replaced misery with a youthful exuberance to which was added a passion for the theater and music.

After finishing school in Taganrog, Chekhov went to Moscow, where he studied medicine at the University on scholarship. To help with his family's finances, he started publishing articles, tales, jokes, and anecdotes. By the time that he earned his medical degree in 1884, his main interest was writing. His medical practice furnished him with constant contact with uninhibited human beings who in their weakened states provided him with an infinite amount of material— and skepticism. He wrote that medicine was his "legal wife" and that literature was his "mistress."

Chekhov's literary reputation grew with the publication of his collection *Motley Stories* (1886). In 1888 he was awarded the Pushkin Prize for another collection, *In the Twilight*. This, and publication of his story "The Steppe" (1888), established him as one of Russia's leading writers.

All of Chekhov's writing reflects the man himself. From age fourteen, when he had his first attack of pleurisy, until his death, he was often desperately ill. He understood the importance of what he called "life's trifles" and rarely neglected these in his writing. In the conduct of his life he was the epitome of all that was kind, generous, witty, and humane, and he was an inveterate optimist. On his deathbed, he wrote: "life and people are becoming better and better, wiser and more honorable. . . ." But he did not believe in shifting responsibility for one's behavior to circumstances and society. The human being, he intensely believed, was perfectly competent to judge right from wrong. This did not make him popular with the future socialist revolutionaries, and adverse criticisms of his work were at times purely political.

Chekhov has been known best in the English-speaking world for his plays, which he wrote in the last years of his life: *The Seagull* (1896), *Uncle Vanya* (1897), *The Three Sisters* (1901), and *The Cherry Orchard* (1904). His stories, however, were greatly admired from the beginning and were translated into many European languages soon after publication in Russia.

In 1901 Chekhov married the actress Olga Knipper, who played leading roles in several of his plays that were staged by the Moscow Art Theater. He died of tuberculosis on July 2, 1904, at a German health resort in Badenweiler.

Table of Contents

Introduction

Why a collection of stories describing women by Anton Pavlov Chekhov today? Are they relevant today? His characters are from a specific historic time, a specific place, but the problems may be generated from the same source. When our forefathers and mothers spent all of their time struggling to exist, the complementary natures of men and women were exercised to produce the most for the least—a necessary division of labor. Both worked and loved by doing what came naturally. They did not accept a "media's" instructions as to what their goals should be or how they should satisfy their sexual drives—let alone make love!

When Chekhov began writing, woman in Russia was virtually man's possession. A wife was the slave of her husband. She had no civil identity such as a passport or a resident permit, i.e., she had no legal existence without her husband's permission. She had limited inheritance rights although she could own property. She was magnanimously allowed to inherit one-seventh of her husband's real estate and one-fourth of his personal estate. If she were a peasant woman, she had *no* rights. The evolution of women's awareness began primarily with the emancipation of the serfs in 1861 and the granting of permission for women to attend university lectures. A woman's education before this was whatever the home provided or at the finishing schools for the female gentry, that kept them illiterate and taught them to remain submissive and passive. At this time women of means began to go abroad to schools where they were not treated like sheep. When they returned home, they began to participate in protests, which in the 1880s led to a reactionary movement and the closing of university doors to women until 1897.

Education did become a means to independence. The independent woman's traditional employment, however, was not too different from that of today. Women were typists, sales girls, librarians, elementary school teachers, governesses, and the like. Peasant women were the workhorses in the homes, the fields, and the factories. But women of character and class found ways of overcoming their second-class citizenship without giving up whatever it was that they cherished: status, children, comfort, "freedom," stability, or security. The stories I have selected describe these women in all their complexity. I chose those which I empathized with the most and which I believed would speak to the liberated woman of today. As independent women we may be making a serious mistake in behaving like men when we participate in a man's world. If we cannot "see what we are like," we will continue to pay for our denial of uniqueness. I believe the essential message in all the tales which I have chosen is that women are not men and that humor, love, and work are the components that give meaning to life.

In Chekhov's day women listened with "enraptured faces" to the sound of military trumpets. Today women follow male sports with the same enthusiasm as their men. When Russian women became bored with the men they married for economic security, if they were clever, they had their extramarital relationships, just as today. Men found "pink stockings" more desirable than "blue stockings," so if a woman wanted a man, she played the game even though her husband might stray to a "blue stocking" for some decent conversation with a woman. Office romances are nothing new, as are sexual harassment, wife abuse, low pay, "women ask for it," "she's an albatross around my neck," "women are frivolous, unfaithful, petty, weak, slavish, belong in a convent," and so on.

With great humor, brevity, and some truth, "My Wives" says it all. "A Case History" describes the human tragedy of the well-meaning, passive, gentle woman being dominated by a shrewd, self-serving, arrogant governess. That a woman's revenge can be just as vicious as a man's is the essence of "The Court Investigator." On the other hand, "The Lowest of the Low" is not the story of a beggar but a eulogy in praise of a hard-working peasant woman who performs the kind of selfless, generous act of charity that is rarely exhibited by men whose egocentricity prevents them from giving without a quid pro quo. Women's illusions are a favorite topic, but illusions have a function. "The Sweetie" (translated previously as "The Darling") is full of illusions that are based on a genuine need for love and work in order to cope with the troublesome realities of existence. "Life's Afflictions" describes good deeds and infinite patience as the remedy for disillusions. There's lots of sly comedy in this one. Why not retire to a convent?

"Too Late the Flowers," like Alan Paton's "Too Late the Phalarope," bemoans the tragedy of shortsightedness, a woman's fantasies about men when she is innocent, and the scorn heaped upon her for her self-effacement. A woman who is poor is the most unfortunate of all creatures. In this story Chekhov suffers for both the man and the woman, the crude doctor and the refined lady. He has his work but no love, she has no work but is overflowing with love. Ultimately, these two resolve the enigma and find each other— but too late. In "Anna Around the Neck" the poor, unappreciated, self-effacing woman finds another solution. She exploits her female charms to the hilt and turns into the kind of woman the men admired: a frivolous, pretty vamp.

All the characters define themselves by their behavior. If you're stupid, you behave stupidly; if you're shrewd, you behave shrewdly, and so on. The women are weak, strong, simple, complex, ignorant, intelligent, cruel, generous, vindictive, dominating, self-effacing, cowardly, and courageous, and behave accordingly. Can we say the same thing today? I think so. The differences are minor. The trivialities of life make or break relationships between men and women depending upon how women handle them. Customs permit the outside world to step between two people who probably belong together, and communication is as difficult as it has ever been. There is a lack of appreciation for woman's roles, especially as nurturer, which is not only undervalued but scorned today as it was yesterday. The question remains: Can woman survive if she exists in a state of denial, hypocrisy, suppressed potentiality, desensitization, wretchedness? This is the question Chekhov asks.

It is true that I have excluded some important stories that might belong in this collection. On the other hand, I wanted to select those which were most direct and true. All good stories are not true. I have also included early stories that were never translated before, either because they were not available or probably because they were considered too crude by self-appointed critics. Channing Pollock once said: "A critic is a legless man who teaches running." I hope the reader will agree with me that these stories belong here.

In a letter to his brother Alexander, Chekhov wrote that "the center of gravity should be two: he and she. . . ." My concluding selection, "He and She," finds gravity a bit boring at times, but sticks to it!

For those who wish to object to my too "literal" translation, I can only say that I have tried to retain the original flavor of what was written not in English but in Russian, and at the same time absorb the reader. Ellipses have been retained throughout the text as they are in the original stories. Their purpose was to indicate hesitation in the thought or action, and to suggest passage of time.

—Paula P. Ross

At the Cottage

I love you. You are my life, my happiness—my all! Forgive me for acknowledging this, but I no longer have the strength to suffer and be silent. I beg you, not for reciprocity but for sympathy. Please be in the old arbor at eight o'clock this evening. . . . I consider signing my name superfluous, but do not be frightened by anonymity. I am young, and good looking. . . . Do you need anything else?"

Having read this note, summer resident Pavel Ivanich Vihodtsev, an upright family man, shrugged his shoulders and scratched his head in perplexity.

"What kind of devilishness is this?" he thought.

"I'm a married man and suddenly here's this strange, stupid note! Who wrote this?"

Pavel Ivanich waved the letter before his eyes and read it again and spat.

"I love you," he mimicked. "You've found someone wet behind the ears! That's the kind that will hurry to you in the arbor! I, mother mine, I've weaned myself from this kind of romantic *fleur d'amour*. H'm! It must be some kind of mischievous, good-for-nothing. . . . Women! Anyhow, it must be, dear God, a hussy in order to write such a note to a stranger, and a married man at that! Downright demoralized!"

In all the eight years of his married life, Pavel Ivanich had become unaccustomed to flirtations and had not received any notes, besides congratulations, and because he was not a vain boaster, the aforementioned note puzzled and upset him.

An hour later he was lying on a couch and thought:

"Of course, I'm not a young boy and will not rush to hold this rendezvous, but all the same it would be interesting to know who wrote this? H'm. . . . The handwriting, doubtless, is a woman's. . . . The note was written with sincerity, from the heart, and is hardly a joke. . . . Probably some kind of psychotic widow. . . . Widows are generally light-headed and eccentric. H'm. . . . Who could it be?"

To answer this question was even more difficult, since in the entire summer colony Pavel Ivanich did not know any women except wives.

"Strange. . . ." He could not figure it out. " 'I love you.' . . . How could she have come to fall in love with me? Amazing woman! To fall in love this way, without rhyme or reason, isn't even acquainted with me, doesn't know me, what kind of person I am. . . . It must be that she is still very young and romantically inclined if she can fall in love after two or three glances. . . . But . . . who is she?"

Suddenly Pavel Ivanich recalled that yesterday, and the day before yesterday, when he was taking a walk around the vicinity of the cottages, several times he had met a young blonde in a light blue blouse and with a little snub nose. The blonde did give him the once over every now and then, and when he sat on a bench, she sat down beside him. . . .

"Was she the one?" thought Vihodtsev. "Can't be! It's really delicate; an ephemeral human being could fall in love with such an old, worn out ogre like myself? It's not possible!"

At dinner Pavel Ivanich glanced dully at his wife and considered:

"She's written that she's young and good-looking. . . . That means she's not old. . . . H'm. . . . She spoke sincerely, and honestly, I'm not so old and mean that it would be impossible for me to fall in love. . . . A woman loves me! And love isn't bad for anyone—you can even fall in love with an old goat. . . ."

"What are you pondering about?" asked his wife.

"That . . . I have a headache . . . ," lied Pavel Ivanich.

He decided that it was foolish to attract attention over such a bagatelle as a love note; he laughed at it and its author, but—alas!—man is his own worst enemy. After dinner Pavel Ivanich lay on his bed and along with planning to sleep, he thought:

"But really, excuse me, she hopes that I will come! What a little dummy! I imagine that it will be unnerving and upsetting for her when she doesn't find me in the arbor! . . . No, I will not go. . . . So!"

But, I repeat, man is his own worst enemy.

"However, all the same, I'll go out of curiosity . . . ," he thought a half hour later. "I'll go and take a look from afar to find out what kind of a prank this is. . . . Interesting to observe! Only to have a laugh! Honestly, why not have a little laugh if opportunity presents itself?"

Pavel Ivanich got out of bed and began to dress.

"Where are you going all dressed up?" asked his wife, noting that he had put on a clean shirt and a fashionable tie.

"Just . . . to take a walk. . . . I have a headache for some reason. . . . Ehem. . . ."

Pavel Ivanich had dressed up, waited for eight o'clock, and then left the house. When his eyes observed the bright green setting, overflowing with the light of the setting sun, the colorful figures of the well-dressed cottagers, male and female, his heart began to thump.

"Which one is she?" he thought, shyly sneaking a look at the cottagers' faces. "But, there is no blonde. . . . H'm. . . . If she wrote it, she's probably sitting in the arbor now."

Vihodtsev entered the side street at the end of which behind the young foliage of tall lime trees was found the "old arbor." . . . He quietly moved towards it. . . .

"I'll look from afar . . . ," he thought, hesitatingly moving forward. "Now, why am I shy? I'm not really going for a rendezvous! What a fool! Go boldly! What if I did go into the arbor? But, but . . . not for anything!"

Pavel Ivanich's heart beat even faster. Involuntarily, not wanting this himself, he immediately imagined himself in the dimly lit arbor. In his imagination flashed an elegant blonde in a light blue blouse and with a little snub nose. . . . He imagined that she would be ashamed of her love and her whole body would tremble as she modestly approached him, breathing ardently and . . . suddenly embracing him.

"If I weren't married, this would be nothing," he thought, erasing from his mind these sinful thoughts. "However . . . once in one's life it wouldn't hurt to experience, or you'll die not knowing what sort of thing this is. And my wife . . . but what about her? Thank God, for eight years I haven't strayed one step. . . . Eight years of impeccable duty! For her it will be . . . vexing even. . . . I'll take a chance, and with bad luck, might be unfaithful!"

His whole body trembling and holding his breath, Pavel Ivanich walked towards the arbor, which was densely covered with wild grape vines and ivy. He glanced into it. The smell of mold and dampness hit him. . . .

"It seems no one's there . . . ," he thought, entering the arbor, and then saw a human silhouette in the corner. . . .

The silhouette belonged to a man. Peering intently at him, Pavel Ivanich recognized his brother-in-law, Mitu, a student who was living with them at the cottage.

"Oh, it's you?" he muttered in a displeased voice, taking off his hat and sitting down.

"Yes, I . . . ," answered Mitu.

Several minutes went by in silence.

"Excuse me, Pavel Ivanich," began Mitu, "but I beg you to leave me here alone. . . . I'm trying to concentrate on my dissertation and the presence of others distracts me."

"Well, go to some dark sidestreet," Pavel Ivanich incisively remarked. "It is easier to think in the fresh air, and . . . I had wished to be able to take a nap on the bench. . . . It's not so hot here. . . ."

"You need to sleep and I need to think of my composition . . . ," grumbled Mitu. "The composition is more important. . . ."

Silence reigned again. . . . Pavel Ivanich, who had already given his free will over to his imagination, but in reality heard steps, jumped up suddenly and exclaimed in a whining voice:

"Well, I beg you, Mitu! You are younger than I and you must respect . . . I don't feel well and . . . I want to sleep. . . . Leave!"

"That's egotistical. . . . Why is it undoubtedly right that you are entitled to be here and not I? The principle is not apparent. . . ."

"Okay, please! I am an egoist, a despot, a fool, but I beg you! For the first time in my life, I plead! Respect my wishes!"

Mitu turned his head away. . . .

"What an animal . . . ," thought Pavel Ivanich. "With him around there won't be any rendezvous! It will be impossible!"

"Listen, Mitu," he said. "I beg you for the last time. . . . Show that you are a wise, humane, and learned person!"

"I don't understand why you want to stick around?" Mitu shrugged his shoulders. "I have said I will remain because of principle."

At this time, suddenly a female face with a snub nose glanced into the arbor.

Seeing Mitu and Pavel Ivanich, the face frowned and disappeared.

"She left!" Pavel Ivanich thought and looked angrily at Mitu. "She saw this scoundrel and left! It's all over!"

Waiting a bit more, Vihodtsev got up, put on his hat and declared:

"You're an animal, a scoundrel, and a villain! Yes! A beast! You're low-down and stupid! I don't want to have anything more to do with you!"

"Much obliged!" muttered Mitu, also getting up and putting on his hat. "You know that by your presence you have done me such a dirty trick that I will not forgive you even on my death bed!"

Pavel Ivanich left the arbor so angry that he had lost all self-control, and speedily headed for his cottage. . . . Even seeing the dining table all set for supper did not calm him down.

"Once in my life to have such an opportunity," he continued to agitate himself, "and to have it interfered with! Now she's insulted . . . devastated!"

During supper Pavel Ivanich and Mitu stared at their plates and sullenly remained silent. They both harbored an infinite hatred toward each other.

"What are you smiling about?" Pavel Ivanich snapped at his wife. "Only a fool laughs without a reason!"

His wife looked at his sour puss and burst out laughing.

"What was that note you received this morning?" she asked him.

"I? . . . None at all . . . ," answered a confused Pavel Ivanich. "You're making something up. . . . It's your imagination."

"Come on, tell us about it! Fess up, you received it! After all, I sent this note to you! Word of honor, I did! Ha-ha!"

Pavel Ivanich blushed and directed his attention to his dinner plate.

"Stupid jokes," he muttered.

"What was I to do? You yourself could justify it. We had to get the floors washed today, and how were you to be gotten out of the house? Only in this way could you be gotten rid of. . . . Now, now, don't be angry, silly. . . . So that it wouldn't be boring for you in the arbor, you must know that I sent Mitu the same kind of note! Mitu, were you in the arbor?"

Mitu smirked and stopped looking with hatred at his competitor.

1886

The Pink Stocking

T he day was rainy and dreary. The sky had been cloudy for some time and the end of the rain was not in sight. Outside it was all slush, puddles, and wet black crows, and inside the rooms were so cold and dark that it was necessary to fire up the stoves.

Ivan Petrovich Samov is strutting back and forth in his study and grumbling about the weather. The raindrops like tears on the window panes and the darkness of the rooms depress him. He is unbearably bored and has no way of killing time. . . . The newspaper hasn't been delivered yet, it was impossible to go hunting, and it was still far from time to dine. . . .

Samov is not alone in his study. Sitting at his desk is Madame Samov, a small, good-looking little dame in a sheer blouse and pink stockings. She is diligently writing a letter. Every time Ivan Petrovich walks by her, he looks over her shoulders to see what she has written. He sees large, far from perfect script, narrow and scraggly, with impossible tails and flourishes. The paper is full of blots, corrections, and fingerprints. Madame Samov does not like carrying over so she writes to the very edge of the paper—with enormous effort and cascading downward. . . .

"Lidochka, to whom are you writing so much?" asks Samov, seeing that his wife is starting to write on a sixth page.

"To my sister, Vera. . . ."

"Hm . . . it is long! It will be really tedious to read!"

"Take and read it, only there is really nothing interesting. . . ."

Samov takes the written sheets and continues to pace while read-

21

ing. Lidochka rests her elbows on the back of the chair and follows the expressions on his face. After the first page he pulled a long face and appeared dumbfounded. . . . By the third page Samov frowns and slowly scratches the back of his neck. By the fourth page he stops, timidly looks at his wife, and falls to thinking. A bit later, sighing, he renews reading. . . . His face expresses incredulity and even fright. . . .

"No, this is impossible!" he grumbles, finishing reading and flinging the sheets on the desk. "Decidedly impossible!"

"What is it?" asks frightened Lidochka.

"What is it! You wrote six pages, spent two hours writing, and . . . and it is nothing to you! If there were just one little evidence of thought! You read, read, and some kind of blankness takes over, as if you're deciphering the Chinese gibberish on tea boxes! Oof!"

"Yes, that's true, Vanya . . . ," says the blushing Lidochka. "I wrote carelessly. . . ."

"Why the hell carelessly? Even when one writes carelessly, there is thought and harmony, there is substance, but you . . . excuse me, I can't even find a name for it! It's sheer balderdash! Words and phrases but not the slightest bit of substance. Your whole letter, word for word, reminds me of the babble of two little kids: 'We had *blini* today!' 'A soldier visited us!' It's shocking! You drag things out, repeat yourself. . . . Thoughts hop around like dervishes in a cage. You don't distinguish beginnings and endings. . . . How is this possible?"

"If I wrote with care," Lidochka tries to justify herself, "then there wouldn't be any mistakes. . . ."

"Ugh, I'm no longer speaking of mistakes! It is screaming poor grammar! It is an insult to the reader when there are no lines, no commas, no periods, and the spelling! The handwriting? It's not handwriting but a desperate effort. I'm not making jokes, Lid. . . . I was amazed and agitated by your letter. . . . You must not be angry, darling, but I really did not realize that your grammar was so lousy. . . . And besides, with your background—you belong to educated, intellectual circles, you are the wife of an academician, daughter of a general! Tell me, didn't you ever study anywhere?"

"How is it? I completed studies at the Pension von Mebki."

Samov shrugs his shoulders and heaves a sigh, and continues pacing. Lidochka is aware of her ignorance and is ashamed, and also sighs and casts her eyes down. About ten minutes pass in silence.

"Listen, Lidochka, you know that really this is terrible!" exclaims Samov, suddenly stopping in front of his wife and looking at her as if in shock. "You are a mother. . . . Do you understand? A mother! How will you be able to teach your children if you yourself know nothing? You have a good brain, but what use is it if it hasn't even elementary knowledge in it? Well, I don't give a hang if you don't know anything. . . . The children will learn in school, but you know practically nothing about moral training! You make such a botch of things that it makes me sick."

Samov shrugs his shoulders again, thrusts his hands into the flaps of his jacket, and continues to pace. . . . He is appalled and vexed, but at the same time he is sorry for Lidochka, who does not protest, but only blinks her eyes. . . . It is difficult and unfortunate for both of them. . . . Because of their distress they do not notice how time is flying and that dinner time was approaching.

Sitting down at the table, Samov, liking to eat elegantly and restfully, drinks a large glass of wine and shifts the conversation to another topic. Lidochka listens to him, nods agreement, but suddenly when the soup was served, her eyes filled with tears, and she began to whimper.

"It's my mother's fault!" she cries, wiping her tears away with her napkin. "Everybody advised her to send me to the high school, and I certainly would have been sent to college from there!"

"To college . . . high school . . . ," grumbles Samov. "That's the limit, little mother! What's the use of those 'blue stockings'? The 'blue stocking' . . . what the deuce! She's neither a woman nor a man, and thus is in the middle of a half, neither here nor there. . . . I detest 'blue stockings'! I would never marry an intellectual. . . ."

"You aren't clear . . . ," says Lidochka. "You are angry that I'm a know-nothing, and at the same time you hate erudite women; you resent that I write thoughtlessly, but in spite of that you don't want me to know anything."

"You're nit-picking about words, darling," says Samov, and out of ennui pours himself another drink. . . .

Under the influence of the wine and the satisfying dinner, Samov feels more pleasant, kinder, and gentler. He sees how his good-looking wife has a disturbed face as she is preparing the salad, and he is overwhelmed by a burst of love for his wife, condescending and all-forgiving. . . .

"Poor thing, I discouraged her today for no reason," he thought. "Why did I say such unfortunate words to her? She is, it is true, a little dummy to me, uncivilized, narrow, but . . . a medal has two sides and *audiatur et altera pars.** It may be a thousand times more correct, as some say, that female lack of intelligence is fundamental to femininity. . . . She is called, I suggest, to love her husband, give birth to children, and to toss the salad, so why the hell does she need to be educated? Of course!"

Along with these thoughts he recalls how learned women generally are difficult, how demanding they are, stern and stubborn, and how, on the other hand, it is easy to live with stupid little Lidochka, who is never vain, doesn't comprehend much, and does not easily criticize. Life with Lidochka is peaceful and you don't risk not being in control. . . .

"Forget about them, these smart, educated women! It's better and more peaceful to live with the simple ones . . . ," he thinks, taking a plate of chicken from Lidochka.

Recollecting that a sophisticated man does want to converse a bit and exchange ideas with a smart and educated woman . . . "So what?" thinks Samov. "When I want to chat with an intellectual I'll go to Natalie Andreevna . . . or to Maria Frantceva. . . . Very simple!"

1886

---

*"the opposite side needs to be heard"

The Nincompoop

T he other day I called to my office the governess of my children, Julia Vasilevna. It was time to settle accounts.

"Please be seated, Julia Vasilevna," I said to her. "We must do some calculating. Certainly you need money, but you have such good manners that you do not make a request. . . . Now. . . . We agreed upon thirty rubles a month. . . ."

"Upon forty . . ."

"No, upon thirty . . . I have it recorded. . . . I have always paid the governesses thirty rubles. . . . Let's see, you have spent two months here. . . ."

"Two months and five days . . ."

"Exactly two months . . . I have it recorded. It means you are entitled to sixty rubles. . . . Subtract nine Sundays—you know you were not occupied with Kolya on Sundays, and only went strolling—and three holidays. . . ."

Julia Vasilevna flushed and wanted to have a chance to protest but . . . not a word from her!

"Three holidays. Subtract, it follows, twelve rubles. . . . Four days when Kolya was sick and you were free of him and only had Vara. . . . You had a toothache for three days and my wife permitted you to be free after dinner. . . . That's twelve plus seven—nineteen. Deduct . . . that leaves . . . hmm . . . forty-one rubles. Correct?"

Julia Vasilevna's left eye reddened and became moist. Her chin quivered. She coughed nervously, blew her nose, but—not a word from her! . . .

"On New Year's Eve you broke a china cup and saucer. Subtract two rubles. . . . The cup is much more valuable—it is a family heirloom, but . . . we'll forget about that! What haven't we lost! Later, because you did not keep your eyes on Kolya, he climbed a tree and tore his jacket. . . . Subtract ten. . . . The maid, also because you were negligent and did not watch her, stole Vara's boots. You must be responsible for everything. You are paid a salary. And so, this means, another five rubles must be subtracted. . . . On the tenth of January I gave you ten rubles. . . ."

"I didn't get them!" whispered Julia Vasilevna.

"But I have it recorded!"

"Oh, well . . . forget it."

"From forty-one rubles subtract twenty-seven—this leaves fourteen."

Both her eyes were now full of tears. . . . Perspiration appeared on the long, pretty little nose. Poor girl!

"Only once was I given anything," she said with a quivering voice. "I had three rubles from your wife. . . . No more. . . ."

"Really? Wouldn't you know it, I don't have it recorded! Subtract three from fourteen and that leaves eleven rubles. . . . Here's your money, my pretty one! Three . . . three, three . . . one and one. . . . Take it please!"

And I gave her eleven rubles. . . . She took them with shaking fingers and put them in her pocket.

"*Merci,*" she whispered.

I jumped up and paced the room. I was overcome with anger.

"What are you saying *merci* for?" I asked.

"For the money . . ."

"But you know I fleeced you, damn it, robbed you! You know I stole from you! For this you thank me?"

"In other places I was not given all . . ."

"Not given? And not so subtly! I was playing a joke on you, teaching you a cruel lesson. I will give you all eighty rubles I owe you! They are ready for you in this envelope! But, is it possible that such meanness is common? Why didn't you protest? Why are you silent? Is it possible that on this earth there is one so slow to respond? Is it possible that there really is such a nincompoop?"

She smiled bitterly, and I could see from her face: "It is possible!"

I asked for her forgiveness for the cruel lesson and to her great amazement gave her the eighty rubles. She shyly *mercied* me and left. . . . My eyes watched her leave and I thought: "How easy it is to be strong in this world!"

1883

The Good Fortune of Being a Woman

I t was the funeral of Lieutenant-General Zapuperin. In the home of the dead man funereal music droned. Commanding words filled the air. Crowds rushed from all sides wanting to take a look at the casket as it was being carried out. In the crowd were the bureaucrats Probkin and Svistkov, and they were pressing to get near the exit. They were accompanied by their wives.

"No further, sirs!"

They were stopped by one of the assistants of the police as they approached the boundary line. He had a kindly, sympathetic face.

"No further, sirs! Please back up a little! Gentlemen, you know we aren't the ones making the rules! Please, back up! Even so, however, the ladies can come through. . . . Please, Mesdames, but . . . you, gentlemen, for God's sake . . ."

The wives of Probkin and Svistkov blushed at the unexpected kindness of the police assistant and plunged through the line, while their husbands remained on the side of the living wall. They were left to contemplate the backs of the pedestrians and the guards on horseback.

"They got through!" enviously exclaimed Probkin and looked, almost with hatred, at the retreating dames. "Really, those chignons are fortunate! The male sex will never have such privileges as those given the female. What's so special about them? Women can say the most ordinary things, full of prejudices, and get away with it, but we men, even though we are state councillors, can't get away with anything."

"Your reasoning is strange, gentlemen!" exclaimed the police assistant, looking reproachfully at Probkin. "To let you in now would start

28

an ugly pushing and shoving; ladies, on the other hand, because of their delicateness, would never permit themselves anything of the kind!"

"Enough, please!" exclaimed the angry Probkin. "Dames in a crowd always push first. A man seeks to come to the point, but a dame pushes and spreads her arms so that her clothes won't get crushed. Enough said! The female sex always has the advantage. They don't even allow women to be soldiers, and they are admitted free to evening dances, and are free from corporal punishment. Tell me why they deserve such privileges? A babe drops her handkerchief, you pick it up; she enters the room, you get up and give her your seat; she leaves and you conduct her. . . . Let's talk about rank! In order to become district councillors, you and I need to work at it all our lives, while a dame in a half-hour will get herself engaged to a district councillor—and immediately she's somebody. In order for me to become a prince or a count I'd have to conquer all of society, be Shipki's son-in-law, attend ministries, while some, forgive me Lord, Varenka or Katenka, still wet behind the ears, twirls her train before a count, screws up her eyes—and becomes somebody. You, you are now the provincial secretary. . . . It can be said that you achieved rank with blood and sweat, but your Maria Fomishna? How did she get to be the wife of the provincial secretary? From being the daughter of a priest straight to an official's wife? A fine official's wife! Let her near our work and she'll take no time in checking all your comings and goings."

"That's why a woman gives birth in pain," noted Svistkov.

"Big deal! If she would stand before the powers that be when they are letting loose the cold weather, they would show her consideration. They are privileged in everything! Any babe or dame in our set can blurt out to a general what you wouldn't dare to say even if you were to be flogged. Yes . . . your Maria Fomishna can boldly walk arm-in-arm with the state councillor, but you just take the state councillor by the arm! Take him, try it! In our house, just below us, brother, there lives some kind of professor and his wife. A general, understand, he has the First Order of Anna, but you can hear how his wife nags: 'Fool! Fool! Fool!' And you know she's just a simple hag from the lower-middle classes. However, if you're legally tied, so be it. . . . From time immemorial it's been so laid out, that legally tied can berate, but take those not legally bound! What do they permit themselves! I'll never forget one situation. This guy was almost dead and his surviving parents had to be called to say the prayers.

"Remember last year, when our general left on vacation to his country home, he took me with him to take care of correspondence. . . . It was petty work which only took about an hour. He finished his end of it and went out to the woods for a walk or to listen to his lackey's gossip. Our general—he's a bachelor. The house—had everything— servants like dogs, but no wife to give instructions. The workers were all dissipated, disobedient . . . and over the boss was a hag, the housekeeper Vera Nikitishna. She pours the tea, orders the dinners, and yells at the servants. . . . A hag, as you are my brother, dirty, venomous, and has a satanic look. Fat, red-faced, shrill. . . . When she begins to yell at someone, the screech is so high that even saints couldn't stand it. Even her berating wasn't as exasperating as the shrieking. Lord! Nobody could get away from her. Not only the servants, but me too—the rogue bullied me. But I figured to myself, just wait. I'll grab a minute with the general and tell him everything about you. He's too absorbed, I thought, and doesn't notice what's going on with the servants—how they are robbing him, how the people are muttering—wait a bit, I'll open his eyes.

"And, brother, did I open his eyes. I opened his eyes so that my own eyes were almost closed forever, so that now when I recall it, it makes me feel sick.

"I'm walking in the corridor once and I suddenly hear a shriek. At first I thought that a pig was being slaughtered; then I cocked an ear and hear that it's Vera Nikitishna quarreling with someone. 'You creep! You're such a bitch! Devil! . . .' Who was that? I'm thinking. And suddenly, brother, I see the door open and out runs our general, all red, eyes puffed out, his hair as if the devil had blown on it, and she's following him: 'Scoundrel! Devil!' "

"You're lying!"

"Word of honor. You know that threw me into a funk. Our general rushed into his office. I'm standing in the corridor, and like a fool I don't understand anything. A simple, uneducated hag, a cook, smelly—and she permits herself such words and deeds! That meant, I thought, that the general wanted to fire her, and she, thinking there weren't any witnesses, allowed herself to rail against him. It was time for me to get moving! It tore me up. . . . I went to her room and said: 'How dare you, worthless reprobate, to say such things to a superior personage? You think that he is such a weak old man that no one will take his part?' You know I took it upon myself to smack her fat cheeks twice. She let out a shriek, brother, bellowed out as if it were three times worse than it was, sorry to say. I closed my ears and went out into the woods."

"About two hours later, a boy runs to meet me. 'Please, the master wants you.' "

"I go. I enter. He's sitting, scowling like a turkey and does not look at me."

" 'What is this?' he says. 'Are you trying to take over my home?' 'How is that,' I ask. 'If,' I add, 'you are speaking about Nikitishna, your honor, then I stepped in for your sake.' 'It's none of your business,' he says, 'to meddle into the family affairs of others!' Do you understand? Family affairs! Then he began, brother, to throw the book at me and began to make it so hot for me that I almost dropped dead! He went on and on, laid the law down to me, and then suddenly, brother, he roared with laughter for no reason at all. 'And how,' he asks, 'how were you able to do this? How did you get so brave? Amazing! But, I hope, my friend, that this all remains between the two of us. . . . I understand your warmth but it is agreed that you can no longer stay in my home.'

"There, brother! It was even amazing to him how I could strike such a peahen. The hag has blinded him! He's a big shot, has the Order of the White Eagle, has no boss over him, but submits to a woman! Brother, the privileges of the female sex!"

"But. . . . Take your hat off! They're bringing out the general. . . . So many decorations, holy smoke! But really, they let the dames in ahead of us, but what do they really understand about all these decorations?"

The music died down.

1885

The Sweetie

Olyenka was the daughter of a retired middle-level government employee, Plemyanikov. She was sitting on the porch of their home, seemingly deep in thought. It was hot, the pestering flies were troublesome, but it was pleasant to contemplate that it would soon be evening. Dark rain clouds were approaching from the east and from time to time the breeze felt damp.

In the middle of the yard stood Kukin, a private theatrical entrepreneur and manager of the Tivoli, the local amusement park. He had rented the cottage in her back yard. He was looking up at the sky.

"Again!" he exclaimed remorsefully. "It's going to rain again! Every day rain, rain, rain—as if on purpose! It's really a millstone around my neck! It'll be the death of me! Every day my losses are dreadful!"

He threw up his hands and turning to Olyenka, he continued:

"There you have it, Olga Semyonovna, such is our life. It's enough to make you cry! You work, you strive, you worry, you have sleepless nights, you're always thinking about how to improve things—and what for? On the other hand, you have the public—ignorant, barbarous. You present them with the best operettas, enchantment, magnificent couplets, but is this really desirable? Do they understand any of this? What they want is the vulgar primitive shows they have in the markets! Give them low-level trash! On the other hand, look at the weather. Practically every evening it is raining. It's been raining constantly since the tenth of May, all of the rest of May and June—

32

a disaster! I don't have any customers, so how am I to pay the rent, pay the actors?"

On the next day toward evening the clouds again were approaching and Kukin roared with a hysterical laugh:

"So what? Go ahead! Go ahead, at least immerse the whole park, at least drown me! You'd do me a favor to take me away from this world where there is no luck for me! The actors are suing me! What kind of a sentence will I get? Probably hard labor in Siberia! Probably on a scaffold! Ha-ha-ha!"

Olyenka listened quietly and seriously to Kukin, and it happened that tears began to fill her eyes. Finally, Kukin's misery touched her so that she fell in love with him. He was a little guy, emaciated, with a jaundiced-looking face and hair combed across his forehead; he spoke with a thin tenor voice, and when he spoke his mouth was distorted, and he always looked desperate, but all the same, he awoke in her genuine, deep feeling.

She could not live without having someone to love. Earlier she had loved her Papa, and he was now ill, always sitting in an armchair in a dark room and having difficulty with breathing. She had loved her aunt, who had at times, maybe once or twice a year, come to Bryansk; and still earlier when she was in junior high, she had loved her French teacher.

This was a quiet, good-natured, long-suffering genteel woman with a meek, gentle look, and very healthy. Looking at her full, rosy cheeks, on her soft white neck with its dark birthmark, on her kind, naive smile which remained on her face while she listened to something pleasant, men thought, "Hm, not so bad . . . ," and also smiled, and the female guests in the middle of a conversation could not refrain from grasping her hands and exclaiming in a burst of delight:

"What a sweetie you are!"

The house in which she had lived since birth and which was willed to her was located at the edge of the town, Tsiganska, not far from the park, Tivoli. In the evenings and nights you could hear the music from the park, how the rockets burst and crackled, and it seemed to her that Kukin was struggling with his fate and was defending himself against his chief enemy—the indifferent public. Her heart sweetly sank, she couldn't sleep, and when toward morning he returned home, she quietly knocked on the small window to her bedroom, and through the curtain she revealed only her face and one shoulder, while smiling sweetly. . . .

He proposed to her and they got married. And when he saw that her shoulders were full and strong like her throat, he spread out his hands and exclaimed:

"What a sweetie you are!"

He was happy, but since on the wedding day and during the night it rained, the look of despair did not leave his face.

The married couple lived well. She took care of the ticket window, looked after maintenance in the park, kept the books, and paid the workers. Her rosy cheeks, sweet, naive smile, so like an aura, flashed in the ticket window, behind the scenes, and in the snack bar. She now told her acquaintances that the most remarkable, the most important and necessary thing in the world was the theater. The theater provided the only true delight and one could only become well-educated and humane by learning from the theater.

"But does the public really understand this?" she would ask. "They need buffoonery! Yesterday we performed *Faust Turned Inside Out,* and almost all the loges were empty, but if we and Vanechkoy had put on some kind of banality, you can be sure the theater would be sold out. Tomorrow Vanechkoy and I will put on *Orpheus in Hell,* do come."

And whatever Kukin said about the theater and about the actors, she repeated it. Just as he did, she despised the public for its indifference to art, and for its ignorance. She interfered at rehearsals, corrected the actors, commented on the playing of the musicians, and when the local paper gave an uncomplimentary review of the theater, she cried and then went to the editor to have it out with him.

The actors loved her and called her "Vanechkoy and I" and "the sweetie." She was sorry for them and lent them a good bit, and if it so happened that they cheated her, she secretly cried and didn't let her husband know.

They lived well in the winter too. They rented a theater in town and sublet it for short periods to a Ukrainian troupe, to a magician, and to local amateurs. Olyenka put on a little weight and shone from pleasure while Kukin got thinner and more jaundiced, and moaned about the frightful losses, even though everything went well all winter. He coughed at night and she would make him drink raspberry and lime-blossom liquor, rubbed him with cologne, and muffled him in her soft shawls.

"How nice it is for me to have you!" she said perfectly sincerely, while stroking his hair. "How dear you are to me!"

During Lent he drove to Moscow to hire a troupe, and she couldn't sleep without him, and sat by the window all the time and gazed at the stars. At this time she compared herself with the chickens who also couldn't sleep and exhibited restlessness when the rooster wasn't in the henhouse.

Kukin was detained in Moscow and wrote that he would return by Easter and was making arrangements for the Tivoli. But on Monday before Easter, late in the evening, suddenly was heard a loud, ominous knock at the gate. Someone was banging on the gate and it sounded like thumping on a keg: boom! boom! boom! The sleepy cook, shuffling her bare feet along the lawn, hurried to open the gate.

"Be so kind as to open quickly!" someone with a deep basso voice cried out. "There is a telegram for you!"

Olyenka had gotten telegrams from her husband before, but for some reason she grew weak in the knees this time. She opened the telegram with shaking hands and read the following:

"Ivan Petrovich's death occurred suddenly today. Will wait until Tuesday for the funeral."

So it was stated in the telegram, "funeral" and the still not comprehended "occurred"; the signature was that of the opera troupe's director.

"My darling!" sobbed Olyenka. "My sweet Vasechka, my darling! Why did we meet? Why did I know and love you? For whom are you casting aside your poor, unfortunate Olyenka?"

They buried Kukin on Tuesday in one of Moscow's cemeteries. Olyenka returned home on Wednesday and as soon as she entered her room, she threw herself on the bed and sobbed so loudly that she could be heard on the street and in her neighbors' yards.

"What a sweetie!" exclaimed the neighbors, crossing themselves. "Dear Olyenka Semyonovna, little mother, how deeply affected she is!"

Three months passed. Olyenka, melancholy and in deep-mourning clothes, was returning from early mass. It so happened that walking alongside her, also returning from church, was one of her neighbors. Vasily Andreich Pustavalov was the forest supervisor for the merchant, Babakaev. He wore a straw hat and a white jacket with gold buttons and he looked more like landed gentry than a tradesman.

"Everything has its reason, Olga Semyonovna," he spoke gravely, with feeling in his voice, "and if someone close to us dies, it means that God wills it so, and in that case, we should remember this and submit to his will."

Walking Olyenka up to the gate, he said good-bye and went on his way. After this she could hear his grave voice every day and could hardly close her eyes without his dark beard presenting itself in her imagination. She was very attracted to him. It wasn't long before an older woman of slight acquaintance had coffee with her, and as soon as she sat down to the table immediately spoke about Pustavalov, that he was a fine, solid person and that all the unmarried women were after him. Three days later, Pustavalov himself came. He stayed only ten minutes, said little, but Olyenka fell in love with him—so much so that she couldn't sleep all night long, as if in a fever. In the morning she sent for the elderly woman. Soon after, they became engaged and then married.

Pustavalov and Olyenka as a married couple lived well. Usually, he remained in the lumber yard until lunch, and then left to do other jobs while Olyenka took his place. She stayed in the office 'til evening, did the bookkeeping, and released materials.

"The value of the forest now increases by twenty percent every year," she told customers and acquaintances. "Just think, previously we dealt only with local supplies of lumber, now Vasechka has to travel to Mogilyovska province. And the cost!" she would exclaim, covering both cheeks with her hands. "It's expensive!"

It seemed to her that she had been dealing in lumber for a long, long time; that lumber was the most important and necessary thing in life and that there was something for her that was dear, touching, in the words "beam," "shingle," "two-by-fours," "shutters," "not warped,""inventory." . . . At night she dreamt of mountains of boards and shingles, long endless lines of supply, stretching far beyond the town. She dreamt a whole regiment of two-by-fours and four-by-fours were attacking the lumber office, and how the boards, beams, and slabs knocked and gave off the booming sound of dry wood; all were falling and rising, pushing each other around. Olyenka screamed in her sleep and Pustavalov spoke tenderly to her:

"Olyenka, what's wrong, darling? Make the sign of the cross."

Whatever thoughts her husband had, she had the same ones. If he thought it was too warm in the room or that business was a little slow, she thought the same thing. Her husband didn't like any kind of entertainment, and on days off he sat at home and she did the same.

"You always stay at home or at the office," remarked her acquaintances. "You ought to go to the theater, dear, or to the circus."

"Vasechka and I never go to the theater," she replied sedately. "We are working people, we don't need triviality. What's in the theater that's worth anything?"

On Saturdays they attended evening service, on holidays they attended the earliest morning service, and returning from church walked arm-in-arm and with loving looks. They both emitted a lovely fragrance, and her silk clothing swished pleasantly. When they arrived home, they drank their tea with rich bread and a variety of jams, and then had some turnovers. Every noon one could smell in their yard and beyond the gates into the street the soup and roast lamb or duck, and on fast days—fish. And you couldn't pass their gate without having one's appetite aroused. The samovar was always hot in the office and the customers were always offered tea and bagels. Once a week they went to the bathhouse together, and both returned from there nicely flushed.

"No matter what, we live well," remarked Olyenka to her acquaintances. "Thank God. If only everyone could live like Vasechka and I do!"

When Pustavalov drove to Mogilyovska province for lumber,

she was terribly bored and spent the night crying and not sleeping. Sometimes the army veterinarian, Smirnin, came over in the evening. He was a young man who rented the cottage in the back yard. He told her about his experiences or played cards with her, and this was pleasant for her. Most interesting to her were the stories about his personal family life; he was married and had a son, but was separated from his wife since she had changed toward him and now he hated her. He sent her forty rubles a month for the son's maintenance. And hearing about this, Olyenka sighed and nodded her head, and she pitied him.

"Lord save us," she exclaimed as she lit his way to the steps and parted with him. "Thank you for lifting my boredom. God and the heavenly mother keep you well. . . ."

She spoke all this so sedately, so discreetly, imitating her husband. The veterinarian was already out the door but she called to him:

"You know, Vladimir Platonich, you should reconcile yourself with your wife. Forgive her for the sake of your son! The little boy probably understands everything."

When Pustavalov returned, she confided to him in a hushed voice the veterinarian's unhappy family life, and both sighed, nodded their heads, and then by some strange trend of thoughts, both went before the icon, bowed to the ground, and prayed that God would send them children.

And so the Pustavalovs lived quietly restrained and lovingly for six years. But one winter, Vasily Andreich having drunk hot tea, left the yard office without his cap in order to release some lumber, got chilled, and became ill. The best doctors attended him but the sickness continued. After being ill for four months he died, and Olyenka was a widow again.

"Why did you desert me, my darling?" she sobbed as they buried her husband. "How am I going to live without you, wretched, unfortunate creature that I am? You good people, have pity on me, an utter orphan with no one of my own. . . ."

All her clothing was now black and she foreswore forever gloves and hats, left the house rarely, and then only to go to church or the cemetery, and lived at home as if in a convent. After six months she took off her mourning attire and opened up the shutters on the windows. It was not long before she was seen at times in the mornings with her cook, going to the market, but how she lived now and what went on in her house was a matter of conjecture. For example, it was surmised by those who saw her in her garden drinking tea with the veterinarian while he read the newspaper to her that she was now involved with him. When she met one of her lady friends at the post office, she had told her:

"In this town we don't have proper veterinarian supervision and because of this we have a great deal of sickness. You often hear of people becoming sick from milk, and becoming infected from horses and cows. You must get involved in the health of domestic animals just as much as in the health of people."

She repeated the ideas of the veterinarian and now was of the same opinion as he in all things. It was obvious that she could not exist even for a year without being tied to someone and had found new happiness at home in the rented cottage. Others would have been criticized for this, but no one could think ill of Olyenka and everything in her life was sympathetically understood. She and the veterinarian didn't tell anyone of the change in their relationship and did try to keep it undercover, but they were unsuccessful because Olyenka couldn't keep a secret.

He had some guests, colleagues of his in the field, and while pouring them tea or offering them some dinner, she began to speak of the plague affecting the cattle, of the tuberculosis of domestic animals, of manure disposal in town. . . . He became terribly embarrassed and when the guests left, he held her hand and sternly scolded her:

"I really must beg you not to speak of that which you do not understand! When we veterinarians speak among ourselves, please don't intrude. That's the limit of boredom!"

She looked at him in amazement and alarm and asked:

"Valodechka, what can I talk about?"

And with tears in her eyes she embraced him, begged him not to be angry, and they both were happy again.

But this reconciliation didn't last long. The veterinarian left with his colleagues, never to return, since his regiment was transferred somewhere very far away—possibly to Siberia. Olyenka was left alone.

Now she was really alone. Her father had died long ago and his armchair had been put in the attic, where it was full of dust and minus a leg. She became skinny and lost her good looks. The people who met her in the street did not look at her as previously, nor did they smile. It was obvious that her best years had passed, were left behind, and now a new life was beginning, unknown, and of which it was better not to think. In the evenings Olyenka sat on the porch and she could hear the music from the Tivoli and the bursting of the rockets, but this no longer evoked any response from her. She looked apathetically at her empty courtyard. Her mind was a blank. She wished for nothing, and later when night came, she went to bed and dreamt of her empty yard. She ate and drank as if she had no desire to do so.

Perhaps worst of all, she now had no opinions of any kind. She saw what was going on around her and understood everything, but could not form opinions and so did not know what to talk about. And how terrible it was not to have an opinion of any kind! You see, for example, how a bottle stands, or how rain falls, or how a *muzhik* is going along on his cart, but what that bottle is for, or the rain, or the *muzhik,* what kind of thoughts they have, you can't tell and even for a thousand rubles, you wouldn't have anything to say. In the presence of Kukin and Pustavalov and later with the veterinarian Olyenka could explain everything and would give her opinion of anything, but now in her thoughts and her heart there was some kind of emptiness—Just as in the courtyard. It was as weird and as sharp as if she had stuffed herself with bitter wormwood.

The town was growing slowly in every direction. The section where free Gypsies had roamed was now called a street, and the park where the Tivoli had been and the lumber yard were gone. There were homes making up a row of side streets. How time flies! Olyenka's house darkened, the roof became rusty, the barn was falling over to one side, and the whole exterior was overgrown with weeds and sharp nettles. Olyenka herself had aged and grown unattractive. In the summer she sat on the porch, and as before, her spirit was empty and irksome, and was as bitter as the wormwood. In the winter she sat by the window and looked out at the snow.

But then there is a breath of spring in the air, and the breeze carries the ring of cathedral bells, and suddenly for a moment the memory of the past sweetly grabs her heart and her eyes overflow with abundant tears, but only for a moment, and then again there is the emptiness and she has no idea why she is living. Her black kitten, Briska, nuzzles her and softly meows, but this tenderness does not touch Olyenka. What does she need this for? She needed love that would consume her being, her heart, her mind, would give her thoughts, the direction of her life, and would warm her aging blood. She shoves the black Briska from her lap and says to her with annoyance:

"Go away, go away. . . . It's no use!"

And so day after day, year after year—not one bit of joy and no opinions. This, Mavra, the cook, eloquently reported.

One hot July day toward evening, when the town cattle were being chased and the whole courtyard was being filled with clouds of dust, suddenly someone knocked on the gate. Olyenka went herself to open it and when she glanced out, she was stunned: behind the gate stood the veterinarian, Smirnin, already grey and dressed in civilian clothes. In a moment it all came back to her, she could not restrain herself, she cried out and laid her head upon his breast, not saying a word, and in the strength of the emotional upheaval she was not even aware of how they both entered the house and sat down to tea.

"My darling!" she sputtered, trembling with joy. "Vladimir Platonich! From where did God deliver you?"

"I want to settle here now," he related to her. "I've handed in my resignation and came to see how I could get along outside the army and to have a stable life. It is time my son entered the middle school. He is grown now. Also, I want you to know, I'm reconciled with my wife."

"Where is she now?" asked Olyenka.

"She and my son are in the hotel while I find an apartment."

"Lord, dear man, take my home! Isn't it an apartment? Ah, Lord, I don't want any rent from you," exclaimed the agitated Olyenka and again began to cry. "Live here, the cottage is enough for me. Lord, what joy for me!"

The next day the roof was being painted and the walls whitewashed, and Olyenka, with her hands on her hips, walked about the courtyard supervising the work. Her face shone with the smile she had been known for in the past, she was completely revived, refreshed as if she had awakened from a long sleep. The wife of the veterinarian arrived. She was a skinny, unattractive woman with short bobbed hair and a fretful expression. With her was the little boy, Sasha. He was small for his age (he was already ten years old), chubby, with bright blue eyes and dimples in his cheeks. He barely entered the yard when he ran after the cat, and you could hear his merry, joyful laugh.

"Auntie, is this your cat?" he asked Olyenka. "When she has kittens, please give us one. Mama is dreadfully afraid of mice."

Olyenka chatted with him, gave him some tea, and in her breast her heart suddenly warmed and blissfully contracted, as if the child were her own son. In the evening when he sat at the table doing his homework, she looked at him with tenderness and sympathy and whispered:

"My darling, my beauty, my dear child, and you were born so bright, so pure."

He read: "A piece of dry land surrounded on all sides by water is called an island."

"A piece of dry land is called an island," she repeated, and this was the first opinion she stated with conviction after several years of silence and mental void.

And she already had opinions of her own, and after breakfast she spoke to Sasha's parents about how difficult it was for children to learn anything in the middle schools, but all the same it was better to get a classical education than a vocational one. The path is then paved for you if you want to become a doctor or an engineer.

Sasha began to attend the middle school. His mother went away to Kharkov to her sister's and did not return; his father left every day for some place to oversee the movement of some cattle, and it so happened that sometimes he wasn't home for three days. It seemed to Olyenka that they had really deserted Sasha and that he was neglected at home and was dying from hunger. She moved him to a small room in her cottage so he could be close to her.

And so a half-year passed that Sasha lived with her in the cottage. Every morning Olyenka would go into his room; he slept soundly, with a hand under his cheek, not seeming to breathe. She was sorry she had to awaken him.

"Little Sasha," she said warmly, "get up, darling! It's time for school."

He gets up, gets dressed, says his prayers, and then sits down to drink his tea. He drinks three glasses and eats two large sweet buns and half of a French loaf with butter. He really hadn't completely awakened yet and wasn't in a good mood.

"Dear little Sasha, you haven't learned your assignment," Olyenka says to him, looking at him as if she were accompanying him on a long journey. "I'm very concerned about you. Be sure to try hard, darling, learn. . . . Listen to your teacher."

"Oh, please, leave me alone!" exclaims Sasha.

After that he goes out on the street to go to school by himself, a little boy with a big peaked hat with his school bag on his back. Olyenka goes quietly behind him.

"Little Sasha!" she calls to him.

He looks around and she puts into his hand a date or a sugarplum. When they turn into the crossroad where the school stood, he becomes ashamed that a tall, husky woman is walking behind him. He turns around and says to her:

"Auntie, go home. I can get there now by myself."

She stops and watches him steadily until he disappears into the entrance of the school. How she loves him! None of her other attachments had been so deep; never before was her soul so subdued, so wholeheartedly, so selflessly, with such delight as now, when more and more her maternal instinct was being aroused. For someone else's child, for the dimples on his cheeks, for his peaked cap, she would have given her life, would have given it with joy, with tears of tender love. Why? Who knows—why?

After accompanying Sasha to the school, she returns home quiet, contented, peaceful now that she is able to love; her face has become more alive during the last six months, more pleasant, shining. Those who encounter her, experience pleasure when looking at her and say to her:

"Greetings, sweet Olga Semyonovna! How are you, sweetie?"

"School work is very tough nowadays," she relates at the market. "Imagine, yesterday in the first class they were assigned to memorize a fable, and translate from Latin, and solve a problem. . . . How can a little fellow manage this?"

She begins to talk about the teachers, the lessons, the textbooks—repeating the same things that Sasha said about them.

They have dinner together at three o'clock, and in the evening they prepare his assignments and complain. Tucking him into bed, she takes a long time blessing him and whispering prayers. Later when she goes to bed, she dreams about the future, far off and cloudy, when Sasha finishes all his schooling and becomes a doctor or an engineer. He will have a large home of his own, horses, a carriage, will be married and have children of his own. . . . She falls asleep always thinking of the same thing and tears trickle down her cheeks from her closed eyes. The little black cat lies by her side and purrs:

Mur . . . mur . . . mur. . . .

Suddenly there is a loud knock at the gate. Olyenka wakes up and is numbed by fear; her heart beats wildly. A minute passes and again a knock.

"It's a telegram from Kharkov," she thinks, and her whole body begins to tremble. "The mother wants Sasha with her in Kharkov. . . . O, Lord!"

She is desperate; her head, feet, and hands are growing cold and it seems to her that no person on earth is as unfortunate as she. Another minute passes, a voice is heard: the veterinarian has returned home from the club.

"Thank God," she thinks.

Slowly the weight lifts from her heart, again it becomes light. She lies down and thinks of Sasha, who is sleeping soundly in the next room and once in a while says in his sleep:

"I'll let you have it! Get away! Don't be a smart aleck!"

1898

Name-Day Celebration

I

After the dinner with its eight courses and endless conversations, celebrating the name day of Olga Mihighlovna's husband, she went out into the garden. The necessity to be continually smiling and conversing, the noise of the dishes, the scatterbrained servants, the long religious rituals, and the corset which she wore in order to hide her pregnancy from the guests wore her out to the point of being unendurable. She wanted to distance herself from the house, to sit down in the shade and rest, and to think about the child who was due within two months. She had gotten into the habit of having these thoughts so that when she turned left from the broad avenue onto a narrow path they came to her. Here in the dense shade provided by the plum and cherry trees with the brushing of dry branches against her neck and shoulders, and with cobwebs resting on her face, in her thoughts there arose a little human being of unknown sex and with vague features. It seemed to her that it was not the cobwebs that were gently stimulating her face and neck, but the child she was carrying. When at the end of the path there appeared a weak wattle fence and behind it pot-bellied beehives with tile covers, when in the still, stagnant air the smell of hay and honey and the buzzing of bees could be heard, the little human inside her completely possessed Olga Mihighlovna. She sat down on the bench woven from vines, near a hut, and took to thinking.

At the same time as she approached the bench, sat down, and

began to think, along with the thoughts of the infant arose that of the adults which she had just left. She was terribly disturbed that, as the hostess, she had left her guests; she recalled how at dinner her husband, Peter Dmitrich, and her uncle, Nikolay Nikolaich, argued about the judgment of the barristers, about publications, and about women's education. Her husband, as usual, argued in order to show off before the guests his own conservatism, but more important, in order to disagree with her uncle, whom he disliked. Her uncle contradicted him and picked on every word in order to show the dinner guests that he, the uncle, despite his fifty-nine years, retained youthful enthusiasm and freedom of thought. And toward the end of dinner, even Olga Mihighlovna could not refrain from clumsily defending women's education—not that she wanted to annoy her husband, who, in her opinion, was being dishonest. The guests were bored with this argument, but they found it necessary to enter into the debate, even though they had nothing to do with the judgments of the barristers or women's education. . . .

Olga Mihighlovna sat on the side of the fence that was near the hut. The sun had hidden behind the clouds and the trees and the air were dreary, as when rain is about to fall; but in spite of this, it was hot and stifling. The weeds under the trees had been cut the day before Peter's nameday, but had not been removed, and were unpleasant looking as were the motley faded flowers with their heavy sweet smell. It was quiet. Behind the woven fence, the bees hummed monotonously. . . .

Some unexpected steps and voices could be heard. Someone was walking along the path near the apiary.

"It's so close!" declared a woman's voice. "Do you think it's going to rain?"

"It will, my lovely, but not until tonight," answered gloomily a very familiar male voice. "It's going to be a downpour."

Olga Mihighlovna decided that if she hurried and hid herself in the hut, they wouldn't notice her and would go by, and she wouldn't have to speak and force a smile. She lifted her skirt, bent down, and entered the hut. At the same time her face, neck, and hands were overcome with the heat and the closeness of the steamlike air.

If it were not for the closeness and the smell of the unswept cut grain, the dill, and grapevines, which made it difficult to breathe, here under the straw roof and in the dark it would have been perfect to hide from the guests and to think about the child. It was cozy and still.

"What a nice little place this is!" the woman's voice exclaimed. "Let's sit down here, Peter Dmitrich."

Olga Mihighlovna began to look through a crack between two pieces of wood. She saw her husband, Peter Dmitrich, and a guest, Lybochka Sheller, an eighteen-year-old girl who had just completed her studies at the Institute. Peter Dmitrich, with his hat tilted back, dull and lazy from having drunk a good deal at dinner, walked through the clippings around the fence and was kicking them into a pile. Lybochka, pink from the heat and, as always, pretty, stood with her hands behind her back and followed the lazy movements of his large, handsome body.

Olga Mihighlovna knew that women found her husband attractive and—she did not like to see him with them. There wasn't anything unusual that Peter Dmitrich was lazily piling up the weeds in order to make a seat for Lybochka and himself and to chatter about nonsense. There wasn't anything special about the way Lybochka was looking directly at him, but all the same Olga Mihighlovna felt annoyed with her husband and felt both fear and pleasure that she could eavesdrop.

"Sit down, you charmer," said Peter Dmitrich, sitting down on the dry weeds and stretching out. "Like this. Now, tell me all about something."

"Indeed! I'll start telling you and you'll fall asleep."

"I fall asleep? Allah be praised! How could I fall asleep when such eyes are looking at me?"

There was nothing exceptional in her husband's words or that he stretched out in the presence of a guest and with his hat tilted back. He was spoiled by women, and he knew that they were attracted to him, and that in his relations with them he had a special manner, which, as everyone noted, suited him. He conducted himself with Lybochka in this way as with all women. All the same, Olga Mihighlovna was jealous.

"Tell me, please," began Lybochka after some silence. "Is it true that you are being prosecuted?"

"I? Yes, I happened. . . . It's some malicious carryings-on, my pretty."

"But why?"

"For nothing. It's . . . all a lot of politics," yawned Peter Dmitrich. "A battle between the left and the right. I, as an obfuscator and conservative, had dared to include in an official paper an expression insulting to such innocent Gladstones as our regional justices of the peace, Kuzma Grigorevich Vostrakov and Vladimir Pavlovich Vladimirov."

Peter Dmitrich yawned again and continued:

"We have such a system that you can say anything you want about the sun or about the moon, but Lord protect you if you touch the liberals! Lord protect you! A liberal—he is like the most foul dry mushroom, which, if you accidentally touch it with your fingers, will cover you with a cloud of dust."

"What happened to you?"

"Nothing unusual. The spark that set the forest on fire was pure nonsense. One teacher, a shabby person of bellringing parentage, gives Vostrakov a petition against an innkeeper, accusing him of insulting words and actions in a public place. It was obvious to all that both the teacher and the innkeeper were dead drunk and both conducted themselves badly. If there were any insults, they were mutual. It followed that Vostrakov should have fined them both for disturbing the peace and thrown them both out of the chamber—and that's all. But how do we handle it? For us, in the first place, the first consideration is not the person, not the fact, but the firm and the label. No matter what kind of a scoundrel the teacher might be, he's always right because he's a teacher; the innkeeper is always wrong, because he is an innkeeper and a *kulak*. Vostrakov had the innkeeper arrested and brought the matter before the congress. The congress solemnly approved Vostrakov's sentence. So, I remained a minority. . . . I got a little hot. . . . And that was all."

Peter Dmitrich spoke calmly, with carefree irony. All the same the discussed judgment bothered him greatly. Olga Mihighlovna recalled how, when he returned from this badly conducted session, he had tried to hide from everyone how concerned he was, and how disgusted he was with himself. Being an intelligent man, he could not help but feel that he had strayed a long way from his own way of thinking; that several lies were needed in order to hide this feeling from himself and from other people. There had been many unnecessary conversations, much grumbling and insincere laughs over that which was not laughable! Knowing that they were going to bring him before the court, he suddenly became depressed, didn't sleep well, and more often than usual, stood by the windows and tapped a tune on the panes. And he was ashamed to let his wife know how disturbed he was, and it annoyed her. . . .

"They say you were in the Poltavska *gubernya?*" asked Lybochka.

"Yes, I was," answered Peter Dmitrich. "I returned day before yesterday."

"Is it really lovely there?"

"Yes, lovely. Even very lovely. I must tell you I was there at harvest time, and in the Ukraine harvest time is an exceedingly poetic time. We have here a large home, a large garden, many people, and so much bustling that you cannot see how they are mowing; nothing that is going on is noted. Over there on the farm you have one hundred and fifty meadows spread out before you: no matter at which window you stand, you can see the reapers. In the meadow they are mowing, in the garden they are mowing, and there are no guests and no bustling so that you cannot avoid seeing, hearing, and feeling only the haymaking. Outdoors and in the rooms you have the fragrance of hay, and from sunrise to sunset the scythes are ringing. In general, Hahlandiya is a charming country. Believe it, when I drank water with the cranes at the wells, or the vile vodka in the Jewish taverns, or when in the evening I heard the sound of the Hahlantskoy violins and tambourines, a fascinating thought enticed me—to settle down at my farm far from these assemblies, intellectual conversations, philosophical women, long dinners. . . ."

Peter Dmitrich was not lying. He was exhausted and wished to rest. He rode to the Poltavska *gubernya* only to avoid his office, his household servants, his acquaintances, and all that could remind him of his wounded self-respect and his mistakes.

Lybochka suddenly jumped up and was frantically waving her hands.

"A bee, a bee!" she shrieked. "It will sting me!"

"Relax, it won't sting you!" said Peter Dmitrich. "What a coward you are!"

"No, no, no!" screamed Lybochka, and staring at the bee, quickly ran back.

Peter Dmitrich walked after her and looked at her retreat with kindness and sadness. Is it possible that looking at her, he thought of his farm, of being alone, and—who knows? It is possible that he even thought of how warm and cozy life would be for him on his farm, even if his wife were this young girl—young, pure, fresh, not corrupted by lectures, not pregnant. . . .

When the voices and the steps quieted, Olga Mihighlovna left the hut and set out for the house. She felt like crying. She was already extremely jealous of her husband. She understood that Peter Dmitrich was exhausted and that he was unhappy with himself and was ashamed, and when ashamed, he avoided those close to him and opened up to outsiders. She also understood that Lybochka was not dangerous, just as the other women who were now drinking coffee in the house were not. But in general it was all incomprehensible, fearful, and it seemed to her that Peter Dmitrich only half belonged to her.

"He has no right!" she sputtered, trying to rationalize her jealousy and her aggravation with her husband. "He has no right whatsoever. I'm going to tell him off right now!"

She decided to find her husband immediately and tell him everything: it's lousy, infinitely lousy, that he is attractive to other women and collects them like manna from the heavens. It was unjust and dishonorable that he should share with others that which rightfully belongs to his wife; hides his soul and conscience from his wife in order to open up to the first good-looking face he meets. What wrong has his wife done him? Of what can she be accused? Finally, his lying had already bored her for a long time: he constantly shows off, flirts, never says what he thinks, and it seems that he makes an effort to appear different from what he is and what he needs to be. Why this lying? Was she joined to an honest man? If he lies, he offends both himself and those to whom he lies, and has no respect for that about which he lies. Is it possible that he does not understand that when he shows off and makes trouble for the judicial bureau, or argues about prerogatives of power at dinner only in order to irritate his uncle—is it possible that he does not understand that he doesn't give a damn about the court . . . and himself, and all those who hear and see him?

Coming out on to the large path, Olga Mihighlovna made it appear that she was taking care of her duties as a hostess. On the terrace men were drinking liquors and eating berries; one of them, a court investigator, a sturdy old man and a joker and a wit, appeared to be telling an uncensored anecdote, but seeing the hostess, abruptly closed his thick lips, stared at her, and bowed. Olga Mihighlovna did not like the travelling supervisors. She was not attracted to their awkward, ceremonious wives, to their gossip, their frequent visits, and their flattery of her husband, whom they all disliked. Now that they had drunk and eaten their fill, but were not preparing to leave, she felt that their presence was intolerable, but in order not to appear unpleasant, she smiled affably at the court investigator and shook her finger at him. She walked across the hall and through the drawing room with a smiling face and with the appearance that she was going to attend to something and straighten it out. "Please, dear God, don't have any of them stay!" she thought, but she made herself stop in the drawing room in order to politely listen to a young man who was playing the piano. Pausing for a moment, she then called out: "Bravo, bravo, Monsieur Georges!" and clapping her hands twice, went on.

She found her husband in the study. He was sitting at the desk deep in thought. He was not the Peter Dmitrich who argued at dinner and the one the guests knew, but another one—fatigued, guilty, and displeased with himself—the one only known to his wife. He had probably gone to the study to have a cigarette. Before him lay the open cigarette case, full of cigarettes; one hand was lowered into a desk drawer. Reaching for a cigarette, it had remained as if paralyzed.

Olga Mihighlovna felt sorry for him. It was clear as day to her that he was exhausted and could not find a place to rest, or perhaps, was struggling with himself. Olga Mihighlovna walked quietly toward the desk. She wanted to show him that she had forgotten the dinner argument and was no longer angry. She closed the cigarette case and put it into her husband's side pocket.

"What shall I say to him?" she thought. "I will say that a lie is like a forest; the further you go into it, the more difficult it is to get out of it. I will say: you led yourself into a false position and went much too far; you insulted people who were bound to you and who had done you no harm. Go and excuse yourself to them, laugh at yourself, and you will feel better. And if you want quiet and solitude, we will go away together."

Meeting his wife's eyes, Peter Dmitrich immediately changed the expression on his face to the one he had at dinner and in the garden— indifferent and slightly derisive; he yawned and got up from the chair.

"It is five o'clock now," he said, glancing at the clock. "If the guests are merciful and leave by eleven, we still have six hours to endure. It's lively, I must say!"

And whistling something, he left the study slowly with his usual solid gait. His firm steps could be heard as he crossed the hall, then into the drawing room; how he laughed soundly and told the young musician "Bravo, bravo!" Soon his steps were silenced; he probably went into the garden. And now not jealousy or anxiety, but genuine hate of his steps, of his insincere laugh and voice, took possession of Olga Mihighlovna. She went to the window and looked out into the garden. Peter Dmitrich was already walking along the lane. With one hand in his pocket and snapping the fingers of the other, with his head slightly leaning back, he walked firmly, waddling, and with the appearance that he was pleased with himself, with the dinner, with his digestion, and with nature. . . .

Two little schoolboys appeared on the path, the sons of the landowner Chizhevski, who had just arrived. With them was the student-tutor in a white tunic and very narrow britches. Having come up to Peter Dmitrich, the children and the student stopped and congratulated him on his name day. He leaned over elegantly and touched the childrens' cheeks and carelessly gave the student his hand without glancing at him. The student may have praised the weather and compared it with Petersburg's because Peter Dmitrich declared loudly, not in the tone he would have used to a guest, but that with a bailiff or with the investigator:

"What? Did you have cold weather in Petersburg? Here we have, dear fellow, prevailing healthy air and abundantly fruitful land. Ah? What?"

And putting one hand in his pocket and snapping the fingers of the other, he strode farther. While he was not hidden by hazelnut bushes, Olga Mihighlovna watched the back of his neck and was perplexed. Where did a thirty-four-year-old man get the solid gait of a general? What was the source of this firm, elegant walk? What was the source of this supercilious, vibrating voice; where did all those *whats, ah yeses,* and *good fellows* come from?

Olga Mihighlovna recalled how in the first months of marriage, in order not to be bored when alone at home, she rode into town to the council meetings where sometimes, along with her godfather, Count Alexey Petrovich, Peter Dmitrich presided as chairman. In the seat of the chairman, in a uniform and with his chain denoting his rank on his chest, he changed completely. The grand gestures, the loud voice, the *whats* and *yeses,* the casual tone. . . . All his usual human warmth that was his alone, which Olga Mihighlovna had become accustomed to see in him at home, disappeared in the grandeur, and Peter Dmitrich was not sitting in the chair but some other individual whom all called Mr. President. The consciousness that he was endowed with power did not allow him to sit still, and he sought out the instance to ring the bell, sternly glare at the public, and to shout. . . . What made him nearsighted and deaf? Why did he suddenly start to see and hear badly and to grandly frown so that it was necessary to speak louder and come closer to the table? From the height of grandeur he badly distinguished faces and sounds, so that it seemed at these moments that if Olga Mihighlovna herself approached him he would have shouted: "What is your name?" He addressed the peasant witnesses with the informal "you" and shouted at the people so that his voice was heard even out on the street, and he was impossible with the lawyers.

When it came time to speak with the barrister, Peter Dmitrich sat a little sideways from him and stared at the ceiling, wishing in this way to show him that the barrister was not really necessary there, and that he neither recognized nor listened to him. If the local attorney was dismally dressed, he became all ears and considered the attorney with a supercilious and demeaning look, that is to say, "What miserable lawyers we now have!" He interrupted them with, "What is it you wish to say?" if a florid attorney made use of a foreign word and, for example, instead of "fictitious" pronounced "factitious." Peter Dmitrich would become suddenly alert and would ask: "What? How come? Factitious? What does that mean?" And then would didactically note: "Words which you do not understand are not necessary." And the attorney, completing his statement, leaves the table, red and in a sweat, while Peter Dmitrich smiles with self-satisfaction, glories in the victory, and leans back in the chair. In his dealings with the attorneys he often irritated Count Alexey Petrovich, as when once, for example, he said: "Defense, be a little brief!" This would come out naturally from the old and kindly, but from Peter Dmitrich it seemed vulgar and strained.

II

Applause resounded. The young pianist had stopped playing. Olga Mihighlovna was reminded of her guests and hurried to the drawing room.

"I have listened with delight," she said, walking toward the piano. "I heard you with pleasure. You are wonderfully talented! But, don't you find our piano in poor condition?"

At this time the two schoolboys and their tutor came into the drawing room.

"My God, Mitya and Kolya?" Olga Mihighlovna declared in a drawling and delighted manner, going to meet them. "How you have grown! I hardly recognized you! And where is your Mama?"

"Congratulations to you and to the one whose name day it is," began the student loquaciously. "I wish you all the best. Katherine Andreevna sends her congratulations and begs to be excused. She is not well."

"She is, after all, not well! I have been awaiting her all day! Have you arrived recently from Petersburg?" Olga Mihighlovna asked the student. "What is the weather like there now?" And, not waiting for an answer, she glanced kindly on the schoolboys and repeated: "How you have grown! Not so long ago you arrived here with your nanny and now you are already schoolboys! The old get old and the young grow. . . . Have you eaten?"

"Oh, don't trouble yourself, please!" said the tutor.

"Isn't it true that you haven't eaten?"

"For goodness sake, don't trouble yourself!"

"But, you do want to eat, don't you?" asked Olga Mihighlovna in a rude and harsh voice, impatiently and with annoyance—this came out involuntarily, so at once she coughed, smiled, and flushed. "How you have grown!" she said softly.

"Don't trouble yourself, please!" repeated the student-tutor.

The tutor begged her not to trouble herself, but the schoolboys were silent. It was obvious all three wanted to eat. Olga Mihighlovna led them to the dinner table and ordered Vasily to set it.

"Your Mama is naughty," she said as she seated them. "She has really forgotten me. She is naughty, naughty, naughty. . . . You tell her that. And what is your major?" she asked the student-tutor.

"Medicine."

"Well, I have a weakness for doctors, imagine. I'm sorry my husband is not a doctor. How much courage it must take, for example, to operate or dissect a corpse! Terrible! Aren't you afraid? I would, I know, die of fright. You will, of course, have some vodka?"

"Don't trouble yourself, please."

"After being on the road, you need a drink. I'm a woman, but I take a drink sometimes too. But Mitya and Kolya will drink some wine. The wine is weak, have no fear. What smart young fellows they truly are! Almost marriageable."

Olga Mihighlovna spoke without stopping. She knew from experience that it was much easier and more comfortable to talk and to hold her guests' attention than to listen. When talking, it was not necessary to pay strict attention, invent answers to questions, and to change the expressions on one's face. However, involuntarily, she asked a serious question, and the student gave a long discourse which she was forced to listen to. He knew that she had attended lectures, and in addressing her he did his best to appear very serious.

"What is your major?" she asked, having forgotten that she had already asked that question.

"Medicine."

Olga Mihighlovna remembered that she had not been with the ladies for quite a while.

"Really? That means you will be a doctor?" she said while getting up to go. "That's fine. I wish that I had taken medical classes. Do have your fill, gentlemen, and then come out into the garden. I will introduce you to some young ladies."

She left and glanced at the clock: it was five minutes to six. She was amazed that time was going so slowly, and was horrified that until midnight when the guests would leave, there remained six hours. How to kill these six hours? How would she express herself? How was she to conduct herself with her husband?

There wasn't a soul in the drawing room or on the terrace. The guests had all spread themselves throughout the garden.

"I must propose a walk among the birches or a boat ride before tea," Olga Mihighlovna thought, and hurried to the croquet court from which could be heard voices and laughter. "And settle the old folks with a game of cards."

Coming to meet her from the croquet court was the butler, Grigory, carrying empty bottles.

"Where are the ladies?" she asked him.

"In the raspberry patch. The master is there too."

"Ah, gentlemen, my God!" someone shouted desperately from the croquet court. "I've told you the same thing a thousand times! In order to know the Bulgarians you have to see them! You can't judge them by what you read in the papers!"

From this outcry or from something else, Olga Mihighlovna suddenly felt extremely weak throughout her whole body, especially in her legs and shoulders. She had no desire to speak, to listen, or to move.

"Grigory," she began wearily and with great effort, "when you are serving tea to someone, will you please not turn to me, don't ask me, or speak of anything? . . . Serve everything yourself and . . . and don't make any noise with your feet. I beg you. . . . I cannot because . . ."

She did not finish and continued toward the croquet court, but on the way she remembered the ladies and turned toward the raspberry patch. The sky, the air, and the trees were overcast as before and promising rain. It was hot and close; a huge flock of shrieking crows, predicting foul weather, were descending upon the garden. The closer you came to the kitchen garden, the more abandoned, dark, and narrow became the paths. On one of these, hidden by the thicket, were some wild pear trees, sour cherries, young oaks, and hops. A whole cloud of small black gnats surrounded Olga Mihighlovna. She covered her face with her hands and began to think compulsively of the infant within her. . . . Grigory, Mitya, Kolya, faces of peasants arriving in the morning to congratulate flashed across her mind. . . .

She heard someone's steps and opened her eyes. Coming briskly toward her was Uncle Nikolay Nikolaich.

"Is that you, my dear? I'm happy to run into you . . . ," he began, breathing heavily. "A word with you." He wiped his shaven, red chin with his handkerchief and then suddenly stepped back, spread out his hands, and opened his eyes wide. "Little mother, how long is this going to continue?" he spoke quickly, breathlessly. "I ask you: what's the limit? I'm not speaking of his insolent ugly looks that demoralize all around him, that he insults me and every honorable man and all which is sacred and best to the thinking person. I am saying, let him at least be proper! What's the point? He shouts, roars, gives himself airs, makes of himself some kind of Bonaparte, and doesn't allow a word to be said. . . . Who the hell knows what he's up to? These magnificent gestures, the laughter of an army general, the condescending tone! Permit me to ask you: what is he up to? I ask you: What is he up to? A husband of his wife, with a title to a petty estate, who was fortunate enough to marry a rich woman! An upstart and a young cadet—there are many of these! The liberal type! I swear to God that either he is a megalomaniac or, as that old penpusher Count Alexey Petrovich, now in his dotage, says, that today's children and youth mature late and play drivers and generals until they're forty!"

"That's true, true . . . ," agreed Olga Mihighlovna. "Please let me go by."

"Tell me what you think now; why these goings on?" continued her uncle, not letting her pass. "What will come of this game of conservatives and generals? He's already been brought to trial! He's been hit! I'm glad! He's shouted and knocked around to the point that he's been called to the bench. And not just the local court but the court chamber. It's impossible to imagine anything worse! In addition, he argues with everybody! Today, for example. . . . Today is his name day and look, neither the Vostrakovs, nor the Yahontovs, nor the Vladimirovs, nor Shevyd, nor Count ——. . . . Why, it seems, that even that more conservative Count Alexey Petrovich, didn't show up. And he'll never come again. You'll see, he won't come!"

"Ah, my God, and what have I to do with it?" asked Olga Mihighlovna.

"What to do with it? You are his wife! You are intelligent, you've attended lectures, and it is in your power to make an honorable worker out of him!"

"When you attend lectures they don't tell you how to influence aggressive people. It appears that I must beg all of you to forgive me for having attended lectures!" Olga Mihighlovna said sharply. "Listen, Uncle, if all day long your ears will be subjected to the same tune, you will not stay seated in the same place, but will run off. I've already heard the same thing for days the whole year around, one and the same thing. Lord, finally, you must have sympathy for me!"

The uncle made a very serious face, then looked searchingly at her and restrained a derisive smile.

"So that's the way it is!" he sang out in his old voice. "Sorry!" he declared and bowed ceremoniously. "If you yourself have fallen under his influence and have changed your convictions, you should have said so earlier. I'm sorry!"

"Yes, I betrayed my convictions!" she shouted. "Be gratified!"

"I'm sorry!"

The uncle bowed ceremoniously for the last time, somehow sideways, and all shrunken, shuffled and turned back.

"Fool," thought Olga Mihighlovna. "He ought to go home."

She found the ladies and the young among the raspberry bushes. Some were eating raspberries; others, who had already had enough berries, wandered about the rows of strawberries or were in the sweet peas. Not far from the raspberry patch, around the branches of an apple tree that was supported by poles taken from an old burned-out garden, Peter Dmitrich was cutting the grass. His hair had fallen down over his forehead, his jacket was unbuttoned, and his watch chain had fallen out of its buttonhole. In every step and in every stroke of the scythe was the apparent feeling of the knowledge and presence of great physical strength. Near him stood Lybochka and the daughters of Colonel Bykreev, a neighbor, Natalia and Valentina, or, as they were known, Nata and Vata—two anemic blondes who were oversensitive of their fullness, sixteen or seventeen years old, in white kerchiefs, and strikingly alike. Peter Dmitrich was teaching them how to mow.

"It's very simple," he said. "You only have to know how to hold the scythe and not be too eager; that is, not to put any more effort into it than necessary. So! . . . Now do you want to try?" He handed the scythe to Lybochka. "Now then!"

Lybochka clumsily took the scythe in her hand and immediately blushed and laughed.

"Don't be timid, Lybov Alexandra!" shouted Olga Mihighlovna loudly, so that the young ladies could hear and know that she was nearby. "Have courage! You must learn! If you become followers of Tolstoy, you'll have to know how to mow."

Lybochka lifted the scythe, but again laughed, and weakened by laughter, at once let it go. She was at the same time both ashamed and pleased that she was being spoken to as an adult. Nata, not smiling and not timid, and having a serious, cold face, took the scythe, waved it, and entangled it in the grass. Vata, also not smiling, serious and cold like her sister, took the scythe and thrust it into the ground. Having done this, the sisters, arm-in-arm, went toward the raspberries.

Peter Dmitrich laughed and joked like a little boy, and this mood of childlike joking, when he was exceptionally kind, made him immensely more attractive than anything else. Olga Mihighlovna loved him when he was like this. However, this boyish clowning usually did not last very long. Thus, it was at this time, having joked with the scythe, he found it necessary for some reason to add a serious inflection to his humor.

"When I mow I feel myself, you know, healthier and more normal," he said. "If I were forced to be satisfied only with an intellectual life, I think I would go out of my mind. I feel that I was not born an intellectual. I should be mowing, plowing, planting, training horses. . . ."

Peter Dmitrich and the ladies then began a conversation about the advantages of physical labor, about culture, and later about the detriments of money and about property. Listening to her husband, for some reason Olga Mihighlovna was reminded of her dowry.

"The time will come," she thought, "when he will not forgive me for being wealthier than he is. He is proud and ambitious. Perhaps he will come to hate me because he will be obligated to me for a great deal."

She was standing near Colonel Bykreev, who was eating raspberries and also taking part in the conversation.

"I think," he said, making way for Olga Mihighlovna and Peter Dmitrich, "the ripest are here. . . . And so, in the opinion of Proudhon," he continued, raising his voice, "property is robbery. I admit that I do not acknowledge Proudhon and do not value his philosophy. For me, the French are not authorities; forget about them!"

"Well, what concerns Proudhonites and all such Bakunites, I'm one of the riff-raff," said Peter Dmitrich. "When the discussion is about philosophy, turn to my wife. She's attended lectures and knows all these, the Schopenhauers and Proudhons through and through. . . ."

Olga Mihighlovna became a little blue again. She returned to the narrow path in the garden again, past the apple and pear trees, and again made it appear that she was going to some very important task. She arrived at the gardener's hut. . . . On the doorstep sat the gardener's wife, Varvara, and her four small children with their large, shorn heads. Varvara was also pregnant and was expecting to give birth, according to her calculations, about the Prophet Elijah's day. They greeted each other, and after silently looking her and the children over, Olga Mihighlovna asked:

"Well now, how do you feel?"

"Nothing to complain about. . . ."

Silence descended. It was as if both women understood each other without words.

"It's frightening to give birth the first time," said Olga Mihighlovna, thoughtfully adding, "It seems to me that I won't be able to carry it out, and that I'll die."

"And it appeared so to me, and here I am really alive. . . . So what!"

Varvara, pregnant already for the fifth time and experienced, looked at her mistress a little condescendingly and spoke to her with a didactic tone, and Olga Mihighlovna involuntarily felt her an authority; she wanted to speak of her fear, of the unborn child, of her sensations, but she was intimidated and did not want to appear to Varvara as petty and naive.

"Olga, we're going home!" called Peter Dmitrich from the raspberry patch.

Olga Mihighlovna liked being silent, to wait and to keep looking at Varvara. She would have agreed to remain so, silent and without obligations, until nightfall. But it was necessary to go. She hardly left the hut when Lybochka, Vata, and Nata ran for about seven feet to meet her, and then both sisters stopped on the spot together. Lybochka ran up and threw her arms around her neck.

"Darling! Wonderful! Priceless!" she exclaimed, kissing her face and neck. "Let's have tea on the island!"

"On the island! On the island!" Vata and Nata also exclaimed simultaneously, not smiling.

"But you know it's going to rain, my darlings."

"It won't, it won't!" cried Lybochka, making a sad face. "Everybody is agreeable. Dearest, kindest!"

"Over there everybody is getting ready to have tea on the island," said the approaching Peter Dmitrich. "We'll spread it out. . . . We'll all go on the small boats, and the samovar and everything else must be sent with the servants in the carriage."

He came alongside his wife and took her by the arm. Olga Mihighlovna wanted to say something unpleasant to her husband, something cutting, if only to mention the dowry—the harsher, it seemed, the better. She thought it over and said:

"Why didn't Count Alexey Petrovich come? How unfortunate!"

"I'm very happy that he didn't show up," lied Peter Dmitrich. "That crackpot has bored me to death."

"You know you were awaiting him impatiently right up to dinner!"

III

Within a half-hour all the guests were clustering on the shore around the piles where the boats were moored. They were all chattering, laughing, and from excessive bustling could not settle themselves in the boats. Three of the boats were already full of passengers and two were empty. The keys for these two had been misplaced and messengers had been sent to the house to find them. One said that Grigory had the keys, another that they were with the steward; a third suggested that a blacksmith be called to break the locks. And they all spoke at once, interrupting and deafening each other. Peter Dmitrich was impatiently pacing the shore and shouted:

"What a hell of a mess! The keys are always to lie on the window sill in the foyer! Who dared to take them from there? The steward can, if he wishes, bring his own boat!"

The keys were finally found. Then it was discovered that two of the paddles were defective. Pandemonium arose again. Peter Dmitrich, having become bored with striding, jumped into the long, narrow canoe which had been carved from a poplar tree, and while rocking it almost fell into the water, and then cast off from the shore. One after the other, with loud laughter and shrieks from the ladies, the other boats struck out.

The cloudy white sky, the trees on the shore, the rushes, the boats with people and paddles were all reflected in the water as in a mirror; under the boats, deep down, in the bottomless depth were the sky and the flying birds. On one of the banks was a tall country estate hidden completely by trees; on another was a sloping, wide green floodplain with waterfalls. The boats floated about three hundred fifty feet. Behind the wistfully bending pussy willows on the ascending shore were huts and a herd of cows; singing could be heard, drunken cries, and the sounds of an accordion.

Here and there along the river the fishermen's boats poked about in order to place their nets for the night. In one of the dugouts sat some pretty poor amateur musicians playing on homemade violins and violoncellos.

Olga Mihighlovna was sitting near the rudder. She smiled affably and talked a great deal in order to keep her guests entertained, while she watched her husband out of the corner of her eye. He paddled his canoe ahead of all the others, standing and manipulating one paddle. The light cone-shaped canoe, which the guests called murderous, and which Peter Dmitrich himself for some reason called *Penderakly,* was moving rapidly. It appeared lively and clever and, it seemed, disliked the strong Peter Dmitrich and awaited the right moment in order to tip him. Olga Mihighlovna, observing her husband, felt repelled by his handsomeness, which so pleased everyone: the back of his neck, his stance, his familiarity with women. Sitting in the small boat, she was jealous and at the same time she winced every minute and feared that the unsteady canoe would tip and create grief.

"Slow down, Peter!" she cried, and her heart stopped from fear. "Sit down! We know you're daring!"

She was bothered too by the people who were in the boat with her. They were all ordinary, intelligent people mostly, but now everyone of them appeared unusually stupid. In everyone she only saw fraud. "There," she thought, "paddling is a young brunette in gold-rimmed glasses with a handsome chin, a well-fed, rich, and ever-lucky mother's son, whom they all consider an honorable, free-thinking, progressive person. It's not even a year since he left the university and came to live in the district, but already talks about himself as: 'We, district councillors.' But not a year will pass and he, like many others, will become bored and go to Petersburg, and in order to justify his flight, will tell everyone that the district council will never be of use and that he was deceived. And, from the other boat, not taking her eyes away from him, his young wife looks at him and believes that he is a 'district councillor' and who, after a year, will believe that the district council is of no use. And here was the well-built, carefully shaven young country gentleman in a straw hat with a wide ribbon and with an expensive cigar held by his teeth. This one here likes to say: 'It's time to discard fantasies and get to the business at hand!' He has Yorkshire pigs, Butler's hives, turnips, pineapples, an oil-mill, a cheese dairy, and Italian double-entry bookkeeping. But every summer, in order to live with his mistress in the Crimea, he sells trees from his forest for cutting and piles them up on his private land. And here is Uncle Nikolay Nikolaich, who is angry with Peter Dmitrich, but all the same for some reason doesn't go home!"

Olga Mihighlovna glanced at the other boats and there she saw only uninteresting cranks and actors, or narrow-minded people. She thought about them, those she knew from the district, and could not think of a single one of whom she could say or think something better. They were all, it seemed to her, untalented, pale, short-witted, narrow, fraudulent, heartless, who never spoke what they thought or did what they wanted to. Boredom and despair were choking her; she wanted to stop smiling immediately, jump up and cry, "You bore me!" and then jump out of the boat and swim to shore.

"Ladies and gentlemen, let's tow Peter Dmitrich!" someone shouted.

"A tow-line! A tow-line!" joined in the rest. "Olga Mihighlovna, grab your husband's tow-line."

In order to be able to tow him, Olga Mihighlovna, who was sitting at the helm, could not lose a minute in catching the chain at the nose of *Penderakly*. When she leaned over for the chain, Peter Dmitrich frowned and looked at her with alarm.

"You mustn't catch cold!" he said.

"If you're afraid for me and the child, why are you tormenting me so?" thought Olga Mihighlovna.

Peter Dmitrich declared himself defeated and not wishing to be part of the towing, jumped from *Penderakly* into the boat, which was already packed without him, jumped so clumsily that the boat listed so severely that all in it shrieked from fear.

"He jumped in order to be attractive to the women," thought Olga Mihighlovna. "He knows that it looks attractive. . . ."

She thought that from boredom, from aggravation, from strained smiles and discomfort, something was going on in her whole body, and her hands and feet began to tremble. In order to hide this trembling she forced herself to speak even louder, to laugh, and to move around. . . .

"In case I suddenly begin to cry," she thought, "I'll say I have a toothache. . . ."

The boats finally pulled in on the island, Good Hope. The peninsula was so named because it was formed at a bend on the river in a sharp corner and was covered with an old growth of birches, oaks, willows, and poplars. Tables were already set up under the trees, the samovars were steaming, and Vasily and Grigory were fussing around the dishes in their frock coats and knitted white gloves. On another shore opposite Good Hope stood the carriages, having arrived with the supplies. Baskets and bundles of provisions from the carriage were transported in a dugout resembling the canoe, *Penderakly*. The expression of the butlers, the drivers, and even the peasants who sat in the dugout was one of festivity such as only children and servants exhibited.

While Olga Mihighlovna started the tea and poured the first glasses, the guests busied themselves with liquors and sweets. Then began the turmoil customary on picnics when the tea was being drunk, and which was very boring and tiring for the hosts. Grigory and Vasily had hardly succeeded in handing it out when hands with empty glasses were stretched out toward Olga Mihighlovna. One wanted no sugar, another a little stronger, and a third a little weaker, a fourth thanked her. All this Olga Mihighlovna had to remember and then call out: "Ivan Petrovich, yours was without sugar?" or "Gentlemen, who asked for a bit weaker?" But the ones who asked for it weaker or without sugar had forgotten and were involved in pleasant chatter and took the first glass available. Some dejected-looking figures, like shadows, moved apart from the table and gave the appearance of looking for mushrooms in the grass, or reading labels on boxes— it was these who were not holding glasses. "Have you had some tea?" Olga Mihighlovna asked and the one to whom the question was addressed asked her not to trouble herself and said: "I'm waiting a little," although for the hostess it was more desirable that the guests not wait, but hurry.

Some were involved in conversations and drank their tea slowly, holding their glasses for a half-hour; others, however, especially those who drank a lot after dinner, did not leave the table but drank cup after cup, so that Olga Mihighlovna had trouble keeping their cups full. One young cut-up drank his tea while sucking a piece of sugar and repeating over and over again: "I love, sinner that I am, to treat myself to a Chinese herb." Along with this he would take a deep breath and ask: "Allow me just one more little crock!" He drank a great deal, bit on his sugar noisily, and thought it all a great joke and original, and that he was superbly imitating the merchants. No one perceived that all this nonsense was tormenting the hostess, and it was difficult to perceive as Olga Mihighlovna constantly smiled affably and chattered nonsense.

But she did not feel well. She was irritated by the large number of people, the laughter, the questions, the joker, the unexpected slipping and falling of the butler, and the children running around the table; she was annoyed that Vata looked like Nata, and Kolya like Mitya, and that you couldn't distinguish which one had had his tea and which one hadn't. She felt that her strained affable smile was becoming unpleasant looking and that any minute she would begin to cry.

"Ladies and gentlemen, rain!" shrieked someone.

They all looked up at the sky.

"Yes, indeed, it is raining . . . ," confirmed Peter Dmitrich and wiped his cheek.

Only a few drops fell from the sky and there wasn't a full-fledged rain as yet, but the guests forsook the tea and rushed. At first they all wanted to ride in the carriages, but after thinking it over, headed for the boats. Olga Mihighlovna, under the pretext that she had to hurry in order to take care of the arrangements for supper, begged permission to be unsociable and to ride home in a carriage.

Having been seated in the carriage, she immediately gave herself a respite from smiling. She rode through the village with an angry face, and with an angry face responded to the bows of the peasants met along the way. Arriving at home, she went in by the back entrance to the bedroom and lay down on her husband's bed.

"Lord, my God," she whispered, "why this drudgery? Why are these people lounging about here and making it seem that they're having a good time? Why am I smiling and lying? I don't understand!"

Steps and voices were heard. The guests were returning.

"So what," thought Olga Mihighlovna. "I'll lie here a bit longer."

But a maid came into the bedroom and said:

"Mistress, Maria Grigoryevna is leaving!"

Olga Mihighlovna jumped up, straightened her hair, and hurried out of the bedroom.

"Maria Grigoryevna, what's this?" she began with a hurt voice, going to meet Maria Grigoryevna. "Where are you hurrying to?"

"It's impossible for me to stay, my dear! I have already stayed too long. My children are waiting for me at home."

"Oh, you are naughty! Why didn't you bring the children with you?"

"Darling, if it will please you, I'll bring them sometime on a weekday, but today . . ."

"Oh, please do," interrupted Olga Mihighlovna. "It will make me so happy! Your children are so sweet! Kiss them all. . . . But, honestly, you hurt me! Why you are hurrying, I don't understand!"

"It's impossible, impossible. . . . Farewell, dear. Take care of yourself. You know in your condition . . ."

And they exchanged kisses. Having accompanied the guest to her carriage, Olga Mihighlovna went into the drawing room to the ladies. There the lights were already lit and the men were being seated to play cards.

IV

After supper the guests started to leave at a quarter to one. Accompanying the guests, Olga Mihighlovna stood on the porch and said:

"Really, you should have shawls! It has become cool. God forbid you should catch cold!"

"Don't concern yourself, Olga Mihighlovna!" replied the guests getting into their carriages. "Farewell! We're looking forward to your visiting us! Don't disappoint us!"

"Whoa!" the coachman held back the horses.

"Let's go, Dennis! Farewell, Olga Mihighlovna!"

"Kiss the children for me!"

The carriage moved and instantly disappeared in the darkness. In the red circle cast by the lamp on the road, another pair or troika appeared with impatient horses and silhouettes of the coachman with hands outstretched before him. The kisses began again, with reproaches and requests to come again or to take shawls. Peter Dmitrich hurried out of the entrance to help the ladies into their carriages.

"Go now on the Yefremov road," he instructed the coachman. "Mankino is closer, but the road is bad. You won't overturn on a good road. Farewell, my lovely! A thousand compliments to your artistic creator!"

"Farewell, dear Olga Mihighlovna! Get inside or you'll catch cold out here! It's damp!"

"Whoa! Stop prancing!"

"What kind of horses do you have?" asked Peter Dmitrich.

"They were bought during Lent in Highdarov," answered the coachman.

"Elegant little horses. . . ."

And Peter Dmitrich smacked the lead horse on his hindquarters.

"Go on, move! God grant you good luck!"

Finally the last guest drove away. The red circle on the road had moved to the side, narrowed, and died out—Vasily had taken the lamp from the porch. In the past, after accompanying the leaving guests, Peter Dmitrich and Olga Mihighlovna usually began to race into the hall, clapping their hands and singing: "They've left! They've left! They've left!" But now Olga Mihighlovna could not do this. She went into the bedroom, undressed, and lay down on the bed.

It seemed to her that she would fall asleep immediately and that she would sleep soundly. Her legs and shoulders ached painfully, her head had grown heavy from conversing, and her whole body, as previously, did not feel right. Covering her head, she lay still for several minutes, then glanced from under the covers at the lamp, listened to the silence, and smiled.

"Wonderful, wonderful . . . ," she whispered, pulling up her legs, which seemed to her had become longer from all the walking. "I must sleep, must sleep. . . ."

Her legs would not settle down, and her whole body felt uncomfortable so she rolled over to the other side. But in the bedroom there was a large fly buzzing and it was disturbingly thumping against the ceiling. The careful steps of Grigory and Vasily in the hallway could also be heard as they removed the tables. It became obvious to Olga Mihighlovna that she would not fall asleep or be comfortable until all these sounds would quiet down. And she impatiently rolled over on the other side.

Her husband's voice could be heard from the drawing room. It must be that someone had remained for the night and Peter Dmitrich was addressing them and speaking loudly:

"I did not say that Alexey Petrovich was a fraud. But, he appears thus, because you gentlemen, as a matter of fact, strive to see in him what is not there. In his foolishness an original mind is seen and in his familiarity toward everyone, good nature. In the complete absence of opinions is seen conservatism. I will allow even, that he is indeed a conservative of the '84 type. But in reality, is that conservatism?"

Peter Dmitrich, who was angry with Count Alexey Petrovich, his guests, and himself, unburdened his heart. He swore at the count and the guests, and sadly at himself, and was ready to tell and confess whatever he felt like doing. After accompanying his guest to his room, Peter Dmitrich strutted back and forth in the drawing room, crossed into the dining room and into the corridor, into the pantry, and then again into the drawing room, and at last into the bedroom.

Olga Mihighlovna was lying on her back, covered only to the waist (she was already too warm), and with an irate face was following the fly that was thumping the ceiling.

"Who stayed for the night?" she asked.

"Yegorov."

Peter Dmitrich undressed and lay down in his bed. He quietly lit a cigarette and also began to follow the fly. His look was grim and disturbed. Keeping silent for about five minutes, Olga Mihighlovna stared at his handsome profile. It seemed to her that if for some reason her husband turned his face toward her and said: "Olya, I'm depressed," she would laugh, or cry, and then she would feel better. She thought about her aching legs, and that her whole body was uncomfortable because of her tense spirit.

"Peter, what are you thinking about?" she asked.

"So, so, nothing much . . . ," he answered.

"Lately you've been keeping secrets from me. That's not right."

"Why isn't it right?" Peter Dmitrich answered drily and not at once. "We all have private lives, and therefore, secrets are unavoidable."

"Private life, one's own secrets . . . these are just words! Can't you see you're hurting me?" declared Olga Mihighlovna, rising up and sitting on the bed. "If your soul is distressed, why do you hide it from me? And why do you find it easier to be more candid with other women than with your wife? I heard, you see, how you unloaded to Lybochka today in the bee garden."

"Well, congratulations. I'm glad you heard!"

That meant: leave me alone, don't disturb my thoughts! Olga Mihighlovna was exasperated. The vexation, hate, and anger that had been brewing in her as the day went by suddenly boiled over; she now did not want to postpone until the next day telling her husband everything, but to hurt him, to have revenge. Controlling herself so that she would not scream, she said:

"You know that that's all nasty, nasty, and nasty! I hated you all day today—that's what you have done!"

Peter Dmitrich also raised himself to a sitting position.

"Vile, vile, vile!" continued Olga Mihighlovna, her whole body beginning to tremble. "There's nothing to congratulate. You'd better congratulate yourself! Shame, for shame! Things have gotten to such a stage that you are ashamed to remain in the same room with your wife! You're a fraud! I see through you and understand your every move!"

"Olya, as long as you're in such a state, please warn me and I will sleep in the study."

Having said this, Peter Dmitrich took his pillow and left the bedroom. Olga Mihighlovna had not expected this. She sat silently with an open mouth and a shaking body, stared at the door behind which her husband had hid himself, and tried to understand what this meant. Was this one of those methods that deceitful people use in arguments when they are wrong, or was this an insult thoughtfully carried out against her self-respect? What did it mean? Olga Mihighlovna recalled that her first cousin, an officer and a "gay blade," had often laughingly told her that when during the night "my wife begins to nag me," he usually takes his pillow and whistling, leaves for his study, and his wife remains in a stupid and ridiculous situation. This officer was married to a rich, capricious, and dull woman whom he did not respect and only tolerated.

Olga Mihighlovna jumped from her bed. In her opinion, only one thing was left for her: to dress quickly and leave this house forever. The house belonged to her, but so much the worse for Peter Dmitrich. Not thinking it over, whether this was or was not necessary, she rushed into the study to inform her husband of her decision ("woman's logic" flashed across her mind) and in farewell to say again something insulting, foul. . . .

Peter Dmitrich was lying on the couch and gave the appearance of reading the newspaper. On the small table beside him a candle burned. You could not see his face behind the newspaper.

"Try to enlighten me as to what this means? I ask you!"

"I ask you . . . ," mimicked Peter Dmitrich, not showing his face. "I'm tired of this, Olya! Honestly, I'm exhausted and I can't handle this now. . . . We can fight tomorrow."

"No, I understand you perfectly!" continued Olga Mihighlovna. "You hate me! Yes, yes! You hate me because I'm wealthier than you are! You'll never forgive me for this and will always lie to me!

("Woman's logic!" again flashed across her mind.) Right now, I know you're laughing at me. . . . I'm even convinced that you married me only to be qualified for the council and to have these lousy horses. . . . Oh, I'm miserable!"

Peter Dmitrich threw down the newspaper and got up. The unexpected assault stunned him. He smiled, a child's helpless smile, and looked with perplexity at his wife, and as if defending himself from blows, stretched his hands toward her and pleadingly said:

"Olya!"

And, expecting that she would say something even more awful, he leaned against the back of the couch, and his huge figure seemed to take on the helplessness of a child, just as his smile did.

"Olya, how can you say that?" he whispered.

Olga Mihighlovna came to herself. She suddenly felt her insane love for this person, remembered that he was her husband, Peter Dmitrich, without whom she could not live for a day, and who also loved her to distraction. She sobbed loudly, not sounding like herself, grabbed her head with her hands, and ran back into the bedroom.

She fell on the bed and her small, hysterical sobs, disturbing her breathing and causing cramps in her hands and legs, bounced around the room. Recalling that there were several guests spending the night, she hid her head under the pillow in order to stifle the sound of the sobbing, but the pillow fell on the floor and she too almost fell when she reached for it. She pulled the covers over her face, but her hands were disobedient and convulsively plucked at whatever she tried to get hold of.

It seemed to her that all was lost, that the lies, which she had said in order to hurt her husband, had shattered her life. Her husband would not forgive her. The insults that she had cast upon him were of the kind which you could not smooth away with caresses, or with vows. How could she convince her husband that she herself could not believe she had said these things?

"Finished, finished!" she screamed, not noticing that the pillow had again fallen on the floor. "For God's sake, for God's sake!"

The guest and servants were, no doubt, awakened by her screams. Tomorrow everyone in the district would know that she had been hysterical and all would blame Peter Dmitrich for this. She tried to control herself, but the sobbing became louder and louder every minute.

"For God's sake!" she shrieked in a strange voice and did not know why she was screaming this. "For God's sake!"

It seemed to her that the bedstead was collapsing under her and that her legs were caught in the covers. Peter Dmitrich entered the room in his dressing gown with a candle in his hands.

"Olya, enough!" he exclaimed.

She got up on her knees in bed and squinting from the light, through her sobs said:

"Understand me . . . understand me!"

"Here, drink!" he said, handing her some water.

She obediently took the glass and started to drink, but the water spilled and wet her hands, breast, and knees.

"I must now be terribly hideous!" she thought.

Peter Dmitrich gently lay her down on the bed and covered her, then took the candle and left.

"For God's sake!" Olga Mihighlovna screamed again. "Peter, try to understand, try to understand!"

Suddenly something squeezed her in the lower part of her stomach and back so strongly that her crying broke off, and she bit the pillow from pain. As the pain receded, she started to sob again.

The maid came in, straightened the covers over her, and asked with alarm:

"Mistress, darling, what's wrong?"

"Leave!" said Peter Dmitrich sternly, coming up to the bed.

"Understand me, understand me . . . ," began Olga Mihighlovna.

"Olya, I beg you, calm down!" he said. "I didn't want to hurt you. I wouldn't have left the bedroom if I had known that it would upset you so. I was simply exhausted. On my word of honor, I say this to you."

"Understand me. You lied, I lied. . . ."

"I understand. . . . Now, now, it's all right! I understand . . . ," Peter Dmitrich said gently, sitting down on her bed. "You were feverish when you said that, it's understandable. . . . I swear to God that

I love you more than anything in the world, and when I married you, I never considered that you were rich. I have never needed nor did I ever value anything in terms of money and, therefore, cannot sense the difference between your wealth and mine. I have always considered us equally wealthy. And if I have been dishonest in little things . . . that is, of course, true. My life up to this time has not been very serious, so that it was impossible to get along without little lies. It's difficult for me, too, now. Let's drop this topic, for God's sake! . . ."

Olga Mihighlovna again felt a sharp pain and grabbed her husband's hands.

"It hurts, it hurts, it hurts!" she exclaimed quickly. "Oh, it hurts!"

"The devil with these guests!" muttered Peter Dmitrich, getting up. "You shouldn't have had to ride to the island today!" he cried. "Fool that I am that I didn't stop you! Lord, my God!"

He scratched his head in vexation, gave it up as a bad job, and left the bedroom.

Later he came in every now and then, sat by her on the bed, and spoke a great deal, first very caressingly, then crossly, but she could hardly hear him. The sobs alternated with the terrible pain, and every new pain was stronger and lasted longer. At first when in pain, she held her breath and bit the pillow, but later began to scream with an ugly, rending sound. Once, seeing her husband by her side, she remembered that she had hurt him, and not being able to judge whether it was her husband or delirium, grabbed his hand with both of hers and began to kiss it.

"You lied, I lied . . . ," she began to justify herself. "Understand, understand. . . . They wore me out, they made me lose patience. . . ."

"Olya, we're not alone!" Peter Dmitrich said.

Olga Mihighlovna picked up her head and saw Varvara, who was on her knees before the chest of drawers and was pulling out the lowest drawer. The top drawers were already pulled out. Finishing with the chest, Varvara stood up, red from the effort, and with a cold, solemn face took to opening the large chest.

"Maria, I can't open it!" she whispered. "Maybe you can open it."

The maid, Maria, scraped around the candlestick in order to

replace the candle with a new one. She then went to Varvara to help her open up the chest.

"Nothing should be left closed," whispered Varvara. "This chest should be open too! Master," she addressed Peter Dmitrich, "you should send for Father Mihighel, so that he would open up the holy gates! It's a must!"

"Do whatever you want," said Peter Dmitrich gasping, "only, dear God, get the doctor or the midwife here as soon as possible! Did Vasily go? Send someone else too. Send your husband!"

"I'm giving birth," observed Olga Mihighlovna. "Varvara," she moaned. "You know he will be born dead!"

"No, no, mistress . . . ," whispered Varvara. "God willing, he'll be alive!" (In the pressure of the moment she mispronounced "alive"!) "He'll be alive!"

When Olga Mihighlovna regained consciousness for a second time, she no longer sobbed and did not toss about from pain but only moaned. She could not keep from moaning even in those intervals when there was no pain. The candles were still burning but the morning light was already breaking through the shutters. It was probably around five o'clock in the morning. In the bedroom at the little round table sat a strange woman in a white apron and with a very modest physical appearance. From her appearance it was obvious that she had been sitting there for a long time. Olga Mihighlovna guessed that she was the midwife.

"Will it be over soon?" she asked, and in her voice she heard some kind of peculiar, unrecognizable note which had never been there before. "It must be that I'm dying from childbirth," she thought.

Peter Dmitrich came cautiously into the bedroom, dressed for the day, and stood at the window with his back to his wife. He lifted the shade and looked out the window.

"It's a downpour!" he said.

"What time is it?" asked Olga Mihighlovna in order once more to hear the unrecognizable note in her voice.

"Quarter to six," answered the midwife.

"So what, if I'm really dying?" thought Olga Mihighlovna, looking at her husband's head and at the window panes, against which the rain was pelting. "How will he live without me? With whom will he drink tea, dine, converse in the evening, sleep?"

And he appeared to her as a little orphan; she became sorry for him, and she wanted to say something nice to him, kind, comforting. She recalled how in the spring he had been ready to buy himself some foxhounds and how she, who felt the amusement was cruel and dangerous, had prevented him from doing so.

"Peter, buy yourself some foxhounds!" she moaned.

He released the shade and went to the bed, wishing to say something, but at this moment Olga Mihighlovna felt pain and screamed in an unpleasant, heart-rending voice.

She had become spiritless from the pain, frequent cries, and groans. She could hear, see, and sometimes speak, but she understood poorly and recognized only that she was in pain, or that she would soon be in pain. It seemed to her that the name-day party was long, long ago, not yesterday, but a year ago, and that this new painful life was longer than her childhood, her days in school, at the university, being married, and would continue still longer, without end. She saw how they brought the midwife tea, how they called her for lunch at noon, and later to have dinner; she saw Peter Dmitrich's custom of coming in, standing for hours at the window, and then going out; how some strange men, the maid, Varvara, were in the habit of coming in. . . . Varvara only said: "It will be, it will be," and got angry when anyone closed the drawers in the highboy. Olga Mihighlovna saw how the light changed in the room and in the windows: that it was twilight, then dark like fog, then bright like daylight, as it was yesterday during dinner, then again twilight. . . . And all these changes were dragged out, like childhood, classes at college, lectures. . . .

In the evening two doctors—one bony and bald with a wide red beard, and the other with a Semitic face, dark and wearing cheap glasses—were performing some kind of operation on Olga Mihighlovna. She was completely indifferent to the fact that strange men were touching her body. She no longer had any shame, or pain, and anyone could do what they wanted to her. At this time, if someone had attacked her with a knife, or insulted Peter Dmitrich, or took from her the right to the infant, she would not have said a word.

During the operation she was given chloroform. When she awoke later, the pains still continued and were unbearable. It was night. Olga Mihighlovna recalled that just on this kind of night with the quiet, with the small lamp, with the midwife sitting motionless by the bed, with the open drawers of the highboy, with Peter Dmitrich standing at the window, that it was already very, very long ago. . . .

V

"I didn't die . . . ," thought Olga Mihighlovna when she began to understand again what was going on around her and when she was no longer in pain.

Through the two wide-open windows in the bedroom could be seen a bright summer day. From behind the windows in the garden, not letting up for a second, came the sounds of sparrows and magpies.

The drawers of the highboy were closed, and her husband's bed was made. Neither the midwife, nor Varvara, nor the maid were in the bedroom. Only Peter Dmitrich, as before, stood motionless by the window and was looking out into the garden. No infant's cries could be heard, no one was there with congratulations, and no one was jubilant; it was obvious that the infant was not born alive.

"Peter!" Olga Mihighlovna called out to her husband.

Peter Dmitrich looked back. Much time must have elapsed since the last guest had left and since Olga Mihighlovna had hurt her husband. It was noticeable that Peter Dmitrich's cheeks were sunken and that he had become thin.

"What is it?" he asked, coming to the bed.

He looked aside, moved his lips, and smiled like a helpless child.

"Is it all over?" asked Olga Mihighlovna.

Peter Dmitrich wanted to answer, but his lips trembled and his mouth took on a senile, wry twist, such as the toothless Uncle Nikolay Nikolaich had.

"Olya!" he said, wringing his hands, and his eyes suddenly filled with large tears. "Olya! I don't need your qualification, nor your dowry. . . . I don't need anything! Why didn't we protect our child? Ah, what's there to say!"

He waved his hand and left the bedroom.

Olga Mihighlovna had already decided the same thing. Her head was still foggy from the chloroform, and her soul was empty. The obtuse indifference to life that she had felt when the two doctors were operating had not left her yet.

1888

Wretchedness

Sofia Petrovna, a pretty twenty-five-year-old woman, the wife of notary Lubyantsev, walked quietly along the wooded path with her neighbor at the cottage, barrister Ilin. It was five o'clock in the afternoon. Above the path puffy white clouds were thick. Here and there openings of light blue sky were being swallowed. The clouds were still, as if chained to the tops of the tall old pines. It was quiet and stuffy.

Further ahead, the path cut into a slight embankment along which at this time an armed sentry walked. Just past the embankment was a large white church with six cupolas and a rusty roof. . . .

"I didn't expect to see you here," said Sofia Petrovna. Her eyes were cast on the ground and she was poking last year's leaves with the end of her parasol. "But, I am now happy that I have met you. I need to speak to you seriously and conclusively. I beg you, Ivan Mihighlovich, that if you truly love me and respect me, that you will cease your pursuit! You follow me like a shadow; you are forever looking at me with indecent eyes, brightened with lovelight; you write me strange notes, and . . . and I don't know when all this will end. Dear God, why is this going on?"

Ilin was silent. Sofia Petrovna took a few steps and continued:

"And this sharp change in you occurred in the last two or three weeks, after we've known each other for five years. You are a stranger to me, Ivan Mihighlovich!"

Sofia Petrovna glanced from the corner of her eyes upon her companion. He, screwing up his eyes, stared at the billowing clouds.

His face appeared angry, capricious, distracted—like that of a person who is suffering and who at the same time is obliged to listen to nonsense.

"It's amazing that you can't understand!" continued Lubyantseva, shrugging her shoulders. "You know that you are indulging in an unadmirable game. I'm married. I love and respect my husband. . . . I have a daughter. . . . Really, don't you place any value on this? Besides, as an old friend, you know how I feel about the family. . . . The family is the foundation of everything. . . ."

Ilin groaned with annoyance and sighed.

"Family foundations . . . ," he muttered. "Oh, Lord."

"Yes, yes. . . . I love my husband, respect him, and in any case, I value family contentment. I would sooner kill myself than be the cause of André's and his daughter's unhappiness. So, I beg you, Ivan Mihighlovich, for God's sake, leave me in peace. Let us be as before, good and fine friends, and discard those sighs and groans that are not part of your personality. It is decided and ended! It's better not to say a word about this. Let us talk about something else."

Sofia Petrovna glanced again at Ilin's face. Ilin looked up. He was pale and was bitterly biting his trembling lips. Lubyantseva could not understand why he was angry, or what was making him indignant, but his paleness touched her.

"Don't be angry. We will be friends . . . ," she said gently. "Agreed? I give you my hand."

Ilin took her tiny, soft hand in both his, pressed it, and slowly raised it to his lips.

"I'm not a schoolboy," he grumbled. "I'm not at all tempted by friendship with a beloved woman."

"Enough, enough! It is decided and ended. We've come to a bench. Let's sit down. . . ."

Sofia Petrovna's soul was filled with the sweet sensation of relief: the most difficult and ticklish had been said. The troubling question was decided and concluded. She could now sigh lightly and look directly into Ilin's face. She glanced at him, and the egotistical feeling of superiority of the loved woman over the man in love pleasantly caressed her. It pleased her that this strong, huge man with a courageous, angry face with a large black beard, who was wise, educated, and, as it was said, talented, sat obediently beside her with his head downcast. They sat for two or three minutes without a word.

"Nothing is decided or ended yet . . . ," began Ilin. "You are speaking to me as if you were reading from some script: 'I love and respect my husband . . . familial foundations. . . .' All of this I know without your telling me, and can tell you even more of the same. Sincerely and honorably I say to you, that I consider my behavior criminal and immoral. What more can be said? Instead of feeding the nightingale with wretched words, you would do better to teach me. What am I to do?"

"I have already told you: go away!"

"As you well know, I have already attempted to leave five times and each time have turned back after having gone half way! I can show you my one-way tickets and they are all unused. I do not have the choice to run from you! I struggle, struggle terribly, but no matter what the devil I'm capable of, I have no endurance; I'm weak, faint-hearted! I can't struggle with my nature! Don't you understand? I can't! I run from my nature, but she grabs me by my coattails. It is a vulgar, vile weakness!"

Ilin flushed, arose, and walked around the bench.

"Furious like a dog!" he muttered, clenching his fists. "I hate and despise myself! My God, I'm like a profligate juvenile, chasing after someone else's wife, write idiotic notes, abase myself. . . . Ugh!"

Ilin grabbed himself by the head, groaned, and sat down.

"And on top of this, your insincerity!" he continued hotly. "If you object to my ugly game, why did you come here? What drew you here? In my letters I begged for only direct, unequivocal answers—yes or no, but you, instead of a direct answer strive every day 'unwillingly' to meet with me and treat me to recitations from a script!"

Lubyantseva became frightened and flushed. She suddenly felt awkward, as a proper woman comes to feel when she is accidentally caught undressed.

"It's as if you suspect that I have been playing with you," she mumbled. "I always gave you a direct answer and . . . and today I begged you!"

"Ah, does one really plead in such matters? If you had from

the beginning told me 'Go away!' I would have left long ago, but you did not say this to me. Not once did you give me a direct answer. Strange indecisiveness! Really, either you are playing with me, or . . ."

Ilin did not finish his sentence and leaned his head on his fists. Sofia Petrovna began to recall her behavior from beginning to end. She recalled that for days, not only in her actions but in her secret thoughts, she was against getting involved with Ilin; but at the same time, she felt that there was a grain of truth in the barrister's words. And not knowing what the truth was, what she thought, she could not find what to say to Ilin in reply to his complaint. It was awkward being silent, so she shrugged her shoulders and said:

"So I'm the guilty one."

"I'm not accusing you of insincerity," gasped Ilin. "It just came out that way. . . . Your insincerity was natural and proper conduct. If people immediately warmed up and began to speak sincerely, then everything would go to hell."

Sofia Petrovna was not into philosophy, but she was glad to have the chance to change the subject and asked:

"Why is that?"

"Because sincerity is only for savages and animals. Once civilization, for example, introduced into our lives the necessity for such comforts as female virtue, there was no place left for sincerity. . . ."

Ilin angrily poked his cane in the sand. Lubyantseva listened to him, understood very little, but the conversation pleased her. More than anything else she liked, as ordinary women do, that a talented individual speaks to her "from the top of his head." So, she was exceedingly happy to see how the pale, lively, and still angry young person was aroused. She did not understand much, but it was clear to her that this attractive boldness of a contemporary person such as he did not indulge in worthless mental exercises, but decides the large questions and manages the final outcomes.

Suddenly, she cut herself short; she was falling for him, and it was frightening.

"Forgive me, but I don't understand," she hurried to say. "Why did you speak of insincerity? I repeat again my plea: be a kind, good friend; leave me in peace! I plead sincerely!"

"All right, I will continue to struggle with myself!" Ilin breathed in. "I will be glad to try. . . . Only hardly anything will come out of my struggle. Either I'll put a bullet into my brain or . . . do the most stupid thing, and have a bout of hard drinking. It makes me sick! Everybody has his limits even in struggles with one's nature. Tell me, how does one struggle with insanity? If you drink wine, how can you overcome the stimulation? How can I help it if your vision is imbedded in my soul and persistently, day and night, stands before my eyes, just as this pine tree does right here? So, you must learn what a feat I have to perform in order to free myself from this miserable, wretched situation, when all my thoughts, desires, dreams do not belong to me but to some demon who has settled in me. I love you, love you to distraction, have cast aside work and those close to me, have forgotten my God! Never in my life have I loved this way!"

Sofia Petrovna, not expecting such a turn of events, moved away from Ilin and looked with fright upon his face. His eyes were full of tears, his lips were trembling, and his whole face was flooded with a hungry, pleading appearance.

"I love you!" he mumbled, bringing his eyes close to her large, frightened eyes. "You are so beautiful! I suffer now, but I swear I could spend the rest of my life suffering and staring into your eyes. But . . . you are silent. I beg you!"

Sofia Petrovna, as if caught unawares, quickly began to think of words with which she could restrain Ilin. "I will leave!" she decided, but could not make the move in order to get up because Ilin was on his knees at her feet. . . . He embraced her knees, stared into her face, and spoke passionately, warmly, beautifully. In her fear and frenzy she did not hear his words; why now, at this dangerous moment, when her knees were being pleasantly pressed, as in a warm bath, with some kind of angry spitefulness was she searching to be rational in her reactions? She was angry because instead of protesting virtuously, she was filled with weakness, sluggishness, and futility like a drunkard up to his knees in the ocean. It was as if in the depths of her being some distant small splinter teased maliciously: "Why don't you leave? Does this mean that the inevitable is occurring? Yes?"

Seeking sense within herself, she could not understand why she did not pull her hand away to which Ilin was sticking like a leech. And why was she hastily looking around, simultaneously with Ilin, to the right and left, to see if anyone was observing what was going on? The pines and the clouds stood motionless and looked on sternly, like old uncles, seeing the nonsense, but as if obliged not to report to the authorities because they had been paid off. A sentinel-like trunk stood on the embankment and it seemed to be observing the bench.

"Let it look!" thought Sofia Petrovna.

"Look . . . you must listen!" she finally remarked with anxiety in her voice. "Why go on? What will come of this?"

"I don't know, I don't know," he whispered, waving away the unpleasant questions with his hand.

The loud, jangling whistle of a locomotive was heard. This external, cold sound of ordinary activity made Ilin rouse himself.

"I don't have any more time. . . . It is time for me to leave!" she said, getting up quickly. "The train is coming. . . . André is arriving. I must see to his dinner."

Sofia Petrovna turned her burning face toward the railroad embankment. The locomotive slowly passed by first, and after this could be seen the cars. It was not the cottager's train but a freight train. One after another, the long chain stretched along the white background of the church, like the days of human existence, seemingly without end.

Finally, the train came to an end and the last car with its chimney and conductor disappeared behind the verdant trees and bushes. Sofia Petrovna turned sharply and not looking at Ilin, quickly went back toward the path. She had regained control over herself. Red with shame, she was outraged with herself and not with Ilin—with her own faintheartedness, her own shamelessness . . . that she, a moral and decent woman, had permitted a man other than her husband to embrace her knees. She thought of only one thing now: how to get as quickly as possible to her cottage and her family.

The barrister could barely keep up with her. Turning from the entrance to the narrow path, she glanced at him briefly, seeing only the sand on his knees, and motioned with her hand that he should leave her.

Arriving home, Sofia Petrovna stood motionless in her room for about five minutes, glanced at the window, and then at her desk.

"Vile hussy!" she castigated herself. "Hussy!"

Angry with herself, she recalled all the details, not hiding anything, of the days when she had objected to Ilin's courting, and what it was that had *drawn* her to meet him in order to clarify their relationship. However, when he threw himself at her feet, she had felt unusual pleasure. Recalling everything, not having any compassion for herself, and choking with shame, it would have made her happy had she been able to slap herself.

"Poor André," she thought, and while thinking, she tried to put a tender look upon her face. "Varya, my poor daughter, does not know what a mother she has! Forgive me, darlings! I love you very, very much!"

And, wishing to convince herself that she was still a good wife and mother, and that her "principles" of which she had spoken to Ilin had remained intact, Sofia Petrovna hurried into the kitchen and scolded the cook for not having the table ready for André Ilich. She strove to picture the tired and hungry husband, expressing her sympathy for him, and set the table herself for him, which she had never done previously. Then she searched out Varya, her daughter, lifted her in her arms, and embraced her warmly. The little girl seemed heavy and cold to her, but she did not want to admit this to herself, and then took to enlightening her about how fine, honorable, and good her daddy was.

To balance things out, when André Ilich soon arrived, she hardly greeted him. The overflow of affected feelings had already passed, not having proved anything and only making her irritable and angry with herself for lying. She sat by a window, pained and angry. Only in poverty can people comprehend how difficult it is to control one's feelings and thoughts. Sofia Petrovna later recounted that she was overcome by "confusion in which it was as difficult to be discriminating as it was to count swiftly flying sparrows." Because of the fact, for example, that she was not happy about the arrival of her husband,

and that she was not pleased by the way he attacked his dinner, she suddenly concluded that she had begun to hate her husband.

André Ilich, languid from fatigue and hunger, while waiting for his soup, pounced upon the sausage and ate it greedily, chewing noisily and moving his temples.

"Good God," Sofia Petrovna thought. "I love and respect him, but why does he chew so repulsively?"

The chaos in her thoughts was no less than in her feelings. Lubyantseva, like all those who are inexperienced in battle with unpleasant thoughts, tried with all her might not to think of her distress. And the more intensely she tried, the more vividly Ilin stood out in her imagination, with the sand on his knees, the billowing clouds, the train. . . .

"Why did I, dimwit, go there today?" she tortured herself. "Am I really so weak that I'm incapable of controlling myself?"

Fear makes mountains out of molehills. When André Ilich finished eating, she had already decided: she would tell all to her husband and flee from danger!

"I need, André, to speak seriously with you," she began after dinner, when her husband had taken off his jacket and shoes in order to lie down for a rest.

"Yes?"

"Let us leave here!"

"Hm. . . . Where to? It's too early to go to town."

"No, lets take a trip or something like that. . . ."

"To travel . . . ," mumbled the notary, stretching. "I've dreamed of that, too, but where's the money to come from, and who will take my place at the office?"

And, thinking it over a little, he added:

"Really, you're bored. Go yourself, if you wish!"

Sofia Petrovna agreed, but at the same time she had imagined that Ilin would be thrilled to be able to go with her in the same train, in the same coach. . . . As she thought, she looked at her husband who was no longer hungry, but still tired. Why did her glance stop at his very small feet, almost feminine, covered with striped socks with threads sticking out at the tips of both?

Behind the lowered shade a bee buzzed and beat against the window pane. Sofia Petrovna looked at the threads, listened to the bee, and imagined how she would go. . . . She would be sitting opposite Ilin night and day, he not taking his eyes away from her, angry at his weakness and pale from an aching spirit. He would exaggerate his degenerate immaturity, scold her, pull at his hair, waiting, however, for darkness to catch a time when the passengers would be asleep or going out to the station in order to fall on his knees before her and embrace her legs as on the bench. . . .

She took hold of herself. What was she dreaming?

"Listen, I won't go alone!" she said. "You must go with me!"

"Fantasy, dear little Sofia!" sighed Lubyantsev. "We must be serious. Wishing is all that's possible."

"You will come when you know the score!" thought Sofia Petrovna.

Having decided to go away no matter what, she felt herself free of danger. Little by little her thoughts became proper. She grew gay and even allowed herself to think of everything: how not to think, not to dream, but all the same to go away! While her husband napped, it gradually became evening. . . . She stayed in the living room and played the piano. The liveliness of evening goings-on behind the windows, the sounds of the music, and, more important, the thought that she had a good head and had coped with a disaster had absolutely cheered her up. Other women—her peaceful conscience said to her— in her position, truly would not have resisted and would have been knocked off their feet as if by the wind, but she had blushed with shame, suffered, and now ran from danger, which might or might not have existed! Her virtuousness and decisiveness so pleased her that she even glanced at herself in the mirror several times.

When it got dark, guests arrived. The men settled in the dining room to play cards and the ladies took up the living room and the terrace. Ilin showed up after everyone else. He was sullen and gloomy, as if he were ill. He sat on the corner of the divan and did not get up the whole evening. Ordinarily he was jovial and talkative, but this time he sat silently, frowned, and scratched around his eyes. When he had to answer someone's question, he forced a smile, using only his upper lip, and answered jerkily and unpleasantly. Five times he tried to make a witty remark, but they all came out stiff and crude. It appeared to Sofia Petrovna that he was close to hysteria. It was only now, while sitting at the piano, she saw clearly for the first time that this unhappy man was not joking and that his spirit was sick and that he was lost. Because of her he was losing the best days of his youth and career, wasting his last rubles on a cottage, and had left his mother and sister to the mercy of fate; but more important, he was exhausted by the agonizing struggle with himself. Simply from ordinary human kindness, it followed that one had to consider him seriously. . . .

She recognized this clearly, so much so that her heart ached, and if at that time she had gone up to Ilin and told him "No!" her voice would have been so weak that it would have been difficult to hear. But, she approached him and did not say this, or even thought of this. . . . The small-mindedness and egoism of a youthful temperament never, it seems, became so strongly apparent in her as on this evening. She recognized that Ilin was wretched and was sitting on the divan as if on hot coals. She was pained for him, but at the same time the presence of a person who passionately loved her filled her spirit with solemnity and the feeling of her own strength. She felt her youth, her beauty, her unapproachability and—luckily she had decided to go away!—on this evening she released herself completely. She flirted, laughed incessantly, sang with special feeling and inspiration. Everything made her merry and everything became humorous for her. It was funny to recall the time on the bench and of the observation of the watchman. The guests amused her, and the crude wit of Ilin and his tiepin, which she had never noticed previously. The tiepin looked like a little red snake with diamond eyes. This little snake seemed so ridiculous to her that she would have been ready to cover it with kisses.

Sofia Petrovna tremulously sang love songs with something of a half-drunk fervor, and as if tantalizing someone else's grief, she selected the saddest, melancholy songs that wailed of lost hopes, of the past, of old age. . . . "Old age approaches closer and closer . . . ," she sang. And what had old age to do with her?

"It seems that something is going on in me that is wrong," she thought from time to time while laughing and singing.

The guests departed at about midnight. Ilin was the last to leave. Sofia Petrovna was seized by an eagerness to walk him to the bottom step of the terrace. She wished to let him know that she was going away with her husband and to see what an effect this news would have upon him.

The moon was hiding behind the clouds, but it was still somewhat bright so that Sofia Petrovna saw how the wind played with his coattails and with the awnings of the terrace. It was obvious also how pale Ilin was, how strained his smile was, and how his upper lip was curled.

"Sonya, my dear little Sonya . . . my precious woman!" he mumbled, preventing her from speaking. "My sweet one, my darling!"

In this burst of tenderness, with tears in his voice, he showered her with caressing words, one sweeter than the other, and even permitted himself to address her with the familiar form of "you," as one does with a wife or a mistress. He unexpectedly put one arm around her waist and took hold of her elbow with the other.

"Darling, my lovely," he whispered, kissing the back of her neck. "Be sincere, come with me now!"

She released herself from his embrace and raised her head in order to burst out with indignation and to be outraged, but the outrage did not show, and all her praiseworthy good intentions and virtue remained only in order to speak the phrase which all ordinary women say under similar circumstances:

"You're out of your mind!"

"True, let's go!" continued Ilin. "Right now, and there on the bench, I was convinced that you, Sonya, are as weak as I. . . . Remain weak! You love me and now fruitlessly struggle with your conscience. . . ."

Seeing that she was leaving him, he grabbed her lacy sleeve and quickly added:

"If not today, tomorrow, for the time will come to yield! Why drag it out? My darling, dear Sonya, the verdict has been issued; why deny its fulfillment? Why deceive yourself?"

Sofia Petrovna pulled herself away from him and dashed through the door. Returning to the living room, she mechanically closed the piano, took a long look at the sheet music, and sat down. She could neither stand nor think. . . . From the excitement and fervor there only remained in her a terrible weakness with a feeling of indolence and tedium. Her conscience whispered to her that she had behaved stupidly during the evening, like a goofy young girl—that she had just been embraced on the terrace, and still felt some kind of awkwardness in her waist and around her elbow. There wasn't a soul in the living room and only one candle was burning. Lubyantseva sat on the round stool before the piano, not moving, somehow waiting for something. Being consumed by the utter impossibility and darkness, she was seized, nevertheless, by an intense, unexpected desire. As if a python had paralyzed her limbs and her soul, the desire grew with every second and no longer irritated her as previously, but was obvious to her in all its nakedness.

She sat motionless for half an hour, constantly thinking of Ilin, then indolently rose and trudged to the bedroom. André Ilich was already in bed. She sat by the open window and repulsed her desire. The "muddles" in her head were no longer there, and all her thoughts and feelings jostled each other around one clear purpose. She would have tried to struggle with it, but instantly gave up. She now understood how strong and implacable the enemy was. In order to battle with it, it was necessary to be strong and guarded, and her birthright, upbringing, and experience gave her nothing upon which she could lean.

"Immoral! Filthy female!" she scathed herself for her weakness. "What kind of a woman are you?"

Her outraged decency was so repelled by this weakness that she derided herself with every disparaging word she knew, with many insulting, demeaning truths. So, she told herself, you've never been moral, you've not fallen before only because the opportunity wasn't there—and your struggle all day has been a game and a comedy. . . .

"Let's assume that there has been a struggle," she thought, "but what a struggle! Merchants struggle before they sell, but all the same they sell. It was a good fight: like milk, it will be curdled in one day! In one day!"

She knew that it was not emotional feelings which were impelling her not to leave home, nor the personality of Ilin, but that which awaited her in the future. She would be just one of the many summer mistresses, a strolling madame!

"How they killed the mother near the little fledgling," someone sang haltingly in a hoarse tenor outside the window.

"If you're to go, the time is now," Sofia Petrovna thought. Her heart suddenly began to beat with a frightening strength.

"André!" she nearly screamed. "Listen, we . . . we are going to go? Yes?"

"Yes . . . I already told you: go by yourself!"

"But listen a little . . . ," she spurted out. "If you don't go with me, you risk losing me! I, it seems, am really in love!"

"With whom?" André Ilich asked.

"It wouldn't make any difference to you who it is!" shouted Sofia Petrovna.

André Ilich raised himself, lowered his legs, and looked with amazement at the dark figure of his wife.

"Fantasy!" he yawned.

He didn't believe it, but all the same, he became frightened. Thinking it over and asking his wife some unimportant questions, he declared his view of the family, of infidelity. . . . He spoke listlessly for about ten minutes and then lay down. His maxim was a failure. This world is full of opinions and more than half of them belong to people who have never been in trouble!

In spite of the late hour, behind the windows summer residents were still moving about. Sofia Petrovna threw over herself a light cape, stood up, and thought. . . . She was still held by a determination to tell her sleeping husband:

"Are you sleeping? I'm going for a walk. . . . Do you want to come with me?"

That was her last hope. Not receiving an answer, she went out. The air was fresh and breezy. She neither felt the breeze nor the darkness, but walked and walked. . . . An overwhelming strength drove her on, and it seemed that if she stopped, it would have given her back a push.

"Immoral!" she muttered mechanically. "Fiend!"

She gasped for breath, flushed from shame; she did not feel her legs beneath her, but only that which moved her forward, and that which was stronger than her shame, and her reason, and her fear. . . .

1886

The Long Tongue

N atalia Mihighlovna, a young lady, having arrived in the morning from Yalta, was eating and indefatigably chattering, describing to her husband the wonders of the Crimea. Her husband was overjoyed and looked lovingly at her enraptured face. He listened and from time to time asked questions. . . .

Among the questions he asked was: "But they say that the cost of living is unusually high?"

"How can I tell you? As far as I am concerned, the high prices are greatly exaggerated, Daddy. It's not as bad as it's painted. I, for example, with Julia Petrovna, had a very comfortable and decent room for twenty rubles a night. All, my darling, depends on how you know how to live. Of course, if you want to go into the mountains, somewhere . . . for example, to Ai-Petri, you have to take a horse and a guide . . . so then, of course, it's expensive. Terribly, terribly expensive! But, Vasechka, what moun . . . tains! Picture to yourself high, high mountains . . . a thousand times higher than the church. . . . Above are clouds, clouds, clouds. . . . Below are huge boulders, boulders, boulders. . . . And the pines. . . . Oh, I can't bear to remember them!"

"By the way . . . when you weren't here, I read in one of the magazines about the Tartar guides from that place. . . . What villains! Are they really such unusual people?"

Natalia Mihighlovna made a scornful face and shook her head.

"The ordinary Tartar is nothing unique," she said. "Though, I only saw them from a distance, in passing. . . . They were pointed out to me, but I didn't pay any attention. I always felt, Daddy, biased toward these Circassians, Greeks . . . Moors!"

"They say they're passionate Don Juans."

"That may be! There are villains who . . ."

Natalia Mihighlovna suddenly got up, as if she remembered something terrible, looked at her husband for some seconds with frightened eyes, and said, dragging out every word:

"Vasechka, I tell you, there is immorality! Oh, what immorality! Not, however, you know, from the ordinary or middle classes, but the female aristocracy, those stuck-up high society women! Simply terrible. I couldn't believe my own eyes! I won't forget it 'til the day I die! I suppose one can forget to some extent in order to. . . . Oh, Vasechka, I don't even want to talk about it! Take my travelling companion, Julia Petrovna. . . . A wonderful husband, two children . . . belongs to the right circle, always posing as saintly, and—suddenly, you can imagine for yourself. . . . Only, Daddy, this is, of course, *entre nous*. Give me your word of honor that you won't tell anyone!"

"What have you imagined! Naturally, I won't say a word."

"Word of honor? To be sure! I trust you. . . ."

The young lady laid down her fork, put a secretive look on her face, and whispered:

"Imagine this. . . . Julia Petrovna took a trip up the mountains. . . . The weather was wonderful! She is riding in front with her guide, and I am a little behind them. We rode about three or four versts, when suddenly—get the picture, Vasechka—Julia screams and grasps her breasts. Her guide, the Tartar, grabs her around the waist, otherwise she would have fallen from the saddle. . . . I, with my guide, rode up to her. . . . 'What is it? What's the matter?' 'Oh,' she cries, 'I'm dying! I'm faint! I can't ride any farther!' Imagine my fright! 'So we'll go back,' I say! 'No, I tell you, Natalia, I can't even ride back! If I go only one more step, I will die from pain! I'm having spasms!' And she begs, pleads for God's sake, that I and my Syleman return to town and return with her tension-releasing drops which help her."

"Hold up a bit. . . . I really don't understand you," mumbled her husband, scratching his head. "Earlier you said that you only saw these Tartars from a distance, and now you tell me about some kind of Syleman."

"But, you are again picking on a word!" frowned the little woman, not a little confused. "I can't stand your suspiciousness! I can't stand it! It's stupid, it's silly!"

"I'm not being picky, but . . . why tell falsehoods? So you were riding with Tartars, so that's that, all right. But . . . why equivocate?"

"Hmm!. . . . What a strange man!" thought the exasperated little dame.

"Jealous of Syleman! I imagine, if you were to go up the mountains, it would be without a guide! I can imagine it! You don't know anything about life in that place, and you don't understand it. It would be better if you remained silent. Absolutely silent! Without a guide you can't take one step."

"Of course!"

"Please, none of those dumb smiles! I'm not some kind of Julia to you. I'm not making excuses for her, but I . . . psss! I don't pose as a saint, but up to this time, I haven't lost control of myself. Syleman did not take liberties with me. No way! Mametkyl dallied by Julia all the time, but in my place, as soon as eleven o'clock struck, immediately: 'Syleman, march! Time to leave.' And my stupid Tartar got moving. By me, Daddy, he was ruled with an iron fist. When he equivocated over the bill or anything else, I would immediately demand: 'How come? What's this? What's that?' So his heart sank to his boots. . . . Ha, ha, ha. . . . His eyes, Vasechka, understand, were very dark, like coal, and his little Tartar mouth was so stupid looking that it was funny. . . . That's how I stopped him! So!"

"I can imagine . . . ," mumbled her husband, rolling beads out of the bread.

"It's stupid, Vasechka! I really know what thoughts you're having! I know what you think. . . . But I tell you truly, that even when we were walking, he never crossed the line. For example, we were riding up the mountains, or to the waterfall, Uchan-Su. I always told him: 'Syleman, ride in the back! So!' And the poor thing always rode in the back. . . . Even at the time . . . in the most pathetic situations I told him: 'All the same you must not forget that you are only a Tartar and I am the wife of a state councillor!' Ha, ha . . ."

The little woman laughed, then quickly looking around and putting on a frightened look, whispered:

"But Julia! Oh, that Julia! I understand, Vasechka, why it is necessary not to play around, and why not to take a vacation from the emptiness of society! All that can . . . make jokes, be welcoming, and nobody will criticize you, but to look at this seriously, and to make scenes. . . . No, if you wish, I don't understand! Imagine, she became jealous! Now wasn't that dumb? Once Mametkyl, her passion, came to her place. . . . She wasn't home. . . . So, I called him to come over to mine. . . . We began to talk about this and that. . . . You know, very amusing things! The evening passed unnoticed. Suddenly Julia rushed in. . . . She pounced on me, on Mametkyl . . . made a scene. . . . Phew! I can't understand that, Vasechka. . . ."

Vasechka snorted, frowned, and stomped around the room.

"You had a high time there and nothing to tell!" he grumbled, smiling sardonically.

"But, how sil . . . ly!" Natalia Mihighlovna was insulted. "I know what you are thinking! You always have such vile thoughts! I won't tell you anything. I won't!"

The little woman pouted and became silent.

1886

Chorus Girl

Once, when she was younger, more beautiful, and her voice lovelier, Nikolay Petrovich Kolpakov, an admirer, was at her summer cottage sitting in the mezzanine. It was unbearably hot and humid. Kolpakov had just eaten and drunk a bottle of cheap port wine. He was in a bad mood and did not feel well. They were both bored and were waiting for the heat to let up so that they could take a walk.

Suddenly, the doorbell rang. Kolpakov, who did not have his jacket on and was wearing slippers, jumped up and looked questioningly at Pasha.

"It must be the mailman or possibly a girlfriend," commented the singer.

Kolpakov was not bothered by the mailman or a girlfriend, but, just in case, he picked up his jacket and went into the adjacent room and Pasha hurried to the door. To her great amazement, standing on the threshold was not the mailman nor a girlfriend, but an unknown woman, young, lovely, well-dressed, and from all appearances, respectable.

The strange woman was pale and was breathing heavily, as if she had just climbed a long stairway.

"What can I do for you?" asked Pasha.

The young woman did not answer at once. She came forward, slowly looked over the room, and sat down, seeming not to be able to stand, either from fatigue or illness; her pale lips trembled as she tried to say something.

"Is my husband here?" she finally asked, raising to Pasha her large eyes whose lids were red from much crying.

"What husband?" Pasha whispered, suddenly so afraid that her hands and feet grew cold. "What husband?" she repeated, starting to tremble.

"My husband . . . Nikolay Petrovich Kolpakov."

"No . . . no, Madame. . . . I don't know your husband."

A moment of silence passed. The unknown woman wiped her pale lips several times with a handkerchief as if trying to overcome her internal shivering, and held her breath as Pasha stood motionless, seeming rooted, and stared at her, uncomprehending and fearful.

"So you say, he isn't here?" asked the lady, now with a hard voice and with a strange smile.

"I . . . I don't know about whom you are asking."

"You're wicked, vile, loathsome!" exclaimed the stranger, looking over Pasha with hate and revulsion. "Yes, yes . . . you are wicked. I'm very, very happy that I'm finally able to say that to you!"

Pasha felt that she had given the impression of something truly villainous and ugly to this woman in black with angry eyes and with delicate white fingers, and she became ashamed of her full red cheeks, the pock mark on her nose, and the curls on her forehead which she could not comb back. And it seemed to her that if she were slender, had no powder on, and had no curls, that she could have hidden that she was dishonorable, and it wouldn't have been so frightening and shameful to stand before this mysterious woman whom she did not know.

"Where is my husband?" continued the woman. "However, if he is not here, it makes no difference to me, for I must tell you that embezzlement has been discovered and Nikolay Petrovich is being sought. They want to arrest him. This is what you have wrought!"

The lady arose and excitedly walked around the room. Pasha watched her and fear kept her from understanding.

"Today they will find and arrest him," said the lady and sobbed, and in this sound could be heard hurt and grief. "I know who led him to this kind of horror! Vile, loathsome! Repulsive, mercenary creature!" (The lady's lips curled, and her nose twitched from revulsion.) "I am weak . . . listen, you fallen woman! I am weak, you are stronger than I, is there anyone to intercede for me and for my children? God sees everything! He is just! He will exact payment from you for every one of my tears, for all my sleepless nights! The time will come when you will recall what I've said!"

Silence reigned again. The woman strutted about the room cracking her knuckles while Pasha continued to watch her, dumbfounded, not perceiving, not understanding, and waiting for something terrible.

"I, Madame, know nothing!" she repeated and suddenly began to cry.

"You lie!" screamed the lady and her eyes flashed angrily. "I know everything! I have known about you for a long time! I know that in the last month he has been with you every day!"

"Yes. So what? What of it? I have many guests, and I don't force anyone to come. He is free to come and go."

"I tell you: embezzlement was detected! He embezzled on the job someone else's money! For the sake of this . . . for the likes of you, for your sake he decided to commit a crime. Listen," said the lady with a firm intonation and placing herself directly before Pasha. "You cannot have any principles for you live only to cause evil, that is your purpose, but it is impossible to think that you have fallen so low that you don't have some human feeling left! He has a wife, children. . . . If they convict him and send him away, the children and I will starve to death. . . . You must understand that! Meanwhile there is a means to save him and us from poverty and disgrace. If I can bring nine hundred rubles today, they will leave him alone. Only nine hundred rubles!"

"What nine hundred rubles?" Pasha asked quietly. "I . . . I know nothing. . . . I didn't take any."

"I'm not begging you for nine hundred rubles. . . . You don't have any money. I'm asking for something else. . . . Men usually give valuable jewels to women like you. Return to me only those which my husband gave you."

"Madame, he has never given me any gifts!" screamed Pasha, beginning to understand.

"Where's the money? He has spent his, mine, and that of others.

. . . Where has all this gotten to? Listen, I beg you! I was overwrought and said unpleasant things to you, but I excuse myself. You must hate me, I know, but if you are capable of suffering, step into my shoes! I plead with you, return the things to me!"

"Hm . . . ," said Pasha, shrugging her shoulders. "I would be happy to, but, Lord strike me dead, I've been given nothing. Believe it, I have a clear conscience. However, you are right," the singer was confused. "I was brought two little pieces. If it pleases you, I will give them to you."

Pasha pulled out one of the drawers in her dressing table and took from it a hollow gold bracelet and a narrow little ring with a ruby.

"Please!" she said, handing the visitor these things.

The lady sobbed and her face trembled. She was insulted.

"What is this you are giving me?" she said. "I'm not asking for charity, but for that which does not belong to you, which you, making use of your circumstances, got out of my husband . . . that weak, unhappy human being. . . . When I saw you with my husband on Thursday on the pier, you had on valuable brooches and bracelets. Consequently, it's no use playing tricks on me, innocent little lamb! I beg you for the last time: Are you going to give me the things or not?"

"Really, how strange you are," said Pasha, beginning to be insulted. "I tell you truly that from your Nikolay Petrovich I have nothing but this ring and bracelet. He sent me only sweets."

"Sweet cakes . . . ," the stranger bitterly laughed. "At home the children have nothing and here, sweet cakes. You definitely will not return the things?"

Not receiving an answer, the lady sat down, and thought about something, and stared at one spot.

"What's to be done now?" she muttered. "If I don't get nine hundred rubles, he is lost, and I and the children are lost. Shall I kill this viper or get on my knees before her?"

The lady covered her face with her handkerchief and sobbed.

"I beg you!" could be heard through her sobs. "You have, as you know, destroyed and debauched my husband, now save him.

. . . If you have no feeling for him, but the children . . . the children. . . . What are the children guilty of?"

Pasha pictured small children who were out on the street and were crying from hunger, and she too sobbed.

"What can I do, Madame?" she said. "You say I am loathsome and destroyed Nikolay Petrovich, but I, before the true God . . . swear to you, I have nothing useful from him. . . . In our chorus only Motey is paid highly and we all exist from hand to mouth. Nikolay Petrovich is an educated and refined gentleman, so I received him. We must receive someone like that."

"I beg you! Give me the things! I cry . . . lower myself. If you please, I will get on my knees! If you please!"

Pasha shrieked in fright and wrung her hands. She felt that this pale, beautiful lady, who expressed herself elegantly as in the theater, could at the same time be on her knees before her simply from pride and arrogance in order to remain superior and demean the chorus girl.

"All right, I will give you everything!" declared Pasha, beginning to fuss around and wiping her eyes. "If you please. Only they are not from Nikolay Petrovich. I received them from other guests. As you wish. . . ."

Pasha opened the top drawer of the dresser, took from it brooches with diamonds, a string of corals, several rings, and a bracelet, and gave them to the lady.

"Take these, if you wish, only I have nothing from your husband. Take them, get rich!" continued Pasha, offended by the threat of the woman to get on her knees. "And if you are the honorable . . . his legal wife, then I would keep him to myself. So be it! I did not ask him to come to me. He came on his own. . . ."

The lady, through her tears, looked over the things being given her and said:

"This is not everything. . . . There's only about five hundred rubles worth."

Pasha impetuously took from the drawer a gold watch, a cigarette case, and cuff links and said, spreading out her hands:

"I have nothing else. . . . You can search me!"

The visitor sighed and with shaking hands wrapped the objects in her scarf, and, not saying a word, not even nodding her head, left.

The door of the adjacent room opened, and Kolpakov entered. He was pale and was nervously shaking his head as if he had just drunk something very bitter; his eyes glistened with tears.

"What kind of things did you bring me?" Pasha cast at him. "When, may I ask you?"

"Things . . . that is nothing . . . things!" Kolpakov repeated and shook his head. "My God! She cried before you, lowered herself. . . ."

"I ask you: what kind of things did you bring me?" cried Pasha.

"My God, she, a respectable, proud, pure . . . she was even ready to get on her knees . . . before this babe! And I drove her to this! I permitted it!"

He shook his head and groaned:

"No, I will never forgive myself for this! I will never forgive it! Get away from me . . . you trash!" he exclaimed with repugnance, moving backwards from Pasha and keeping her away with shaking hands. "She wanted to get on her knees and . . . before whom? Before you! Oh, my God!"

He quickly dressed himself, and with apparent disgust avoided Pasha, took himself toward the door, and left.

Pasha laid down and burst into tears. She already had regrets about the things which she had given away in a moment of excitement, and that hurt. She recalled how three years ago, a merchant beat her for no reason, and her crying became even louder.

1893

Ninotchka

|T| he door is being opened quietly and my good friend enters. Pavel Sergeyevich Viklenev is a young person, but is old-looking and is unwell. He is stooped, long-nosed, and skinny. In general, he is not good-looking and because his physiognomy is so unpretentious, gentle, and dull, every time you look at him you get a strange desire to take it into your five fingers as if to feel the softheartedness and soulful doughiness.

"What's up?" I ask, looking at his pale face and slightly trembling lips. "Are you ill or have you had another rift with your wife? You look awful!"

Hesitating a little and giving out a cough, Viklenev waves his hand and says: "Would you do something for me with Ninotchka! Dear friend, such grief that I couldn't sleep all night and as you can see, I'm barely alive. . . . I'm in a hell of a fix! Others don't get at all upset, take lightly insults, losses, sickness, but I get limp and unwound over a trifle."

"What happened?"

"Nonsense . . . a small family scene. I'll tell you about it if you want. Last evening my Ninotchka didn't go anywhere, stayed at home, and said she wanted to spend the evening with me. I was delighted, of course. In the evenings she usually leaves for a meeting somewhere, but I usually remain at home, alone, so you can imagine how delighted I was by this. However, you've never been married so you can't judge how warm and cozy it feels when coming home from work you find that for which you live. . . . Oh!"

Viklenev describes the charms of family life, wipes the perspiration from his forehead, and continues:

"Ninotchka wanted to spend the evening with me. . . . But you know me! I'm a boring person, dull, and not sharp. What kind of fun is it with me? I'm forever with my blueprints and soil filters. I don't know how to play, or dance a little, or to joke around. I'm good for nothing and Ninotchka, you will agree, is young and worldly. . . . Youth has its rights. . . . Isn't that so? So, I began to show her pictures, a variety of things, and yes . . . telling her about a thing or two. . . . By the way, I remembered some old letters in my desk which were to the point and among these letters were some ludicrous ones! When I was a student, I had some friends who wrote clever, roguish things! When you read what they wrote, you could split your sides laughing. I took these letters from the desk and began to read them to Ninotchka. I read her one letter, then another, and a third . . . and suddenly . . . put on the brakes! In one of the letters a phrase occurred: 'Kate sends you regards.' For a jealous wife such phrases are a dagger and my Ninotchka is an Othello in a skirt.

"My miserable head was showered with questions: Who was this Katenka? How come? What for? I told her this Katenka was like a first love . . . an affair during student days, young and green, and to which couldn't, in no way, be given any importance. Everybody has a Katenka in his youth. You can't avoid it. . . . My Ninotchka doesn't listen! She imagines, the devil knows what, and is in tears. After tears, hysteria.

" 'You,' she screams, 'are vile, fiendish! You have been hiding your past from me. Could be you have some kind of Katenka now, and are hiding this from me!'

"I tried to convince her over and over, but to no avail. . . . Male logic can never defeat woman's. Finally, I begged forgiveness on my knees . . . crawled and whatever you care to imagine. She went to bed hysterical—she in her room and I in mine on a couch. . . . This morning there is no smoothing over. She pouts and stares. She promises to go to her mother's. And she'll really do this—I know what she's like!"

"That's a pretty kettle of fish!"

"I just can't understand women! But allow that Ninotchka is young, likeable, and haughty, you couldn't compose such prose for her as for Katenka. . . . But really, is it so difficult to forgive? Allow that I'm guilty, but I begged forgiveness, crawled on my knees! I, if you want to know, even . . . cried!"

"Yes, women are a great puzzle."

"Dear friend, you have lots of influence on Ninotchka, she respects you, sees an authority in you. I beg you go to her, exercise your influence, and move her into seeing that she's wrong. . . . I suffer, dear friend! . . . If this situation continues for another day, I won't be able to stand it. Begone, my friend!"

"But do you think it will be all right?"

"Why wouldn't it be all right? You've been friends almost since childhood and she believes you. . . . Be kind and go to her!"

The tearful pleas of Viklenev move me. I dress and drive to his wife.

I find Ninotchka in her favorite pursuit: she is sitting on the couch with legs crossed, gazing blankly with her pretty little eyes, and doing nothing. . . . Seeing me, she jumps up from the couch and runs to me. . . . Then she takes a quick look around, shuts the door, and light as a feather hangs on my neck. (Don't, dear reader, think that there is a misprint here. It's been a year since I shared with Viklenev his marital obligations.)

"What have you been up to again, you imp?" I ask Ninotchka, seating her beside me.

"What is it?"

"You have again contrived torture for your husband! He has come to me today with the tale about Katenka."

"Oh, that! He's found someone to complain to!"

"What happened?"

"Some nonsense. . . . It was boring yesterday evening. . . . I was angry because I had no place to go, so out of vexation I took on his Katenka. I cried from boredom, and how can you explain such tears to him?"

"But you know, dear heart, that it is cruel, inhuman. He is so high-strung and you and your scenes only make him more so."

"Not at all. He loves it when I'm jealous. . . . Nothing is so distracting as false jealousy. . . . But let's leave this conversation. . . . I don't like it when you start talking about my wimp. . . . He's bored me enough. . . . It's better that we drink tea. . . ."

"All the same, stop torturing him. . . . It's too pathetic to see. He describes family happiness so sincerely and honorably and has such faith in your love that it puts one in awe. You really can somehow control yourself, be nice, lie. . . . Only one word from you is enough for him to feel himself in seventh heaven."

Ninotchka pouts and frowns, but all the same when Viklenev enters a little later and timidly looks at me, she smiles happily and looks at him fondly.

"You came just in time for tea!" she says to him. "You always know when I'm home, and never are late. . . . Would you like cream or lemon?"

Viklenev, not expecting such a reception, is moved. He kisses his wife's hand with feeling, embraces me, and this embrace is so awkward and out of place that Ninotchka and I both blush. . . .

"Blessed are the peacemakers!" joyfully prattles the happy husband. "Why did you succeed in convincing her? Because you are a man of the world, have travelled in high society, know all subtleties of the woman's heart! Ha-ha-ha! I'm a lout and sluggard. Only one word needs to be said and I'll say ten. . . . It's only necessary to kiss a little hand or something else, but I don't even begin to do anything! Ha-ha-ha!"

After tea Viklenev takes me into his study, takes hold of one of my buttons, and mutters:

"I don't know how to thank you, my dear fellow. You know how I suffered, tortured myself, and now how happy I am—more than I can handle! And this is not the first time you got me out of a terrible mess. My dear friend, don't deny me! I have one little thing . . . a small locomotive which I put together myself. . . . I received a medal for it at an exhibit. . . . Take it as a sign of recognition . . . friendship! . . . Do me this favor."

It is understandable that I try to refuse in every way possible, but Viklenev is implacable and I, like it or not, take his dear little gift.

Days pass, weeks, months . . . and sooner or later the damn truth becomes obvious to Viklenev in all its vile magnitude. Learning by chance of the truth, he becomes terribly pale, lies on his couch, and stares dully at the ceiling. . . . He doesn't say a word about this. But the pain inflicted upon his soul must be expressed in some kind of action, and so he starts to toss torturously from side to side on his couch. With these movements he organizes his weak-willed nature.

Within a week, a little straightened out after his staggering news, Viklenev approaches me. We are both embarrassed and cannot face each other. I begin, for no reason at all, to talk through my hat about free love, conjugal egoism, and being resigned to one's fate.

"It's not about that," he abruptly interrupts me. "I understand all this very well. No one can be blamed for his feelings. I'm interested in another aspect of the matter that is purely practical. I, dear friend, don't know beans about life, or what is the right thing to do, or the customs of high society, and in this I'm a wimp. You, my dear fellow, can help me. Tell me how to behave toward Ninotchka now. Should she continue to live with me, or would you consider it preferable that she should come to you?"

It did not take us long to come to a decision arrived upon mutually: Ninotchka stays with Viklenev. I visit her whenever I take it into my head to do so, and Viklenev disappears to a corner room that was a pantry at one time. This room is a bit damp and dark. The entrance is through the kitchen. You can, therefore, shut yourself away exceedingly well and be out of everyone's way.

1885

Life's Afflictions

According to the observations of sophisticated people, it is not easy even for the old priests to keep separate from the local life. Moreover, they often detect in their own maturity stinginess and greed, and over-anxiety about health, faintheartedness, obstinacy, unhappiness, etc.

—P. Nechaev, *Practical Guide for Priests*

T he only daughter of Anna Mihighlovna Lebyedeva, a colonel's wife, died when a young bride. The consequence of this death was another one: the old mother, devastated by what she felt was a visitation from God, felt that all of her past was dead, beyond retrieving, and that now a second life was beginning, one which had nothing in common with the first one.

She began to lead a bustling and disorderly life. Before doing anything else, she sent a thousand rubles to Afon and donated half of her family's silver to the church's cemetery. Shortly afterwards she stopped smoking and swore never to eat meat. But none of this gave her surcease, and, on the contrary, her consciousness of old age and the proximity of death became sharper and more pronounced. Anna Mihighlovna then sold her city home for next to nothing, and without any planning, hastily returned to her country home.

There comes a time in the consciousness of a person, in whatever form it might be, when the question arises about the reasons for existence and reveals a vigorous necessity to contemplate death. This does not require sacrifices, nor fasting, nor vegetarianism.

Fortunately for Anna Mihighlovna, after she arrived in her rural home in Zhenino, fate placed her in a situation which sustained her for a long time. It caused her to forget about old age and the proximity of death. It so happened that on the day she arrived, her cook Martin spilled boiling water over both of his legs. The servants ran for the local doctor but he was not at home. Anna Mihighlovna, even though squeamish but sympathetic, washed Martin's wounds, put an ointment on them, and bandaged both legs. She sat all night by his bed. Thanks to her efforts, Martin stopped groaning and fell asleep.

Her soul, as she recounted later, "revived." As if disclosed to her on the palms of her hands, her purpose in life became known to her. . . . Pale, with swollen eyes, she thankfully kissed the brow of the sleeping Martin and then said her prayers.

After this Lebyedeva kept herself busy healing. She recalled her sinful and disorderly past existence with revulsion. She no longer had nothing to do—her days were filled with much healing.

Besides this, among her admirers were doctors from whom she learned a thing or two. This and other things came in handy when needed. She wrote prescriptions, several books, a newspaper called *Doctor,* and boldly treated illnesses. In the beginning, her patients were only from Zhenino, but later they came from all the surrounding villages.

"Imagine, my dear!" she boasted to the priest's wife, three months after her arrival. "Sixteen patients came to me yesterday, and today twenty! I'm so worn out that I can hardly stand on my own two feet. All my opium was used up, imagine! In Gyrina there's an epidemic of dysentery!"

Every morning when she awoke, she remembered that people in pain awaited her and a pleasant chill ran through her. She dressed hastily, drank her tea, and then began receiving patients. The procedure of receiving patients gave her an inexpressible pleasure. First, she would list the patients very slowly in a notebook, as if wishing to prolong the pleasure, and then would call in each patient according to his turn.

The more a patient was suffering, the more filthy and repulsive was his ailment, the sweeter was the work to her. Nothing gave her as much satisfaction as the thought that she was fighting her own squeamishness. She did not spare herself and purposely strove to bury herself in rotting wounds. There were moments when, aware of her lack of knowledge and the unendurable stink of wounds, she fell into a kind of ecstatic cynicism, and a desire to restrain her nature was revealed to her. In these moments it seemed to her that she had reached the peak of her calling.

She adored her patients. She had a sneaking feeling that they were her saviors, but rationally she wanted to see them not as isolated individuals, not as peasants, but as an abstraction—*the people*! She was, therefore, unusually tender and shy, and blushed before them when she made a mistake, and when treating them always had a guilty look.

After receiving patients until late afternoon, worn out and flushed from the strain and her body aching, she rushed to her quarters to involve herself in reading. She read medical books or those of Russian authors who best suited her mood.

Living this new life, Anna Mihighlovna felt herself renewed, content, and almost happy. Greater fulfillment in her life she did not wish. Moreover, as though to complete her happiness, as in the manner of a dessert, conditions occurred that made possible a reconciliation with her husband, toward whom she had retained feelings of guilt. Seventeen years ago, soon after the birth of her daughter, she changed toward her husband and left him. She had not seen him since that time. He was somewhere in the south, serving as a battalion commander. About two times a year he had written to the daughter, who had carefully hidden the letters from the mother.

Anna Mihighlovna unexpectedly received a long letter from her husband after the death of the daughter. With the feeble handwriting of an old man, he wrote that with the death of his daughter he had lost the last thing that had given meaning to his life, and that he was old and sick and was awaiting death, which, at the same time, he feared. He complained that he was bored and annoyed by everything, could not get along with people, and could not wait until he could give up the battalion and get away from all the petty squabbles. In closing, he begged his wife for God's sake to pray for him, take care of herself, and not become despondent.

The two old people entered into an enthusiastic correspondence. To some degree it could be perceived from the letters that followed, which were always tearful and depressing, that the colonel was feeling terrified not only from the loss of his daughter and his aches and pains: he was in debt, was in trouble with his superiors and with other officers, had neglected his battalion until it was hopelessly weakened, and so forth. The correspondence between the couple continued for about two years and concluded with the old man's retirement, when he came to live in Zhenino.

He arrived on a February afternoon. His wife's buildings were hidden behind tall snowdrifts. In the transparent blue atmosphere together with the brittle, crackling frost, there was a deathly silence.

Anna Mihighlovna was looking out a window when he stepped out of the sleigh. She did not recognize her husband. He was a small, bent-over old man, already apparently unstrung and senile. Anna Mihighlovna's eyes first fell upon the folds of old skin around his long neck and upon his thin little legs that looked mechanical with their tightly bent knees. While settling with the driver, he took a long time to say something and, as if in conclusion, angrily spat.

"Even to speak to you is disgusting!" A senile grumbling was heard by Anna Mihighlovna. "Understand, that for you to ask for a tip is immoral! Everyone should surely get only what he has earned!"

When he entered the foyer, Anna Mihighlovna saw a jaundiced face, not even given a little color by the frost, with puffy red eyes and a thin beard in which grey hairs were mixed with red. Arkadey Petrovich embraced his wife with one arm and kissed her forehead. Glancing at each other, the two old people, as if frightened of something, were strangely confused. It was as if they were ashamed of their old age.

"You're just in time!" Anna Mihighlovna hastily addressed him. "The table was set only this minute. You'll eat well after being on the road!"

They sat down to dinner. The first course was eaten in silence. Arkadey Petrovich took a thick notebook out of his pocket and glanced at some notes while his wife diligently prepared the salad. There was a great deal to talk about from the past, but neither was concerned about the past. Both felt that any recollection of their daughter would bring forth sharp pain and tears. And from the past, like from a deep vinegar barrel, there would be emitted oppressiveness and gloom. . . .

"You're not eating any meat!" noted Arkadey Petrovich.

"True, I have taken a vow not to eat meat," his wife quietly answered.

"Well? It's not unhealthy. If you analyze its chemical content, you'll find the Lenten foods and fish have the same chemical elements as meat. In truth, there are no Lenten foods. ('What am I saying this for?' thought the old man.) For example, the pickle is the same as meat, as chicken . . ."

"No. . . . When I eat a pickle I know that no life was lost and that no blood was shed. . . ."

"That, my dear, is an optical illusion. With the pickle you are eating a great deal of infusoria, and who is to say that a pickle has no life? Plants really are organisms too! Or fish?"

"Why am I speaking such nonsense?" Arkadey Petrovich thought once more and then immediately began talking about the successes that chemistry was achieving.

"Simply miraculous!" he declared while having difficulty chewing his bread. "Soon the chemists will be able to produce milk and will succeed, pardon me, to meat! Yes! Within a thousand years in every home together with a kitchen will be a chemical laboratory where from nothing substantial, like gases and similar substances . . . anything one wishes will be prepared!"

Anna Mihighlovna looked at his disturbed, shifting, bloodshot eyes and listened. She felt that the old man spoke of chemistry to avoid speaking of anything else, but this did not deter her from considering his theorizing about Lenten foods and meat.

"Are you retired as a general?" she asked him when he suddenly became silent and began to blow his nose.

"Ah yes, a general. . . . Your Excellency. . . ."

The general spoke throughout the whole dinner, never letting up, displaying extraordinary loquaciousness—a trait which in their youth ages ago, Anna Mihighlovna never knew of him. His constant jabbering gave her a headache.

After dinner he went to his room for a rest, but in spite of his exhaustion, he could not fall asleep. When the "old woman" came to his room before evening tea, he was lying curled under the coverlet, staring at the ceiling and letting out intermittent gasps.

"What's bothering you, Arkadey?" Anna Mihighlovna glanced at his grey and worn-out face and was frightened.

"Nothing, nothing," he muttered. "Rheumatism."

"Why won't you tell me? Maybe I can help you."

"Help is impossible."

"If it's rheumatism, then an iodine rubdown . . . internally one takes sodium bicarbonate. . . ."

"That's all nonsense. . . . I've been doctoring for eight years. . . . Stop stamping your feet!" he suddenly yelled at the elderly maid, staring maliciously at her. "You stomp around like a horse!"

Anna Mihighlovna and the maid were unaccustomed to such a tone, exchanged glances, and reddened. Noting their discomfiture, the general frowned and turned his face to the wall.

"I must forewarn you, dear Anna," he groaned. "I have an intolerable character! In old age I have become grumpy. . . ."

"You must break yourself of this habit," sighed Anna Mihighlovna.

"It's easy to say 'must'! We mustn't have pain, but nature doesn't listen to our 'must'! But you, dear Anna, leave. . . . When I feel bad, the presence of people annoys me. . . . It's difficult to talk. . . ."

The days, the weeks, the months went by, and Arkadey Petrovich, little by little, became acclimated to his new circumstances: he became accustomed to them and others became accustomed to him. At first he remained inside, not going out, but his age and the burden of his intolerable disposition was felt in the whole village of Zhenino. He usually awoke very early—about four o'clock in the morning. His day began with a penetrating senile cough, waking Anna Mihighlovna and all the servants. In order to kill time somehow, from early morning to dinner time, if rheumatism did not lock his legs, he roamed about all the rooms and carped about the disorder he saw everywhere. Everything annoyed him: the sloth of the servants, loud footsteps, the crowing of the roosters, smoke from the kitchen, church bells. . . . He grumbled, railed against and chased the servants, but after every scolding would hold his head in his hands and declare with a tearful voice:

"God, what a disposition I have! An unbearable disposition!"

At dinner he ate a great deal and spoke incessantly. He spoke about socialism, about the new reforms in the army, about hygiene. Anna Mihighlovna listened and felt that all this was said only to avoid talking about their daughter and the past. In each other's presence they both still felt awkward, as if there were something to be ashamed of.

Only in the evenings, when twilight drifted into the rooms and a cricket croaked dismally behind the stove, did this awkwardness disappear. At this time they sat silently alongside each other, and their souls seemed to whisper about that which neither could decide to express aloud. At this time they warmed each other with the remainder of life's warmth, perfectly understanding what each was thinking. However, when the maid brought in the lamp, the old man again would begin to chatter or grumble about the disorder.

He had nothing to do. Anna Mihighlovna wanted to involve him with her medications, but when the first patient arrived, he yawned and became depressed! She tried to involve him in reading, but this too failed. He was accustomed to reading sporadically while in the army and did not know how to concentrate on reading for hours. It was enough for him to read five or six pages, after which he grew weary and removed his glasses.

Spring came. The general abruptly changed his way of life. When in the green fields of the estate and in the village fresh paths were formed, and in the trees before the windows birds were building nests, he unexpectedly, for Anna Mihighlovna, began to go to church. He went to church not only on holidays but daily. Such religious assiduity began with the requiem mass, which the old man without his wife's knowledge had celebrated for the daughter. During the whole time of the mass, he had remained on his knees bowed to the ground and cried, and it seemed to him that he prayed earnestly. But this was not prayer. Surrendering wholly to a father's feeling, painting in his memory the features of his beloved daughter, he stared at the icons and whispered:

"Shyrochka! My beloved child! My angel!"

It was an attack of the yearnings of senility, but the old man imagined that in him there was a response, an upheaval. On the next day he was again drawn to the church, on the third also. . . . He returned from the church refreshed, shining, and with a smile on his face. At dinner the theme of his incessant babbling was religion and theological questions.

Several times she found him in his room turning pages of the Bible. But, unfortunately, the religious attraction did not last very long. After one especially severe attack of rheumatism, which continued a whole week, he stopped going to church, as if he did not remember that he needed to go to mass. . . .

He now suddenly needed company.

"I don't understand how one can live without company!" he began to grumble. "I must visit the neighbors! It is stupid, barren, that while I'm alive, I don't involve myself in the world's affairs!"

Anna Mihighlovna ordered horses for him. He visited the neighbors, but did not go a second time. His necessity for company was satisfied with mincing around the village and finding fault with the peasants.

One morning he was sitting in the dining room before an open window drinking tea. In front of the window in the front yard around the lilac and gooseberry bushes some peasants were sitting on the benches. They had come to Anna Mihighlovna to be treated. The old man focused his eyes upon them for a long time and then thundered:

"*Ces moujiks.** . . . Cause of civic embarrassment. . . . Instead of curing you of your sickness, it would be better if you went somewhere to be cured of your baseness and filth."

Anna Mihighlovna, who adored her patients, stopped pouring tea and with wordless amazement looked at her husband. The patients, having never seen anything in her home but gentleness and warm sympathy, were also amazed and picked themselves up to leave.

"Yes, gentlemen peasants . . . *ces moujiks* . . . ," continued the general. "You are amazed by me. You are very amazed! Well, you are beasts aren't you?"

---

*"These muzhiks"

The old man turned to Anna Mihighlovna.

"The traveling council gave them a loan for sowing oats and they've gone and drank it up, not one of them, not two, but all! The saloon keeper has no place to sow oats. . . . Right?"

The general turned toward the peasants.

"Yes? That's right, isn't it?"

"Stop, Arkadey!" whispered Anna Mihighlovna.

"Do you think the council got the oats for nothing? What kind of citizens are you, if you don't respect your own, or that of others, general welfare? You drank up the oats . . . denuded the forest and drank that up too. . . . You pilfer everything without exception. . . . My wife heals you and you plundered her factory. . . . Was that right?"

"Enough!" groaned the general's lady.

"It's time you came to your senses," Lebyedev continued to harangue. "It's shameful to look at you! You here, you redhead, came here to be treated. Your leg hurts? But, you didn't take the trouble to wash your feet. . . . You're the epitome of filth! You hope, you ignoramus, that they'll be washed here? Knock it into your head that these *moujiks* think they can ride all over people. A priest married a local joiner, one Fedor. The joiner didn't even give him a kopeck. 'Poverty!' he says. 'I can't.' Okay. So the priest asks this Fedor, 'Just make me a little shelf for books.' . . . What do you think? He came to the priest five times to get paid! Now, isn't he an animal? He didn't pay the priest himself, but . . ."

"The priest has a lot of money without it," one of the patients interjected sullenly in a deep voice.

"How do you know?" blurted out the general, jumping up and thrusting his head out of the window. "Have you looked into the priest's pocket? But even if he were a millionaire, you don't have any right to use his services without paying! You don't give anybody anything for nothing, so don't take anything from anybody else for nothing!"

He turned to his wife:

"You can't imagine what kind of villainy they are capable of! You'd do better to be around when they get together and talk to each other than to attend their court trials. They're robbers!"

The general didn't quiet down even when the patients were being received. He seized upon every patient, mimicked them, declared all the illnesses due to drunkenness and debauchery.

"You, skinny!" poking his finger into the chest of one of them. "What's wrong with you? There's nothing here! You drank it up! You drank up the oats, didn't you?"

"Say what you want," sighed the patient. "We were better off under the aristocracy."

"Stuff and nonsense! You're lying!" exclaimed the general. "You aren't saying that with sincerity, but simply to say something flattering!"

On the next day he again sat by the window and fumed at the patients. This activity was a diversion for him and he began to sit at the window every day. Anna Mihighlovna, seeing that her husband did not let up, began receiving her patients in the warehouse, but the general picked himself up and came to the warehouse. The old woman bore this "trial" quietly, but outwardly demonstrated her protest by flushing and giving the berated patients money. However, when the patients, whom the general intensely disliked, began to come to her less and less frequently, she could no longer endure it. Once at dinner when the general made a joke at the expense of the patients, her blood boiled and her face convulsed.

"I have asked you to leave my patients in peace," she spoke sternly. "If you feel the necessity to let off steam, attack me, but leave them alone. . . . Thanks to you they have stopped coming to me for treatment."

"Aha, they have stopped!" exclaimed the general. "They were insulted! Jupiter, you are angry, and that means you can't be right. Ha, ha. . . . But that, dear Annie, that's good, that they've stopped coming. I'm very pleased. . . . Actually, your treatment doesn't achieve anything but harm! Instead of going to the council's hospital to the doctor, who uses scientific means, they come to you to be healed with baking soda and castor oil. Tremendous harm!"

Anna Mihighlovna stared at the old man, thought it over, and suddenly became pale.

"Of course," continued the talkative general, "in medicine, above all, knowledge is necessary, and after that, philanthropy. Without knowledge, it's quackery, and according to the law you don't have the right to treat the sick. In my opinion, you'd be infinitely more useful to the sick if you would out-and-out chase them to a doctor than to begin to treat them yourself."

He became silent for a moment and then continued.

"If you don't like my handling of them, so be it. I will stop saying anything; however, according to my conscience, sincerity toward them is infinitely better than silence and politeness. Alexander Macedonian is a huge man, but it doesn't follow that he should smash chairs; so with the Russian people—a great people but it doesn't follow that one cannot tell them the truth. You shouldn't make a lap dog from people. These *moujiks* are persons like you and me with the same needs, and you shouldn't pray for them and nurse them, but teach, straighten out, reprimand . . ."

"We can't teach them," interrupted the general's lady. "We can learn from them."

"How's that?"

"There's much . . . if only . . . industriousness . . ."

"Industriousness? What? You said industriousness?"

The general choked, jumped up from behind the table, and stomped about the room. . . .

"And I didn't work?" he shot out. "Nevertheless . . . I'm an intellectual, not a *moujik*. Where am I to labor? I . . . I'm an intellectual!"

The old man was really insulted, and his face took on the expression of a capricious little boy.

"Thousands of soldiers have been under me. . . . I was willing to die in the war; I've had rheumatism all my life, and . . . I didn't work! And you're telling me that these people of yours can teach me how to strain myself? Of course, I've not really suffered? I lost my daughter . . . that, which bound me to life in this cursed old age! And I haven't suffered!"

By this unexpected recollection of their daughter, the old people were brought to tears and wiped their eyes with the napkins.

"And we haven't suffered!" sobbed the general, letting his tears flow freely. "They have a purpose in life. They have faith and we only question . . . questions and fear! We don't suffer!"

The two old people felt sympathetic toward each other. They sat snuggled close for about two hours and cried a bit. After this they were able to look directly at each other and dared to speak of their daughter, of the past, and of the awful future.

In the evening they went to sleep in the same room. The old man did not let up talking and his wife's sleep was disturbed.

"Lord, what a character I have!" he declared. "Now why did I tell you all that? They were all illusions. People, especially in old age, naturally live with illusions. With my jabbering I've taken away from you your last bit of comfort. You could have continued to treat your *moujiks,* and not eat meat. So what? The devil got my tongue! You can't exist on illusions. Well-known writers are, it appears, wise, but they can't get along without illusions. That lover of yours wrote seven volumes about 'the people'!"

An hour went by. The general turned over and continued:

"And why, precisely, in a person's old age does he keep track of feelings and criticizes his own behavior? Why doesn't he do this in his youth? Old age is intolerant of this too. . . . Really. . . . When one is young, all life passes by without being observed and is hardly aware of its existence. In old age every little sensation is hammered into one's head and raises heaps of questions."

The old couple fell asleep late and awoke early. As a matter of fact, after Anna Mihighlovna stopped treating patients, they slept little and badly. Because of this, life seemed twice as long. . . . They shortened the nights with conversation, but during the workless days they loitered about the rooms or the garden, and glanced questioningly into each other's eyes.

At the end of the summer, fate sent them one more "illusion." Anna Mihighlovna came upon her husband who was taken up with an interesting activity; he was sitting at the table greedily eating a grated radish with hempseed oil. The veins of his face were trembling and saliva was dripping from the corners of his mouth.

"Have one, Annie!" he offered. "It's magnificent!"

Anna Mihighlovna hesitantly tasted the radish and then began to eat it. Soon her face also exhibited greediness.

"You know, it would be tasty . . . ," said the general that same day before lying down to sleep. "It would be pleasant, just as the Jews do, to steam the belly of a pike, put some caviar on it with some green onion . . . refreshing . . ."

"Why not? Pike is easy to get!"

The undressed, barefoot general took himself to the kitchen, awoke the cook, and ordered him to get some pike.

In the morning Anna Mihighlovna got the urge for sturgeon and Martin the cook had to go on the double to town for sturgeon.

"Oh," exclaimed the startled old lady. "I forgot to tell him to buy some peppermint cakes while he was there! I have a yearning for something sweet."

The old people then gave themselves up to gustatory experiences. They were constantly in the kitchen indulging in creative cooking. The general strained his brain and recalled his army bachelor life when he had to involve himself in culinary activity. Contrived from many foods invented by him, they both especially liked one that was prepared from rice, grated cheese, eggs, and sauce from well-done meat. The dish had a lot of pepper and bay leaves.

With this piquant dish the last "illusion" was concluded. Its fate was to be the last "delight" of both lives.

"It looks like rain," remarked the general one September evening. He was beginning to have some kind of an attack. "I'd better not eat any more of this rice. It's too heavy."

The general's lady stretched herself on her bed and took a deep breath. The atmosphere was stifling her. Just as the old man, she too felt a weight in the pit of her stomach.

"And, devil take it, my legs are itching," muttered the old man. "From my heels to my knees there's something that is making them itch. Damn it, it's unbearable! But, I'm interfering with your sleep. . . . Forgive me. . . ."

An hour passed quietly. Anna Mihighlovna gradually forgot about the weight in the pit of her stomach. The old man sat up in bed, put his head on his knees, and stayed that way for a long time. He then started scratching his calves. The harder his fingers worked, the worse became the itch. A little later the miserable old man slipped out of bed and began to limp about the room. He looked out the window. There he could see the bright light of the moon and the fall's nippy weather gradually forcing the seasonal demise of nature. It was evident that the grey, cold fog clouded the faded grass and that the forest did not sleep and shook with the remaining yellow bits of leaves.

The general sat down on the floor, embraced his knees, and put his head on them.

"Annie!" he called out.

The sensitive old woman rolled over and opened her eyes.

"I was thinking, Annie," began the old man. "Are you sleeping? I think that the most natural support of old age must be children. How do you feel? Once there are no children a person must involve himself in something else. It is healthy, when one is old, to be a writer, a painter, a scientist. . . . Gladstone has said that when he has nothing to do, he studies ancient classics and—distracts himself. If he has to retire, he will have something to fill his life. It wouldn't be bad to become a mystic, or . . . or . . ."

The old man scratched his legs and continued:

"And it does happen that the old become childish. You know, they want to plant a tree, wear medals and ribbons, involve themselves in spiritualism. . . ."

The light snoring of the old lady could be heard. The general picked himself up and again looked out the window. The cold spread gloomily over the room, and the mist lay over the forest and enveloped the trunks of the trees.

"How many more months to spring?" thought the old man, placing his forehead against the cold glass. "October . . . November . . . December. . . . Six months!"

And these six months appeared for some reason to be infinitely long—long like his old age. He limped across the room and sat on the bed.

"Annie!" he called out.

"What?"

"Is your apothecary locked?"

"No, why?"

"Nothing. . . . I want to rub my legs with iodine."

Silence descends again.

"Annie!" The old man woke his wife again.

"Are the bottles labeled?"

"They are, they are. . . ."

The general slowly lit a candle and left the room.

The sleepy Anna Mihighlovna heard the shuffling of bare feet and the tinkling of glass for a long time. Finally, he returned, grunted, and lay down.

In the morning he did not awake. He simply died or died from walking to the apothecary. Anna Mihighlovna did not know. But there was no reason for her to seek the reason for his death. . . .

Once again she began to bustle about in a disorderly, convulsive manner. She renewed the donations, the fasting, the vows, the collections for pilgrims. . . .

"To the nunnery!" she whispered, leaning out of fear against her old maid. "To the nunnery!"

1886

Anna Around the Neck

I

There wasn't even a light snack after the wedding ceremony. The bride and groom drank one goblet apiece, changed their clothes, and drove away to the railway station. Instead of a merry wedding ball and dinner, instead of music and dancing, there was a pilgrimage of two hundred versts to a monastery. Many of the guests approved of this, saying that Modest Alexeich was already of high rank and not young and that an elaborate wedding celebration might not have been, sad to say, in good taste. Also, it would have been unseemly to listen to merry music when a fifty-two-year-old bureaucrat was being married to a young girl who had just reached eighteen.

It was also said that this drive to the monastery was undertaken by Modest Alexeich, a person with principles, for the specific purpose to let his young wife understand that even when married, he would give priority to religion and morality.

The bride and groom were accompanied by a crowd of servants and relatives who remained at the railroad station in order to shout "hurrah" when the train moved. Peter Leontich, the bride's father, in a top hat and in his teacher's uniform, already drunk and very pale, squeezed up to the window of the train, and with a drink in his hand spoke pleadingly:

"Annie! Anna, Anna, one word!"

Anna leaned toward him from the window, and he whispered

123

something to her, smothering her with the smell of his alcoholic paregoric. He blew it into her ear—it was not necessary to understand anything—made the sign of the cross over her face, her breast, her hands; while doing this, he was gasping for breath and his eyes glistened with tears. Anna's brothers Peter and Andy, schoolboys, were pulling him away, tugging at his jacket, and whispering disconcertedly:

"Daddy, leave it. . . . Daddy, don't!"

As the train moved, Anna saw how her father ran a bit after the coach, staggering and spilling his wine, and there was on his wine-swollen face something that was pathetic, good. . . .

"Hu-rr-rah!" he shouted.

The bride and groom were finally alone. Modest Alexeich examined the compartment, placed their things on the shelves, sat across from his young wife, and smiled. He was a man of average height, a bit stout, puffy, and very self-satisfied. He had long sideburns and no mustache, and he had a cleanly shaved, round, sharply outlined chin that looked like a heel. The most characteristic feature of his face was the absence of a mustache. This freshly shaved naked place, shaking like jelly, gradually drifted toward his fat cheeks. He carried himself sedately with deliberate movements and mild manners.

"It is impossible now for me to forget one occasion," he said, smiling. "Five years ago, when Kosorotov received the Order of Anna of the second degree, and came to give his thanks to his superiors, His Honor expressed himself thus: 'It means that you have now three Annas. One in your buttonhole and two around your neck.' It must be told that at that time Kosorotov's wife had just returned. She was a shrewish and flighty woman whose name was Anna. I hope that when I receive the Order of Anna of the second degree, that the grantor will not have the occasion to say the same thing to me."

His small eyes smiled. She also smiled, shaken by the thought that this person could at any moment kiss her with his moist lips— and that she now had no right to repulse him. The gentle movements of his swollen body frightened her—she felt both terrified and dirty. He rose, slowly removed his medal of honor from around his neck, took off his jacket and vest, and put on his dressing gown.

"This is better now," he said and sat down by Anna.

She recalled how painful the wedding was, when it seemed to her that the priest and the guests and all who were in the church looked pityingly at her. Why did she, such a sweet and good girl, marry this old, uninteresting gentleman? And yet, this morning she had still been thrilled that everything was going so well, but during the marriage ceremony and now in the compartment, she felt guilty, deceived, and laughable. Here she was married to a rich man, but she was still without money. Her wedding dress was sewn on credit, and when her father and brothers were seeing her off, she could see by their faces that they didn't have a kopeck. Were they going to have any supper? And tomorrow? And it seemed to her that her father and the boys were now sitting at the table without her, and that they were hungry and were experiencing the same kind of sadness that they felt the first night after their mother's funeral.

"Oh, how miserable I am!" she thought. "Why am I so miserable?"

With the awkwardness of a sober man not accustomed to associating with women, Modest Alexeich held her around the waist and patted her shoulders, while she thought about money, about her mother, and of her mother's death. When her mother died, her father, Peter Leontich, who was an art and calligraphy teacher in the high school, began to drink, and they became impoverished. The boys didn't have boots or galoshes, the father was brought before the local justice of the peace, and the bailiff came and made an inventory of their furniture. . . . What shame! Anna had to look after her drunken father, knit socks for her brothers, do the marketing. When her beauty, youth, and elegant manners were admired, it seemed to her that the world saw her cheap hat and the holes in her shoes which she had covered with black ink. At night there were persistent tears and disturbing thoughts that her father would soon be dismissed from the school for incompetence and that he could not bear this and would soon die just like her mother.

It so happened that some women who knew her got busy searching for a good husband for Anna. Soon this same Modest Alexeich showed up. He was not young and good looking, but had money. He had one hundred thousand in the bank and an inherited estate from which he received rent. He was a person with principles and was held in high esteem by the powers that be. They told Anna that this man had influence. It wouldn't cost him anything, they told her, to ask His Honor to write a note to the director of the school and even to the trustee, so that Peter Leontich would not be fired.

While she recalled these details, music resounded suddenly near the window. The loud noise of voices was also heard. The train had stopped at a small station.

Behind the platform in the crowd were lively performers on an accordion and a squeaky, cheap violin. Behind the tall birches and poplars, and behind the summer homes lit by the moonlight, one could hear the sounds of a military band. It appeared that there was a dance at the summer homes. Summer residents and townspeople strolled on the platform, arriving in good weather to breathe the clean air. Artinov was also there. He was the proprietor of the resort, a wealthy man, tall with dark brown hair, who resembled an Armenian with his bulging eyes and foreign clothes. He had on a shirt that was unbuttoned over his chest and wore high boots with spurs. From his shoulders hung a black cloak, dragging on the ground like a train. With their sharp mugs lowered, two borzois followed him.

Tears still glistened in Anna's eyes, but she no longer was having recollections about her mother, nor about money, nor of her wedding, but was shaking the hands of school acquaintances and officers who knew her, while she laughed gaily and spoke rapidly:

"Hello! How are you?"

She stepped out on to the little moonlit square and stood so that all could see her in her new magnificent dress and hat.

"Why are we standing here?" she asked.

"There's a siding here," she was told. "We're awaiting the mail train."

Noting that Artinov was looking at her, she coquettishly screwed up her eyes and spoke loudly in French. Because her voice rang out beautifully, and the music could be heard, and the moonlight was reflected in the pond, and because Artinov, a well-known Don Juan and rogue, was looking at her intensely and with obvious curiosity, she suddenly felt happy. And when the train moved and an officer with whom she was acquainted saluted her, she hummed the polka being played by the army band, the sounds of which came from behind the trees. She returned to her compartment feeling as if she had been convinced beyond doubt at this small station that she was going to be fortunate no matter what.

The "young couple" remained at the monastery for two days and then returned to the town. They lived in a government-owned apartment. When Modest Alexeich left for work, Anna played the piano, or cried from boredom, or lay on the couch and read novels and looked at the latest fashion magazine.

At dinner Modest Alexeich ate a great deal and talked about politics, appointments, transfers, and awards; that it was necessary to work and that family life was not about comforts but about duty; that a kopeck saved is a ruble earned; and that above all else on earth he valued religion and morality. Holding his knife in his fist like a sword, he would say: "Every individual must assume his responsibilities!"

So, Anna listened to him. She was frightened and could not eat, usually leaving the table hungry. After dinner her husband napped and snored loudly. She would go to her room.

Her father and the boys looked upon her as somehow odd. It seemed as if when she came to see them they blamed her for marrying an unlovable, irksome, stingy man for money. The rustle of her gown, her bracelets, and in general her ladylike appearance restrained and offended them. In her presence they were somewhat confused and didn't know what to talk about. At the same time they loved her as they had in the past and had still not become accustomed to dine without her. She would sit and eat with them cabbage soup, groats, and small potatoes fried in lamb's fat, which had a candlelike odor. Peter Leontich would pour from the decanter with a shaking hand and would drink hastily, greedily, and would then drink a second glass, then a third. . . . Little Peter and Andy would take the decanter away. In embarrassment they would say: "Don't, Daddy. . . . Enough, Daddy."

Anna was also troubled and begged him not to drink anymore. He suddenly blew up and banged his fist on the table. "I will not permit anyone to tell me what to do!" he screamed. "You boys, little girl—I'll turn you all out!" But in his voice there was evidence of weakness, goodness, and no one was afraid of him. He usually got dressed up after dinner. Pale, with a nicked chin after shaving, stretching out his thin neck, he would spend a half-hour in front of the mirror, preening, brushing his hair, curling his mustache, spraying himself with perfume. Tying his tie in a bow, then putting on his gloves and his top hat, he left to give private lessons. If it were a holiday, he remained at home and painted or played the hissing and sobbing harmonium and alternately sang or angrily accused the boys: "Scoundrels! Villains! You've ruined the instrument!"

Anna's husband played cards in the evening with his co-workers. They all lived under the same roof in the government-owned building. The wives of these bureaucrats gathered at the same time. They were homely, tastelessly dressed, and crude like cooks. In the apartment arose gossip as tasteless and ugly as the wives themselves.

It so happened that Modest Alexeich went with Anna to the theater. During the intermission he didn't let her get one step away from him but walked with her on his arm around the foyer and the corridors. Bowing to someone he would whisper to Anna: "State Councillor. . . . He receives the big shots at his home," or "has means . . . owns his own home."

When they walked by the buffet, Anna often felt like having something sweet. She loved chocolate and apple turnovers, but she had no money and was loath to ask her husband. He would take a pear in his hand, press it with his fingers, and ask tentatively:

"How much is it?"

"Twenty-five kopecks."

"You don't say so!" he exclaimed and put the pear back; but since it was awkward to leave the buffet without buying something, he asked for seltzer water and emptied the whole bottle so that tears glistened in his eyes. At this time Anna would hate him.

Or, he would suddenly flush and quickly tell her: "Bow to this old lady!"

"But I'm not acquainted with her."

"No matter. She is the wife of the chief of the fiscal bureau! Bow, I tell you," he barked insistently. "Your head won't fall off."

Anna bowed and her head didn't fall off, but it was depressing.

She did everything her husband wanted and was angry with herself for doing so, and that he had betrayed her just as if she were the worst little goose. She married him only for money and now she had even less than she had before she married. Even her father had given her a few rubles, and now—not even a paltry kopeck. Simply to take it secretly or ask for it, she could not.

She was afraid of her husband. He made her tremble. It seemed to her that she had borne in her soul this fear of him for a long time. As a child, the most impressive and fearful strength, like that of a cloudburst or like a moving locomotive ready to crush her, was that of the picture of her school principal. Another such force, which was always spoken of in the family circle and of which for some reason they were all fearful, was that of the superintendent—and he was a lot weaker. . . . And among these too were the teachers with their shaved upper lips, stern and implacable appearance—and now finally, Modest Alexeich, a person with principles who even resembled the principal. In Anna's imagination all these powers blended into one and appeared as an enormous, frightful white bear, pressing down upon the weak and guilty—like her father—and she was afraid to oppose him in anything and forced herself to smile, and expressed a feigned pleasure when he crudely caressed her with his embraces and profaned her. She was inundated with fear.

Only once did Peter Leontich dare to ask her husband for a loan of fifty rubles in order to pay some kind of ugly debt—oh, how painful that was!

"All right, I'll give it to you," said Modest Alexeich, considering it, "but I warn you that I will not help you again until you stop drinking. For a person holding a state position that kind of weakness is shameful. I can not but remind you of the well-known fact that many capable people have been destroyed by this obsession. Among these, if they had abstained from drinking, it is possible that in time they could have become VIPs with high-ranking positions."

The statements were drawn out with: "because of this . . . ," "the result of this situation . . . ," "it is obvious that what is said . . . ," and poor Peter Leontich suffered from being humbled and experienced a dire need for a drink.

When the boys visited Anna in their customary torn boots and worn trousers, they also had to listen to such admonitions.

"Every human being has responsibilities!" Modest Alexeich would say to them.

And he never gave her money. Instead he gave Anna gifts of rings, bracelets, and brooches, saying that these things were good to have available for a rainy day. He often looked into her dresser drawer to check whether the things were all there.

II

Meanwhile winter arrived. It was still long before Christmas. In the local newspaper it was announced that on the twentieth of December the usual winter ball would take place in the nobility's assembly hall.

Every evening when through playing cards, an excited Modest Alexeich would whisper with the other bureaucrats, looking at Anna in a preoccupied manner, and later walk back and forth for a long time, deep in thought. Finally, late one evening, he stopped before Anna and said:

"You have to have an evening gown sewn. Do you understand? Only, please, get the advice of Maria Grigorevich and Natalie Kuzmich."

He gave her a hundred rubles. She took it but ordered an evening gown without conferring with anyone. She did speak to her father and tried to picture to herself how her mother dressed for a ball. Her deceased mother always dressed in the latest fashion. She had always spent time with Anna and dressed her elegantly, like a doll. She taught her to speak French and dance the mazurka superbly. (Before her marriage she had been a governess.) Anna, like her mother, could remake an old dress into a new one; wash gloves in cleaning fluid; rent jewelry; and, like her mother, knew how to use her eyes, slur her words, hold attractive poses, be ecstatic when necessary, and look enthralled and amazed. From her father, she had dark eyes and hair, and a touchy sensitivity which was always apparent.

A half-hour before it was time to leave for the ball, Modest

Alexeich entered her room without his frock coat in order to put on his ribbon of rank before her pier glass. He was so thrilled by her beauty, by the brilliance of her new billowy costume, that he stroked his sideburns with self-satisfaction.

"You are really something . . . so wonderful! Darling Anna!" He went on and on and then changed to a solemn tone. "I have made you happy and today you can make me happy! Please introduce yourself to the wife of His Honor. For God's sake! Through her I can be promoted to a senior lecturer!"

They left for the ball. They arrived at the nobility's assembly hall and drove up to the attended entrance. The lobby and its cloakroom were full of furs and obsequious footmen, and women in décolleté gowns hiding behind fans from the draft. It smelled of gaslight and soldiers. When Anna went up the stairs on her husband's arm, she heard the music and saw her whole self in the enormous mirror illuminated by many lights. Her soul awoke with gladness and with the same kind of happiness she had experienced on the moonlit night at the small railroad station. She walked proudly, self-assuredly, and for the first time did not feel like a little girl, but like a woman. Unconsciously, she imitated her deceased mother in her walk and manners. For the first time in her life she felt wealthy and free. Even the presence of her husband did not restrain her. Stepping over the threshold into the ballroom, she instinctively guessed that the proximity of her old husband did not in any way reduce her, but on the contrary, placed upon her the stamp of tantalizing mystery which so pleases men.

In the large ballroom the orchestra had already begun to play and the dancing had started. The formal rooms were filled with the effects of high society, colorfulness, music, bustling, and after casting her eyes around the ballroom, she thought: "Oh, how wonderful!" She noted at once several of her acquaintances in the crowd, all of whom she had met previously at evening parties or on walks. There were officers, teachers, lawyers, officials, landowners—and His Honor, and Artinov, and women from the highest society—formally dressed and very décolleté—beautiful and ugly. Many had already taken up their positions in the little booths and pavilions of the philanthropic bazaar where they were to begin the business for the benefit of the poor.

A huge officer wearing epaulets—she recognized him from Old Kiev Street where she had gone to high school, and now remembered his name, as if he had arisen from under the ground—invited her for the waltz, and it seemed she flew away from her husband. It was as if she were sailing on a boat in a violent storm and her husband had remained on a distant shore. . . . She danced with ardor, with abandon—the waltz, the polka, the cadrill—passing from hand to hand, enlivened by the music and the hubbub, blending Russian with French, burring her voice, laughing, and not thinking of her husband now, of anyone or anything.

She was a great success with the men, and it could not be otherwise. She was breathless from excitement, convulsively squeezed her fan, and wanted a drink. Her father, Peter Leontich, in a wrinkled frock coat which smelled from cleaning fluid, approached her, extending a dish of pink ice cream.

"You are bewitching today," he said, looking at her with delight, "and never before have I been so sorry that you rushed into marriage. . . . Why? I know you did it for our sake, but . . ." With trembling hands he took out a bundle of money and continued: "Today I received payment for a lesson and can repay my debt to your husband."

She thrust the saucer into his hand and then, bowing to someone, was rushed away, and in passing saw over the shoulder of her partner how her father glided over the parquet floor, embraced a woman, and dashed off with her across the ballroom.

"How sweet he is when he's sober!" she thought.

She danced the mazurka with the enormous officer. He stepped impressively, with a strong tread—a hulk in a uniform leading with his shoulders and chest, hardly tapping his feet. He definitely did not want to dance, but she fluttered around teasing him with her beauty and her exposed throat. Her eyes blazed with excitement and her movements were passionate while he moved indifferently and offered her his arms sympathetically—like a king.

"Bravo, bravo!" was the general outcry.

Little by little even the huge officer lost his seriousness and became energized, and having already been conquered by her charm, joined in the excitement and moved quickly, youthfully, while she only moved her shoulders and gazed playfully as if she were the queen and he the slave. In that moment it seemed to her that the whole ballroom was looking at them and all these people were thrilled and envious of them. The officer hardly succeeded in thanking her when the assembly parted and the men lined up somehow strangely with lowered arms. . . . His Honor came toward her, staring steadily at her and smiling all sugar and honey while smacking his lips, as was his custom when he saw a pretty woman.

"I'm very happy, very happy," he began. "I'm going to order that your husband be put into the brig for having kept such a treasure in hiding from us up to this time. I am going to give you a request from my wife," he continued, offering her his arm. "You must help us. . . . Mmm. . . . Yes. We must grant you a prize for beauty . . . like in America. . . . Mm. . . . Yes. . . . Americans. . . . My wife impatiently awaits you."

He led her to a booth attended by an old dame, the lower part of whose face was disproportionately so large that it appeared as if she held a large stone in her mouth.

"Help us," she said through her nose in a singsong voice. "All the good-looking women work at the charity bazaar and you are the only one who for some reason has passed it up. Why don't you want to help us?"

After she left, Anna took her place at the silver samovar and cups. A brisk business began at once. Anna accepted not less than a ruble for a cup of tea and she induced the huge officer to drink three cups. Artinov, the rich man with bulging eyes, short-winded, but not in the strange clothing that Anna had seen him wearing in the summer but in a frockcoat like everyone else, drank a glass of champagne while not taking his eyes off of Anna, and paid a hundred rubles. He then drank a cup of tea and paid another hundred— all of this without saying a word, and wheezing from asthma. Anna attracted buyers. She took their money, and was firmly convinced that her smiles and looks were giving nothing but great pleasure to these people. It was her understanding now that she was created exclusively for this noisy, brilliant, laughing life with music, dancing, and bowing. Her former fear of power which had approached and threatened to crush her now seemed laughable. She was no longer afraid and was only sorry that her mother was not there. Along with her, she would have been delighted by her current conquests.

Peter Leontich, pale but still able to walk without staggering, came to the booth and asked for a glass of cognac. Anna blushed, expecting that he would say something unseemly (she was already ashamed that she had such a poor, eccentric father), but he drank, withdrew from his wallet ten rubles, and respectfully withdrew, not saying a word. A little later she saw how he participated in the Grand Round, but by this time he was staggering and to the great confusion of his partner was calling out something. Anna remembered how three years ago he had behaved in the same way at a ball—reeling and calling out—and finally the police officer had driven him home to sleep, and on the next day the director had threatened to fire him. This was not a welcome recollection.

When the samovars were empty and the exhausted do-gooders turned over their receipts to the old dame with the stone in her mouth, Artinov led Anna on his arm to where they were serving supper for all the participants at the charity ball. About twenty people were having supper—no more—but it was very noisy. His Honor offered a toast: "In this luxurious dining room it is appropriate to drink to the inexpensive dining rooms that were the reasons for today's bazaar." The brigadier general proposed to drink "to the strength before which even the artillery flinches," and all reached out, clinking their glasses with the ladies. It was very, very delightful!

When Anna came home it was already getting light and the cooks were going to the market. Happy, tipsy, full of new impressions, exhausted, she undressed, fell into bed, and fell asleep instantly.

At two o'clock the maid awoke her and told her that Mr. Artinov had come to visit. She quickly dressed and went to the drawing room. Shortly after Artinov, His Honor arrived to thank her for participating in the charity bazaar. Looking at her sweetly and murmuring, he kissed her hand and before he left asked her for permission to come again. She stood in the middle of the drawing room amazed and delighted, not believing in this change in her life—this amazing change—that had occurred so suddenly.

At the same time her husband, Modest Alexeich, entered. . . . And he too now stood before her with the same fawning, sweet, groveling, respectful expression which she had become accustomed to seeing on his face in the presence of the powerful and notable. With pleasure, with indignation, with scorn, convinced that she would get away with it, she said distinctly enunciating every word:

"Get out, you blockhead!"

After this Anna never had a free day. She took part in picnics, in strolls, in plays. She returned every day toward morning and lay down on the floor in the drawing room and later described touchingly how she had slept under the flowers. She needed a lot of money, but she was no longer afraid of Modest Alexeich and spent his money as if it were her own. She didn't ask—she didn't need to—she simply sent him the bills or notes such as: "Give the bearer of this note two hundred rubles," or "Pay one hundred and fifty rubles immediately."

At Easter time Modest Alexeich received the Order of Anna of the second degree. When he went to proffer thanks, His Honor put his newspaper aside and leaned back in his armchair.

"It means that you now have three Annas," he said, examining his white hands and pink fingernails, "one in your buttonhole and two around the neck."

Modest Alexeich warily put two fingers to his lips in order not to laugh aloud and said:

"It now remains to await for the arrival of little Vladimir into the world. May I be so bold as to ask Your Honor who the godparents will be?"

He was hinting about the rank of Vladimir IV and was already imagining how he would tell everyone about this pun, successful in its aptness and daring, and wanted still to say something as apropos, but His Honor nodded his head and again buried himself in his newspaper.

All the while Anna was taking rides in troikas, went on hunts with Artinov, acted in one-act plays, dined out, and was more and more rarely at home. They now dined alone. Peter Leontich drank more than ever, had no money, and the harmonium was sold long ago in order to pay debts. The boys now never let him go out on the street alone and followed him in case he fell. Once when on the Old Kiev Drive, they met Anna with Artinov sitting on the coach box as drivers of a trotting pair. Peter Leontich removed his top hat and prepared to call something out, but young Peter and Andy took him by the arms and begged him:

"Don't, Daddy. . . . Enough, Daddy. . . ."

1895

At the Home of the Marshal's Widow

O n the first of April of every year, on the day of the martyr
Saint Trefon, on the name day of the late district marshal
Trefon Lvovichev Zavzetov, there are unusual goings-on. On this
day the marshal's widow, Lubov Petrovna, since the decease of her
husband, has a requiem service performed, and after the mass, prayers
of thanks are given to the good Lord. The whole district drives up
for the requiem service. Here you will see the current marshal, Krumov;
the president of the land council, Marfutkin; the permanent member,
Potrashkov; both the district justices of the peace; the district police
officer, Krinolinov; two local police officers; the rural doctor, Dvornyagin, smelling of iodine; all the local landowners, big and small; and
so on. All together there are gathered about fifty people.

Exactly at twelve o'clock noon the guests stretch and from all
the rooms gather together in the ballroom. On the floor there are
rugs so the footsteps are quiet, but the solemnity of the occasion
makes the company instinctively go on tiptoe and straighten their
attire with their hands, near the entrance. In the ballroom all is ready.
Father Evmeni, a little old man in a tall, faded *kamilavka,** is putting
on the black vestments. Deacon Konkordiev, red as a crab, is already
robed and is quietly turning the pages of the prayer book and slipping
markers into it. At the door, leading into the foyer, Deacon Luka,
with puffy fat cheeks and bulging eyes, is fanning the censer. The

*tall cylindrical headwear widened at the top which Orthodox priests wear as
a sign of their distinction

137

room is gradually filling up with a bluish transparent smoke and with the smell of incense. The local teacher, Gelikonski, a young man in a new baggy jacket and with large blackheads on his frightened face, is distributing wax candles that are on a German silver tray. The hostess, Lubov Petrovna, stands in front near a little table with *kytay** and is prematurely bringing her handkerchief up to her face. The silence is broken only rarely by deep sighs. All the faces are strained, solemn. . . .

The requiem begins. Streams of blue smoke flow from the censer and play in the slanting rays of the sun. The lit candles flicker weakly. The singing, at first shrill and deafening, soon becomes softer and more elegant after the singers, little by little, become accustomed to the acoustical conditions of the room. The motifs are all mournful, plaintive. . . . The guests gradually become attuned to the melancholy tone and are plunged into deep reverie. In their minds are thoughts about the brevity of human life, about human frailty, and about worldly vanity. . . .

The deceased, Zavzetov, is remembered; he was solid and red-cheeked, and could drink a bottle of champagne with one gulp, and could break a mirror with his forehead. And when they sang "with the holy have repose," the sobbing of the hostess was heard and the guests began to gloomily shift their weight from foot to foot. The more sensitive began to clear their throats and wipe around their eyelids. The president of the land council, Marfutkin, wishing to submerge his unpleasant feelings, leans toward the ear of the district police officer and whispers:

"I was at Ivan Fedorich's yesterday. Peter Petrovich and I made a grand slam without a trump card. By God . . . Olga Andrevna got so furious that her false tooth fell out of her mouth."

But now they are singing "Eternal Memory." Gelikonski is politely collecting the candles, and the requiem is ending. A minute of bustling follows and then the changing of the vestments and prayers of supplication. After the prayers, while Father Evmeni disrobes, the

---

*a dish made with rice and honey, sometimes with raisins, which is eaten at funerals

guests wipe their hands and cough, and the hostess talks abut the virtues of the deceased, Trefon Lvovichev.

"Please, dear guests, have something to eat!" she entreats the guests with a deep sigh when she completes her eulogy.

The guests try not to push and not to step upon each other while hurrying to the dining room. . . . Lunch awaits them there. The lunch is so lush that Deacon Konkordiev at the sight of it considers it his obligation every year to make a helpless gesture with his hands and shake his head with amazement and say:

"Supernatural! This, Father Evmeni, does not so much resemble human nourishment as the sacrifices brought to the gods."

The lunch was truly unusual. On the table was all that could be provided by flora and fauna, but there was only one thing about it that was supernatural: on the table was everything but . . . alcoholic drinks. Lubov Petrovna had made a vow never to have cards or alcoholic drinks in her home—the two things which destroyed her husband. So, on the table there stood only bottles of vinegar and oil, as if to make fun of and as punishment for the feasters, most of whom were awful drunkards and carousers.

"Please eat, ladies and gentlemen!" invites the marshal's widow. "Only, please forgive me, there is no vodka in my house. . . . I never have it. . . ."

The guests move toward the table and hesitatingly approach the pies. But the eating does not seem to catch on. In the tinkling of forks, in the cutting, in the swallowing, there appears a kind of laziness, an apathy. . . . It is obvious that something is missing.

"It feels as if something is missing," whispers one officer to another. "I had this kind of feeling when my wife ran away with the engineer. . . . I can't eat!"

Marfutkin, before beginning to eat, takes a long time rummaging in his pockets to find a handkerchief.

"My handkerchief is in my overcoat! I will go look for it," he recalled loudly and went to the foyer where his coat was hanging.

He returns from the foyer with oily eyes and attacks the pies with a good appetite.

"Wouldn't you say it's disgusting to eat without something to drink?" he whispers to Father Evmeni. "Step into the foyer, Father, and you will find a bottle in my coat. . . . Only be careful and don't make any noise with the bottle."

Father Evmeni remembers that he has to show something to Lyka and steps mincingly to the foyer.

"Father, a word . . . in secret!" Dvornyagin catches up with him.

"What a fur coat I bought secondhand!" brags Krumov. "It's worth a thousand and I gave, you won't believe it . . . only two hundred and fifty!"

At any other time the guests would have treated this information indifferently, but at this time they expressed amazement and incredulity. Finally, they all crowd into the foyer to look at the coat and continue looking until the doctor's Mekeshka secretly carries out five empty bottles. . . . When the boiled sturgeon is served, Marfutkin remembers that he left his cigarette case in his sleigh and goes to the stable. So that he wouldn't be bored going alone, he takes the deacon with him, for whom it was necessary, by the way, to take a look at the horses. . . .

During the evening of this same day, Lubov Petrovna sits in her study and writes a letter to her old Petersburg girlfriend.

"Today, following the example of previous years," she writes among other things, "there was at my home a requiem service for my dead husband. At the service were all my neighbors. They are a crude, simple people, but what hearts! I entertained them royally but, of course, as in the past years, there was not a drop of alcoholic drinks. From the time when he died of overindulgence, I made a vow to instill sobriety in our district and in this way to redeem his sins.

"Father Evmeni is enthusiastic about my task and helps me with word and action. Oh, *ma chère,* if you only knew how my bears love me! The president of the land council, Marfutkin, took hold of my hand after the lunch, held it to his lips, and ridiculously shaking his head, started to cry. There are no words for such feeling! Father Evmeni, that amazing little old fellow, sat beside me, and, looking at me with tear-filled eyes, babbled for a long time like a child. I did not understand his words, but I know how to understand sincere feelings.

"The district police officer, that handsome man of whom I have written you, stood before me on his knees, and wanted to read poems of his own composition (he is our poet), but . . . could not gather the strength . . . staggered and fell. . . . The giant became hysterical. . . . You can imagine my delight!

"It did not pass, however, without unpleasantness. The poor president of our social society, Alalikin, a heavy, apoplectic person, felt poorly and lay on the sofa unconscious for two hours. It became necessary to revive him with water. . . . Thanks to Dr. Dvornyagin, who brought a bottle of cognac with him from his apothecary and moistened his eyelids with it, he soon came to himself and was driven home. . . ."

1885

The Lowest of the Low

K ind Sir! Be so good as to turn your attention to this unhappy, hungry human being. I haven't eaten for three days . . . don't even have the five kopecks needed for a bed overnight. . . . I swear before God! For eight years I served as a village teacher and lost my position by some shenanigans of the board. I was a victim of false denunciation. I have been without a job for a year now."

The barrister Skvortsov glanced at the grayish, torn jacket of the pleader, at his dull eyes bloodshot from drinking, with red spots on his cheeks, and it appeared to him that he had already seen this person.

"They are now proposing a position to me in the Kalyshsk province," continued the pleader, "but I don't have the means to get there. Help me, do me the kindly act! It is shameful to beg, but . . . the circumstances require it."

Skvortsov looked down at the beggar's galoshes, of which one was heavy and the other light, and instantly remembered.

"Listen, the day before yesterday, it seems, I met you at Sadov," he said, "but then you told me that you were a student and not a village teacher; a student who was expelled. Remember?"

"No . . . no, that can't be!" babbled the pleader. "I'm a village teacher, and if you wish, I can show you my credentials."

"They'll lie for you! You called yourself a student and even recounted to me what you were expelled for. Remember?"

Skvortsov flushed and with a look of loathing moved away from the ragged beggar. "That's false, charitable sir!" he mimicked him angrily. "It's a swindle! I'll take you to the police station, the devil with the likes of you! You're poor and hungry, but that doesn't give you the right to tell naked, unscrupulous lies."

The beggar grabbed hold of a door handle and, confused like a trapped thief, looked for escape.

"I . . . I'm not lying, sir . . . ," he mumbled. "I can show you my papers."

"Who will believe you?" continued the indignant Skvortsov. "To exploit the sympathy society has for the village teachers and the students—how low, spurious, vile can you get! It's disgusting!"

Skvortsov moved away and with the most uncharitable look chastised the beggar. The unabashed lying of the beggar aroused in him such disgust and aversion for it offended that which he, Skvortsov, loved and valued in himself: goodness, sensitivity, compassion for the unfortunate. The lying and attempt to make use of a current charity "subject" defiled the alms, which he from purity of intentions liked to give to the poor. The ragged fellow began to justify himself, swear to his veracity, but then became silent and ashamedly lowered his head.

"Sir!" he said, putting his hand to his heart. "Really, I . . . lied! I'm not a student and not a village teacher. That was all fiction! I was a member of a Russian choir, but they threw me out because of my drinking. So, what am I to do? Believe me God, it is impossible without lies! When I tell the truth, nobody will give me anything. Speak the truth and you'll die from hunger and freeze to death without a place to spend the night! You rightfully argue, I understand, but . . . what am I to do?"

"What to do? You ask what are you to do?" exploded Skvortsov coming closer to him. "Work, that's what is to be done! You need to work!"

"To work . . . I understand that myself, but where can I get work?"

"Nonsense! You are young, healthy, strong, and can always find work if only you want to. But you are really lazy, spoiled, a drunkard! You smell as strong as a pigsty from vodka! You have become an incorrigible liar and are worn out to the marrow of your bones. You are capable only of begging and lying! If you sometime deign to lower yourself and work, you must have an office, or the Russian choir . . . a type of position where you do nothing but get paid money for it! Why can't you do menial work? Most likely you won't look for menial work in the yards or the factories! You're just a pretender!"

"It's just as you say, really," declared the pleader, and bitterly laughed. "Who will hire me for menial work? It's too late for me to apply to the managers because in business you have to start when you're young, and in the yards no one will hire me because it is impossible for me to poke my nose in. . . . In the factory they won't hire me because I have no trade. I don't know how to do anything."

"Nonsense! You can always rationalize! Can you find it impossible to chop wood?"

"I don't refuse, but now even the good wood choppers are sitting around without work."

"Come on, all you spongers talk that way. Make you a proposition and you reject it. Would you like to chop wood at my place?"

"If you wish, I will chop. . . ."

"Good, we'll see. . . . Excellent. . . . We'll see!"

Skvortsov didn't waste any time, and without malice, rubbed his hands together and called his cook from the kitchen.

"Olga," he said, turning toward her, "take this gentleman to the woodshed and show him the wood that needs to be chopped."

The ragged fellow shrugged his shoulders as if he did not understand, and hesitatingly followed the cook. It was obvious from the way he walked that he agreed to chop wood not because he was hungry and wanted to work, but simply from self-respect and shame, having been taken at his word. It was also noticeable that he had been terribly weakened by alcohol, was unhealthy, and hadn't the slightest inclination to work.

Skvortsov quickly returned to his dining room. There, from the French windows opening out into the courtyard, could be seen the woodshed and everything that went on in the yard. Standing by a window, Skvortsov saw how the cook and the ragged one went through the back door to the yard and across the dirty snow toward the woodshed. Olga could be seen angrily looking over her companion and opening the door by pushing with her elbows and furiously slamming the door.

"Honestly, we've disturbed her coffee break," thought Skvortsov. "What a malevolent creature!"

Later he observed how the "teacher" and "student" sat down on a chopping block and, resting his red cheeks on his fists, appeared deep in thought about something. The hag threw the ax down at his feet, spit in disgust, and, it could be seen from the movement of her lips, cursed him. The ragged fellow indecisively dragged a log toward himself, placed it between his legs, and timorously struck it with the ax. The log began to sway and then fell. The ragged fellow moved it near himself, blew on his cold hands, and again hit it with the ax so cautiously that it looked as if he were afraid he might hook his galoshes or chop off his fingers. The log fell again.

Skvortsov's anger had already left him, and he began to feel a little guilty and ashamed that he had berated a person as ruined, alcoholic, and who perhaps was sick, and to hire him to do menial work out in the cold.

"Well, so be it," he thought, going out of the dining room into his study. "It's of benefit to him after all."

Within an hour Olga showed up and said that the wood was chopped.

"Okay. Give him a fifty-kopeck piece," said Skvortsov. "If he wants, tell him to come to chop wood on the first of every month. We'll always find work for him."

On the first, the ragged fellow appeared and again earned a fifty-kopeck piece, although he could hardly stand on his feet. From that time on he often showed up in the yard, and every time they found work for him: he would shovel snow, clean the barn, beat the dust out of the rugs and mattresses. Each time he received from twenty to thirty kopecks for his work, and once was even given some old britches.

Skvortsov had to move to other quarters and hired him to help with packing and moving the furniture. This time the ragged fellow was sober, gloomy, and silent. He hardly applied himself to the furniture, walked with a hanging head behind the wagons, and didn't even try to do the work; he shivered from the cold and appeared confused when the carriers laughed at his idleness, his weakness, and his torn nobleman's coat. When the move was finished, Skvortsov ordered that he be brought to him.

"Well, I see my words had an effect upon you," he said, giving him a ruble. "This is for your work. I see that you are sober and are not loathe to work. What is you name?"

"Lyshkov."

"I, Lyshkov, can now offer you other, cleaner work. Can you write?"

"I can, sir."

"Take this letter tomorrow to my friend and you will receive from him a copying position. Work and don't drink, and don't forget that which I said to you. Good-bye!"

Skvortsov, satisfied that he had set a person on the straight and narrow path, affectionately patted Lyshkov on the back and even offered him his hand in farewell. Lyshkov took the letter, left, and never again came to the yard for work.

Two years passed. Once while standing at a theater box office and paying for his ticket, Skvortsov saw alongside him a short man in a coat with a lambskin collar and wearing a shabby, sealskin hat. The man shyly asked the cashier for a ticket in the gallery and paid for it with five-kopeck copper coins.

"Lyshkov, is it you?" asked Skvortsov, recognizing his former woodchopper. "Well, how are things? What are you doing? Are you living well?"

"Not bad. I now work for a notary. I'm paid thirty-five rubles, sir."

"Well, praise God. That's excellent! I'm happy for you. Very, very happy, Lyshkov. You know in some ways you are my godchild. You know that I put you on the right road. Remember how I laid into you? It looked as if you wanted the earth to open and swallow you. Well, thanks, dear man, you didn't forget my words."

"Thanks to you," said Lyshkov. "If I hadn't come to your place then, very likely I would still be calling myself a teacher or a student. Yes, I was saved at your place, and was able to get out of the hole."

"I'm very happy, very happy."

"Thank you for your good advice and for the work. Your words at that time were excellent. I am grateful to you and to your cook, may God give good health to that fine, noble woman. You spoke superbly then and I am obligated to you, of course, for a new life, but the one who really saved me was your cook, Olga."

"By what means?"

"In this way. It happened when I came to your place to chop wood, she starts out: 'Oh you, drunkard! You're damned! You're beyond redemption!' And then sitting opposite me, becoming depressed, she looks me in the eye and cries: 'You poor devil! There's no place in heaven or on earth for you. You drunkard, you'll burn in hell! You'll burn!' And more in the same vein, you know. How much blood and tears she shed for me, I can't tell you. But most important—she chopped the wood for me! You know, I, sir, didn't split one log. She did all of it! Why she saved me, why I changed, why after watching her I stopped drinking, I cannot tell you. I only know that her words and generous deeds made for a change of heart in me. She straightened me out and I will never forget it. However, it is time. The bell is ringing."

Lyshkov bowed and left for the gallery.

1887

Mother-in-Law Solicitor

I t occurred one marvelous morning exactly one month after the marriage of Michel Puzirev with Lizie Mamymina.* Michel had drunk his morning coffee and was looking for his hat in order to leave for work, when his mother-in-law entered.

"I would like to keep you back, Michel, for a few minutes," she said. "Don't be annoyed, my dear. . . . I know that sons-in-law don't like to speak with mothers-in-law, but we, it seems . . . are not opposed to each other, Michel. We don't behave like a mother-in-law and a son-in-law, but like intelligent adults. . . . We have much in common. . . . Isn't this true?"

The mother-in-law and the son-in-law sat down together on the sofa.

"What can I do for you, dear mother?"

"You are such a wise person, Michel, very wise; I, too, am not stupid. . . . We understand each other, I hope. I have been thinking of talking to you for some time, *mon petit*. . . . Tell me candidly, for the sake of . . . for the sake of all that is holy, what do you wish to make of my daughter?"

The son-in-law's eyes widened.

"I, you know, agree with you. . . . Let it be! Why? Learning is good, and life without literature is impossible. . . . One must know poetry! I understand! It is pleasant to have an educated wife. . . . I myself was educated and understand. . . . But why, *mon ange,* be extreme?"

---

*"Mommy's Girl"

148

"That is? I don't understand you at all. . . ."

"I don't understand your attitude toward my Lizie! You married her, but is she really your wife, your friend? She is your victim! The lessons, the books, and the various theories . . . all these are fine but, my dear, don't forget that she is my daughter! I will not permit it! She is my body and my blood! You are killing her! Not a month has passed since your marriage, but she already appears to be held on a leash by you! She sits with you all day long behind a book, reads those dull journals! Copying some kind of pages! Really, is this what a wife should do? You don't take her out, you don't let her live! She doesn't mix in society, she doesn't dance! It's hard to believe! She hasn't once been to a ball in all this time! Not once!"

"She hasn't once been to a ball because she hasn't wanted to. Talk to her yourself. . . . You'll find out what her opinion is of your balls and dances. No, *ma chère!* She objects to your indolence! If she sits for whole days behind books at work, believe it, no one has forced this assiduity upon her. . . . That is why I love her. . . . In this matter I know better and beg you in the future not to interfere in our affairs. Liza will say it herself, if she finds it necessary to say anything. . . ."

"You think so? You really can not see how quiet and subdued she is? Love has tied her tongue! If it were not for me, you would put a yoke upon her, my dear sir! Yes, sir! You're a tyrant, a despot! Please change your ways today!"

"I don't even want to listen. . . ."

"You don't want to? And it's not necessary! Big deal! I wouldn't have spoken to you but for Liza! I'm sorry for her! She begged me to speak to you!"

"Now, you're telling a fib. . . . That's a lie, admit it. . . ."

"A lie? Take a look, you crude darling!"

The mother-in-law jumped up and grabbed the doorknob. The door flung open and Michel saw his Liza. She stood on the threshold, wrung her hands, and sobbed. Her sweet little face was covered with tears. Michel rushed toward her. . . .

"You heard? Tell her! So she may understand her daughter!"

"Mama . . . Mama says the truth," wailed Liza. "I can't bear this life. . . . I am suffering. . . ."

"How . . . how come! Strange. . . . Why didn't you tell me yourself about this?"

"I . . . I . . . you would be angry. . . ."

"But really, you yourself constantly expounded against idleness! You said that you loved me for my convictions, that you objected to the way people in your set lived! I too loved you for that! Right up to our marriage you scorned, were repelled by this vain life! How did this change come about?"

"I was afraid then that you wouldn't want to marry me. . . . Darling Michel! Let's go today to Maria Petrovna's reception!"

And Liza fell upon Michel's chest.

"Now, you see! Are you convinced now?" exclaimed the mother-in-law and triumphantly left the room. . . .

"Oh, you silly" groaned Michel.

"Who's silly?" asked Liza.

"The one who was mistaken!"

1883

The Boa Constrictor and the Bunny

P eter Semyenich, a dissipated and bald fellow in a velvet jacket with crimson lapels, stroked his fluffy sideburns and continued:

"But there is, *mon cher,* if you wish, there is one more method. This method is the most subtle, clever, venomous, and the most dangerous for husbands. He must understand the psychology and be a connoisseur of the female heart. Besides this *conditio sine qua non** is patience, patience, and patience. He who doesn't know how to wait and be patient, cannot do this. By this means, in order to seduce someone's wife, you must keep yourself away from her as far as possible. Finding her attractive, a kind of ailment, you stop being at her house, meet her as little as possible, stealing only a glance, and be satisfied with conversing with her. Here you behave aloof. Everything you do is in the nature of hypnotism. She must not see, but must feel your presence, just as the rabbit feels the stare of the snake. You hypnotize her with your gaze, your venomous tongue, but the husband can serve as the really best transmitting wire.

"For example, I am in love with one N. N. and want to seduce her. I meet her husband at the club or in the theater.

" 'And how is your wife?' I ask among other things. 'I say, she's a lovely woman! I find her extremely attractive! The devil knows how attractive!'

" 'Hm. . . . What do you find so attractive?' asks the pleased husband.

---

*"an indispensable condition"

151

" 'The most charming, poetic creation, which even a stone could be moved to love! You husbands, however, are prosaic and know your wives only in the first month after marriage. . . . Acknowledge and be glad that fate sent you such a wife! At this time in our lives such women are a necessity . . . precisely such!'

" 'What's so special about her?' asks the dumbfounded husband.

" 'For pity's sake, she's a beauty, full of grace, life, and integrity, poetic, sincere, and at the same time mysterious! If you once love such a woman, you love intensely, with all the ardor you can muster. . . .'

"And more in the same vein. The husband on the same day, lying down to sleep, can't keep from telling his wife:

" 'I saw Peter Semyenich. He praised you fantastically. He was ecstatic. . . . You're a great beauty, graceful, mysterious. . . . As if to love you would be something extraordinary. Talk about laying it on thick. . . . Ha . . . ha!'

"After this, not seeing her, I again arrange to meet with the husband.

" 'By the way, my friend,' I say to him. 'Yesterday an artist was at my house. He had received an order from some prince: for two thousand rubles he was to paint the head of a typical Russian beauty. He asked me to find a model for him. I wanted to send him to your wife but I felt somewhat reticent. Your wife would be perfect! What a charming little head! I find it a hell of a pity that this wonderful model is not seen by the artists! A hell of a pity!'

"It would have to be a very alienated husband not to pass this on to his wife. In the morning the wife looks in the mirror for a long time and thinks: 'Where did he get the idea that I have a pure Russian face?'

"After this, when she looks in the mirror, there isn't a time when she does not think of me. Along with this, the accidental encounters with her husband continue. After one of these meetings, the husband comes home and begins to scrutinize his wife's face.

" 'What are you looking for?' she asks.

" 'That kook, Peter Semyenich, discovered that one of your eyes is darker than the other. I can't see that if my life depended on it!'

"His wife looks in the mirror again. She examines herself for a long time and thinks: 'Yes, it seems that the left eye is a little darker than the right eye. . . . No, it seems that the right is darker than the left. . . . Though, it could be, that it appeared that way to him!'

"After the eighth or ninth meeting, the husband says to his wife: 'I saw Peter Semyenich at the theater. He asked to be forgiven that he hasn't paid you a visit: there just hasn't been any time! He says he's terribly busy. It seems it's been almost four months since he's been here. . . . I reproached him for this, and he excused himself and said that he will come here when he finishes some kind of assignment.'

" 'And when will he be finished?' asks the wife.

" 'He says not earlier than a year or two. What kind of job this windbag has, only the devil knows! A kook, really! He stood close to me, as if with a knife at my throat: "Why doesn't your wife go on the stage? With such," he says, "heavenly looks, with such potential and sensitivity, it is a sin to remain at home." "She," he says, "should cast away everything and go thither, whither her inner voice calls her. The ordinary limits on behavior were not created for her. Such," says he, "natures as hers are found only outside time and space." '

"The wife, of course, sadly understands this as rhetoric, but all the same, melts and is transported with delight.

" 'What nonsense!' she says, trying to appear indifferent. 'And what else did he say?'

" ' "If I weren't," he says "so involved, I'd take her away from you." 'So what,' I said, 'take her, I won't insist on a duel.' "You," he shouts, "don't understand her! You need to know her! She has," he says, "an unusual nature, a strong, wistful appearance. My only regret," he says, "is that I'm not a Turgenev, or I would have long ago written about her." 'Ha-ha. . . . I'd give you to him! Well, I think, brother, if you'd live with her a couple of years, you'd sing another song. . . . Idiot!'

"And the poor wife is gradually consumed by a passionate desire to meet with me. I'm the one man who understands her, and it's only to me she can confide copiously! But I stubbornly stay away and do not see her. She hasn't seen me for a long time but my agonizingly sweet venom has already poisoned her. The husband, yawning, passes my words on to her, and it seems to her that she hears my voice, sees the gleam in my eyes.

"The time is coming to make the catch. One evening the husband comes home and says:

" 'I met Peter Semyenich. He was very dull, depressed, and crestfallen.'

" 'From what? What happened to him?'

" 'It's impossible to figure it out. He's complaining that he's overcome with grief. "I," he says, "am all alone," he says. "There isn't anyone who is close to me, no friends, not a soul who would understand me and be in harmony with my soul. No one understands me," he says, "I want only one thing now: death. . . ." '

" 'What idiocy!' says the wife, and thinks, 'Poor guy! I understand him completely! I too am lonely, only he understands me; who, if not I, could understand the state of his soul?'

"The wife is all fired up. She intensely wants to go to N——skey Boulevard and look, if only briefly, upon this person who was able to understand her, and who was now in anguish. Who knows? She might speak with him, speak words of comfort to him, it was possible that his suffering might cease. She could tell him he had a friend who understands him and values him, so that his soul might be revived.

" 'No, that's impossible . . . wild,' she thinks. 'It is illogical even to think that. Perhaps, I can still fall in love with someone fine, but that's crazy . . . stupid.'

"At last, when her husband falls asleep, she raises her hot head, puts her finger to her lips, and ruminates: What if she took the risk and went out now? Later she could lie and say that she hurried to the apothecary, or to the dentist.

" 'I'll go!' she decides.

"She had a plan ready: out of the house by the back steps, to the boulevard by cab. On the boulevard she would go by his house, take a look, and return. In this way she wouldn't compromise herself nor her husband.

"She dresses, quietly leaves the house, and hurries to the boulevard. The boulevard is dark, empty. The barren trees sleep. There is no one around. However, she does see a silhouette. That must be he. Her whole body trembles; forgetting herself, she slowly approaches me. I go toward her. For a moment we stand silent and look into each other's eyes. A minute passes silently and . . . the bunny whole-heartedly allows herself to be swallowed by the boa constrictor."

1887

The Bride-to-Be

I

I t was already ten o'clock in the evening and a full moon shone over the garden. In the Shumin's home they had just finished the daily evening prayers, which were dictated by Marfa Mihighlovna, the grandmother, and now Nadya—who had just gone out into the garden for a minute—could see that the table in the foyer was being set for the hors d'oeuvres, and her grandmother was bustling about in her splendid silk gown. Father André, a high priest from the cathedral, was having a conversation with her mother, Nina Ivanovna, who in the evening light from the window, for some reason, seemed very young. Nearby stood Father André's son, André Andreich, listening attentively.

It was quiet in the garden, cool and dark, and peaceful shadows lay across the ground. One could hear how, from some distant, very distant spot beyond the town, frogs were croaking. May was in the air, wonderful May! One could take deep breaths, and want to think that one was in some other place, somewhere in the sky, above the trees, far away from the town, where in the fields and woods spring had returned to life—secret, marvelous, rich and holy, incomprehensible to a weak, imperfect human being. And, for some inexplicable reason, one wanted to cry.

Nadya was already twenty-three; from the time she was sixteen she had dreamt passionately of marriage, and now she was the fiancée of André Andreich, the same man who was standing at the window.

She liked him and the date had already been set for the seventh of September, but meanwhile she was unhappy, her nights were sleepless, she had lost the ability to be merry. . . . From the basement where the kitchen was, one could hear through the open window how others were laughing, how they were chopping food, how they were banging the door against the pulley. It smelled of roast turkey and marinated cherries. And it seemed to her that now all her life would be like this, without change, endless!

Someone came out of the house and had stopped on the porch. It was Alexander Timofeich, or more intimately, Sasha, a guest, who arrived from Moscow about ten days ago. Once upon a time, long ago, her grandmother was visited from time to time by a distant relative, Maria Petrovna, an impoverished, genteel widow—a small, emaciated, sickly woman. She had a son, Sasha. For some reason he was spoken of as a fine artist, and when his mother died, her grandmother, for the sake of saving his soul, sent him to Moscow to a technical art school. He attended the art school for about two years and was barely fifteen when he had completed the architectural section in a rather plodding way. He never became an architect, but got a job in Moscow producing lithographs. Almost every summer he stayed at her grandmother's in order to rest and improve his health because usually he was very ill.

He now wore a buttoned jacket with tails and shabby canvas trousers that were frayed at the bottom. His shirt wasn't ironed and his whole appearance was somehow worn looking. He was extremely thin, with enormous eyes; long, thin fingers; bearded; dark; but all the same, handsome. He behaved at the Shumin's like a close relative and felt at home there. The room which he occupied had now for a long time been known as "Sasha's room." While standing on the porch, he saw Nadya and went to her.

"Everything is fine with you," he said.

"Of course, fine. You should stay until the fall."

"Yes, seems I'll have to. Very likely I'll be here until September."

He laughed for no reason and sat down beside her.

"I'm sitting and looking at my mother from here," said Nadya. "She seems so young from here! My mother, of course, is weak."

And after being silent, she added, "All the same she is an unusual woman."

"Yes, she is attractive," agreed Sasha. "Your mother in her own way, of course, is a very good and kind woman, but . . . how can I tell you? Early this morning I went down to your kitchen, and there four servants slept on the floor, had no beds, and in the place of beds were rags, stench, bedbugs, cockroaches. The same was true twenty years ago—nothing has changed. As far as your grandmother is concerned, God be with her, she can't change; but you know that your mother speaks perfect French, performs in plays. She should be able to, it seems, understand."

As Sasha spoke, he pointed two long, emaciated fingers before the listener.

"Everything here is somehow preposterous from lack of use," he continued. "Hell, nobody does anything. Your mother strolls around all day like some duchess; your grandmother also does nothing; you—also. And your betrothed, André Andreich, he doesn't do anything either."

Nadya had heard all this last year and, it seemed, the previous year. She knew that Sasha could not think differently, and that in the past it had amused her, but now for some reason, it depressed her.

"That's all old hat and bored me long ago," she said and arose. "If only you could think up something newer."

He laughed and also rose, and they both went into the house. She—tall, beautiful, classy—appeared alongside him very healthy and smartly dressed; she felt this, and it made her sorry for him and, for some reason, awkward.

"And you talk too much," she said. "You've just said something about my André, but you really don't know him."

"My André . . . the deuce with him, with your André! I'm only sorry for your youth."

When they entered the foyer, the others were already seated for supper. The grandmother, or as those at home called her, Granny, was very heavy, unattractive, with thick eyebrows and a mustache, was speaking loudly, and by her voice and manner of speech it was obvious she ran the home. She owned the commercial stands at the pavilion and the old house with its colonnades and garden, but she prayed and cried every morning that God would save her from ruin. Her daughter-in-law, Nadya's mother, Nina Ivanovna, was fair-haired, with a tightly bound waist, pince-nez, and diamond rings on every finger. Father André, a little old man, shrunken, toothless, and with a face that looked as if he were getting ready to say something very funny, was there; and his son, André Andreich, Nadya's fiancé, sturdy and handsome, with curly hair, resembling an artist or a painter— all three were conversing about hypnotism.

"You will improve in a week at my home," said Granny, addressing Sasha, "only eat better. What a sight you are!" she exclaimed. "You look terrible! You are now an authentic prodigal son."

"Having squandered the wealth provided by the father," quoted Father André slowly with laughing eyes, "he is doomed to graze with animals devoid of reasoning power."

"I love my daddy," said André Andreich as he patted his father on the back. "Great old man. Good old boy."

They all became silent. Sasha suddenly laughed and put his napkin up to his mouth.

"Is it true you believe in hypnotism?" asked Father André of Nina Ivanovna.

"I cannot, of course, confirm that I believe," answered Nina Ivanovna, putting on a very serious face, even a stern look. "But it is necessary to recognize that in nature there is much that is mysterious and unknown."

"I agree with you perfectly, although I must add that for myself, faith considerably reduces our sphere of mystery."

They were served a large, juicy turkey. Father André and Nina Ivanovna continued their conversation. And Nina Ivanovna's diamonds shone on her fingers, and then her eyes shone with tears as she became agitated.

"Although I don't dare to argue with you," she said, "you agree that many problems in life remain unsolved!"

"Not one, I assure you."

After supper André played the violin and Nina Ivanovna accompanied him on the piano. He had graduated from the university ten years ago with a degree in philology, but held no position, had no definite business, and rarely took part in philanthropic concerts; in the town he was called an artist.

André Andreich played; everyone quietly listened. On the table the samovar quietly gurgled, but only Sasha drank tea. Later when the clock struck twelve, a violin string broke; everyone laughed, started moving about, and began to leave.

Having seen off her fiancé, Nadya went to her room on the upper floor, which she shared with her mother. The lower floor was her grandmother's. On the first floor in the reception room they were dampening the fires, but Sasha continued to sit and drink tea. He sat over his tea for a long time like a Muscovite, drinking as many as seven cups at a time. Nadya, after she had undressed and lay in bed, could hear the servants for a long time as they cleaned up and how Granny scolded. Finally, all became quiet and only every now and then Sasha's deep coughing could be heard from his room on the lower floor.

II

When Nadya awoke, it must have been about two hours before dawn. Somewhere in the distance the watchman could be heard. Sleep had left her; lying in the very soft bed was uncomfortable. Nadya, as in all the past May nights, sat up in bed and began to think. But the thoughts were the same as those which she had had the nights before—monotonous, unnecessary, persistent thoughts about how André Andreich had started to court her and then proposed marriage; how she had agreed and later gradually began to value this good, wise person. So why now that little time remained before the marriage had she begun to experience fright, uncertainty, as if she were expecting something vague and troublesome?

"Tik-tok, tik-tok . . . ," lazily knocked the guard. "Tik-tok. . . ."

The garden could be seen through the large, old window. In the distance the thick lilac bush was in bloom, sleepy and limp from the cold, and a thick white cloud was slowly floating toward the lilac, as if wanting to cover it. Far away in the trees sleepy crows were cawing.

"My God, why am I so depressed?"

It may be that every bride-to-be feels this way before the wedding. Who knows? Or, in this case, is it Sasha's influence? But really, Sasha for several years has been repeating the same thing as if it were something he had read, and when saying it, he seems simple and strange. However, why can't she get Sasha out of her head?

The guard had stopped knocking long ago. Under the window and in the garden the birds were noisy, the cloud left the garden, everything was illuminated by the spring brightness, as if it were smiling. Soon the whole garden, warmed by the sun and treated kindly, came alive, and drops of dew, like diamonds, glistened on the leaves; and the garden, neglected long ago, this morning seemed young and beautiful.

Granny was already up. Sasha coughed his deep, coarse cough. The setting up of the samovar downstairs could be heard, and how chairs were being moved around.

Time passed slowly. Nadya had been awake for a long time, had been walking in the garden, and yet the morning dragged on.

Here is Nina Ivanovna, tear-stained, holding a glass of mineral water. She was involved in spiritualism, homeopathy, read a great deal, liked to talk about the doubts she was subject to, and from all this, it seemed to Nadya, that she had locked inside a deep, secret thought. Nadya kissed her mother and walked alongside her.

"Why were you crying, Mama?" she asked.

"Last night I began reading a story which described an old man and his daughter. The old man heard somewhere that a supervisor was in love with his daughter. I didn't read it all, for there was one place where it was difficult to refrain from crying," said Nina Ivanovna and gulped a drink from her glass. "This morning I recalled it and again broke into tears."

"And for me these are depressing days," said Nadya, pausing. "Why can't I sleep nights?"

"I don't know, dear. When I can't sleep nights I close my eyes tightly, like this, and I describe for myself Anna Karenina, the way she walked and how she talked, or I imagine something historical from the ancient world."

Nadya felt that her mother didn't understand her and couldn't understand her. She felt this for the first time in her life, and it became fearful, so she wanted to conceal this; she left and went into her own room.

At two o'clock they all sat down to dinner. It was Wednesday, a fast day, so the grandmother, served Lenten* borsch and fish with porridge.

In order to tease the grandmother, Sasha ate his own soup with meat and the Lenten borsch. He joked the whole time they were eating, but the jokes did not sound funny. The intent was to admonish and moralize, and was not amusing. Before he would make a pun, he raised his extremely long, emaciated as if dead, fingers. It made one think that he was very ill and, sorry to say, that he was not long for this world. Pity for him could drive one to tears.

After dinner the grandmother went to her room to rest. Nina Ivanovna briefly played the piano and then she too left.

"Ah, dear Nadya," Sasha began his usual after-dinner conversation. "If only you would listen to me! If only!"

She was sitting deep down in an old armchair with eyes closed, while he quietly walked up and down the room.

"If only you would go away to school!" he said. "Only enlightened and holy people are interesting; only they are indispensable. Only when there are more such people will we have a better world. Your town will then gradually disappear—all will fall topsy-turvy, all will change, as if by magic. There will then be huge, magnificent houses, incredible gardens, unusual fountains, remarkable people. . . . But that is not important. What is important is what occupies our minds now, what is in the mind now. Evil will not exist because every person will be a believer, and everyone will know why he exists, and not a single one will seek support from the throng. Dear, darling, leave! Show everyone that this immobile, dull, sinful life bores you. At least show this to yourself!"

"It's impossible, Sasha. I'm getting married."

---

*If you're a believer, you don't eat meat along with dairy products. "Lenten" implies "no meat," and not time of year.

"Eh, so what! Who needs it?"

They went out into the garden and walked a little.

"If one is objective, my dear, it is necessary to consider, to understand, how dirty, how immoral, this indolent life of yours is," continued Sasha. "Consider that if, for example, you and your mother and your grandmother don't work, that means that someone else works in your place, that you consume the product of the labor of others. Can you really say that is clean and not dirty?"

Nadya wanted to say: "Yes, that's true." She wanted to say that she understood, but tears filled her eyes. She suddenly clammed up, felt compassion for everyone, and went to her room.

André Andreich usually came early in the evening and played the violin for a long time. In general, he was not talkative and loved the violin, perhaps because while playing one had to be silent. At eleven o'clock, getting ready to go home and already in his coat, he embraced Nadya and began to greedily kiss her face, shoulders, and hands.

"My precious, my darling, my beautiful!" he sputtered. "Oh how lucky I am! I'm out of my mind from ecstasy!"

It seemed to her that she had heard all this long ago, very long ago, or read it some place . . . in a novel—an old, torn novel discarded long ago!

Sasha was sitting in the drawing room at a table, drinking tea, having placed the saucer on his five long fingers; Granny had set the cards for a game of patience; Nina Ivanovna was reading. The light was flickering in the lamp before the icon and all seemed quiet and prosperous. Nadya said goodnight and went upstairs to her room, lay down, and immediately fell asleep. But, as the night before, dawn was just breaking when she awoke. Sleep had left her and her soul felt disturbed, heavy. She sat up, placed her head on her knees, and thought about her fiancé, about marriage. . . . She remembered for some reason that her mother had not loved her late husband and now she had nothing; she lived completely dependent upon her mother-in-law, Granny. No matter how much she tried, she could not imagine why up to this time she had seen something special in her mother, something unusual, why she did not notice that she was a plain, ordinary, unhappy woman.

Down below, Sasha also was not asleep—his coughing could be heard. "This strange, ingenuous person," thought Nadya. In his dreams were all these wondrous salons, unusual fountains, but for Nadya there was a feeling of absurdity. So why in his ingenuousness, even in the wonderful absurdity of her leaving to become educated, that although she hardly gave it a thought, did her whole heart and her whole bosom become cold, overflowing with a feeling of joy and excitement?

"It is better not to think, better not to think," she whispered. "It is imperative not to think of this!"

III

Sasha suddenly became bored in the middle of June and began to prepare to return to Moscow.

"I can't bear to live in this town," he declared gloomily. "No running water, no sewers! I'm repelled by the food: the kitchen is impossibly filthy. . . ."

"Wait a bit, prodigal son!" for some reason in a whisper persuaded the grandmother, "the seventh of September is the wedding!"

"I don't wish to stay."

"You should stay with us until September!"

"I don't want to now. I must work!"

The summer was damp and cold, the trees were wet, everything in the garden looked cheerless and despondent, as if it too would really like to work. In the rooms, upstairs and downstairs, strange women's voices could be heard and a sewing machine clattered in the grandmother's quarters: they were hurrying to finish the dowry. Nadya was to get six fur coats, and the most expensive, according to the grandmother, was worth three thousand rubles! The vanity got on Sasha's nerves; he sat in his room and fumed, but all the same, he was convinced to remain, and he gave his word that he would leave no sooner than the first of July.

Time flew. On Saint Peter's day, the twenty-ninth of June, after dinner André Andreich went with Nadya to Moscow Street in order to look over once again the house which they had leased and which for some time was being prepared for the young couple. The house was two-storied, but only the upper floor was ready. In the reception room was a polished floor of painted parquet, chairs made from soft wood, a piano, and a music stand for the violin. The room smelled of paint. On the wall in a gold frame hung a large colorful picture: it was a nude female and near her stood a purple vase with a broken handle.

"A marvellous picture," exclaimed André Andreich and gave a sigh of deep respect. "It is by the artist Shishmachevski."

Beyond was the living room with a round table, sofa, and armchair, both covered in bright blue material. Over the sofa hung a large photographic portrait of Father André in his *kamilavka,* a tall piece of headgear worn by the Orthodox priests, and wearing his decorative ribbons and medals. Then they went into the dining room, which had a buffet, and after this, the bedroom. Here in the twilight two beds stood side by side. It appeared that when they furnished the bedroom, they assumed that everything would be very fine and it could not be different. André Andreich led Nadya through the rooms and held her around the waist the whole time. She felt weak, guilty; hated all these rooms, the beds, the chairs; and she felt disgusted by the nude. It was now clear to her that she had never loved him. But, how to say this, tell it to whom, and why, she did not understand and could not understand, although she had been thinking this for days and nights. . . . He held her around the waist, spoke so tenderly, modestly, how lucky he was, how much he had yearned for this— his own quarters; and she saw in all this only banality—stupid, naive, intolerable banality—and his arm around her waist seemed to her stiff and cold like a hoop. She was ready at a minute's notice to flee, to begin to sob, and to throw herself out the window. André Andreich took her to the bathroom and here touched the faucet set into the wall, and suddenly water trickled out.

"How do you like it?" he said and burst out laughing. "I ordered a hundred-gallon tank installed in the garret and we will now have water here."

They walked through the yard, then out into the street, and hired a cab. Thick clouds of dust rose and it seemed that soon rain would fall.

"Are you cold?" asked André Andreich, squinting from the dust. She kept silent.

"Yesterday, Sasha, you recall, reproached me for not doing anything," he said, hesitating for a moment. "Why, he's right! Infinitely right! I don't do anything and I can't do anything. My darling, why is this so? Why is it so against my nature to even think that I might at some time put on a cap with a visor and go into the service? Why is it so alien to me, when I see a lawyer, or a Latin teacher, or a member of the council? Oh Mother Russia! Oh Mother Russia! How many of us do you still bear that are indolent and useless! Oh Longsuffering One, how many on your back like me!"

And from that—that, he did nothing—he generalized and saw this as a characterization of the time.

"When we are married," he continued, "we will go together to the village, my darling, and work there! We will buy a small plot of land with a garden and a stream; we will work hard, observe life. . . . Oh, how good that will be!"

He took off his cap and his hair was blown about by the wind, and she listened to him and thought: "God, if only I could get home! God!" Just as they were nearing her house they ran into Father André.

"Here comes Father!" André Andreich was delighted and waved his cap. "I love my daddy, it is true," he said, while paying the cabby. "He's a nice old boy! Good old boy!"

Nadya entered the house, angry, sick, knowing that there would be guests the whole evening, and it would be necessary to entertain them, to smile, to listen to the violin, to listen to all kinds of nonsense, and to talk only about the wedding. The grandmother, important, splendid in her silk gown, haughty, as she always seemed when there were guests, sat by the samovar. Father André with his usual sly smile entered.

"I have the pleasure and happy consolation to see you in good health," he addressed the grandmother, and it was difficult to tell whether he was joking or speaking seriously.

IV

The wind buffeted the windows and the roof; its whistling could be heard, and in the stove the house ghost plaintively and morosely sang his song. It was one o'clock in the morning. All were in bed, but no one was sleeping, and to Nadya it seemed that downstairs they were playing the violin. A sharp bang was heard. It must be that one of the outside shutters had broken off. A minute later Nina Ivanovna in a nightgown entered Nadya's room carrying a candle.

"What was that noise, Nadya?" she asked.

Her mother, with her hair in one braid, with a timid smile, seemed older on this stormy night, unattractive, and not very tall. Nadya recalled that it wasn't so long ago that she had thought her mother very unique and proudly listened to what she had to say. At this moment she couldn't remember anything she had said; whatever came to her mind was useless and insignificant.

The noise from the stove was deep and sonorous and even sounded like "Oh . . . o, my Go . . . d!" Nadya sat up in bed and suddenly pulled at her hair and sobbed.

"Mama, Mama," she cried out. "My very own, if only you knew what is happening with me! I beg you, plead with you, permit me to leave! I plead!"

"Where to?" asked Nina Ivanovna, not understanding, and sat down on the bed.

"Where do you want to go?"

Nadya cried for a long time and could not say a word.

"Permit me to leave this town!" she finally exclaimed. "The wedding is impossible and will not occur, you must understand! I don't love this man. . . . And I cannot speak about him."

"No, my dear heart, no," quickly stated Nina Ivanovna, terribly frightened. "You will calm down—you're in a bad mood. This will pass. Truly, you were annoyed by André. Lovers' quarrels aren't serious."

"Well, leave, Mama, leave!" sobbed Nadya.

"Yes," said Nina Ivanovna, pausing a little. "It hasn't been long since you were a little girl, and now a bride-to-be. It is the nature of things that there is continual metabolism. You will not notice how you age and become a mother, and will have an unmanageable daughter such as I have."

"Darling, my sweet, you are wise, but you are unhappy," said Nadya, "you are very unhappy—why are you saying such nonsense? For God's sake, what for?"

Nina Ivanovna wanted to say something but could not say a word, sobbed, and went back to her room. The deep tones droned in the stove and unexpectedly became alarming. Nadya jumped from her bed and hastily went to her mother. Nina Ivanovna, tear-stained, lay in her bed, covered by a blue blanket, and held a book in her hand.

"Mama, listen to me!" exclaimed Nadya. "I beg you, think about it and understand it! Try to understand the extent to which our lives are petty and humiliating. My eyes have been opened. I now see everything. And, what is your André Andreich? You know he is not intelligent, Mama! Lord, my God! Understand, Mama, he's stupid!"

Nina Ivanovna abruptly sat up.

"You and your grandmother torment me!" she said and sobbed. "I want to live! To live!" she repeated and several times beat her breast with a clenched fist. "Give me freedom! I'm still young. I want to live, and you have made me into an old woman! . . ."

She cried bitterly, laid down, and curled up under the cover, and looked tiny, pathetic, and foolish. Nadya went to her room, dressed, and sitting by the window, awaited the morning. She sat all night deep in thought, while outside the shutter banged and the wind whistled.

In the morning the grandmother complained that the wind had damaged the apple trees and felled one old plum tree. It was dull, dingy, and cheerless even though a fire had been lit. Everyone complained about the cold, and rain pattered on the windows. After tea Nadya went to Sasha's room and not saying a word, knelt in the corner near his chair and covered her face with her hands.

"What is it?" asked Sasha.

"I can't . . . ," she uttered. "How I could have lived here before, I don't understand, don't comprehend! I despise my fiancé, I despise myself, I despise this slothful, thoughtless life. . . ."

"Well, well . . . ," said Sasha, not as yet understanding the situation. "It's nothing. . . . It will be all right."

"I am bored stiff by this life," continued Nadya. "I can't bear it here for one more day. I'm going to leave tomorrow. Take me with you, for God's sake!"

Sasha looked for a moment at her in amazement; he finally understood and became as delighted as a child. He waved his hands and began to tap with his slippers, as if he were dancing from joy.

"Wonderful!" he said, rubbing his hands together. "God, how splendid that is!"

She looked at him, not blinking, with large, loving eyes as if fascinated, expecting that he would now say something remarkable and candid which he considered important. He still hadn't said anything to her, but she already knew that something new and bold was opening up before her, something that she had been unaware of before, and she looked at him, full of expectations, ready for everything, even death.

"Tomorrow I leave," he said, having thought it over, "and you will go with me to see me off. . . . I will take your things in my trunk and I will get your ticket; when the third bell is rung, you will get on the train—we will travel together. You will go with me as far as Moscow, and from there you will travel alone to Petersburg. Do you have a passport?"

"I have one."

"I swear to you that you will not be sorry and will not be remorseful," said Sasha enthusiastically. "You will leave, and you will learn. Fate is leading you there. When you overturn your life, everything changes. Most important—to overturn one's life means that what is left behind is unnecessary. So, well then, will we travel tomorrow?"

"Oh, yes! For God's sake!"

It seemed to Nadya that she was very agitated, that she had a heavy weight upon her heart, and as never before, that from now up to the actual departure she would suffer and have torturous thoughts. But when she got to her room upstairs and lay down on the bed, she fell into a deep sleep with a tear-stained face, with a smile, until the evening.

V

They sent for a cab. Nadya, already in a hat and coat, went upstairs in order to see her mother one more time without anyone else around. She stood in her own room by her bed, which was still warm, and after looking all over, she went softly to her mother's room. Nina Ivanovna was asleep and the room was quiet. Nadya kissed her mother, straightened her mother's hair, stood for a few moments . . . then hurriedly returned downstairs.

Outside the rain was torrential. The cabman, soaked even with a cover overhead, was standing by the entrance.

"You won't be able to fit in with him, Nadya," declared the grandmother, when the servant was putting in the trunk. "Why do you want to see him off in such weather? You'd better stay home. Look how hard it's raining!"

Nadya wanted to say something but couldn't. Sasha seated Nadya and covered her legs with a plaid rug. Then he settled himself beside her.

"Make good time! Lord bless you!" shouted the grandmother from the porch. "You, Sasha, write us from Moscow!"

"I will. Farewell, Granny."

"May the heavenly queen protect you!"

"Well, sister, wait a bit!" said Sasha.

Nadya had begun to cry. It was now clear to her that she was irrevocably leaving, which she had up to this time not believed, even when she parted with her grandmother, even when she was looking at her mother. Farewell, town! And suddenly she recalled everything: André and his father, and the new apartment, and the nude with the vase; and all this no longer frightened her, was not oppressive, but was naive, small, and receded into the distant past. When they settled in the passenger car and the train moved, the whole past, so large and serious, was squeezed into a small lump, and turned into a huge, expansive future, to which up to this time she had been inattentive. The rain beat upon the car's windows; only the fields were visible; the telegraph poles flashed by with birds on the lines. Without warning, her breathing became difficult, she was overwhelmed by gladness: she became aware that she was traveling to freedom, she was traveling to learn—that which not very long ago was derisively called "leaving to become a Cossack." She laughed and cried and prayed.

"Never mind!" said Sasha, grinning. "Never mind!"

VI

The fall passed and after the fall, the winter. Nadya was now terribly homesick and every day thought about her mother and her grandmother, and thought about Sasha. Letters came from home, gentle, well-wishing, and it seemed that all had been forgiven and forgotten. In May after exams, healthy and happy, she travelled home, and on the way stopped in Moscow in order to meet with Sasha. He was the same as last summer: bearded, with an uncombed head of hair, in the same jacket and canvas trousers, and with those enormous, marvelous eyes. But his appearance was unhealthy, tortured; he had even aged and become thinner, and coughed the whole time. And, for some reason, he appeared to Nadya ignorant and provincial.

"My God, Nadya has arrived!" he exclaimed, joyfully laughing. "My very own, dear heart!"

They sat in the lithograph workroom, where it was smoky and smelled oppressively of paints. Later they went to his room, where it was smoky too and full of globs of spit. On the table beside the cold samovar was a cracked saucer with a dark paper napkin; on the table and on the floor were clumps of dead flies. It was evident by everything that the personal life of Sasha had been slovenly and that he lived any old way, with complete disdain for comfort, and if anyone spoke to him about his personal happiness, of his personal life, of love for him, he would understand nothing and would only laugh.

"Nothing went amiss. All went well," reported Nadya hastily. "Mama came to see me in Petersburg in the fall and said that grandmother was not angry and only goes often to my room and blesses the walls."

Sasha looked delighted, coughed a little, and spoke with a hoarse voice. Nadya watched him and could not determine whether he was seriously ill or if it only seemed so to her.

"Sasha, my precious," she said, "it is true that you are sick!"

"No, it's nothing. Sick, but not very. . . ."

"Oh, dear God," Nadya was disturbed. "Why don't you get medical care, why don't you take care of your health? My darling, dear Sasha," she declared, and her eyes filled with tears, and for some reason André came to mind, and the nude with the vase, and the entire past, which now seemed so distant, like childhood; and she cried because Sasha no longer seemed so new, intellectual, interesting, as he had the previous year. "Dear Sasha, you are very, very ill. I would do all I could to make you less pale and thin. I'm so obliged to you! You can't imagine how much you have done for me, my dear Sasha! In reality, you are now the closest, the one person that I belong to."

They sat for a while, talked for a while. Now that Nadya had spent the winter in Petersburg away from Sasha, away from his words, his smile, his whole physiognomy announced it had outlived its time, was obsolete, in its prime long ago, and was possibly already on its way to its grave.

"Day after tomorrow I'm going on the Volga," said Sasha. "Well, and later for *kymis** to the steppes to be healed. I want to drink *kymis*. I am going with a friend and his wife. His wife is a remarkable person. I talk with her all the time and tell her she should leave to become educated. I want my own life to be turned over."

Having finished talking, they drove to the train station. Sasha treated her to tea and apples, and as the train moved he, smiling, waved his handkerchief. It was apparent even from his legs that he was very ill and did not have long to live.

Nadya arrived in her home town in the afternoon. When she was on her way home from the station, the streets seemed very wide and the houses small and flat. There were no people about and they met only a German builder in a red coat. All the houses looked as though covered by dust.

---

*"fermented goat milk"

The grandmother, already really old, still stout and unattractive, held Nadya with her hands and cried for a long time, pressed her face to her shoulders, and could not pull herself away. Nina Ivanovna had also greatly aged and lost her good looks, as if completely pinched, but was still tightly corseted, and diamonds glittered on her fingers.

"My darling!" she exclaimed, her whole body trembling. "My darling!"

After this they sat and cried silently. It could be seen that both the grandmother and mother felt that the past was lost forever and could never return. They no longer had status in society, nor the former honors, nor the right to invite guests. That is how it is when in the midst of a genteel, untroubled life, suddenly, let us say, police appear in the night, conduct a search, and the owner is turned out of his home, which he has squandered and forfeited—and bids farewell forever to his genteel, untroubled life!

Nadya went upstairs and saw the same bed, the same windows with the white, unblemished curtains, and from the windows the same garden full of sunshine, joyous, noisy. She fingered her table, sat down, considered. She was well-fed and drank her tea with delicious thick cream, but this no longer held her; emptiness filled the rooms, and the ceilings were low. In the evening she lay down to sleep, covered herself, and for some reason it seemed ridiculous to lie in this warm, very soft bed.

Nina Ivanovna came in for a minute and sat looking guilt-ridden, timid and cautious.

"Well, how are things, Nadya?" she asked, and after a pause: "Are you content? Very content?"

"I am content, Mama."

Nina Ivanovna arose, blessed Nadya and the windows.

"And I, as you can see, have become religious," she said. "You know, I'm now involved with philosophy and am always thinking, thinking. . . . And many things have become bright as day for me. It seems to me that, first of all, life should pass as if through a prism."

"Tell me, Mama, how is grandmother's health?"

"As if nothing had happened. When you went away with Sasha

and the telegram came from you, Grandmother read it and fainted; she lay motionless for three days. Then she prayed and cried. And now it doesn't matter."

She stood up and walked about the room.

"Tik-tok . . . ," knocked the guard. "Tik-tok, tik-tok. . . ."

"First of all, it is necessary that all of life should pass as if through a prism," she said, "that is, in other words, it is necessary that conscious life be reduced to its simplest elements, as into seven basic colors, and every element must be studied separately."

Nina Ivanovna spoke some more and Nadya did not hear when she left, for she had fallen soundly asleep.

May went by and June came. Nadya had become accustomed to being home. The grandmother fussed around the samovar, breathing heavily. Nina Ivanovna talked about her philosophy in the evenings. As in the past she lived in the house like a ward, and had to turn to the grandmother for every kopeck. There were a great many flies in the house, and the ceilings in the rooms, it seemed, became lower and lower. Granny and Nina Ivanovna never went out into the street from fear that they might meet Father André and André Andreich. Nadya walked about the garden, about the street, looked at the homes, at the dull fences, and it seemed to her that everything in the town had grown older, had outlived its time, and was only waiting, not exactly for its demise, not exactly for the beginning of something young and fresh. Oh, if only that new, enlightened life would quickly arrive, when it would be possible to look directly and boldly into the eyes of one's fate, recognize oneself as right, to be happy, free! Sooner or later that life would come! The time would come when from grandmother's house, where everything is so arranged that four servants can't live any differently than in one basement room in filth— the time would come when there wouldn't remain a trace of this house and it would be forgotten; no one would remember it. And Nadya was only amused by some little boys from the neighboring courtyard. When she walked in the garden, they banged on the fence and with laughter teased her:

"Old maid! Old maid!"

A letter came from Sasha from Saratov, a city on the Volga.

He wrote with his easy, flowing handwriting that the trip on the Volga went very well, but that in Saratov he was sick for a while, lost his voice, and for two weeks now lay in the hospital. She understood what this meant and had a premonition, much like a certainty, which seized her. But it was disturbing for her that this premonition and thoughts about Sasha did not agitate her as they had earlier. She passionately wanted to live, wanted to be in Petersburg. Her association with Sasha still presented itself fondly, but in the distant, distant past! She spent a sleepless night and in the morning sat by the window as if listening for something. And really, voices were heard from downstairs. An alarmed grandmother was speedily asking questions of someone. After this sobs could be heard. . . . When Nadya went downstairs, the grandmother was in the corner before the icon, praying, and her face was tear-stained. A telegram lay on the table.

Nadya walked about the room for a long time, listened to the crying grandmother, then took the telegram and read it. It informed that yesterday morning in Saratov, Alexander Timofeich, or simply Sasha, had died from tuberculosis.

The grandmother and Nina Ivanovna went to church to order services for the dead, and Nadya walked about the rooms for hours deep in thought. She clearly recognized that her life had turned over just as Sasha had wished, that she was alone here, a stranger, unneeded, and that here there was nothing necessary for her; all of the past had been stripped away from her and had disappeared, as if burned, and the ashes had been blown away by the wind.

"Farewell, dear Sasha!" she thought, and pictured for herself a future life that would be new, liberal, spacious; and this future life, still unclear, full of secrets, attracted and lured her.

She went upstairs to her room to pack, and on the next day in the morning parted with her relatives and, animated, cheerful, forsook the town forever, just as she had planned.

1903

The Tale of Lady NN

Once at twilight, about nine years ago at haying time, Peter Sergeich, performing his duties as the court investigator, and I were going on horseback to the train station for the mail.

The weather was fabulous, but on the way back we heard the rolling of thunder and saw an angry black cloud moving directly toward us. The cloud kept coming closer to us and we to it.

Against this background our house and the church appeared white and the tall poplars were silver. The air was full of the aroma of the end of the haying and the coming rain.

My companion was in fine form. He laughed and spoke nonsense. He said that it wouldn't be bad if we suddenly ran into a medieval castle with notched towers, covered with moss and full of owls, so that we could hide there from the rain and so that eventually lightning would strike us. . . .

Over the fields of rye and oats sped the first blast of wind, and the dust swirled in the air. Peter Sergeich broke into laughter and spurred on his horse.

"Great!" he shouted. "Super!"

I, infected by his excitement and the thought that I would soon be soaked to the bones and even possibly killed by lightning, also began to laugh.

The whirlwind and the galloping, so that you can hardly catch your breath from the wind and feel like a bird, thrills and tickles the breast. When we rode into our courtyard, the wind had stopped and torrential rain was falling on the grass and the roofs. The stable was abandoned.

Peter Sergeich unsaddled the horses himself and led them to their stalls. Waiting for him to finish, I stood at the entrance and watched the slanting bands of rain. The penetrating, exciting fragrance of the hay was even stronger here than in the fields. The clouds and the rain had made it dark.

"What a strike!" exclaimed Peter Sergeich, coming alongside me after one very strong crash of thunder, when it seemed the heavens had burst across the fields. "What do you think of it?"

He stood by me at the entrance and breathing heavily from the fast ride, stared at me. I noticed that he was admiring me. "Natalie Vladimirovna," he said, "I would give up everything in order just to stand like this much longer and look at you. You are beautiful today."

His eyes were looking rapturously and pleadingly. His face was pale. On his beard and mustache shone raindrops, which also seemed to look lovingly upon me.

"I love you," he said. "I love you and am happy that I can see you. I know that you cannot be my wife, and I do not ask for anything. I don't need anything, only to tell you that I love you. Be silent, don't answer, don't pay attention to me, but only be aware that you are dear to me, and allow me to look at you."

His rapture was passed on to me. I looked at his animated face, heard his voice that blended with the sound of the rain, and as if bewitched, I could not move.

I wanted to be able to look at his shining eyes forever, and listen to his words.

"You are silent—and beautiful!" exclaimed Peter Sergeich. "Don't say anything."

I felt wonderful. I laughed from pleasure and ran in the rain to the house. He also laughed and leaping, ran after me.

Both of us, noisily like children, wet, huffing and puffing, stomping up the steps, ran into the house. My father and brother, unaccustomed to seeing me laughing and merry, looked with amazement at me and also started laughing.

The threatening clouds passed, the thunder stopped, but on Peter Sergeich's beard the raindrops still glistened. He sang all evening until supper, whistled, played boisterously with the dog, chasing her around the rooms so that he almost knocked over the servant with the samovar. At supper he ate a great deal, spoke foolishness, and asserted that when you eat fresh cucumbers, the scent of spring pervades the mouth.

When I lay down to sleep, I lit a candle and opened my window wide. An undefined feeling embraced my spirit. I noted that I was free, healthy, distinguished, and wealthy and that I was loved, but most important, that I was distinguished and wealthy—distinguished and wealthy. My God! How good that was. . . . Later, curling up in bed feeling a little cold, which had hit me from the garden together with the dampness, I tried to understand, did I love Peter Sergeich or not. . . . And not solving anything, fell asleep.

In the morning when I saw the shimmering rays of the sun upon my bed, and the shadows of the branches from the lime tree, the memory of the day before came alive for me. Life was rich, full of variety and charm. Singing, I dressed quickly and ran into the garden. . . .

And what happened after this? What happened—was nothing. In the winter when we lived in town, Peter Sergeich came to see us now and then. Country acquaintances are only fascinating in the country and in the summer; in town in the winter they lose half of their charm. When you serve them tea in the city, it seems that they wear strange jackets and that they stir their tea too long. But even in town Peter Sergeich sometimes spoke of love, but it didn't come out in the same way as in the country. In the city the wall between us was felt stronger than in the country: I was distinguished and wealthy, and he was poor and wasn't even an aristocrat, but the son of a deacon. He performed the duties of a court investigator, and nothing else. Both of us, I because of my youth and he—God only knows why—considered this wall very high and thick, and he, when at our house in town, had a strained smile and criticized high society, and was gloomily silent when there was anyone else in the living room.

There wasn't a wall that could not be overcome. The heroes

of contemporary novels, several of which I was familiar with, were too proud, had no guts, were lazy and indecisive, reconciled with the thought that they were not successful and that life had hoodwinked them. In place of struggling for what they wanted, they only criticized, called the world evil, and became oblivious that their criticisms would gradually turn into platitudes.

I was loved, happiness was within reach and seemed to live shoulder to shoulder with me. I lived in clover, did not try to understand myself, not knowing what I waited for and what I wanted from life, and time passed and passed. . . . People with their love passed by me, bright days and warm nights flashed by, the nightingales sang, the fragrance of hay—all this, precious, wonderful in my recollections, for me as for everyone passed quickly, leaving no traces, not appreciated, and disappeared like the clouds. . . . Where has it all gone?

My father died, I grew old; everything that was pleasing, that flattered, that gave hope has disappeared. The sound of rain, the crash of thunder, thoughts of happiness, conversations about love—all of that is only a memory, and I see before me a flat, empty future: on the plain there isn't a living soul, and on the horizon it is dark, frightful. . . .

There's the bell. . . . It's Peter Sergeich. When in the winter I see barren trees and remember how green they were for me in the summer, I whisper:

"Oh, my darlings!"

And when I see people with whom I spent the spring of my life, I feel melancholy, warm, and I whisper the same words. It has been a long time now since my father recommended that Peter Sergeich be transferred to the city. He has aged a little and has drifted somewhat away from us. He has already stopped speaking of his love, does not speak nonsense, hates his work, for some reason is ill and disillusioned, has given up hope, and lives half-heartedly. He sits by the fireplace; silently stares into the fire. . . . I, not knowing what to say, ask: "Well, what is it?"

"Nothing," he answered. And again silence. The red glare from the fire crosses his pained face.

I remembered the past and unexpectedly my shoulders shudder, my head falls, and I cry bitterly. It had become unbearably sad for me, and this person and the past were passionately desired, and that which life was now denying us. I no longer thought of how distinguished and wealthy I was. I sobbed hysterically, pressing my temples, and mumbled:

"My God, my God, life has passed me by. . . ."

He sat, silent, and did not say to me: "Don't cry." He understood that I needed to cry and the time had come for tears. I saw from his eyes that he was sorry for me; and I too was sorry for him, and vexed with this proud failure who was unable to settle neither my life nor his own.

When I accompanied him to the foyer, it seemed to me he deliberately took a long time putting on his coat. He kissed my hand a few times and stared for a long time at my tear-stained face. I think that he recalled the storm then, the torrential rain, our laughter, my former face. He wanted to say something to me, and he would have been glad to say it, but he said nothing and only shook his head and tightly held my hand. God be with him!

Having accompanied him to the door, I returned to the study and sat on the rug before the fireplace. The red coals were covered with ashes and were dying out. The frost was still angrily knocking against the window and in the brick chimney the wind howled about something.

The maid entered and thinking that I had fallen asleep, called me. . . .

1887

My Wives:
Letter to the Editor
by Raul Blue Beard

Dear Sir!
   The operetta *Bluebeard* that aroused in your readers laughter and gained laurels for Messrs. Lodio, Chernov, and others, drew from me only bitter feelings. The reaction was not simply one of insult, I'm sorry to say, but of sadness . . . sincere grief that for the last dozen years the lies of the press and the stage were in the mold of Adam's sin. It does not concern the existence of the operetta, nor even touches the circumstances that the author had no right to bring in my private life and uncover my family secrets. I am concerned only about the details upon which the public shapes its opinion of me, Raul Blue Beard. All these details are scandalous lies which I consider it necessary, dear sir, to dispute by means of your respectable magazine before pursuing legal means to expose the naked lie of the author, of Mr. Lentovski's connivance in this disreputable vice and covering it up.

   First of all, dear sir, I by no means am a ladies' man, as the author found it convenient to describe in his operetta. I am not crazy about women. I would be happy not to know them at all, but am I guilty because "I am a man: I count nothing that is human indifferent to me"? Besides having the right to choose, a person is still drawn by the "laws of necessity."

   I must choose one or the other: either join the category of madcaps, whom the medics love so, printing their observations on the front pages of newspapers, or sign a marriage contract. There is no middle way between these two undesirables. I married. Yes, I married and during the time of my married life—day and night—I envied that sluggard who didn't need feminine companionship and didn't have to support a wife, and it could happen a father-in-law and a mother-in-law—or his own mother. . . . You can agree that this doesn't sound like a womanizer.

Furthermore, the writer states that the day after the wedding I poisoned my wives—after the first night. In order not to put upon me such a cock-and-bull story, the writer had only to glance in the registration records, or in my service record. But, he did not do this and placed himself in the position of a person, as the saying goes, of a prevaricator. I did not poison my wives on the second day of the honeymoon, nor if you please, as the writer would wish, not without forethought.

The good Lord knows how much moral torment, weighty doubts, agonizing days and weeks that I have lived through before I decided to treat one of these small, vain creatures with morphine or phosphorus!

Not a whim, not carnality of a lazy and gluttonous knight, nor hard-heartedness, but a whole complex of screaming reasons and occurrences forced me to turn toward the kindness of my "doctor." Not an operetta but an entire tragic opera evolved in my soul. After a combination of a life of torture and long draining reflection, I sent to the shop for the phosphorus. (Forgive me, ladies! I do not consider a revolver a proper weapon for you. It is customary to poison rats and women with phosphorus.)

From the characterizations of all seven of my poisoned wives that are mentioned below, it will become evident to you, dear sir, and to the reader, the extent to which the reasons were not strategic that forced me to hold on to my last trump card for familial well-being. I will describe my wives from my diary in the order in which I recorded that which was significant to me under the heading, say, "expenditures for baths, cigars, marriages, and barbers."

*   *   *

No. 1. A petite brunette with long curly hair and large eyes like a young colt. She had style, was sinewy like a spring and beautiful. I was struck by the modesty and gentleness that filled her eyes. How she knew when to be silent—a rare talent which I value in women more than artistic talents! This was a human being, limited, none too clever, but honest and sincere. She confused Pushkin with Pygachev, Europe with America, rarely read, never knew anything, was always amazed by everything, but because of this in her whole life never consciously told even one lie, never made a false move. When it was required to cry, she cried. When a laugh was called for, she laughed. She laughed unconcerned about the appropriateness of time or place. She was natural like a dumb lamb.

The strength of the love of the feline species is proverbial, be biased if you wish, but no kitten loved her cat as this feline female loved me. The whole day, from morning 'til night, she never left me, walked after me, didn't take her eyes off of me, stared at me as if there were notes written on my forehead according to which she breathed, moved, spoke. . . .

The days and hours when she didn't see me she considered irrevocably lost—erased from her book of life. She looked at me silently, rapturously, with amazement. . . .

At night, when I snored like the last lazybones, if she were also sleeping, she saw me in her dreams. If she could keep awake, she prayed before the icon in the corner. If I were a romanticist, I would undoubtedly try to find out what kind of words in the dark of the night loving wives send to heaven for their husbands. What do they want and what are their pleas? How much logic there is in these prayers I can only imagine!

Neither in Testova nor in Moscow did I ever eat anything but what her little fingers prepared. Soup slightly oversalted was in her opinion a mortal sin. Overdone steak was demoralizing. Noting that I was hungry or dissatisfied with the food caused her terrible suffering. But nothing depressed her so much as my ailments. If I coughed or looked as if my stomach bothered me, she paled, developed a cold sweat on her forehead, walked to and fro cracking her knuckles. . . .

Even my briefest absence had her thinking that I was crushed under the carriage wheels, or fell from the bridge into the river, or was killed in an attack. . . . How many tortuous seconds resided in her memory! When I returned home after a few friendly drinks "under the influence" and good humoredly stretched out on the couch with a novel by Gaborio, no scolding, not even kicks, delivered me from a stupid compress on my head, a warm quilted cover, and a glass of lemon tea!

A golden fly is pleasing to observe only when it flies before your eyes for a minute and then flies away in the air, but if it begins to take a stroll on your forehead, tickles your cheek with its little feet, lies on your nose, and will not leave and pays no attention to your waving it away, you finally try to catch it and deprive it of its ability to pester you. My wife was like this fly.

The eternal staring into my eyes, the constant surveillance of my appetite, the steadfast pursuit of my sneezes, coughs, and slight headaches wore me out.

Finally, I couldn't stand it any longer. Her love for me was the cause of her suffering. The eternal silence and the blue meekness of her eyes spoke for her defenselessness.

I poisoned her. . . .

No. 2. She was a woman with an eternally smiling face, dimples in her cheeks, and squinting eyes . . . a very attractive little figure and her clothing was extraordinarily expensive and in enormously good taste. As much as my first wife was meek and a stay-at-home, this one was always on the go, loud and active. A novelist would describe her as a woman made up of nothing but nerves, and I wasn't far from wrong when I described her body as composed evenly of baking soda and vinegar.

This was a good bottle of sauerkraut soup in the moment of uncorking. All organisms known to physiology rush to live, but my wife's blood circulated like an express train rented by an American eccentric. Her pulse was 120 even when she slept. She didn't breathe but panted, did not drink but gulped. She rushed to breathe, to speak, to make love. . . . Her life consisted completely of speedily chasing after sensations. She liked pickles, mustard, pepper, giantlike men, cold showers, wild waltzes. . . .

From me she wanted a continual cannonade, fireworks, duels, and to march against that poor devil, Bobesha. . . . When she saw me in a dressing gown and slippers with a pipe between my teeth, she became beside herself and damned the day and hour when she married the "bear" Raul. There was no way possible to make her understand that I had outlived the ability to be part of that which was now the salt of her life, and that a sweater suited me better than a waltz.

She answered all of my arguments with a wave of her hands and hysterical tricks.

Willy-nilly, in order to escape the screeching and reproaches, I had to waltz, fire the cannon, fight. . . . That kind of life soon wore me out, and I sent for the "doctor." . . .

No. 3. She was a tall, classy, blue-eyed blonde. Her face expressed modesty, but at the same time, personal pride. She was always looking dreamily at the sky and every minute was emitting anguished sighs. She led a regulated existence, had her "own God," and eternally spoke of principles. In those things that she considered a matter of principle, she was merciless.

"It is dishonorable," she told me, "to wear a beard when from it you could make pillows for the poor!"

"Good God, why is she suffering? What is the cause?" I asked myself, listening to her deep sighs. Oh, these were for me communal sorrows!

The human being likes puzzles: Why did I fall in love with this blonde? It was not long before the puzzle was solved. My eyes accidentally fell upon this blonde's diary and in it I ran across the following pearl:

"Wishing to save poor papa, who got mixed up in a commissariat lawsuit, I had to make a sacrifice and listen to the voice of reason. I married the wealthy Raul. Forgive me, my Paul!"

Paul, as was later revealed, worked in a surveyor's office and wrote bad poetry. He never saw his Dulcinea again. . . . Along with her principles, she was "gathered" to her forefathers.

No. 4. A babe with a direct but eternally frightened and amazed look. She was the daughter of a merchant and along with a dowry of 200,000 she brought into my house her murderous habit of playing scales and singing the romantic "Once More I Come Before You." When she wasn't sleeping or eating, she played; when not playing, she sang. The scales made all my poor veins expand (I'm now without veins) and the words of this love song, "I Stand Enchanted," were sung with such a tortuous scream that all the sealing wax in my ears dissolved and the listening apparatus was unstrung.

I endured for a long time but it was evident that sooner or later the suffering itself would take precedence: the "doctor" came, and the scales stopped.

No. 5. This was a long-nosed, smooth-haired woman with a never-smiling, stern look. She was nearsighted and wore glasses. Because she had no taste whatsoever and was vain, she liked to dress simply and strangely: in a black dress with narrow sleeves and a wide belt. . . . It seemed that in whatever she wore there was a kind of flatness, an ironed look—not a single relief, not a single fold!

Her originality attracted me: she was not stupid. She had been educated abroad, somewhere in Germany, had absorbed all of Boklay and Millay, and dreamed of a scientific career. She spoke only of "wisdom." The ideas of spiritualists, positivists, and materialists were constantly pouring from her lips. When I conversed with her for the first time, I felt like an idiot. She surmised from my face that I was stupid, but this did not stop her from observing me from her superior height. On the contrary, she naively began to teach me, as if to put a stop to my stupidity. Smart people, when they are condescending to ignoramuses, are extraordinarily sympathetic!

As we were returning from the church in the wedding carriage, she looked thoughtfully out of the carriage window and told me about the nuptial customs in China. On the first night she revealed to me that my skull reminded her of mongolism. At the same time, she taught me how to measure the skull and declared that phrenology would never succeed as a science. I listened, listened . . . our most profound time of life is when we are listening. . . . She talked and

I blinked my eyes, afraid to show that I didn't understand anything. . . . When I awoke during the night, I saw two eyes concentrating on the ceiling or on my skull. . . .

"Don't disturb me . . . I'm thinking," she would say when I began to make gentle overtures toward her. . . .

Within a week after the wedding, a conviction was established in my noodle: Erudite women are a bit much for the male. Terrible trials! To eternally feel oneself to be taking an exam, to have a serious face constantly before you, and to be afraid to emit a stupid word— you must agree is to be subjected to terrible trials! Like a thief, I surreptitiously placed a little nugget of cyanide in her coffee. Phosphorus from matches would not take care of such a woman!

No. 6. A little girl who enticed me with her naiveté and unpolluted nature. This was a sweet, generous child, who within a month after the wedding proved to be a flirt, mad about the latest fashions, high society, gossip, manners, and visiting. She was a smidgin of trash, squandering my money recklessly and at the same time earnestly keeping up with the specials in the shopkeepers' catalogs.

She was willing to spend hundreds and thousands at the milliners, but gave the cook a hot dressing-down for spending a kopeck too much for sorrel. Frequent hysterics, weary migraines, and slapping the maids she considered great chic.

She married me only because she thought I was sophisticated and changed toward me two days after the wedding. So, at the same time when exterminating rats in the pantry, I poisoned her. . . .

No. 7. This one died because of a mistake: she accidentally drank some poison I had prepared for my mother-in-law. (I was in the process of poisoning my mother-in-law with liquid ammonia.) If it hadn't been for such an incident, she possibly would be alive even now. . . .

I am finished. I think, dear sir, that all that has been written above is sufficient to uncover for the reader the misinformation that the composer of the operetta and Mr. Lentovski provided. He was trapped, truly, by lack of knowledge. In any case, I await from Mr. Lentovski a published clarification, making the appropriate corrections.

Raul Blue Beard

1885

From the Notes of a Hot-Tempered Man

I 'm a serious person, and my brain has a philosophical bent. My profession is that of a financier. I am studying financial law and am writing a dissertation with the title "The Past and the Future of the Dog Tax." You will agree that I decidedly have no time for women, romances, moons, and other such foolishness.

It is morning. Ten o'clock. My *maman* is pouring me a cup of coffee. I drink it and go out on the balcony in order to immediately get to work on my dissertation.

I take a clean sheet of paper, dip my pen in the ink, and painstakingly trace out the title "The Past and the Future of the Dog Tax." Giving it some thought, I write: "A historical review. Judging from several hints found in Herodotus and Seneca, the dog tax begins from . . ."

At this point I hear extremely suspicious steps. I look down from the balcony and see a young woman with a long face and a narrow waist. She is called, it seems, Nadyenka or Varyenka, which, however, is decidedly unimportant. She is looking for something, then seems to notice me, and sings:

"Remember that melody, the absolute bliss. . . ."

I read over what I have written, wish to continue, but at this point the young woman gives the appearance that she has noticed me, and says with a grief-stricken voice:

"Hello, Nikolay Andreich! Imagine how unfortunate I am! While taking a walk yesterday, I lost the clasp from my bracelet!"

Once more I read over the beginning of my dissertation, improve

189

my handwriting, and am about to continue, but the young girl does
not give up.

"Nikolay Andreich," she says, "be so kind as to accompany me
home. The Karelins have a huge dog and I don't dare go alone."

I have no choice, put down my pen, and go downstairs. Nadyenka
or Varyenka takes hold of my arm, and we go toward her cottage.

When it is my fate that I am obliged to walk with a lady or
a young girl on my arm, why is it I always feel as if I'm a hook
on which a heavy fur coat has been hung. Nadyenka or Varyenka,
just between us, has a passionate nature (her grandfather was an
Armenian), and possesses the ability to hang on your arm the weight
of her whole body, and, like a leech, sticks to your side. And that's
the way we walk. . . .

Passing the Karelins, I see the huge dog, which reminds me of
the dog tax. I sadly remember the beginning of my work and sigh.

"What are you sighing about?" asks Nadyenka or Varyenka and
she too sighs.

It is necessary to make a stipulation. Nadyenka or Varyenka
(now I remember that her name is Mashyenka) imagined from somewhere that I was in love with her, and because of that she looked
at me with compassion and with words is trying to heal my wounded
heart.

"Hear me out," she stops and says. "I know why you're sighing.
You're in love, yes! I beg you, in the name of our friendship, believe
it, this girl whom you love, regards you with great respect! She cannot
reciprocate your love, but can she be blamed since her heart for
a long time belonged to another?"

Mashyenka's nose reddens and distends, her eyes fill with tears;
she, apparently, is waiting for an answer from me, but fortunately,
we arrived. . . . On the terrace is Mashyenka's *maman,* a good woman
but with prejudices. Glancing at her daughter's disturbed face, she
gives me a long once-over and takes a deep breath, as if she wished
to say: "Ah. Young man, you don't know how to conceal anything!"

Besides her, several motley girls are sitting on the terrace and
among them is a neighbor from the cottage next to ours, a retired
officer, who had been wounded in the last war in his left temple

and his right thigh. This wretched man, like me, had assigned himself to devote the whole summer to literary labor. He is writing *Memoirs of an Army Man.* Like me, he takes to his honorable work every morning, but really only succeeds writing "I was born in . . ." as under the balcony some kind of Varyenka or Mashyenka appears, and the wounded slave is taken into custody.

All on the terrace are cleaning some kind of ripe berries for jam. I bow and start to leave, but the motley young girls shriek, grab my hat and insist that I stay. I sit down. They hand me a dish with berries and a pin. I begin to clean them. The theme of the conversation of the motley young girls is men. This one is nice; that one is handsome, but not charming; the third isn't handsome, but charming; the fourth wouldn't be bad if only his nose didn't look like a thimble, etc.

"And you, Monsieur Nicolas," Varyenka's *maman* turns toward me, "are not handsome, but charming: There is something in your face. . . . However," she sighs, "in a man, the mind is more important than handsomeness. . . ."

The young girls sigh and cast down their eyes. . . . They also agree that the mind in a man is more important than his looks. I take a side glance into a mirror in order to see how charming I am. I see a shaggy head, a shaggy beard, mustache, eyebrows, hair on my cheeks, hair under my eyes—a whole bush from which in the manner of a Maypole my strong nose sticks out. Not bad, needless to say!

"Nevertheless, Nicolas, you will succeed because of your spiritual qualities," said Nadyenka's *maman,* giving a deep sigh, as if she had confirmed some kind of secret thought.

Nadyenka suffers for me, for from the time of being aware that sitting opposite her is a man in love, it affords her, obviously, the greatest pleasure. Having finished off the men, the girls speak about love. After a long session on love, one of the girls gets up and leaves. Those remaining begin to pick to pieces the one who left. All find that she is stupid, intolerable, ugly, and that all her marbles aren't in place.

Well, thank God, the maid finally comes in with a note from

my *maman,* calling me for dinner. Now it is possible for me to leave this unpleasant company and to continue work on my dissertation. I rise and make my bows to leave. Varyenka's *maman,* Varyenka, and the motley crew of females surround me and inform me that I have no right to leave, as I gave them my word of honor yesterday that I would dine with them, and after dinner to go to the forest for mushrooms. I bow and sit down. In my heart hate is boiling over, I feel that one more minute and I would lose control of myself, I would break down, but delicacy and fear of upsetting the goodwill felt toward me required that I obey the women. And I obey.

We sit down to the table. The wounded officer, on whom the scars made his temples look like chins, when eating looked as if he were harnessed and had a bit in his mouth. I roll little balls out of the bread and think about the dog tax, and knowing my hot temper, work on keeping quiet. Nadyenka watches me with compassion. Served is hodgepodge, tongue with small peas, roast chicken, and compote. I have no appetite, but out of politeness I eat. After dinner, when I'm standing alone on the terrace and smoking, Mashyenka's *maman* comes up to me, presses my hands, and speaks breathlessly:

"Now, Nicolas, don't despair. . . . Such a big heart. . . . such a heart!"

We go to the woods for mushrooms. Varyenka hangs on my arm and sticks to my side. I suffer unbearably, but endure it.

We enter the forest.

"Listen, Monsieur Nicolas," gasps Nadyenka. "What makes you so sad? Why are you silent?"

Strange girl: what can I talk about with her? What do we have in common?

"Now, tell me something . . . ," she begs.

I begin to think about something popular, at the level of her understanding. Having thought it over, I say:

"The destruction of the forests will bring great harm to Russia."

"Nicolas!" gasps Varyenka and her nose reddens. "Nicolas, I see, you shun candid conversation. . . . It's as if you wish to punish with your silence. . . . Your feelings are not reciprocated and you want to suffer in silence, alone. . . . That's terrible, Nicolas!" she exclaims, impetuously taking hold of my hands, and I can see her nostrils are beginning to flare. "What would you say if that girl which you love proposed eternal friendship to you?"

I mutter something incoherent, because I don't have anything definite to say to her. . . . For pity's sake, in the first place, I don't love any girl, and in the second place, of what use would eternal friendship be to me? In the third place, I'm very hot-tempered. Mashyenka or Varyenka covers her face with her hands and says in an undertone, as if to herself:

"He is silent. . . . Obviously, he wants sacrifice on my part. I can't love him, if I still love another! However . . . I'll think it over. . . . Good, I'll think it over. . . . I'll collect all my heart's strength and, it might be, that valuing my own happiness, I will save this human being from suffering!"

I don't understand anything. What kind of a scheme this is. We go further and pick mushrooms. We are silent all the time. Nadyenka's face shows that an internal struggle is going on. We hear the bark of dogs: it reminds me of my dissertation and I sigh loudly. From the openings between the trunks of the trees I see the wounded officer. The poor devil is tortuously limping to the right and to the left; to the right he has the wounded thigh, and on the left hangs one of the motley young girls. His face reflects a resignation to his fate.

We return to the cottage from the forest for tea; then we play croquet, and listen to one of the motley young girls sing the romantic melody, "No, I don't love you! No! No!" When singing the "No" she twists her mouth all the way to her ear.

"*Charmant!*" moan the other girls. "*Charmant!*"

Evening arrives. The repulsive moon creeps out from behind the bushes. The atmosphere is quiet and there is the unpleasant smell of fresh hay. I pick up my hat and want to leave.

"I have to tell you something," significantly whispers Mashyenka to me. "Don't leave."

I have a premonition that this will not be a good thing, but from politeness, I remain. Mashyenka takes hold of my arm and leads me somewhere on the path. Now her whole body reflects readiness for battle. She is pale, breathes deeply, and, it seems, intends to pull off my right arm. What's with her?

"Listen . . . ," she mutters. "No, I can't. . . . No . . ."

She wants to say something but wavers. But from the look on her face, I can see that she's determined. With sparkling eyes and flaring nostrils, she grabs my hand and says recklessly:

"Nicolas, I'm yours! I can't love you, but I promise you faithfulness!"

With this she snuggles against my chest, and then immediately jumps away.

"Someone is coming . . . ," she whispers. "Farewell. . . . To-morrow at eleven o'clock I'll be in the arbor. . . . Farewell!"

And she disappeared. I don't understand anything. I feel my heart beating agonizingly. I go home to my room. "The Past and the Future of the Dog Tax" awaits me, but I can't work anymore. I'm furious. It could even be said, I'm horrified. Damn it, I won't permit being treated like a juvenile! I'm hot-tempered, and it's dangerous to play around with me! When the maid enters to call me to supper, I shout at her: "Leave!" Such a hot-temper bodes nothing good.

It's morning, the next day. It is typical cottage weather, that is, the temperature is below $0°C$, there is a sharp cold wind, rain, mud, and the smell of camphor because my *maman* took her coat out of a trunk. It's a hell of a morning. It's the seventh of August 1887, the time of the solar eclipse. You must note that at the time of eclipse we can all perform a tremendous service for future astronomers. So each of us can: (1) determine the diameter of the sun and the moon, (2) draw the sun's crown, (3) take the temperature, (4) observe at the moment of the eclipse the fauna and flora, (5) note one's own impressions, and so forth. This is so important that I noted it in the margin of "The Past and the Future of the Dog Tax" and at that time determined to observe the eclipse.

We all got up very early. I decided to allocate the work above as follows: I would measure the diameter of the sun and the moon; the wounded officer draws the crown; all the rest would be performed by Mashyenka and the motley young girls. Almost all of us gathered and waited.

"How does the eclipse occur?" asks Mashyenka.

I answer.

"The eclipse of the sun occurs when the moon turns into the same plane as the ecliptic, blends into one line, coinciding with the center of the sun and the earth."

"What does 'ecliptic' mean?"

I enlighten her. Mashyenka, listening attentively, hears me out and then asks:

"Can you see the line coinciding with the center of the sun and the earth through a smoked glass?"

I answer her that this line is a mental boundary.

"If it's mental," asks Varyenka, not comprehending, "how can the moon place itself over the sun?"

I don't answer. I feel that from this naive question my liver begins to enlarge.

"That's all nonsense," says Varyenka's *maman*. "It's impossible to know what will happen in the future, and since you've never been up in the sky, why do you know what will happen with the moon and the sun? It's all a fantasy."

But now a black spot is passing over the sun. All else is commotion. The cows, sheep, and horses are picking up their tails and howling; they are running over the fields in fear. The dogs are whining. The deacon, who at this time was taking the cucumbers from his vegetable garden to his home, was frightened, jumped out of his cart, and hid under the bridge. His horse pulled the cart into someone else's yard, where the cucumbers were eaten by the pigs. Akseezney, not spending the night at home but at the cottage of one of the summer women, jumped out in his underwear, ran to where there was a crowd of people, and shouted in a wild voice:

"Save yourself if you can!"

Many of the cottagers, even the young and beautiful, awakened by the noise, ran out onto the street without their slippers. More of the same occurred, which I have decided not to record.

"Ah, how frightful!" screeched the motley young girls. "Ah, it's terrible!"

"*Mesdames,* observe," I call out to them. "Time is precious!"

I myself rush and measure the diameter. Remembering about the crown, I look for the wounded soldier. He is standing and doing nothing.

"What about it?" I shout. "The crown?"

He shrugs his shoulders and helplessly indicates with his eyes, his arms. The poor beggar has hanging on both arms the motley young girls, clinging to him for life, and keeping him from working. I take a pencil and note the time in seconds. This is important. I record the geographical position at the observed point. This is also important. I want to determine the diameter, but at this time Mashyenka takes my arm and says:

"Don't forget, today at eleven o'clock!"

I release my arm and want to continue my observations for every second was precious, but Varyenka convulsively held my arm and pressed against my side. Pencil, glass, sketches—everything fell on the grass. The deuce knows what else! Finally, it's time to let this girl understand that I'm hot-tempered, that when my temper is aroused, I become furious and then can't control myself!

"Look at me!" she whispers tenderly.

Oh, this is the height of humiliation! You will agree that this kind of playing around with a person's patience can only end badly. Don't blame me if something terrible happens! I will not permit anyone to make a fool of me, humiliate me. Hell, when I'm furious I don't advise anyone to come near me, the devil with everything! I'm ready for anything!

One of the babes notices my furious-looking face, and says, apparently with the purpose of calming me down:

"I, Nikolay Andreich, completed your assignment. I observed the mammals. I saw how before the eclipse the grey dog chased the cat and then wagged her tail for a long time afterwards."

So nothing came of the eclipse. I go home. Thanks to the rain, I don't go out on the balcony to work. The wounded officer risks going out on his balcony and even wrote "I was born in . . . ," and now I see from the window how one of the motley young girls drags him to her cottage. I can't work because I'm still furious and feel my heart palpitating. I don't go to the arbor. That is rude but, you will agree, I can't go because of the rain! At twelve o'clock I receive a note from Mashyenka; in the note are reproaches and a plea to come to the arbor, and she addresses me with a familiar "you." . . . At one o'clock I receive another note, at two o'clock—a third. . . . I have to go. But before I go, I have to think up what I'm going to talk about with her. I will behave like a polite human being. At first, I will tell her that she wrongfully imagines that I love her. However, one does not say such things to women. To tell a woman "I don't love you" is as tactless as to tell a writer "You're a lousy writer." The best thing is to tell Varyenka how I feel about marriage. I put on a warm coat, take an umbrella, and go to the arbor. Knowing my hot temper, I'm afraid that I might say something superfluous. I will do my best to restrain myself.

I am awaited in the arbor. Nadyenka is pale and tear-stained. Seeing me, she cries out joyfully and throws herself around my neck and says:

"At last! You are playing with my patience. Listen, I didn't sleep all night. All I did was think. It seems to me that when I know you intimately, that . . . I will love you."

I sit down and begin to expound my views on marriage. At the beginning, in order not to stray too far, to be as brief as possible, I give a small historical overview. I speak of the weddings of Indians and Egyptians; after that I cross over to later times and some thoughts from Schopenhauer. Mashyenka listens attentively, but suddenly, from a strange inconsistency of ideas, finds it necessary to interrupt me.

"Nicolas, kiss me!" she says.

I'm confused and don't know what to say to her. She repeats her request. I have no choice. I rise, and getting close to her long face I have the same feeling I felt as a child when once it was insisted at the requiem that I kiss my dead grandmother. Not satisfied with my kiss, Varyenka jumps up and impetuously embraces me. At this moment Mashyenka's *maman* shows up at the door of the arbor. Her face appears frightened, she says "tsss!" to someone and disappears, like Mephistopheles in prison.

Confused and furious, I return to my cottage. At home I find Varyenka's *maman,* who with tears in her eyes is embracing my *maman,* and my *maman* is crying and saying:

"I too wanted this!"

Later—how do you like this?—Nadyenka's *maman* comes toward me and says:

"God has blessed you! You will see, love her. . . . Remember that for you she is making a sacrifice. . . ."

And now they are marrying me. As I write this, over me stands the best man, who is hurrying me. These people positively don't know my character! That I'm hot-tempered and can not control myself! Damn it, you'll see what the future will bring! Leading to the altar a hot-tempered, furious person—that, in my way of thinking, is as dumb as putting your hand in the cage of an infuriated tiger. We will see, we will see, what will be!

*   *   *

And so, I'm married. They all congratulate me, and Varyenka presses against me and says:

"Understand, that you now are mine, mine! Say you love me! Say it!"

And as she says this, her nostrils flare.

I learned from the best man that the wounded officer in a clever manner escaped from Heemena.* He let one of the motley young girls know that thanks to the wound in his temple he has brain damage, and because of this he does not have the legal right to marry. What an idea! I also could have presented evidence. One uncle was a drunkard, another uncle was very absent-minded (once, in place of a hat, he put a woman's muff on his head). An aunt constantly played the piano and when meeting men, stuck out her tongue. Besides, there was still my extreme hot temper—a very suspicious symptom.

But why are good ideas always late? Why?

1887

---

*Hymen

The Dear Lessons

F or an educated person not to know foreign languages is a tremendous inconvenience. Vorotov felt this strongly when, having received a degree from the university, he decided to take on in a small way the job of learning a language.

"It's appalling!" he said, catching his breath (in spite of the fact that he was only twenty-six years old, he was overweight, obese, and short-winded). "It's appalling! Without the knowledge of foreign languages, I'm like a bird without wings. Even if I have to put aside my work, it's a must."

So he decided to overcome his natural laziness and learn French and German, and looked for a teacher.

One winter afternoon, when Vorotov was sitting in his office working, the butler informed him that there was an unknown lady asking to see him.

"Ask her to come in," said Vorotov.

Into the office came a young lady, dressed in the latest refined fashion. She, Alice Oseepovna Anket, introduced herself as a teacher of French, and that one of Vorotov's friends had sent her.

"My pleasure! Please be seated!" said Vorotov, taking a deep breath and covering the collar of his nightshirt with the palms of his hands. (In order to breathe more easily, he always worked in his nightshirt.) "Peter Sergeich sent you to me? Yes, yes . . . I did ask him. . . . I'm very pleased!"

Talking it over with Mlle Anket, he bashfully but with curiosity looked her over. She was a genuine, very elegant Frenchwoman, still very young. By her face, pale and dark, by her short curly hair and unnaturally slender waist, she couldn't be more than eighteen years old. Glancing at her wide, beautifully developed shoulders, her handsome black and austere eyes, Vorotov, thinking it over, decided she must be at least twenty-three, maybe even twenty-five; then again it seemed, she was only eighteen. Her expression was cold, businesslike, as that of a person who came to talk about money. Not once did she smile, did not frown, and only a flicker of bewilderment when she realized that she was being asked to teach a grown, heavy person and not children.

"So, Alice Oseepovna," Vorotov said to her, "we will work every day from seven to eight o'clock in the evening. As to your salary— a ruble per lesson suits me. Per lesson one ruble—well then, per lesson one ruble. . . ."

He asked her if she would like tea or coffee, whether the weather was fine, and smiled good-naturedly; smoothing the cover on the table with his palms, he asked amicably about personal details, where she had completed her studies and where she lived.

Alice Oseepovna answered him in a cold, businesslike way that she had studied in a private boarding school and had the right to teach in homes, that her father had died recently from scarlet fever, that her mother was alive and made flowers, and that she, Mlle Anket, taught at a private boarding school until dinner, and after dinner until evening went to wealthy homes and gave lessons.

She left, leaving a trail of faint, very delicate fragrance of feminine clothing. Vorotov didn't work for a long time afterwards. He spent the time sitting at the table, smoothing the green cover with his palms and meditating.

"It's good to see young girls working to earn a piece of bread," he thought. "On the other hand, it's not good to see that necessity does not spare even such elegant and good-looking young women such as Alice Oseepovna. She, too, must carry on the fight for existence. Too bad!"

He had never seen a hard-working Frenchwoman and thought also that this elegantly dressed Alice Oseepovna, with well-developed shoulders and extremely slender waist, in all probability, besides giving lessons, had other employment too.

The following day in the evening, when the clock showed it was five minutes to seven, Alice Oseepovna arrived rosy, from the cold. She opened Margot, the currently used text, which she had brought with her, and began without beating around the bush:

"French grammar has twenty-six letters. The first letter is A, the second B . . ."

"Excuse me," Vorotov interrupted her, smiling. "I must tell you beforehand, Mademoiselle, that you will have to change your method for me. It so happens that I am fluent in Russian, Latin, and Greek. . . . I have studied comparative philology, and it seems to me that we can skip Margot and go directly to reading some literature."

And he informed the Frenchwoman how adults learn languages.

"One of my acquaintances," he told her, "desiring to learn new languages, placed before himself a French, a German, and a Latin Bible, read them in parallel fashion, painstakingly analyzing every word, and what happened? He achieved his goal in less than a year. We will work this way. We will pick an author and start to read him."

The Frenchwoman looked at him in bewilderment. It was obvious that Vorotov's proposition was very naive and foolish. If this strange proposition had been made by a young pupil, she probably would have become angry and scolded, but since here was an adult, and a very heavy one at that, whom it was impossible to scold, she only shrugged her shoulders barely noticeably and said:

"As you wish."

Vorotov rummaged in a bookcase and withdrew from it a worn-looking French volume.

"Will this do?" he asked.

"It's all the same to me."

"In that case, let's begin. Lord bless us. Let's begin with the title . . . *Mémoires*."

"Remembrances . . . ," translated Mlle Anket.

"Remembrances . . . ," repeated Vorotov.

Smiling good-naturedly and breathing heavily, he worked on the word *mémoires* for a quarter of an hour, and at the same time with the word *de,* and this fatigued Alice Oseepovna. She answered questions languidly, was confused, and apparently could not understand her pupil and did not try to understand. Vorotov asked her questions, and at the same time contemplated her fair head and thought:

"She doesn't have naturally curly hair, but puts it up. Amazing! She works from morning 'til night and yet succeeds in putting it up."

Exactly at eight o'clock, she arose and said a dry, cold "*Au revoir, monsieur,*" and left the office. And after she left, there remained the same, delicate, subtle, exciting fragrance. The pupil once again did nothing for a long time and sat at the table meditating.

On the following days he became convinced that his teacher was a sweet young lady, serious and precise, but not very educated and did not know how to teach adults. He decided to pay her for the time spent, part with her, and invite another teacher. When she came for the seventh time, he took an envelope with seven rubles in it from his pocket and, holding it in his hands, became very embarrassed and started to say:

"Excuse me, Alice Oseepovna, but I must tell you. . . . I've got to do something very difficult. . . ."

Seeing the envelope, the Frenchwoman guessed what it was all about and for the first time during the lessons, her face quivered and the cold, businesslike look disappeared. She blushed slightly and, dropping her eyes, nervously began to finger her delicate gold chain. Vorotov, seeing her discomfort, understood how precious a ruble was to her, and how difficult it would be for her to lose this job.

"I must tell you . . . ," he mumbled, becoming even more embarrassed, and his heart missed a beat. He quickly put the envelope in his pocket and continued: "Excuse me, I . . . I must leave you for ten minutes. . . ."

And giving the impression that he did not want to discharge her, but simply wanted her permission to leave for a short time, he went into another room and sat there for ten minutes. He returned later even more embarrassed. He had thought that his absence for a short time would allow her to find her own explanation, and it was awkward for him.

The lessons began again.

Vorotov was no longer eager to continue. Recognizing that the lessons were useless, he gave the Frenchwoman a free hand, no longer questioned her, and did not interrupt. She translated, as she wished, ten pages a lesson, and he listened, breathed heavily, and from having nothing else to do, looked at her curly head, her neck, her delicate white hands, and breathed in the scent of her clothing. . . .

He caught himself thinking unseemly thoughts, and was ashamed; or he was moved by her and then felt chagrin and grief because she held herself in such a cold, businesslike way with him, as with a pupil, not smiling, and as if afraid that he might accidentally touch her. This is what he was thinking: how to get her to trust him, to acquaint himself with her on friendly terms, then help her, and to help her to understand how bad her teaching was, poor thing.

One day Alice Oseepovna showed up for the lesson all dressed up in a pink gown, a bit *décolleté*, and gave off a fragrance that seemed as if she were covered by a cloud that was hanging over her, ready to puff, and she would fly off or dissipate like smoke. She apologized, saying she could only give a half-hour lesson as from the lesson she was going directly to a ball.

He gazed upon her naked neck and shoulders, and it seemed to him that he understood why Frenchwomen had the reputation of being frivolous and of easy virtue. He sank in this cloud of aromas, beauty, nakedness, and she, not knowing his thoughts, and truly, not really interested in them, quickly turned the pages and translated at top speed:

"He walked on the street and met a gentleman of his acquaintance and said: 'Where are you hurrying to, it pains me to see your face so pale.' "

The *Mémoires* had been finished long ago and now Alice was translating some other book. Once she came an hour early for the lesson, her excuse being that at seven o'clock she had to drive to the Little Theater. Seeing her off after the lesson, Vorotov dressed and also drove to the theater. He went, so it seemed to him, only to relax, be entertained, and that of Alice he had no thought. He could not submit that a serious person, preparing for a scientific career, would be sluggish and put his work aside and drive to the theater just to meet there a scarcely known, not very smart, minimally educated girl. . . .

But why during the intermission did his heart race, and didn't he even notice how a young boy ran across the foyer and along the corridors impatiently seeking someone? He became annoyed when the intermission ended; but when he saw the familiar pink gown and the beautiful shoulders under the tulle, his heart contracted as if from a presentiment of happiness; he blissfully smiled and for the first time in his life experienced jealousy.

Alice was with two ugly students and an officer. She was laughing, spoke loudly, and was obviously flirting. Vorotov had never seen her like this. One could see that she was happy, content, serious, warm. From what? Why? From, it was possible, that these people were close to her, from the same circle as she. . . . And Vorotov felt the tremendous gap between himself and this circle. He bowed to his teacher, but she coldly acknowledged him and quickly went by. It appeared that she didn't want her boyfriends to know that she had pupils and that she gave lessons because she needed the money.

After the meeting in the theater, Vorotov realized that he was in love. . . . During the following lessons, devouring with his eyes his elegant teacher, he no longer struggled with himself, and gave free rein to his pure and impure thoughts. Alice Oseepovna's face did not stop being cold, and exactly at eight o'clock every evening she calmly said *"Au revoir, monsieur,"* and he felt that she was indifferent to him and would be indifferent and that his position was hopeless.

Sometimes during a lesson he would begin to dream, have hope, make plans, mentally compose the revelation of his love, then recalled that Frenchwomen were frivolous and complaisant, but it was enough for him to look at the teacher's face in order to extinguish these thoughts instantly, as a candle is extinguished when it is windy and is carried out on the terrace of one's summer home. Once when a little tipsy, he forgot himself and, as if in a fever, was not able to contain himself and blocked her path in the hallway when she was leaving after the lesson, and breathless and stammering, started to speak of love:

"You are precious to me! I . . . I love you! Permit me to speak!"

Alice grew pale—probably from fear that after this expression it would be impossible to come there and receive a ruble per lesson. She looked startled and loudly whispered:

"Ah, that is impossible! Don't say such things, I beg you! It is impossible!"

Vorotov didn't sleep all night after this; tortured by shame, he cursed himself and had stressful thoughts. It seemed to him that his revelation had insulted the girl, and that she would never come again.

He decided to find her address in the morning and write her an apology. But Alice came without a letter. She felt awkward at first, but then opened the book and began to translate quickly and fluently, as always:

"O, young gentleman, don't dig up those flowers in my garden which I wish to give to my sick daughter. . . ."

She comes until this day. She has already translated four books, but Vorotov has learned nothing besides the word *mémoires,* and when he is asked about his studies, he gives it up as a lost cause, doesn't answer the question, and changes the subject to the weather.

1887

The Court Investigator

ne fine spring afternoon the district doctor and the court investigator were traveling together to perform a postmortem. The investigator, a man of about thirty-five, thoughtfully stared at the horses and said:

"Nature is full of much that is dark and mysterious, but also in ordinary day-to-day existence, doctor, one often meets with occurrences for which there decidedly is no explanation. I know of several mysterious, puzzling deaths, the reasons for which can only be explained by mystics and spiritualists. A person with a cool head can only explore with his hands. For example, I know of one very intelligent woman who predicted her death, and who died without any apparent reason exactly on the day she predicted. She stated that she would die then and she did."

"There is no effect without a cause," said the doctor. "If death occurs, then there is a reason. As to the prediction, there really is little that is unusual here. All our ladies and hags possess a gift of prophesy and indulge in premonitions."

"So be it, but this lady I'm talking about, doctor, was unique. In her predictions and death there was nothing smacking of an old wives' tale, nor of a lady's superstitions. She was a young woman, healthy, smart, without prejudices. She had wonderful, intelligent, bright, good eyes; her face was open, wise, with a gentle, pure Russian smile in her glance and on her lips. Whether it was a lady's or a peasant's, if you wish, there was nothing about her that was not—beautiful. She was elegant, graceful like this birch tree; her hair was striking! In order that she not be misunderstood by you, I can still add, that this was a human being, full of the most infectious gaiety, carefree—and that wise, gentle quick-thinking which only those thoughtful, straightforward, happy people have. Can there be here any word of mysticism, spiritualism, even premonitions or anything of that kind? She thought all this laughable."

The doctor's buggy stopped by a well. The investigator and the doctor had a drink, stretched, and stood waiting while the driver watered the horses.

"Well, what did this lady die from?" asked the doctor when the buggy was on the road again.

"It was a strange death. One truly beautiful day, her husband comes up to her and says that it wouldn't be stupid to sell the old carriage in the spring and in its place to buy a newer and better one; that it wouldn't be upsetting then to change the left lead horse and to put Bobchinsk (the husband had such a horse) out to pasture.

"The wife heard him out and said:

" 'Do as you like. It's all the same to me now. In the summer I will already be in my grave.'

"The husband, of course, shrugs his shoulders and smiles.

" 'I'm not in the least joking,' she says. 'I'm informing you seriously that I will soon die.'

" 'How soon?'

" 'As soon as I give birth. I will have the child and then I will die.'

"The husband did not give any credence to these words. He does not believe in any kind of premonitions and he knows very well that women who are pregnant like to be capricious and in general are disposed to depressing thoughts. A day went by and the wife repeated to him that she would die immediately after giving birth. And after that, she repeated the same thing, but he laughed and called her a peasant, superstitious, and a hysterical woman.

"The thought of the nearness of death became an idée fixe of the wife. When the husband would not listen to her, she went into the kitchen and spoke there of her coming death with the nanny and the cook:

" 'I don't have long left to live, dear nanny. As soon as I give birth, I will die. I wouldn't want to die so soon, of course, but I already know that that is my fate.'

"The nanny and the cook, of course, were in tears. It so happened that a priest's wife or a landowner's wife came to visit. She would lead the guest to a corner in order to unburden her heart—always one and the same thing, about her approaching death. She spoke seriously, with an unpleasant smile, even with an angry face, not permitting any argument. She had always dressed fashionably, but now as her death approached, she gave it up and became slatternly; she stopped reading, stopped smiling, stopped dreaming aloud. Moreover, she drove to the cemetery with her aunt and selected the place for her grave, and about five days before she was scheduled to have the baby, she wrote her will.

"Keep in mind that when this was all going on, she was in excellent health, without any hint of any kind of pain or any kind of danger. Giving birth is—a difficult thing, sometimes fatal, but for her, of whom I am speaking, all went on well and there did not seem to be anything to be apprehensive about. Finally, this whole story became irksome for the husband. At dinner, therefore, he grew angry and asked her:

" 'Listen, Natasha, when is this idiocy going to stop?'

" 'It's not idiocy. I'm speaking seriously.'

" 'Nonsense! I would advise you to stop this stupidity so that you yourself won't be conscience-stricken later.'

"Well, the time to give birth arrived. The husband brought the best midwife from the city. It was the first child for the wife, but everything went along splendidly. After the birth was over, the mother asked to see the child. She looked at it and said:

" 'Now, now it is possible to die.'

"She said goodbye, closed her eyes, and within a half-hour died. She was conscious up to the last minute. At least, when in the place of water she was given milk, she whispered quietly:

" 'Why have you given me milk instead of water?'

"Such was the story. As she had predicted, so she died."

The investigator hesitated, sighed, and said:

"Can you enlighten me as to what she might have died from? I give you my word of honor that this is not fiction but fact."

Thinking it over, the doctor looked up at the sky.

"It would be necessary to have an autopsy," he said.

"Why?"

"In order to find the reason for the death. She did not die because she predicted it. She probably poisoned herself."

The investigator sharply turned his face toward the doctor and, screwing up his eyes, asked:

"What has made you conclude that she was poisoned?"

"I have not concluded, I've conjectured. Did she and her husband have a good life together?"

"Hm . . . m . . . not entirely. There was a misunderstanding early after the marriage. It was such an unhappy coincidence of circumstances. The dead woman came upon her husband once with another woman. However, she soon forgave him."

"What came first, the unfaithfulness of the husband or the revelations about death?"

The investigator stared at the doctor as if he wanted to discover the reason he had asked this question.

"Allow," he did not answer at once. "Allow me to try to recollect." The investigator took off his cap and wiped his forehead. "Yes, yes . . . she began to speak of death soon after this incident. Yes, yes."

"Well, you can see. . . . The probability is that she decided to take poison, but in truth she would then kill the child also, so she postponed her suicide until after she gave birth."

"Hardly, hardly . . . that's impossible. She forgave him."

"She forgave quickly, which means she was thinking of something ugly. Young wives don't forgive so easily."

The investigator forced a smile and, in order to hide his very noticeable agitation, began to smoke a cigarette.

"Really, really," he continued. "Such a possibility never entered my thoughts. . . . Yes, and at the same time . . . he's not as guilty as it seems. . . . His infidelity was strange; he didn't even desire it. He came home one night a bit tight and wanted to make love, but his wife was pregnant . . . and here, devil take her, in his path falls a dame who had arrived for a three-day visit, an empty-headed, stupid, ugly hag. It isn't even possible to consider it infidelity. The wife herself looked at this and quickly . . . forgave; there wasn't even any talk about this later. . . ."

"People don't die without a cause," said the doctor.

"That's so, of course, but all the same . . . I can't allow that she poisoned herself. But it's strange that up to this time it never entered my head of the possibility of such a death! . . . No one else thought of this! All were amazed that her predictions came true, and thoughts of the possibility . . . of such a death were far off. . . . Yes, it's not possible that she poisoned herself! No!"

The investigator fell into a trance. The thought of the strange death of the woman did not leave him, and in time the cause would be uncovered. Making a note of what the doctor was dictating to him, he gloomily frowned and wiped his forehead.

"Are there really such poisons that kill within a quarter of an hour, gradually and without pain?" he asked the doctor while he was covering the skull which they had been examining.

"Yes, there is. Morphine, for example."

"Hm. . . . Strange. . . . I recall she had in her room something similar. . . . But hardly!"

On the return trip the investigator looked fatigued, nervously chewed his mustache, and spoke with reluctance.

"Let's go on foot for a bit," he proposed to the doctor. "I'm bored with sitting."

After about a hundred steps the investigator, it appeared to the doctor, had weakened considerably, as if he had been climbing a high mountain. He stopped and, looking at the doctor with strange eyes, like those of a man who is drunk, said:

"My God, if your supposition is correct, you know this . . . this is cruel, inhuman! She poisoned herself in this way to punish another human being! That is really a mortal sin! Oh, my God! Why have you given me this cursed thought, doctor?"

The investigator held his head in despair and continued:

"I have told you about my wife and about myself. Oh, my God! I'm guilty. I injured her, but it was easier to die than to forgive!

Exactly, such is woman's logic . . . cruel, uncharitable logic. Oh, she was cruel in life too. I remember now! It's all clear to me now!"

The investigator spoke these words, at one moment shrugging his shoulders, at another moment taking hold of his head. He sat in the buggy, then went on foot. The new thought imparted to him by the doctor, it seemed, stunned him, poisoned him. He fell apart, weakened in body and soul, and, when they returned to town, said goodbye to the doctor and excused himself even though the night before he had made a dinner date with the doctor.

1887

Zenochka

A group of hunters lying on beds of fresh hay were spending the night in a peasant's hut. The moon shone through the windows, out on the street an accordion sadly wheezed, and the hay gave off a slightly saccharin, provocative scent. The hunters spoke of dogs, of women, of first love, of shots. After these, the bones of known men were scraped clean and a hundred anecdotes were told. The heaviest of the hunters, who in the dark looked like a pile of hay, speaking in a thick staff-officer's basso, loudly yawned and said:

"It's no great feat to be loved: the ladies are created in order to love our brotherhood. But, gentlemen, were any of you ever hated, hated passionately, furiously? Have any of you observed the delights of hate? Yes?"

There was no answer.

"Not one, gentlemen?" inquired the staff-officer's basso. "Well I was hated, hated by a pretty young girl, and from my own experience I could instruct on the first signs of hate. First, gentlemen, this was something like the exact opposite of first love. However, this, which I am going to recount to you, happened when I had not yet had thoughts of either love or hate. I was then eight years old, but that's not relevant here, gentlemen, it is not he that is important, but *she*. Now, I beg for your attention.

"One absolutely beautiful summer night, just before sunset, I and my governess, Zenochka, a very sweet and poetic creation just recently out of college, were sitting in the nursery doing something. Zenochka absentmindedly looked out the window and said:

212

" 'So, we breathe in oxygen. Now tell me, Petya, what do we breathe out?'

" 'Carbon dioxide,' I answered, also looking out the window.

" 'That is so,' agreed Zenochka. 'Plants do just the opposite: they breathe in carbon dioxide and breathe out oxygen. Carbon dioxide is held in seltzer water and in fumes from the samovar. . . . This is a very harmful gas. Near Naples there is a place called Dog's Cave which contains carbon dioxide. If you put a dog in this cave, the dog will gasp for breath and die. This unlucky Dog's Cave near Naples contains a chemical combination such that not a single governess would dare to step into it.'

"Zenochka always earnestly made use of the natural sciences, but what she knew about chemistry was little more than the story of this cave.

"So, she told me to repeat it. I repeated it. She then asked what is the horizon. I answered.

"At this time my father was getting ready to go hunting, while we were ruminating over the horizon and the cave. The dogs ran out, the trace horses impatiently shifted from one foot to the other and teased the coachman, the servants were pushing the wagons to start them, all kinds of things were going on. Beside the shay stood the small buggy in which my mother and sister sat in order to go to the Evanitskis' to a name-day party. To be left at home were I, Zenochka, and my older brother—a student—who had a toothache. You can imagine my envy and boredom!

" 'So, what is it we breathe in?' asked Zenochka, looking out the window.

" 'Oxygen. . . .'

" 'Yes, and the horizon is the name of the place where, it seems to us, that the earth meets the sky. . . .'

"Finally, the shay and, after it, the buggy moved. . . . I saw how Zenochka took out of her pocket some kind of note, convulsively crumpled it and pressed it to her temples, then sighed and looked at the clock.

" 'Keep in mind now,' she said, 'near Naples is a cave which we call a Dog's Cave. . . .' She again looked at the clock and continued: 'Where does it seem to us that heaven and earth meet? . . .'

"The poor thing walked about the room greatly disturbed and once more looked at the clock. There still remained a half-hour for our lesson.

" 'Now, arithmetic,' she said, breathing deeply and with a shaking hand turned the pages of the workbook. 'Do assignment No. 325, and I . . . will return shortly. . . .'

"She went out. I heard how she ran quickly down the stairs, and then saw out the window how her blue dress fluttered across the yard and disappeared through the garden gate. The haste of her movements, her flushed face intrigued me. Where was she rushing to and why? Hindsight is not a factor here. I instantly realized and understood everything: she was running to the garden to take advantage of the absence of my stern parents, to go to the raspberry patch or to pick some sweet cherries for herself! If that was so, then I too, deuce take it, will go and eat sweet cherries! I threw down the workbook and hot-footed to the garden. She was not in the cherry orchard. Passing through the raspberry patch, the gooseberry shrubs, and the watchman's hut, I saw her going toward the pond. She was pale and started at the slightest sound. I stole after her and saw, gentlemen, the following:

"On the banks of the pond, between the thick stalks of two old pussy willows, stood my older brother Sasha; his face showed no sign that he had a toothache. He was watching for Zenochka and his whole body, like the sun, shone with happiness. And Zenochka, as if she were being chased into the Dog's Cave and was becoming breathless from carbon dioxide, was going toward him, barely moving her legs, breathing deeply, and tossing back her head. . . . It was obvious that she was going to a rendezvous for the first time in her life. She now approached. . . . For a half-minute they silently stared at each other as if they did not believe their eyes. As if some unseen power was pushing Zenochka, she put her hands on Sasha's shoulders, placed her head against his jacket. Sasha laughed, mumbled something incoherent, and with the clumsiness of someone very much in love, placed both his palms on Zenochka's face.

"And the weather, gentlemen, was miraculous. . . . The knoll behind which the sun was hiding, the two pussy willows, the green banks, the sky—all this together with Sasha and Zenochka was reflected in the pond. The stillness can be imagined. Above the sedge a million golden butterflies with long whiskers were chasing the cattle. In one word, it was like a painted picture.

"From everything I saw I understood only that Sasha and Zenochka were kissing. It was indecent. If *maman* knew of this, they'd both get it. I felt that for some reason this was shameful. I returned to the nursery, not waiting for the end of the rendezvous. I then sat over my assignment, thought, and imagined. Over my ugly mug flickered a triumphant smile. On the one hand, it was pleasant to be the possessor of someone else's secret; on the other hand, it was also very pleasant to realize that such authorities as Sasha and Zenochka at any minute could be exposed by me for ignorance of polite decorum. Now they were in my power and their peace depended entirely upon my generosity. I'd show them!

"When I laid down to sleep, Zenochka, as was her custom, came into the nursery to check whether I went to bed in my street clothes and if I had said my prayers. I looked at her pretty, happy face and smirked. I was simply bursting with the secret and it begged to be released. It was necessary to hint and savor the effect.

" 'Ah, I know!' I said, smirking. 'He-he!'

" 'What do you mean?'

" 'He-he! I saw how you and Sasha were kissing near the willows. I followed you and saw everything. . . .'

"Zenochka winced, reddened, and, disturbed by my crack, sank down on a chair on which were a glass of water and a candlestick.

" 'I saw how you . . . kissed . . . ,' I repeated, giggling and savoring her confusion. 'Ah! I'm going to tell Mama!'

"Faint-hearted Zenochka stared at me and, convinced that I really knew everything, in despair grabbed me by the hands and muttered in a shaking whisper:

" 'Petya, that's beneath you. . . . I beg you, for God's sake. . . . Be a man . . . don't tell anyone. . . . Decent people don't spy. . . . It's despicable. . . . I beg you. . . .'

"The poor thing, as of fire, was afraid of my mother, who was a virtuous and strict woman. That was one thing, but another, my smirking ugly mug, could not but dirty her first, pure, and poetic love, and you can imagine for yourself the state of her soul. Thanks to me she did not sleep all night, and in the morning appeared for tea with dark circles under her eyes. . . . Meeting Sasha after tea, I couldn't hold back, unable to keep from smirking and boasting:

" 'Aha, I know! I saw how you and Zenochka were kissing yesterday!'

"Sasha looked at me and said:

" 'You're crazy.'

"He wasn't chicken-hearted like Zenochka so the effect was unsuccessful. This egged me on even more. If Sasha wasn't frightened, it was apparent he didn't believe that I saw and knew. 'Just you wait, I'll show you!' I thought.

"Zenochka was involved with me until dinner, but didn't look at me and hesitated when she spoke. Instead of trying to intimidate me, she fawned over me in every way and gave me fives, and didn't complain to my father about my impishness. My age had nothing to do with how I behaved. I exploited her secret as I wished: I didn't learn my lessons; I walked on my hands in the classroom and spoke nonsense. I made a wonderful blackmailer. Well, a week passed. Someone else's secret egged me on and tortured me, like a splinter in my soul. So, no matter what would happen to me, I wanted to let it out and enjoy the effect. And so, one day during dinner, when we had many guests, I smirked stupidly, looked venomously at Zenochka, and said:

" 'Ah, I know. . . . He-he! I saw. . . .'

" 'What do you know?' asked my mother.

"I continued to look sneakily at Zenochka and Sasha. I had to see how the young girl flushed and the angry eyes of Sasha! I bit my tongue and did not continue. Zenochka gradually paled, tightened her lips, and ate nothing more. On the same day during my evening lessons, I saw in Zenochka's face a sharp change. It struck me as sterner, colder, as if depressed, and her eyes looked at me strangely, directly into my eyes, destructively, and I give you my word of honor, not even during the hunt when the wolf is being chased have I seen such stricken and murderous eyes! I understood perfectly their expression when during the lesson she suddenly spoke through clenched teeth:

" 'I hate you! Oh, if you, you vile, disgusting creature, know how I hate you, how repulsive to me is your clipped head, your ugly, protruding ears!'

"But at the same time she became frightened and said:

" 'I'm not saying that to you; I'm repeating a part in a play. . . .'

"Later, gentlemen, during the night, I saw how she came up to my bed and stared at me for a long time. She hated passionately and yet could not live without me.

"Contemplation of my hated ugly mug became a necessity for her. I remember a marvelous summer evening . . . the fragrance of freshly mown hay, the stillness, and so forth. The moon shone. I was walking along a path, thinking of cherry jam. Suddenly approaching me was the pale, beautiful Zenochka; she grabbed me by the hand and, panting, began to explain herself:

" 'Oh how I hate you! I have never wished harm to anyone as to you! Understand that! I want you to understand that!'

"Understand if you will, the moon, the pale face, the impassioned breathing, the stillness . . . even to me, little swine that I was, it was pleasant. I listened to her, looked at her eyes. . . . In the beginning it was satisfying to me and new, but later fear took over, and I shrieked and raced home at breakneck speed.

"I decided that the best thing was—to complain to my *maman.* And I complained and told her incidentally that Sasha had kissed Zenochka. I was stupid and did not know what would follow, otherwise I would have kept the secret to myself. . . . My *maman,* hearing me out, reddened with indignation and said:

" 'It is not your business to speak of this, you are still very young. . . . But, however, what an example for children!'

"My *maman* was not only virtuous but also tactful. She, so as not to make a scandal, did not at once dismiss Zenochka, but handled it gradually, systematically, as in general, decent but intolerable people are gotten rid of. I remember when Zenochka was leaving us, the last look which she cast at our home was directed toward the window where I sat, and I assure you, I remember that look to this day.

"Zenochka soon became my brother's wife. She is the Zenighda Nikolaevna whom you know. I met her again when I was already a young officer. No matter how hard she tried, she could in no way recognize in the mustached young officer the hated Petya. But all the same, she could not treat me as kin. . . . And even now, in spite of my good-natured bald head, meek paunch, and modest outlook, she continues to look crossly at me and is out of sorts when I come to my brother's house. Obviously, hate cannot be forgotten as love is. . . . Oops! I hear that poet, the rooster. Good night! Milord, to the station!"

1887

She Left

Dinner was over. Their stomachs felt satiated; they yawned; their eyes began to narrow from a pleasant drowsiness. The husband smoked a cigar, stretched, and sank down on the couch. The wife sat by his head and hummed. . . . They were both happy.

"Tell me something . . . ," said the husband and yawned.

"What can I tell you? Hm . . . m. . . . Ah, yes! Have you heard this? Sofie Okyrkova got married to that . . . what's his name . . . to that von Tramb! It's scandalous!"

"In what way is it scandalous?"

"Well, you know that Tramb is a rascal! He's such a scoundrel. . . . Such a conscienceless person! He has no principles! He is of honorable lineage! He was the count's supervisor—became rich, now serves on the railroad and steals . . . robbed his sister. . . . In a word, he is a villain and a thief. And to marry such a man? To live with him? It's amazing! Such a moral young girl and . . . well, I never! Not for anything would I marry such a fellow! Even if he were a millionaire! Even if he were incredibly handsome, I would spit on him! I can't imagine marrying a villain!"

The wife jumped up and, flushed, indignant, walked about the room. Her eyes flamed from anger. Her sincerity was obvious.

"This Tramb is such trash! And the women who marry such men are a thousand times foolish and common!"

"Tsk . . . tsk. . . . You, of course, would not marry. . . . No way. . . . But, if you would learn now that I also am a villain . . . what would you do?"

219

"I? I would throw you out! I wouldn't stay with you for a minute! I can only love an honorable person! You know, that if you did only one-hundreth of what Tramb has done, I . . . in the blink of an eye! *Adieu* at that time!"

"Tsk. . . . Hm. . . . What a woman I have. . . . And I never knew. . . . He-he-he. . . . The wench lies and doesn't blush!"

"I never lie! Try to do something villainous and then you will see!"

"Why should I try? You know yourself. . . . I will clean up even more than your von Tramb. . . . Tramb—is a little mosquito in comparison. Your eyes are widening? That's strange . . . ," he paused. "What's my salary?"

"Three thousand a year."

"And how much did the ring that I bought for you last week cost? Two thousand . . . isn't that so? The dress I bought yesterday was five hundred. The summer place was two thousand. . . . He-he-he. Yesterday your daddy touched me for a thousand. . . ."

"But, Pierre, there is additional income. . . ."

"Horses . . . house doctor . . . bills from the milliners. The day before yesterday you lost a hundred rubles at the roulette wheel. . . ."

The husband raised himself a bit, supported his head with his fists, and read the whole indicting riot act to her. Going up to the desk, he showed his wife some of the material evidence. . . .

"Now you see, little mother, that your von Tramb— is nothing, a pickpocket compared with me. . . . *Adieu*! Go and don't judge beforehand!"

I am finished. It may be that the reader will still ask:

"And she left her husband?"

Yes, she left. . . . She went into another room.

1883

A Woman Without Prejudices

Maxim Kyzmich Salyutov is tall, broad-shouldered, and carries himself elegantly. You could say that his build is that of an athlete. He is extraordinarily strong. He can bend a twenty-kopeck coin, pull out a sapling with its roots, lift dumbbells with his teeth, and it is sworn that there is no person on this earth who would dare to fight with him. He is heroic and daring. No one has ever seen him afraid of anything. On the contrary, people fear and blanch before him when he is angry. Both men and women squeal and redden when he shakes hands with them: it hurts! You cannot listen to his magnificent baritone because it is deafening. . . . The strength of this person! Another such individual I've never known.

This wonderful, superhuman, ox-like strength resembled nothing so like a squashed rat he was, when Maxim Kyzmich fell in love with Elaine Gavrilovna! Maxim Kyzmich paled, blushed, trembled, and wouldn't be able to lift a chair when he had to emit from his huge mouth: "I love you!" His strength left him and his enormous figure turned into a huge empty hulk.

He told her he loved her while they were skating. She flew along the ice with the lightness of a feather, and he, chasing after her, trembled, was thrilled by her, and whispered it. His face exhibited suffering. . . . His graceful, nimble legs failed him and became entangled when it came to cutting any kind of fancy design on the ice. . . . Do you think he was afraid of being rejected? No. Elaine Gavrilovna loved him and was eager to have him offer his heart and hands. She was a small, good-looking brunette who was ready

221

any minute to blow up from impatience. . . . He already was thirty years old, not of high rank, wasn't especially wealthy; but making up for all that, he was handsome, sharp, and considered a good catch! He was an excellent dancer, a superb marksman. . . . No one could ride a horse better than he. Once when out riding with her, he leaped across the kind of ditch that would have been difficult for any English jumper! . . .

It was impossible not to love such a man!

And he himself knew that she loved him. He was convinced of this. He suffered, however, from one thought. . . . This thought was stultifying his brain, left him raving, crying, did not allow him to drink, eat, or sleep. . . . It poisoned his life. He was sworn to love, but at the same time, this thought buzzed in his brain and bombarded his temples.

"Be my wife!" he said to Elaine Gavrilovna. "I love you! Wildly, terribly!"

And at the same time he thought:

"Do I have the right to be her husband? No, I don't! If she only knew the kind of past I've had, if someone told her of my past, she'd give me my walking papers! Disgusting, unfortunate past! She is intelligent, rich, educated; she'd spit on me if she knew what a bird I am!"

When Elaine Gavrilovna threw herself around his neck and swore to love him, he did not feel happy.

The thought spoiled everything. Returning from the rink, he bit his lips and thought:

"I'm a scoundrel! If I were an honorable person, I would have told her everything . . . everything! Before telling her I loved her I should have let her in on my secret! But I didn't do this, and I, therefore, am a villain, a scoundrel!"

Elaine Gavrilovna's parents agreed to her marriage with Maxim Kyzmich. They liked the athlete: he was courteous and, as a supervisor, appeared to have great potential. Elaine Gavrilovna felt herself on cloud nine. She was happy. Because of this the poor athlete was far from happy! Until the wedding itself, he was tormented by the thought that the time to tell all was near. . . .

One of his friends, who knew his past like the palm of his hand, tormented him too. . . . The time came when he had to give his friend practically his whole salary to keep him quiet.

"Take her out to dinner at the Hermitage!" advised his friend. "And tell her everything. And lend me twenty-five rubles!"

Poor Maxim Kyzmich lost weight, became haggard. . . . His cheeks became sunken, veins popped up on his fists. If it weren't for the woman he loved, he would have shot himself. . . .

"I'm a scoundrel, a villain!" he thought. "I must tell all before the wedding! Even though they spit on me!"

But he didn't reveal anything before the wedding. He didn't have the courage. The thought that after he made the revelation he would have to part with his beloved was for him the most horrendous of all his thoughts! . . .

The wedding night arrived. The young couple was married, congratulated, and everyone was astonished by their happiness. Poor Maxim Kyzmich received the congratulations, drank, danced, laughed, but was terribly unhappy. "I command myself, animal, to have it all out! We're married, but it's still not too late! We can still part!"

And he did tell his tale. . . .

When bedtime came and the young couple were escorted to the bedroom, conscience and honor took over. . . . Maxim Kyzmich, pale and trembling, not remembering that he was a man, barely breathing, shyly went up to her and taking hold of her hands, said:

"Before we belong to each other, I must . . . must tell you something."

"What's wrong with you, Max? You're . . . pale! You've been pale for days, quiet. . . . Are you ill?"

"I . . . must tell you something, Lanie. . . . Let's sit down. . . . I must hurt you, spoil your happiness . . . but what's to be done? Duty dictates. . . . I will tell you my past. . . ."

Lanie's eyes widened and she grinned.

"Well, tell me . . . only quickly, please. And don't tremble so."

"I, I was . . . born in Tam . . . tam . . . bovye. . . . My parents were uneducated and dreadfully poor. . . . I will tell you what kind of a bird I am. . . . You'll be horrified. Wait . . . you will see. . . . I was a beggar. . . . When I was a boy, I sold apples, pears . . ."

"You?!"

"You're horrified? But, darling, that's not all that's terrible. Oh, miserable creature that I am! You will curse me when you know."

"Well, what is it?"

"Twenty years old . . . I was . . . was . . . forgive me! Don't hurry me! I was . . . a clown in a circus!"

"You?! A clown?"

Salyutov expected a slap in the face and covered his pale face with his hands. . . . He was almost on the verge of fainting. . . .

"You . . . were a clown?"

And Lanie fell off the couch, jumped, ran around. . . .

What was up with her? She held her stomach, convulsed with laughter. . . . Her laughter bounced off the walls and filled the bedroom with laughter, resembling hysteria. . . .

"Ha-ha-ha. . . . You were a clown? You? Maxie, darling! Perform for me! Prove it to me! Ha-ha-ha! Darling!"

She rushed up to Salyutov and embraced him. "Perform for me! Sweetheart! Darling!"

"You are laughing, you unlucky woman? You despise me?"

"Let me see you act! Do you know how to walk on a tightrope? But really!"

She showered her husband's face with kisses, pressed against him, honeyed up to him. . . . It was not noticeable that she was angry. . . . He, not comprehending, happily submitted to the request of his wife.

Approaching the bed, he counted to three and stood on his head, resting his forehead on the edge of the bed. . . .

"Bravo, Max! Bis! Ha-ha! Darling! More!"

Max gave a lurch, jumped on the floor just as he was, and walked on his hands.

In the morning Lanie's parents were terribly bewildered.

"Who is that banging upstairs?" they asked each other. "The newlyweds are still sleeping. It must be a servant acting crazily. Such carryings-on! These infamous creatures!"

The daddy went upstairs, but he found no servants there.

The noise, to his great amazement, was coming from the bedroom of the newlyweds. . . . He stood by the door, shrugged his shoulders, and opened it slightly. . . . Glancing into the bedroom, he shrank back and almost died from shock: in the middle of the bedroom Maxim Kyzmich stood and was carrying out in the open the most desperate *salto mortale**; next to him stood Lanie, applauding. Both of their faces shone with happiness.

1883

---

*"somersault"

Shackled Women

I n the village known as Raybuzhe, opposite the church stands a two-story house with a stone foundation and a metal roof. On the first floor lives the owner and his family, one Philip Ivanov Kashin known by the nickname of Dyoudya,* and on the second floor, where in the summer it is unbearably hot and in the winter just as cold, traveling supervisors, merchants, and landowners are put up. Dyoudya rents plots, stores tobacco, and trades in wood-tar, honey, cattle, and magpies. He has piled up almost eight thousand, which he has in the bank in town.

His oldest son, Fyedor, works in the factory as a senior mechanic and, as the *muzhiks* say of him, has risen so high that he is untouchable. Sofia, his wife, is an unattractive, sickly peasant woman, who lives in the house of her father-in-law, cries constantly, and goes every Sunday to the hospital to be treated. Dyoudya's other son, Alyosha, is a hunchback and he too lives in his father's house. They had recently married him to Barbara, whom they had taken from a poverty-stricken family. She is a young, pretty, healthy, tastefully dressed woman. When the supervisors and merchants stay at Dyoudya's, they always ask that the samovar be served by her and that their beds are made up by her.

One June evening, when the sun was setting and the air was permeated with the fragrance of hay, warm manure, and fresh milk, into Dyoudya's courtyard drove a plain carriage with three passengers:

---

*"Hefty"

226

a man about thirty wearing a suit made of duck cloth; alongside him was a boy of seven or eight in a long black frock coat with large bone buttons; and a young fellow in a red shirt who acted as the coachman.

The young fellow unharnessed the horses and took them out to the street to walk them around. The traveler washed himself, prayed facing the church, then spread out a lap robe alongside the plain carriage and sat down with the boy to eat. He did not eat hurriedly, but sedately, and Dyoudya, having in his time seen many transients, recognized by his manner that this was a man of business—serious and knowing his own worth.

Dyoudya was sitting on the porch in his vest, without a hat, and waited for the traveler to speak. He had become accustomed to having travelers tell him all kinds of stories in the evening before going to bed, and found this very pleasant. His old wife, Afanasia, and his daughter-in-law, Sofia, were milking the cows near the shed. His other daughter-in-law, Barbara, sat by an open window upstairs and was eating sunflower seeds.

"Is the little boy your son?" asked Dyoudya of the traveler.

"No, he's an adopted child, an orphan. I took him in order to save his soul."

They began to converse. The traveler showed himself to be garrulous and eloquent. Dyoudya could tell from the conversation that this was a city person, a homeowner called Matvay Savich, who was now on his way to look over some gardens that he rented from German colonials, and that the boy was called Kyzka. It was a warm evening so no one felt like sleeping. When it grew dark and some faint stars began to flicker in the sky, Matvay Savich began to tell how he took Kyzka to himself. Afanasia and Sofia were standing a little distance away and listened. Kyzka went out to the gates.

"That story, Granddad, is full of unusual details," began Matvay Savich. "And, if I were to tell you everything as it occurred, the whole night would not be long enough. Ten years ago on our street, next door to me, in a small house where there now stands a candle factory and a creamery, lived an old widow, Marfa Simonovna Kaplyntseva, who had two sons: one worked as a conductor on the railways and the other, Vasya, who was my age, lived at home with his Mommy. The deceased Kaplyntsev had kept horses, had five pairs, and sent carters to the city. The widow did not quit the business and managed the carters as well as her late husband had, so that on good days she cleared almost five rubles. The young fellow also had income. He bred pedigreed pigeons and sold them to hunters. Everything, it seemed, was tip-top; he cleans up and squanders and whistles, his pigeons were sky high, and yet he didn't have enough and wanted more. He caught siskens and starlings, built cages. . . . Not much work, but imagine, for this nonsense he cleaned up about ten rubles a month. Well, after some time had passed, the old woman's legs gave way and she became bedridden. Because of this fact, the house was without a mistress, and that's the same as not having an overseer. The old woman got busy and decided to get her Vasya married. A matchmaker was called and five to ten possibilities were chosen, and Vasya went to see the available unmarried women.

"He proposed marriage to Mashenka at the widow Samokvalik's. Not taking a long time to think it over, it was blessed, and in one week all the arrangements were made. The girl was young, about seventeen, small, curly-headed, with a pale and pretty face—she had all the qualities of an upper-class young woman. The dowry was decent: five hundred rubles, a cow, a bed. . . .

"The old woman had had a presentiment that she did not have long to live, and on the third day after the wedding went to the heavenly Jerusalem where there is no pain and no troubled breathing.

"The young couple prayed and started to live together. They lived amicably for about a half-year and then another sorrow beset them. Misfortunes never come singly! Vasya was called up to serve in the army. They took him and gave him no privileges. He was recruited and sent to the Polish Kingdom. If it's God's will, there's nothing you can do. When he said goodbye to his wife in the courtyard, it wasn't so sad, but when he looked into the pigeons' roost, tears streamed from his eyes. It was a sad sight.

"At first, Mashenka, so that she wouldn't be lonely, had her mother live with her. The mother stayed with her until the baby was born, the same Kyzka who is here with me, and then went to her other daughter in Oboyan, who was also married, and left Mashenka alone with the baby.

"There were five carters, all drunks and mischievous, horses and hearses—one could see that the factory building was caving in. The chimney soot was catching on fire. None of this was business a woman could handle, so in a neighborly fashion she began to turn to me for every stupid little thing. So, it comes to pass that you take over, take charge, give advice. . . . It's not unusual, that along with this, you enter the house, drink tea, converse. I was young, smart, liked to talk about many subjects, and she was educated and courteous. She always wore a clean dress, and in the summer carried a parasol. It so happened that I introduced her to religious and political ideas, and she was flattered. She in turn fed me tea and jam. . . . In a word, so as not to stretch it out, I can say, Granddad, that a year didn't pass before I was troubled by indecent thoughts, the enemy of our male sex. So I began to observe that on the days I wasn't with her, I wasn't myself and was bored. And I would find reasons for visiting her. 'It's time that your storm windows were installed,' I would tell her, and spend the whole day there putting on the storms and worked it out so that two were left for the next day. 'Vasiley's pigeons need to be counted so that you don't lose any,' and more of the same. All of this talk was over the fence, so finally, in order that I wouldn't have too far to walk, I made a gate in the fence.

"In this world there's a great deal of evil and dirty tricks which can be blamed on the female sex. We ordinary males aren't the only sinners—the clergy are also seduced. Mashenka didn't reject me. Instead of remembering that she had a husband and should watch out for herself, she fell in love with me. I began to notice that she too was bored, and that she was taking care of everything around the fence, and was peeking through the chinks into my courtyard. Fantasies whirled around in my head. On Holy Thursday I go early in the morning, when it's barely light, to the market. I pass by her gate, and I was dishonorable, but there I was. I looked over—the railing of the gate was raised—and she is standing in the middle of the courtyard, already awake, and feeding the geese. I did not restrain myself but called out. She came up and looked at me through the lattice. Her pale little face, her caressing eyes, a bit sleepy . . . I found her extremely attractive, and I complimented her as if we weren't at the gate, but celebrating a name day. She blushes, laughs, and looks at me with those same eyes and doesn't blink. I lost my head and began to tell her how much I loved her. . . . She opened the gate, let me in, and from that morning we lived as husband and wife."

The hunchbacked Alyosha came into the courtyard from the street, and puffing and panting, without glancing at anyone, ran into the house. In a few minutes he ran out with an accordion and, jingling coins in his pocket, eating sunflower seeds as he ran, disappeared behind the gates.

"Who is that?" asked Matvay Savich.

"My son, Alexey," answered Dyoudya. "He's out on the town, the scoundrel. God gave him a hunchback, so we don't ask much of him."

"He never works, just carouses with the lads," sighed Afanasia. "Before the Easter holidays we married him off, thinking that would be better, but he became even worse."

"It's useless. All we did was make someone else's unmarried daughter happy for nothing," said Dyoudya.

Somewhere behind the church could be heard the singing of a marvelous, mournful song. It was impossible to make out the words, and only the sound of the voices could be heard: two tenors and a bass. Because all were listening, silence pervaded the courtyard. . . . Two of the voices suddenly stopped singing and peeled with laughter, while the third, a tenor, continued singing and hit such a high note that they all involuntarily raised their eyes, as if the voice at its peak reached the sky itself. Barbara came out of the house, and placing her hand over her eyes as if to shield them from the sun, looked in the direction of the church.

"That's the priest's son and his students," she said.

The three voices sang together again. Matvay Savich sighed and continued:

"And that's how things went on, Granddad. About two years later we received a letter from Warsaw from Vasya. He wrote that he was being sent home to recuperate. He was ill. At this time I had cast this folly out of my mind since the unmarried women were after me, but I didn't know how to break it off with Mashenka. I intended to speak to her every day, but didn't know how to approach her so that there wouldn't be any female screeching.

"The letter untied my hands. Mashenka and I read the letter together. She paled, her face became as white as snow, and I said to her: 'Thank God, now,' I say, 'this means you'll be a married woman again.' But she says to me: 'I won't be able to stand living with him.' 'But isn't he your husband?' I say. 'That's easy to say. . . . I never loved him, and I was married to him without my consent. My mother made the decision.' 'But you,' I say, 'don't avoid the issue, fool; tell me: Were you married to him in church or not?' 'I'm married,' she says, 'but I love you and will live with you until I die. I don't care if people laugh. . . . I don't pay any attention to them. . . .' 'You,' I say, 'you are a believer and have read the scriptures. What's written there?'

"I have been given to a husband, and I must live with my husband," said Dyoudya.

" 'Man and wife are as one flesh. We have sinned,' I say, 'but we must be conscience-stricken and fear God. We will confess our guilt to Vasya. He is a mild, modest person—he won't kill us.' And I say, 'It is better on this earth to suffer a husband than to grit one's teeth when one is convicted on the Last Day of Judgment.' The woman doesn't listen, stubbornly sticks to her own view no matter what I say! 'I love you'—and nothing more could be said.

"Vasya arrived on a Saturday early in the morning just before Whitsunday. I could see everything from the fence: He ran into the house, in a minute he came out with Kyzka in his arms, laughing and crying at the same time, kissing Kyzka and looking at the pigeon's shed—wanting not to give up Kyzka and at the same time wanting to go to the pigeons. He was a mild, sensitive person. The day passed happily, quietly, and unpretentiously.

"The bells for vespers were ringing, and I was thinking: tomorrow is Whitsunday' why aren't they decorating the gate and the fence with greenery? I begin to think that something's not right. I went to them. I see that he is sitting on the floor in the middle of the room; his eyes are rolling around like a drunkard's, tears are running down his cheeks, and his hands are trembling. He is taking out of a sack ring-shaped rolls, strands of flowers, honey cakes, and other treats for guests—and is throwing them right and left over the floor. Kyzka—he was three years old then—is crawling around and chewing honey cakes. Mashenka is standing by the stove, pale, trembling all over, and muttering: 'I'm not your wife. I don't want to live with you,' and nonsense such as that. I bowed down to Vasya's feet and said: 'We are guilty before you, Vasiley Maksimich, for Christ's sake forgive us!' Then I got up and spoke these words to Mashenka: 'You, Maria Semenova, I tell you, must now wash Vasiley Maksimich's feet and drink bitter gall. And be an obedient wife, and pray to God for me, so that he,' I say, 'will be merciful, will forgive me for my sins.' As if an angel from heaven had entered me, I read her the riot act and spoke so sincerely that I even shed a tear.

"Anyway, Vasya came to me two days later. 'I,' he says, 'forgive you, Matyousha, you and my wife. God bless you. She was a wife of a soldier, she acted like a woman—young, she found it difficult to take care of herself. She's not the first and won't be the last. But only,' he says, 'I beg you to live as if there had never been anything between you and don't show yourself. And I,' he says, 'will try to please her in every way, so that she will love me again.' He offered me his hand, we had a drink, and he left happy. Well, I thought, thank God, and I became happy too, that everything had turned out so well. But Vasya was barely out of the courtyard when Mashenka arrived. Pure hell! Hanging around my neck, crying, and imploring: 'For God's sake, don't cast me aside. I can't live without you.' "

"What a hussy!" exclaimed Dyoudya.

"I scolded her, stamped my feet, led her out, and locked the door. 'Go,' I yelled, 'to your husband! Don't shame me before the public. Have fear of God!' This tale was repeated every day. One morning I'm standing in my own courtyard around the stable and am repairing a bridle. Suddenly, I see her running through the gate, barefooted, only in a skirt, and straight for me. She grabbed the bridle in her hands, got all dirty from the rosin, and trembling, cries:

'I can't live with someone repulsive. I can't bear it. If you don't love
me, it's better that you should kill me.' I became angry and struck
her several times with the bridle, and at this time Vasya came running
through the gate, and calls out with a desperate voice: 'Don't beat
her! Don't beat her!' But then he himself ran up, and, as if he had
gone completely mad, swung out and began to beat her with his
fists with all his strength, and then knocked her down on the ground
and kicked her with his feet. I started to defend her, but he grabbed
the reins and began to swing about with them. He beat her as if
she were a young colt, screeching: 'Gey-gey-gey!'"

"You should have grabbed the reins," grumbled Barbara, leaving.
"The damn men took advantage of our sister."

"Shut your mouth, you!" Dyoudya shouted at her. "You female
ass!"

" 'Gey-gey-gey!' " continued Matvay Savich. "The driver from
his yard ran in, I called to one of my workers, and the three of
us pulled him away from Mashenka and dragged him home holding
his arms. It was shameful!

"That same day in the evening I went over to see what was
going on. She was lying in bed, completely muffled in moist compresses,
and only her nose and eyes could be seen. She was staring at the
ceiling. I address her: 'Greetings, Maria Semenova!' She keeps still.
Vasya is sitting in the next room, holding his head, and lamenting:
'I'm a scoundrel! I have destroyed my life! Lord, let me die!' I sat
by Mashenka for about a half-hour and admonished her. I tried
to frighten her. 'The righteous,' I said, 'on this earth will go to paradise,
but you will burn in hell with all the sinners. Don't oppose your
husband, go to him and bow down to the floor before him.' But
she didn't let out a peep, didn't blink an eye. It was as if I were
talking to a post.

"On the next day, Vasya got sick. It looked like cholera, and
toward evening I heard that he had died. They buried him. Mashenka
did not go to the cemetery. She probably did not want to show
her shameless face and its bruises. Soon gossip began to spread that
Vasya did not die a natural death, but was done in by Mashenka.
It reached the ears of the authorities. Vasya was exhumed. An autopsy

was performed and they found arsenic in his stomach. It was clear that it had been put in his drink. The police came and took Mashenka, and with her, the innocent Kyzka. She was put in jail. She had overstepped the bounds and God punished her. . . . Within about eight months, she was sentenced.

"I remember how she sat on the bench with a white kerchief and a grey jacket, thin, pale, sharp-eyed. It was sad to see her. Behind her was a soldier with a gun. She showed no sign of recognition of me. There were those in the court who declared that she had poisoned her husband, and others who declared that he had poisoned himself because of grief. I was one of the witnesses. When I was questioned, I answered conscientiously. 'She,' I said, 'sinned. I will not cover anything up. She did not love her husband. She had a temper. . . .' The judges started to consider in the morning and by night came out with this decision: she was condemned to hard labor in Siberia for thirteen years.

"After this sentence, Mashenka remained in our jail for about three months. I visited her, and as a humanitarian brought her tea and sugar. But when she saw me, her whole body began to shake, and, waving her hands, she muttered: 'Get out! Get out!' She pressed Kyzka close to her breast, as if afraid that I would take him away. 'Well,' I say, 'look what you've come to! Eh, Masha, Masha, you're a lost soul! You didn't listen to me when I was teaching you sense, so now you can't complain. It's your own fault,' I say.

"I'm repeating precepts, and she: 'Get out! Get out!'—and presses against the wall, holding on to Kyzka, and trembling. When they took her from us to take her to the provinces, I walked to the train station to see her off and stuffed a ruble into her sack to keep up her spirits. But she never got to Siberia. In the provinces, she developed a fever and died in jail."

"A dog dies a dog's death," commented Dyoudya.

"They returned Kyzka home. . . . I thought and thought, and took him to my house. What else? Even though he was a criminal's offspring, he was a living soul, had been christened. . . . Pitiful. I'll make a good servant out of him, and if I don't have children of my own, I'll even make a merchant of him. Now, when I go anywhere, I take him with me: I'm starting to train him."

While Matvay Savich was telling his story, Kyzka sat near the gate the whole time on a small bench and, supporting his head with both of his hands, was looking up at the sky. In the twilight from a distance he looked like a little stone statue.

"Kyzka, go to sleep!" Matvay Savich shouted to him.

"Yes, it's time," said Dyoudya, getting up. He yawned loudly and added: "We strive to live according to our own wisdom. We don't listen and things don't turn out right for us."

Outside the moon was floating across the sky. It moved quickly in one direction, while the cloud beneath it moved in the other. The cloud moved further away, and the moon now shone over the courtyard. Matvay Savich said his prayers facing the church, wished all a good night, and lay down on the ground near the carriage. Kyzka also said his prayers and lay down in the wagon, and covered himself with his jacket. To be more comfortable, he dug himself a hole in the hay and curled up so that his elbows touched his knees. From the courtyard one could see how Dyoudya lit a candle inside, put on his glasses, and stood in the corner before the icon with his prayer book. He read for a long time and bowed often.

The travelers fell asleep. Afanasia and Sofia went to the wagon and stood looking at Kyzka.

"The little orphan is sleeping," said the old woman. "He's so thin, emaciated, only skin and bones. He doesn't have a mother and no one feeds him on the road."

"My Grishytka, of course, is about two years older," said Sofia. "He lives in bondage at the factory without his mother. The boss probably beats him. When I looked at this boy just now, I was reminded of my Grishytka—my heart almost stopped beating."

A minute passed in silence.

"I don't think he'll remember his mother," said the old woman.

"How can he remember?"

Large tears streamed from Sofia's eyes.

"He's all curled up," she said, sobbing and smiling with tenderness and sadness. "My poor little orphan."

Kyzka sighed and opened his eyes. He saw before him a dirty, wrinkled, tear-stained face and beside it another, older, toothless, with a sharp chin and a hook nose, and above them the fathomless sky with its swiftly moving clouds and the moon, and he cried out in fear. Sofia also cried out. An echo resounded from both of the cries and in the close atmosphere it was unsettling. The watchman in the neighborhood rapped and a dog barked. Matvay Savich mumbled something in his sleep and rolled over.

When both Dyoudya and the old woman were already asleep later in the evening, Sofia went out to the gate and sat down on the bench. She felt stifled and the tears had given her a headache. The street was wide and long. There were about two versts on the right and about the same on the left, and the end could not be seen. The moon had already moved from the courtyard to beyond the church. One side of the street was lit by the moonlight and the shadow made the other side dark. The long shadow from the church, dark and frightening, lay wide and caught Dyoudya's gate and half of the house. The area was deserted and quiet. From the end of the street every now and then, barely audible, the sound of music could be heard. It had to be Alyosha playing on his accordion.

In the shadow by the church fence there was something moving, and it was impossible to tell whether it was a person or a cow, or maybe it was neither and only a big bird was rustling in the trees. But a figure emerged from the shadows, stopped, and said something in a masculine voice, and then hid itself in the side street by the church. A little later about twenty feet from the gates another figure showed up. It walked from the church straight for the gates and, seeing Sofia on the bench, stopped.

"Barbara, is that you?" asked Sofia.

"I should hope so."

It was Barbara. She stood for a minute and then came up to the bench and sat down.

"Where were you walking?" asked Sofia.

Barbara didn't answer.

"You can't walk off this kind of sorrow, young one," said Sofia. "You heard how Mashenka got it with kicks and reins? Look out so that doesn't happen to you."

"Let it."

Barbara laughed behind her shawl and whispered:

"I was strolling with the priest's son."

"You're babbling."

"Really."

"It's a sin!" whispered Sofia.

"Let it be. Why have regrets? A sin is a sin, but it would be better to be struck by lightning than to live as we do. I'm young, healthy, and my husband is a hunchback, repulsive, hard, and worse yet, is cursed by Dyoudya. When I was single I never had enough to eat, I had no shoes, and I left these evils, flattered by Alyosha's wealth and fell into slavery, like a fish in a net, and it would be easier for me to sleep with a monster than with this wretched Alyosha. And what's your life like? You won't look me in the eyes. Your Fyedor drove you out of the factory to his father while he got himself another woman. They took your little boy from you and put him into bondage. You work like a horse, and never hear a kind word. It would have been better if you'd never married. It's better to share a fifty-kopeck piece with a priest's son, better to go begging, better to put your head in a well. . . ."

"It's a sin!" Sofia whispered again.

"So be it."

Somewhere from behind the church came the melancholy singing of the same three voices: two tenors and a bass. And again it was impossible to make out the words.

"They're night owls," laughed Barbara.

And she began to tell in a whisper how she strolled at night with the priest's son, and all about his comrades; how she has strolled with travelling supervisors and merchants. From the melancholy song came a longing for a life that was free. Sofia began to laugh, she felt like a sinner, because it was terrible but sweet to hear, and she was envious; and it made her sad that she had not been a sinner when she was younger and attractive. . . .

In the old church graveyard midnight was struck.

"It's time to sleep," said Sofia, getting up, "but don't let Dyoudya catch you."

They both went quietly across the yard.

"I left and didn't hear what happened later to Mashenka," said Barbara, spreading her bedding under the window.

"She died, he said, in jail. She had poisoned her husband."

Barbara was lying alongside Sofia, thought it over a bit, and then said softly:

"I could do in my Alyosha and not regret it."

"You're speaking idiocy. God be with you."

When Sofia was falling asleep, Barbara leaned over to her and whispered in her ear:

"Let's do in Dyoudya and Alyosha."

Sofia took a deep breath and said nothing, but later opened her eyes, and without blinking an eye, stared for a long time at the sky.

"People would find out," she said.

"No, they wouldn't. Dyoudya is already old, it's time for him to die, and Alyosha, it would be said, died like a dog from drink."

"That's terrible. . . . God will punish."

"Oh, leave it. . . ."

Neither one slept and lay silent, deep in thought.

"It's cold," said Sofia, her whole body beginning to shiver. "It's going to be morning soon. . . . Are you sleeping?"

"No. . . . Don't listen to me, darling," whispered Barbara. "Be angry with them, curse them; I don't know myself what I'm talking about. Sleep, for dawn is already at hand. . . . Sleep. . . ."

They both became silent, calmed down, and were soon asleep.

The old woman, Afanasia, was the first to awake. She awoke Sofia and they both went to the shed to milk the cows. The hunchbacked Alyosha came home, dead drunk, without his accordion. The front of his clothes and his knees were covered with dust and straw—he must have fallen on the road. Swaying about, he straggled into the shed and, without undressing, threw himself into the sleigh and immediately began snoring.

When the rising sun with its bright flames lit up the crosses on the church and then the windows and shone across the courtyard over the damp grass, and the shadows from the trees and the well's sweep stretched out, Matvay Savich jumped up and began to bustle about.

"Kyzka, get up!" he shouted. "It's time to harness the horses! Step lively!"

The morning turmoil began. The young, little Jewess, in a brown kerchief with fringes, brought a horse out to the watering trough in the courtyard. The well's sweep screeched sadly, the well bucket knocked around. . . . Kyzka, sleepy, listless, covered with dew, sat up on the wagon, lazily put on his shirt and listened to the water splashing out of the bucket in the well, and hugged himself from the cold.

"Auntie," shouted Matvay Savich to Sofia. "Give my young man a nudge so that he'll harness up!"

And Dyoudya shouted from the window at the same time:

"Sofia, get a kopeck from the little Jewess for the water! They've gotten into the habit of taking it, damn it!"

Bleating sheep ran back and forth on the street. The peasant women shouted at the shepherd, but he continued to play on his reed pipe, jostled with his whip, or answered them with a hard, hoarse voice. Three of the sheep ran toward the courtyard, and not finding the gates were nosing the fence. Barbara was awakened by the noise, picked up her bedroll, and went into the house.

"You'd at least chase the sheep away!" the old woman shouted at her. "Little lady!"

"And how! I'll decide what I'll do, you tyrants," muttered Barbara as she entered the house.

The wagon was oiled and the horses were harnessed. Dyoudya came out of the house with the bill in his hands, sat on the little porch, and began to add it all up: how much it all came to for the overnight stay, for the oats, and for the water.

"You're charging too much for the oats, Granddad," said Matvay Savich.

"If it's too high, don't take it. We're not bound to you merchants."

When the travelers went to the plain carriage in order to get in and go, they were held up for a minute by a little detail. Kyzka had lost his cap.

"Where did you put it, you little swine?" Matvay Savich shouted angrily. "Where is it?"

Kyzka's face became distorted with fright. He rushed around the wagon and, not finding it there, ran to the gates and then into the shed. The old woman and Sofia helped him look for it.

"I'll pull your ears off!" shouted Matvay Savich. "What a rascal!"

The hat was found under the wagon. Kyzka brushed the hay from it, put it on, and, still with the look of fear on his face as if afraid that he might be struck from behind, diffidently climbed into the plain carriage. Matvay Savich crossed himself, the young man took hold of the reins, and the plain carriage moved from the spot and rolled out of the courtyard.

1891

A Case History

$\boxed{\text{T}}$ he doctor professor received a telegram from Lyaleekov's factory: it requested that he come immediately. The daughter of Madame Lyaleekov, apparently the owner of the factory, was ill, and nothing else could be deciphered from the long, incoherently composed telegram. The professor, however, did not go himself but sent his intern, one Korolev.

It was necessary to go two stations past Moscow and then four versts with horses. At the station a troika awaited Korolev. The coachman had on a cap with a peacock feather and to all questions answered loudly, as if he were a soldier: "Not at all!" "Precisely!" "Yes!" It was Saturday evening and the sun was just beginning to set. Crowds of workers from the factory were walking to the train station and bowed to the troika in which Korolev rode. He was captivated by the evening, the country estates, the summer homes along the way. The birches and the silence surrounded the buildings which, it seemed, were on the eve of a holiday as were the workers. The fields, the forest, and the sun had gathered to rest—and possibly to pray. . . .

Korolev was born and raised in Moscow, was not acquainted with villages and factories, and had never been interested in them nor had he ever been to any. But he had read about factories, and had been a guest of factory owners and had conversed with them. When he saw a factory from a distance or close by, he always reflected that from the outside all was quiet and peaceful, but inside it had to be full of the rank ignorance and the obtuse egoism of the owners, and the boring unhealthy labor of the workers with their squabbles and vodka and vermin. So now, when the workers respectfully, and fearfully, stepped aside for the troika, he saw in their faces, in their visored caps, in their gait, what he surmised as physical uncleanliness, drunkenness, nervousness, and confusion.

The carriage passed through the factory gates. On both sides were the small homes of the workers. The faces of women hanging linens and clothing on the porches flashed by. "Look out!" shouted the coachman, who did not hold back the horses. They crossed a wide, grassless courtyard and on it were five enormous structures with chimneys, each at some distance from the other, and warehouses and barracks. On all of these there appeared to be a gray coating, as if from dust. There were also, like an oasis in a desert, pathetic little gardens and houses with green or red roofs in which the administrators lived.

The coachman suddenly reined in the horses and the carriage stopped by a newly painted gray house. There was a front yard with a lilac bush covered with dust, and a yellow porch smelling strongly of paint.

"Please enter, doctor," could be heard from several voices in unison from the doorway and the foyer. There were also sounds of some kind of commotion. "Please enter, you have been anxiously awaited. . . . It's a desperate situation. This way, please."

Madame Lyaleekova, a stout, aging lady wearing a black silk gown with stylish sleeves, but judging from her face, a simple woman and probably barely literate, looked at the doctor anxiously but did not dare to offer him her hand. By her side stood an individual with short hair, wearing a pince-nez, in a multicolored blouse, obese, and no longer young. The servant addressed her as Christina Dmitrievna, and Korolev guessed that she was the governess. It was obvious that as the only educated person in the house it was her duty to meet and receive the doctor. Because of this, she began immediately and rapidly to set forth the reasons for the illness, with small importunate details, but did not say who was sick and what was the matter.

The doctor and the governess sat and talked while the lady of the house stood motionless at the door, waiting. From the conversation

Korolev learned that the sick person was Liza, a twenty-year-old girl, an heiress, and the only daughter of Madame Lyaleekova. She had been ill for some time and had been treated by a variety of doctors. The night before, her heart had been palpitating so vigorously from evening until morning that no one in the house could sleep and all were afraid that she would die.

"She has been, it could be said, ailing from childhood," reported Christina Dmitrievna in a sing-song voice, now and then wiping her lips with her hand. "The doctors have called it a case of nerves, but when she was little, the doctors gave her gold internally, so I think it might be from that."

They went to the patient. She was an adult, tall and well-built but unattractive, resembling her mother, with tiny eyes, and the lower part of her face was prominent and irregularly proportioned. Her hair was uncombed, she was covered up to her chin, and from the first moment gave Korolev the impression of an unhappy, pitiful human being to whom shelter had been given here from compassion, and it was incredible that she was the heiress to five huge factories.

"I have come," began Korolev, "to treat you. How do you do?"

He introduced himself and then took her hand in his—it was a large, cold, homely hand. She sat up. It was apparent that she was accustomed to being seen by doctors. She was indifferent to the fact that her shoulders and chest were unbared and allowed herself to be examined.

"I had such strong palpitations," she said, "all night, and I was so frightened . . . that I almost died from fright! Give me something to relieve me!"

"I will, I will! Do calm down."

Korolev examined her and shrugged his shoulders.

"This is the way the heart normally beats," he said. "All is well, all is in order. The nerves must be a little overactive, but that too is not unusual. You must believe that the attack is over now and lie down and sleep."

A lamp was brought into the bedroom at this time. The patient squinted her eyes at the light and suddenly grasped her head and sobbed. And the first impression that this poor, unattractive human being had made suddenly disappeared, and Korolev no longer noticed the small eyes nor the coarsely developed lower portion of her face. He saw a gentle, suffering creature who was so sensitive and touching that everything about her became for him elegant, feminine, and simple. He wanted to calm her, not with medicine nor with counsel, but with informal, comforting words.

The mother embraced the patient's head and pressed it to her breast. So much remorse, so much grief on the old woman's face! She, the mother, had nurtured her; watched her grow up; denied her nothing; had her devote her life to learning to speak French, to dance, to know music; had retained many instructors for her; invited the best doctors; kept a governess; and now could not understand where these tears came from, why there was so much torture, and not understanding, was at her wit's end. Her expression was apologetic, anxious, desperate, as if she had omitted something important, that she could have done more, that there was someone else she should have called, but who—she did not know.

"Dear Lizie, you again . . . you again," she exclaimed, holding her daughter closely. "My dear child, my darling, my little daughter, tell me, what's wrong? Have pity on me, tell me."

They both cried bitterly. Korolev sat on the edge of the bed and held Liza's hand.

"Have you cried enough?" he asked kindly. "Really, there is nothing on earth that deserves such tears. Now, we won't cry anymore, it's not necessary. . . ."

And he thought to himself:

"It's time she got married. . . ."

"Our factory doctor gave her a bromide," said the governess, "and I noticed that it only made her worse. In my opinion, she should get some drops for her heart. . . . I forgot what they're called . . . laudanum or something like that."

And again she went into all kinds of details. She interrupted the doctor, confused his words, and her face expressed the proposition that she too was the only educated woman in the house and was obligated to carry on a continual conversation with the doctor, and doubtless about medicine.

Korolev became annoyed.

"I don't find anything unusual," he said upon leaving the bedroom and turning to the mother. "If your daughter has been treated by the factory doctor, he should continue to do so. The treatment up to this time has been correct, and I see no reason for changing doctors. Why change? Such illness is not unusual and it is nothing serious. . . ."

He spoke unhurriedly while putting on his gloves, and Madame Lyaleekova stood stock-still and looked at him with tear-stained eyes.

"There is only a half-hour until the ten o'clock train," he remarked. "I hope that I won't be late."

"But can't you stay with us?" she asked, and again tears streamed down her cheeks. "It's unforgivable to disturb you, but be so kind. . . . For God's sake," she continued in a subdued voice, glancing back to the bedroom door. "Spend the night with us. She is my only child . . . my only daughter. . . . She frightened us so last night, I can't bear to recall it. . . . Don't leave, for God's sake. . . ."

He wanted to tell her that he had a lot of work in Moscow, and that his family was waiting for him to come home. It would be difficult for him to spend the whole evening and night in someone else's home without his personal essentials, but he looked at her face, sighed, and without saying a word, took off his gloves.

They lit all the lamps and candles in the hallway and in the drawing room for him. He sat down at the piano, leafed through the sheet music, and then looked at the landscape paintings and portraits on the walls. The pictures were painted in oils and were in gold frames. There were scenes of the Crimea, a stormy sea with ships on it, a Catholic monk with a wine glass, and they were all hollow, slick, talentless. . . . There wasn't a single attractive, interesting face in the portraits, and all had prominent cheekbones and eyes that stared as if astonished. Lyaleekov, Liza's father, had a small forehead and a self-satisfied face. His baggy uniform hung on his graceless body, and he wore a medal with the mark of the Red Cross on his chest. The refinement was inferior; the opulence thoughtless, accidental, and awkward like the uniform. The polished floors were irritating, the mirrors were irritating, and for some reason reminded him of a merchant entering the baths with a medal around his neck. . . .

Sounds could be heard from the foyer. Someone was peacefully snoring. But suddenly from outdoors could be heard a sharp, jerky metallic noise; such a noise as this Korolev had never heard before and didn't know what it meant. It echoed in his mind strangely and unpleasantly.

"It's obvious I wouldn't live here for anything . . . ," he thought and again perused the sheet music.

"Doctor, please come and have something to eat!" called the governess in an undertone.

He went to have some supper. The table was abundantly spread with hors d'oeuvres and wine, but only two people were to eat: he and Christina Dmitrievna. She drank madeira, ate, and talked rapidly, looking at him through her pince-nez.

"Our workers are very content. At our factory we have plays every winter in which the workers themselves perform. There are recitations with a magic lantern lit, a magnificent tearoom, and, you know, a great deal more. The workers are very devoted to us, and when they heard that Liza had become worse, they prayed for her. The uneducated have feelings too, you know."

"It looks as if there isn't a single man here," said Korolev.

"Not one. Peter Nickanorich died a half-year ago, and we have been left alone. There are only the three of us. In the summer we live here, and in the winter in Moscow on Polyanka Street. I have lived with them as a member of the family for eleven years."

Sturgeon, chicken cutlets, and a fruit dish were served for supper. The wines were expensive French ones.

"Doctor, you mustn't stand on ceremony," remarked Christina Dmitrievna, eating and wiping her mouth with the back of her hand. It was apparent that she was completely pleased wtih her life. "Please, eat."

After supper the doctor was led to a room in which a bed had been prepared for him. But he was not sleepy. The room was close and smelled of paint. He put on his coat and went outside.

It was cool outdoors. The coming dawn was already breaking, and jutting through the dimness, the five buildings appeared with their tall chimneys, and the warehouses and the barracks. It was a holiday and no one was working. The windows were dark but the furnace was still operating in one of the buildings. A crimson flame flared now and again in two of the windows and smoke came out of the chimney. In the distance beyond the courtyard, frogs were croaking and a nightingale sang.

Looking at the factory buildings and the barracks where the workers slept, he once again thought that which always came to his mind when he saw factories. Despite the plays for the workers, the magic lanterns, the factory doctor, the variety of improvements, the appearance of the workers which he had seen on the road from the train station had not improved over that which he had seen during his childhood when there had not yet been factory plays and improvements. He, as a medical man, accurately assessed that the chronic suffering, the basic cause of which was considered unknown, was not curable. He looked at the factories as irrational. Their existence was unavoidable, but why was unclear to him. He did not consider the improvements in the life of the workers as unnecessary, but he equated them to the treatment of incurable illnesses.

"There is misunderstanding here, of course . . . ," he thought, looking at the crimson windows. "From one-and-a-half to two thousand factory workers labor continually in an unhealthy situation, making inferior cotton cloth, live half-starved, and only rarely can they extricate themselves from this nightmare. Hundreds of people look for work, and throughout their lives these hundreds spend their earnings paying fines, are fraudulent, and use foul language. Only two or three, those called the owners, live in comfort, although they don't work at all and despise the poor cloth produced. However, what kind of comforts do they enjoy? Madame Lyaleekova and her daughter were unhappy. It was depressing to look at them. The only one who lived as she wished was Christina Dmitrievna, an aging, inane, single woman with a pince-nez. The conclusion is unavoidable. All five factories operated, producing poor quality cloth to be sold in the eastern markets, for one reason only: in order that Christina Dmitrievna could eat sturgeon and drink madeira."

Suddenly, irritating sounds filled the air—the same ones which Korolev had heard before supper. Near one of the factory buildings someone was striking a metal plank. He struck, and at the same time restrained the sound, so that it came out short, cut-off, and muddy, somewhat like "der . . . der . . . der. . . ." After these there was a half-minute of silence, and in another building other sounds resounded, eleven times just as jerky and unpleasant, but deeper and lower—"drin . . . drin . . . drin. . . ." Apparently the watchmen were striking eleven o'clock.

From the third building could be heard: "dzak . . . dzak . . . dzak. . . ." It was repeated at all the factory buildings and then behind the barracks and the gates. It felt to him as if in the silence of the night these weird sounds with their crimson eyes were the dictates of the devil himself—the dictator of the owners and the workers—who had deceived them and others.

Korolev left the courtyard and went out into the fields.

"Who goes there?" a coarse voice called out to him at the gate.

"As if on an island . . . ," he thought and did not answer.

The nightingales and the frogs could be heard, and the sensation of a night in May was pervasive. From the station came the sound of a train. Drowsy roosters were crowing somewhere, but the night was still and the world was sleeping untroubled. In the fields not far from the factory stood stacked timber which had been prepared for construction. Korolev sat down on one of the boards and continued to think:

"The only one around here who is completely satisfied is the governess, and the factory operates for her comfort. But, she is only the figurehead. More important, the one for whom all is done here is—the devil."

And he thought about the devil, in whom he did not believe, while looking at the two windows through which came light. It seemed to him that with these crimson eyes the devil himself stared at him. The devil, that mysterious power which caused conflict between the strong and the weak, was an ugly fallacy which could in no way be corrected. Such was the natural law that the powerful would control the lives of the weak; but this could only be understood and easily expressed in newspaper editorials and textbooks. In that mess which makes up ordinary existence, in the tangle of petty details which make up the fabric of man's activities, it is no longer a law, but a logical absurdity, when the strong and the weak both are victims of their mutual attitudes, involuntarily submitting to some kind of guiding force that is unrecognized and stands outside of life as a stranger.

So thought Korolev sitting on the planks, and little by little he was overcome by the feeling that this unknown, secret force was nearby and watching. In the midst of this, the east was becoming paler and time was speeding by. The five factories and their chimneys on the colorless background of the coming dawn, alone as if all had died, had a unique appearance—different from that during the day. One completely forgot that inside were steam engines, electricity, and telephones, and one's thoughts were of pile dwellings, of the Stone Age, and the presence of a vulgar, unconscious strength. . . .

Again could be heard:

"Dyer . . . dyer . . . dyer. . . ."

Twelve times. Then silence, silence for a half-minute, and—at the other end of the courtyard reverberated:

"Drin . . . drin . . . drin. . . ."

"Frightfully unpleasant!" thought Korolev.

"Dzak . . . dzak . . . ," came from a third place, jerkily, piercing, as if from vexation: "Dzak . . . dzak. . . ."

It needed four minutes to ring out twelve o'clock. Then all became quiet. Again it felt as if all around had died.

Korolev sat a little longer and then returned to the house, but didn't go to bed for a long time. In the neighboring rooms there was whispering and the shuffling of slippers and bare feet.

"Is she having another attack?" though Korolev.

He left to have another look at the patient. It was already quite light in the rooms. In the hallway on the wall and on the floor a weak bit of sunlight quivered, having penetrated the morning fog. The door to Liza's room was open, and she was sitting in an armchair near the bed. She was wearing a dressing gown and was wrapped in a shawl. Her hair was uncombed. The shades on the windows were down.

"How do you feel?" asked Korolev.

"I thank you."

He took her pulse and brushed back her hair, which had fallen over her forehead.

"You aren't sleeping," he remarked. "The weather is marvelous, it is spring, the nightingales are singing, and here you are sitting in darkness and thinking about something else."

She listened and stared at his face. Her eyes were sad, knowing, and you could see that she wanted to speak to him.

"Does this occur with you often?" he asked.

She moved her lips slightly and answered:

"Often. The nights are almost always difficult."

At this time the watchmen began to beat out two o'clock. "Dyer . . . dyer . . . ," could be heard and she shuddered.

"Are you disturbed by these striking sounds?" he asked.

"I don't know. Everything bothers me here," she answered and became lost in thought. "Everything bothers me. In your voice I hear concern, and from the moment I saw you somehow I knew that I could speak to you about everything."

"Please, say anything you wish."

"I want to tell you what I think. It seems to me that I don't have an illness and that I'm agitated and frightened because nothing can change. Even the healthiest person cannot help being agitated, if, for example, a criminal is walking under his window. They are always trying to cure me," she continued, looking down at her knees and smiling timidly. "I, of course, am very grateful and do not reject the use of curatives, but I would prefer to talk not with a doctor but with someone close to me—with a friend who understood me; convince me that I am right or wrong."

"You have no friends?" asked Korolev.

"I'm alone. I have my mother; I love her, but all the same, I'm alone. That is how my life has taken shape. . . . Solitary people read a great deal, but speak little and rarely listen. Life for them is veiled. They are mystics and often see devils where there aren't any. Lermontov's Tamara was solitary and saw the devil."

"Do you read a great deal?"

"A great deal. I have a lot of free time from morning 'til night.

I read in the daytime and during the nights—when my head is empty and in the place of thoughts there are shadows."

"Do you have visions at night?" asked Korolev.

"No, but I have sensations. . . ."

She smiled again and raised her eyes to the doctor, and again looked pathetic and wise. It seemed that she believed in him, wanted to speak with him earnestly, and her thoughts were the same as his. But she remained silent, perhaps waiting for him to say something.

He did not know what to say to her. It was clear to him that she needed to leave the five factory buildings as soon as possible, and the millions, if she had them—leave behind this devil that she watched during the night. It was also clear to him that she thought this too, and only waited for someone else, whom she trusted, to say so.

But he did not know how to tell her. How to say this? People who are condemned refrain from asking why they are condemned. This is how it was for many very wealthy people who found it awkward to ask why they had so much money, or why they disposed of their wealth so stupidly, or why they didn't get rid of it even though they can see it is the cause of their unhappiness. And if a conversation turns to this topic, it usually becomes embarrassing, clumsy, and extended.

"What can be said?" pondered Korolev. "Is it necessary to say anything?"

So he said what he wanted to, but not directly, but in a roundabout way:

"You are uncomfortable in your situation as the owner of the factories and as a rich heiress. You do not believe in your right to be such, and now, even though you cannot sleep, it is certainly better than if you were content and slept soundly and considered everything was as it should be. Your insomnia is estimable. No matter what, it is a good sign. In fact, it would have been inconceivable for our parents to talk as we are at this moment. Their nights were not disturbed and they slept soundly, but we, our generation, has insomnia, torments itself, discusses a great deal, and makes decisions as to right and wrong about everything. For our children or grandchildren this question—right or wrong—will be decided. They will see more clearly than we can. Life will be better for all some fifty years from now. It's only too bad that we won't be there. It would be interesting to see."

"What will the children and grandchildren do?" asked Liza.

"I don't know. . . . It's possible that they will throw in the towel and leave."

"Where will they go?"

"Where? . . . Wherever they can," said Korolev and laughed. "There are many places a worthwhile, intelligent person can go."

He looked at his watch.

"Although the sun is already rising," he said, "it's time for you to sleep. Undress and sleep as if you were healthy. I'm happy to have known you," he continued while taking hold of her hand. "You are an exceptional, interesting person. Sleep well!"

He went to his room and lay down to sleep.

On the next morning, when the carriage was ready, everyone came out on the porch to accompany him to it. Liza was dressed in a white dress with a flower in her hair, but was pale and sad. She looked at him in the same pathetic and knowing manner as yesterday: smiling, wistful, and with the same expression that she would have liked to say something special, important—for his ears only. The larks were singing and church bells could be heard. The windows of the factories shone in the light. Riding across the courtyard and later on the road to the train station, Korolev no longer thought of the workers nor of the pile-dwellings, nor of the devil, but thought about the time, possibly not too far off, when life would be as bright and joyful as that quiet Sunday morning. He thought of how pleasant such a morning was in the springtime, riding with a troika in a fine carriage and being warmed by the sunshine.

1898

Too Late the Flowers

I

I t happened on one dark, fall "after dinner" in the home of the Princess Preeklonska.

The old princess and the princess Marysya were in the room of the young prince and were wringing their hands and pleading. They were pleading as only unhappy, weeping women can: for Christ's sake, for honor, with the ashes of the father.

The old princess stood motionless before him and wept.

Giving full leeway to her tears and expression, and interrupting Marysya's every word, she laid on the prince cruel and even denouncing words, endearments, and pleas. . . . A thousand times she mentioned the merchant Fyrov, who was protesting their loan, and that the bones of the deceased father were turning in their grave, and so forth. She even mentioned Dr. Toporkov.*

Dr. Toporkov was a splinter in the eye of Princess Preeklonska. His father, Syenkoy, a peasant, had been her husband's valet. Nikifor, his uncle on his mother's side, to this day was the valet to Prince Yegoryshka. Dr. Toporkov himself in his early childhood had had his ears boxed for sloppy cleaning of the princely knives, forks, boots, and samovars. And now he—well, isn't that idiotic?—the young brilliant doctor lives like a gentleman in a devilishly large house and has a fine pair of horses, as if to spite the Preeklonskis, who had

---

*"Awkward," "Coarse," "Crude"

to go on foot and to bargain for a long time when they had to hire a carriage.

"He is respected by everyone," said the old princess, weeping and not wiping away the tears. "All love him, the rich, the beautiful, he's received everywhere . . . your former servant, nephew of Nikifor! It's shameful to tell! Why? Because he conducts himself well, doesn't carouse, doesn't associate with questionable characters. . . . Works from morning 'til night . . . and you? My God, Lord!"

Princess Marysya, a young woman about twenty years old, good-looking, like a heroine in an English novel with wonderful curly flaxen hair, large sensitive eyes the color of the southern sky, pleaded with her brother Yegoryshka with just as much energy.

She spoke at one and the same time as her mother, and kissed her brother through his prickly mustache, which smelled from sour wine, stroked his bald spot and cheeks, and stayed close to him like a frightened lapdog. She spoke only sweet words. The princess was unable to say anything to her brother that sounded caustic. She loved her brother that much! In her opinion, her dissipated brother, Prince Yegoryshka, a discharged hussar, was spokesman of the highest truth and a model of virtue of the highest quality! She was convinced, fanatically convinced, that this drunken imbecile had a heart which could be the envy of fairy-tale heroes. She saw in him an unlucky, misunderstood, unappreciated human being. She excused his drunken dissipation with what seemed almost delight. And how! Yegoryshka had convinced her long ago that he drank because of sorrow: wine and whiskey took the place of unrequited love, which wrenched his soul, and in his associations with depraved whores he was trying to erase from his hussar's head *her* marvelous picture. And what kind of a person was Marysya, what kind of woman considers love a thousand times more valid, apologizing for everything? What is she like?

"Georges!" exclaimed Marysya, snuggling up to him and kissing his haggard, red-nosed face. "You're drinking from grief, that's true. . . . But forget your grief if that's the case! Really, do all unhappy people feel they have to drink? Have patience, have courage, struggle! Be heroic! With a mind like yours, with your sense of honor, with

your big heart, you can bear all the blows of fate! O! You, poor
unlucky creatures, you're all faint-hearted. . . ."

And Marysya (forgive her, dear reader) mentioned Turgenev's
Rudin and took to explaining him to Yegoryshka.

Prince Yegoryshka lay on his bed and his red diminutive eyes
stared at the ceiling. Nothing much was going on in his head, but
in the area of his stomach he felt a pleasant fullness. He had just
eaten, drunk a bottle of red wine, and now, smoking a three-kopeck
cigar, was enjoying a rest. Feelings and thoughts that had nothing
in common were hopping around in his stupefied brain and whimpering
soul. He was sorry for his weeping mother and sister, but at the
same time wanted intensely to chase them out of the room: they
disturbed his desire to take a nap, to snore. He was angry because
they insisted on reading the riot act to him, and at the same he
was disturbed by small digs (in truth, very small) of conscience. He
was dumb, but not so dumb as not to recognize that the Preeklonski
home was really being lost, and that in part because he was a charity
case.

The old princess and Marysya pleaded with him for a long time.
The fires had been lit in the drawing room and some guests had
arrived, but they continued to plead. Finally, Yegoryshka became
bored with lying around and not sleeping. He pulled himself up
ignominiously and said:

"Okay, I'll reform!"

"Word of honor?"

"May God strike me dead!"

The mother and sister took hold of his hands and once again
made him take the oath and swear on his honor, and say may lightning
strike him on the same spot if he didn't stop carrying on his unruly
life. The old princess made him kiss an icon. He kissed the icon
and crossed himself three times. The oath was made; in one word,
it was very genuine.

"We believe you!" said the old princess and Marysya, and they
both embraced Yegoryshka. They believed him. But, how not believe
a word of honor, a desperate oath, and kissing the icon, everything
done together? And where there is love, there is also reckless faith.

They both revived, and shining, resembling the Israelites celebrating the rebuilding of Jerusalem, left to celebrate the reform of Yegoryshka. After seeing the guests out, they sat in a corner and whispered about how their Yegoryshka would reform, how he would lead a new life. . . . They decided that Yegoryshka would go a long way, that he would soon improve their circumstances and they would not have to adapt to extreme poverty—that hateful Rubicon which is crossed by those who survive after all has been squandered. They also decided that Yegoryshka was obliged to marry a rich and beautiful woman. He was so handsome, intelligent, and so knowledgeable that it would be difficult to find a woman who would be so bold as not to love him! The old princess in conclusion gave a biographical sketch of forefathers whom Yegoryshka would soon begin to imitate. Grandfather Preeklonski had been an envoy and spoke all the European languages; father, a commander of one of the most famous regiments; son would be . . . would be . . . what would he be?

"It's to be seen what he will be!" declared the old princess. "You will see!"

Getting into bed together, they continued to talk about the marvelous future. When they fell asleep, their dreams were ecstatic. While sleeping, they smiled from happiness—they were such great dreams. Fate, in truth, rewarded them with dreams for those fears which they endured on the next day. Fate isn't always stingy: sometimes she pays in advance.

Three o'clock in the morning, at the same time when the old princess had dreamed seeing her *bebé* in a splendid general's uniform, and Marysya in her dreams was applauding her brother for a brilliant speech, a plain hired cab drove up to the Preeklonski home. In the cab sat a waiter from the Chateau de Fleurs and held in his arms the noble body of the dead-drunk Prince Yegoryshka. Yegoryshka was completely unconscious and dangled in the arms of the "man" like a duck that had just had its throat cut and was being carried into the kitchen. The cabman jumped from his box and rang the doorbell at the entrance. Nikifor and the cook came out, paid the cabman, and carried the drunken body upstairs. Old Nikifor, not surprised and not horrified, with his usual efficiency undressed the motionless body, laid him in the deep featherbed, and covered him. The maid wasn't told anything. She had long ago become accustomed to her master in this state; that it was necessary to carry him, undress him, cover him, was not in the least surprising or horrific to her. A drunken Yegoryshka was normal for her.

In the morning of the next day occurred that which was horrifying.

About eleven o'clock when the old princess and Marysya were drinking coffee, Nikifor came into the dining room and informed them that something wrong was going on with Prince Yegoryshka.

"One could believe that he is dying!" said Nikifor. "Please come and look!"

The faces of the old princess and Marysya became pale as sheets. A piece of biscuit fell out of the mouth of the old princess. Marysya knocked over her cup and held her breast with her hands to contain the alarmed beating of her heart from the shock.

"He arrived at three in the morning, drunk as usual," added Nikifor with a shaking voice. "As usual . . . but now, God knows, from what he tosses about and groans. . . ."

The old princess and Marysya held on to each other and hurried to Yegoryshka's bedroom.

Yegoryshka, pale green, dishevelled, emaciated, lay under a heavy flannel blanket, panting, shaking, and tossing about. His head and hands could not rest for a moment, but were constantly moving and quivering. Groans were escaping from his chest. On his mustache was a bit of something that looked like blood. If Marysya had leaned over his face, she would have seen a wound on his upper lip and the absence of two upper teeth. From his whole body the smell of fever and liquor exuded.

The old princess and Marysya fell on their knees and sobbed.

"We are the cause of his death!" cried Marysya, taking hold of her head. "Yesterday we showered him with reproaches, and . . . he couldn't bear it! He has a delicate sensitivity! We are guilty, *Maman*!"

With the recognition of their guilt the eyes of both widened and, their bodies trembling uncontrollably, they held on to each other. Trembling people cling to each other in this way when suddenly, with noise and terrible cracking, the ceiling is coming down on them and is about to crush them under its weight.

The cook took it upon herself to run for the doctor. The doctor, Ivan Adolfovich, was a short man with a completely bald head, stupid piglike eyes, and a little round belly. They rejoiced when they saw him as if he were one of their own. He sniffed the air in Yegoryshka's bedroom, took his pulse, gave a big sigh, and frowned.

"Don't upset yourself, your honor!" he said to the old princess in a pleading voice. "I don't know, but, in my opinion, your honor, I don't find that your son is in great, that is to say, danger. . . . It's nothing!"

To Marysya, however, he said something entirely different:

"I don't know, Princess, but, in my opinion . . . in any of my opinions, Princess. In my opinion . . . his honor . . . pff! . . . *schwach** as the Germans say. . . . It all depends . . . depends, that is to say, upon the crisis."

"Is it dangerous?" Marysya asked quietly.

Ivan Adolfovich wrinkled his brow and took to declaring that for any of his opinions, he was given three rubles. He said thank you, was embarrassed, coughed, and left.

When the old princess and Marysya became more rational, they decided to send for someone more illustrious. A famous doctor was expensive, but . . . what was to be done? The life of someone close to you is worth more than money. The cook went for Toporkov. The doctor was not at home. It was necessary to leave a note. Toporkov did not respond to the request quickly. They waited for him with sinking hearts, anxiously, for a day. They waited all night; the morning came. . . . They even wanted to send for another doctor and decided that Toporkov was an ignoramus, and when he would arrive, to call him that to his face so that he wouldn't dare at another time to make others wait so long for him. The other members of the Princess Preeklonski's household, in spite of their own problems, were resentful from the bottom of their hearts.

Finally, at two o'clock on the next day, a carriage drove up to the entrance. Nikifor quickly minced to the door and within a few seconds politely took the heavy overcoat off of his nephew's back.

---

*"He's weak"

Toporkov announced his arrival with a cough, bowed to no one, and went into the patient's room. He strode past the ballroom, the drawing room, and the dining room, not looking at anyone, importantly, like a general. The creaking of his well-shined shoes was heard throughout the house. His huge figure demanded respect. He was stately, important, impressive, and devilishly correct, as if he had been carved from an elephant's tusk. His gold-rimmed glasses, his extreme seriousness, and his immobile face complemented his haughty bearing. By his parentage he was a plebeian, but there was nothing plebeian about him except his well-developed muscles. Everything about him was grand and gentlemanly. His face had a healthy color, was handsome and, if you believed his patients, even very elegant. His neck was as white as a woman's. His hair was soft like silk and beautiful, but, unfortunately, cut very short. Toporkov did not pay much attention to his appearance, and if it were up to him, he would have let it grow down to his collar. His handsome face was too cold and too serious to seem pleasant. Its coldness, seriousness, and immobility did not reveal anything but intense weariness from his daily hard work.

Marysya went to meet Toporkov and, wringing her hands, began to plead. She never before had begged anyone for anything.

"Save him, doctor!" she exclaimed, lifting her large eyes to him. "I beg you! All hope is in you!"

Toporkov passed by Marysya and went to Yegoryshka.

"Open the ventilators!" he commanded, going toward the patient. "Why are the ventilators closed? How can anyone breathe?"

The old princess, Marysya, and Nikifor rushed to the windows and the stove. Since the storm windows had already been put in, there was no ventilation. There was no fire in the stove.

"There are no ventilators," the old princess said timidly.

"Strange. . . . Hm. . . . How to treat under such conditions! I can't do anything!"

Then, raising his voice a little, Toporkov added:

"Carry him into the ballroom! It isn't so stuffy there. Call the servants!"

Nikifor rushed to the bed and stood at its head. The old princess reddened because she had no other servants besides Nikifor, the cook, and the half-blind maid. She took hold of the bed. Marysya also took hold of the bed and pulled with all her strength. The decrepit old man and the two weak women, grunting, picked up the bed and, not believing in their strength, staggering and afraid of dropping it, carried it. The old princess's dress ripped on her shoulders and something tore loose in her stomach, and Marysya's eyes saw a little green and her hands were badly bruised—Yegoryshka was so heavy! And he, medical doctor Toporkov, walked majestically behind the bed and frowned angrily because such trifles were taking up his time. He didn't lift a finger to help the ladies! What an animal! . . .

They placed the bed beside the piano. Toporkov threw off the covers and, asking the old princess questions, took to undressing the turbulent Yegoryshka. He pulled off the shirt in one second.

"Please, subdue yourself! You will not be able to endure it!" remarked Toporkov, hearing the old princess. "Those not needed must leave the room!"

Tapping Yegoryshka's chest and then turning him over on his stomach, he again tapped, quietly puffing as he listened (doctors always puff when listening), and ascertained that it was an uncomplicated drunken fever.

"It will not hurt to put on his shirt," he said in his smooth voice, emphasizing every word.

Giving a few instructions, he wrote a prescription and hurriedly went toward the door. When he had written the prescription, he had asked, among other things, the family name of Yegoryshka.

"Prince Preeklonski," said the old princess.

"Preeklonski?" questioningly repeated Toporkov.

"How quickly you have forgotten the family name of your past . . . landlords!" thought the old princess.

Even in her thoughts the old princess did not dare to use the word "masters." The figure of the former peasant was so imposing!

She went to him in the foyer and with a sinking heart asked:

"Doctor, he's not in danger?"

"I think so."

"In your opinion, he will get well?"

"I dare say," answered the doctor coldly, and, barely nodding, went down the stairway to his horses, who were as stately and grand as he was.

After the doctor left, the old princess and Marysya for the first time in the last weary twenty-four hours breathed freely. The illustriousness of Toporkov gave them hope.

"How considerate he is, how nice!" said the old princess, and in her heart she blessed all the doctors in the world. Mothers love medicine and believe in it when their children are sick!

"What an important gentleman!" noted Nikifor. For a long time now he had not seen anyone in the manor house except the debauched friends of Yegoryshka. It never dawned on the old man that this important gentleman was no other than the same, messy Kolka that more than once he had had to drag out from under the water wagon and flog.

The old princess did not let him know that the doctor was his nephew.

In the evening at sunset, exhausted from grief and fatigue, Marysya suddenly had an attack of violent shivering. This shivering made her fall on her bed. After the shivering came intense warmth and a pain in the side. She was delirious all night and moaned:

"I'm dying, *Maman!*"

Toporkov came in the morning at ten o'clock for one patient and found instead two: Prince Yegoryshka and Marysya. Marysya had double pneumonia.

The home of the Preeklonski princess smelled of Death. She was invisible but terrible, flashed over the heads of the two beds, threatening every minute to take from the old woman both of her children. The old princess was losing her mind from remorse.

"I don't know!" Toporkov told her. "I can't know, I'm not a prophet. It will be clearer in a few days."

He spoke these words drily, coldly, and with them wounded the unfortunate old woman. If only one word of hope! To add to her misery, Toporkov gave practically no instructions for the patients and occupied himself with tapping, listening, and saying that the air was foul, and that the compresses had not been placed correctly and not at the right time. All these latest methods the old woman considered useless, unintelligent nonsense. Day and night she drifted from one bed to the other, forgetting everything else, making vows and praying.

Fever and pneumonia she considered the most fatal of illnesses and when Marysya coughed up some blood, she imagined that this was the end and fainted.

You can picture for yourself the joy when on the seventh day the young princess smiled and said:

"I'm well."

On the seventh day Yegoryshka also revived. The old princess, idolizing him like a demigod, laughing and crying from happiness, approached the arriving Toporkov and said:

"I'm obliged to you, doctor, for saving my children. I am very grateful to you!"

"What is it?"

"I'm much obliged to you! You have saved my children!"

"Ah . . . the seventh day! I had expected it on the fifth. However, it's all the same. Give this powder in the morning and in the evening. Continue the compresses. You can change the heavy covers to lighter ones. Give your son sour liquids. I will come tomorrow in the evening."

And the celebrity, nodding his head, with a measured determined step walked toward the stairway.

II

It was a bright, clear day, a little cold, and one of those spring days when it is hoped that the cold and dampness and heavy boots are on the wane. The air was so clear that one could see the claws of the jackdaws sitting atop the tallest bell tower; the scent of spring saturated everything. Walk out into the street and your cheeks will be covered with a healthy ruddiness, reminding one of a good Crimean apple. The yellow leaves that had fallen long ago, while patiently waiting for the first snow had been trodden underfoot, were golden from the sunshine and gave off a luster like gold coins. Nature is permeated with silence and peace. There isn't a breeze nor a sound.

She is motionless and soundless as if exhausted, and ready for spring and summer, luxuriating under the warming, caressing rays of the sun, and looking at this beginning of peace, you yourself want to be peaceful. . . .

It was this kind of day when Marysya and Yegoryshka sat by a window and awaited the last visit of Toporkov. The sunlight, warming, caressing, came through the windows of the Preeklonskis too: it played around on the carpets, chairs, the piano. Everything was flooded with this light. Marysya and Yegoryshka were looking out the window onto the street and were glorying in their convalescence. Those having recovered from illness, especially if young, are always very happy. They feel and understand the meaning of health, which those who are accustomed to health do not feel or understand. Health is freedom, and who, besides those from whom freedom has been taken away, revel in the consciousness of freedom? Marysya and Yegoryshka felt like freedmen every minute. How wonderful it was! They wanted to breathe, look out the window, get going, live; in short, they had these wishes fulfilled every second. Fyrov, the denial of the loan, the scandals, Yegoryshka's behavior, poverty—all were forgotten. The only things not forgotten were the pleasant, undisturbing things: the fine weather, the coming balls, the good *maman,* and—the doctor. Marysya laughed and talked incessantly. The central theme of the conversation was the doctor, whom they expected momentarily.

"An amazing person, there isn't anything he can't do!" she said. "How perfect is his medical technique! Judge, Georges, what a great feat: to battle with nature and to overcome it!"

As she spoke, she placed an enormous exclamation point with her hands and eyes after every high-flown but sincere phrase.

Yegoryshka listened to the rapturous words of his sister, blinked his eyes, and agreed with her. He, too, respected the stern Toporkov and was convinced that he was obliged to him only, for his recovery. *Maman* sat nearby; beaming, exultant, she shared the joy of her children.

She found it pleasing in the doctor not only that he knew how to treat the sick, but also his "positiveness" which she succeeded in reading in his face.

Old people for some reason find such "positiveness" very desirable. "It's too bad that he . . . he is of such low parentage," said the old princess, timidly glancing at her daughter. "And his profession . . . is not especially clean. He always has to put his hands into all kinds of parts. . . . Phew!"

The young princess flushed and moved to another chair more distant from her mother. These words jarred upon Yegoryshka too.

He had no patience with class arrogance and airs.

If only poverty could teach! It did enter his mind more than once to put on the airs of people who were wealthier than he.

"Today, Mummy," he said, disdainfully shrugging his shoulders. "He who has a head on his shoulders and large pockets in his trousers is well off; he, who instead of using his head, sits on his rear end, and in place of money in his pockets, has soap bubbles, he . . . he's a zero, that's what!"

Yegoryshka was simply parroting someone else's words. He had heard these words two months ago from a seminarian with whom he had been playing a game of billiards.

"I would be happy to exchange my title for his head and pockets," added Yegoryshka.

Marysya raised her eyes in gratitude to her brother.

"I would say more, *Maman,* but you wouldn't understand," she sighed. "Nothing will dissuade you . . . unfortunately!"

The old princess, conventionally taught, was disturbed and tried to justify herself.

"However, in Petersburg, I knew a doctor—a baron," she said. "Yes, yes. . . . And abroad too. . . . It's true. . . . Education means a great deal. Well, yes. . . ."

Toporkov arrived at one o'clock. He entered just as he had the first time: with an air of importance, not glancing at anyone.

"You must not have any alcoholic drinks and avoid as much as possible any overindulgence," he addressed Yegoryshka, while putting down his hat. "Your liver has to be watched. It is remarkably enlarged. The enlargement is the result of alcohol. The only drink you are prescribed is water."

Turning to Marysya, he advised her as to what she was forbidden.

Marysya listened to him attentively, as to an interesting story, fastening her eyes upon the scientist.

"Well? You, I suppose, understand?" Toporkov asked her.

"Oh, yes! *Merci!*"

The visit took exactly four minutes.

Toporkov coughed, took his hat, and nodded. Marysya and Yegoryshka stared at their mother. Marysya even blushed.

The old princess, waddling like a duck, and flushing, went up to the doctor and awkwardly slipped her hand into his white fist.

"Allow me to thank you!" she said.

Yegoryshka and Marysya lowered their eyes. Toporkov lifted his fist to his glasses and saw a roll of banknotes. He was not embarrassed and, not lowering his eyes, he wet his fingers and it could almost not be heard as he counted the banknotes. He counted twenty twenty-five-ruble notes. It was why Nikifor hurried somewhere yesterday with the old princess's bracelets and earrings! A light shadow flickered across Toporkov's face, somewhat like a radiance such as artists paint to depict saints; his mouth curved slightly into a smile. It was apparent that he was very satisfied with the payment. Having counted the money, he put it in his pocket, nodded his head again, and turned toward the door.

The old princess, Marysya, and Yegoryshka stared at the doctor's back and all three felt at once that their hearts were being wrung. Their eyes flooded with tender feeling. This person was leaving and would not come again, and they had become accustomed to his measured steps, distinct voice, and serious face. An idea flashed through the mother's head. She suddenly wanted to be kind to this peasant.

"Poor orphan," she thought. "All alone."

"Doctor," she said in a soft, old-womanish voice.

The doctor turned around.

"What?"

"Won't you have a cup of coffee with us? Be so kind!"

Toporkov frowned and slowly took his watch out of his pocket. He glanced at the watch, thought a bit, and said:

"I'll have some tea."

"Please do sit down! Here!"

Toporkov put his hat aside and sat down: he sat stiffly like a mannequin, his knees bent and shoulders and neck rigid. The old princess and Marysya began to bustle around. Marysya's eyes grew bigger, troubled, as if she had been given an impossible assignment. Nikifor, dressed in his formal black frock and gray gloves, rushed around the rooms. In every corner of the house the sound of china dishes and the ringing of teaspoons could be heard. Yegoryshka was called quietly out of the room for something for a minute.

Toporkov sat for ten minutes waiting for tea. He sat with his eyes on the piano pedals, not moving a limb and not making a sound. Finally, a door opened from the dining room. A glowing Nikifor appeared with a large tray in his hands. On the tray in silver holders were two glasses: One for the doctor and the other for Yegoryshka. Around the glasses, observing strict symmetry, stood the pitchers with cold and hot cream, sugar with tongs, pieces of lemon with a small fork, and sponge cakes.

Behind Nikifor came Yegoryshka, whose face was bloated from pomposity.

The procession was completed by the old princess, whose brow was perspiring, and Marysya, whose eyes had grown larger.

"Please, help yourself!" the old princess said, turning toward Toporkov.

Yegoryshka took a glass, turned aside, and carefully swallowed a mouthful. Toporkov took a glass and also drank a mouthful. The old princess and the young princess sat alongside and concentrated on the doctor's needs.

"It may not be sweet enough for you?" asked the old princess.

"No, it is sweet enough."

And, as could be expected, silence reigned—an uncanny, adversarial time during which, for some reason, it was terribly awkward and disconcerting. The doctor drank and remained silent. It appeared that he was ignoring those around him and saw nothing but the tea before him.

The old princess and Marysya ardently wanted to have a conversation with the learned doctor, but did not know how to begin. Both were afraid to appear stupid. Yegoryshka looked at the doctor, and one could see from his eyes that he was preparing to ask something but could not make up his mind to do it. A deathlike silence fell, disturbed at times only by the sounds of swallowing. Toporkov swallowed very loudly. He, obviously, was not inhibited and drank as he wished. As he swallowed he made noise very much like the sound "glu." The swallow sounded as if it fell from the mouth into a ravine and there splashed against something large and smooth. The silence was broken at times by Yegoryshka. He smacked his lips and chewed as if he were testing the taste of his doctor-guest.

"Is it true what they say, that it is bad for the health to smoke?" Yegoryshka finally asked.

"Nicotine, an alkaloid of tobacco, acts upon the organism as one of the strongest poisons. It is a poison which enters the system with every cigarette in an insignificant quantity. The quantity of the poison, and its effect, depends on the persistence and prolonged necessity to smoke."

The old princess and Marysya exchanged glances: what wisdom! Yegoryshka blinked his eyes and stretched his skinny physiognomy. He, poor wretch, did not understand what the doctor said.

"In our regiment," he began, wanting to shift the technical conversation to something more ordinary, "there was an officer. One Koshechkin, a very fine fellow. He looked incredibly like you! Incredibly! Like two peas in a pod. It would be impossible to distinguish between you! Is he a relative of yours?"

Instead of answering, the doctor swallowed noisily, and the corners of his mouth rose to make a wry and scornful smile. It was noticeable that he held Yegoryshka in contempt.

"Tell me, doctor, am I completely cured?" asked Marysya. "Can I count on being healthy?"

"I suppose so. My prognosis is based on . . ."

The doctor, raising his head and fixing his eyes on Marysya, began to talk about the possible outcome of double pneumonia. He spoke smoothly, emphasizing every word, neither raising nor lowering his voice. They listened to him more intently than could be expected and with pleasure, but, unfortunately, this dried-up person did not know how to popularize and did not consider it necessary to use jargon in order to be understood. He mentioned several times the words "abscess" and "coagulated regeneration," and, in general, spoke very well and beautifully, but none of it was understood. He gave a complete lecture full of medical terms and didn't use a single phrase that could be understood by his listeners. However, this did not keep the listeners from sitting at attention with open mouths and wide eyes, almost in reverence of the learned man. Marysya did not take her eyes off his mouth and took in every word. While looking at him she compared his face with those of the faces she saw every day.

How different was this intelligent, tired face from those dissipated, dull faces of her suitors, friends of Yegoryshka, who bored her daily with their visits! The faces of the carousers and debauchers, from whom Marysya never heard a good, straightforward word, could not hold a candle to this cold, passive, but wise and arrogant face.

"Wonderful face!" thought Marysya, thrilled with the face, the voice, and the words. "What a mind and how expert! Why was Georges a soldier? He too should be a scientist."

Yegoryshka looked kindly at the doctor and thought:

"If he speaks of thought-provoking things to us, it must mean that he considers us intelligent. It's proper that we're in such company. It was terribly stupid, however, to lie about Koshechkin."

When the doctor finished his lecture, the listeners took a deep breath as if they had accomplished some kind of glorious feat.

"How great it is to know so much!" sighed the old princess.

Marysya stood up and, as if she wished to thank the doctor for the lecture, sat down at the piano and struck a few chords. She intensely wanted to involve the doctor in a conversation, delve deeper and more sensitively, and music for her always led to conversation. So, using this method, she wanted to involve this clever, perceptive person.

"That's from Chopin," intruded the old princess, smiling and folding her hands like an instructor. "Wonderful piece! I, too, have dared to capture this marvelous melody, doctor. My pupil—in former times I had a rich voice—do you know her?" And the old princess named a well-known Russian singer.

"She's obliged to me. Yes . . . I gave her lessons. A darling girl!

She was a distant relative of my late husband, the prince. . . . Do you like singing? But, why am I asking you this? Who doesn't love singing?"

Marysya began to play one of her favorite bars from a waltz and turned with a smile. She needed to read the doctor's face, to find out how her playing affected him.

But she didn't succeed in reading anything. His face was, as before, expressionless and dry. He quickly drank his tea.

"I love this part," said Marysya.

"Thank you," said the doctor. "I've had enough tea."

He took his last swallow, stood, and picked up his hat, and did not in any way express a desire to hear the rest of the waltz. The old princess rose quickly. Marysya, embarrassed and hurt, closed the piano.

"You are leaving already," said the old princess, decidedly disappointed. "Can't we offer you something else? It is my hope, doctor . . . that you know the way to our door now. In the evening, sometime. . . . Don't forget us. . . ."

The doctor nodded his head twice, awkwardly took the extended hand of the young princess, and silently went for his overcoat.

"Ice! Wood!" exclaimed the old princess after he left. "It's terrible! He doesn't know how to laugh, such a stick of wood! You wasted your time playing for him, Marie! He only stayed to have some tea! Drank and left!"

"But he's so intelligent, *Maman*! Extremely intelligent! What can he converse about with us? I'm uneducated; Georges kept to himself and was quiet. . . . Really, can we conduct an intelligent conversation? No!"

"He's a plebeian! He's Nikifor's nephew!" said Yegoryshka. "Drinks from the cream pitcher. What is he? Rationally, indifferently, subjectively . . . he comes out a rogue! What kind of a plebeian? What a carriage he has! Take a look! Smart!"

The three of them looked out the window at the carriage, in which the celebrity, in a huge bear-fur coat, sat. The old princess flushed from envy, and Yegoryshka knowingly raised his eyes and whistled. Marysya didn't see the carriage. She was unable to see it:

she was taking in the doctor, who had made a strong impression upon her. Who isn't affected by novelty?

Marysya had never met anyone like Toporkov.

The first snow came, then the second, the third, and the winter set in for a long time with its crackling frost, snowdrifts, and icicles. I don't like the winter and I don't believe those who say they do. The streets are cold, the rooms are dark, the galoshes wet. Severe like a mother-in-law, flat like an old maid, with its eerie moonlit nights, troikas, hunts, concerts, and balls, the winter becomes boring very quickly and is much too long, and poisons more than one shelterless, consumptive life.

The life in the Preeklonski home slipped by in its own way. Yegoryshka and Marysya had completely recovered and even their mother ceased to consider them as ill. The circumstances, as before, were not improved. Their affairs went from bad to worse, and there was less and less money. The old princess pawned and repawned all of her jewels, familial and acquired. Nikifor, as before, went to shops where they had credit for a variety of paltry goods, where gentlemen owed up to three hundred rubles and did not think of repaying. The cook did the same thing, and to whom, from compassion, the shop owner gave his old boots. Fyrov became even more insistent. He would not agree to any postponement and was rude to the old princess when she begged him to hold up protesting the promissory note. With Fyrov's luck, other creditors began to be noisy too. Notaries, the bailiff, and creditors came every morning to the old princess to collect. It seemed a competition had started in the business of bankruptcy.

As before, the pillow of the old princess was never dry of tears. In the daytime the old princess held back, but at night she gave complete leeway to tears and cried all night long up to the morning. You didn't have to go far to find the reason for this weeping. The reasons were right under her nose: they irritated her eyes with their boldness and vividness. Poverty insulted self-respect incessantly. Insulted . . . by whom? By worthless people, a variety of Fyrovs, the cooks, the merchants' wives. Her beloved jewels went to the pawn shops; separating with them wounded the old princess to the very core of her heart. Yegoryshka caroused as before. Marysya was still not completely well. . . . Was there any shortage of reasons for tears? The future looked cloudy, but through the clouds the old princess could see even more ominous signs. The future looked bad. There was no hope for it, only fear of it. . . .

The money became more and more scarce, but Yegoryshka drank more and more, drank persistently, with ferocity, as if he wished to make up for the time lost while ill. He soaked up everything, that which was his and that which was not his. In his dissipation he was bold and cheeky until he got sick. He had no qualms about borrowing money from the first person he could touch for it. He would sit down to cards without a coin in his pocket; it was customary for him to drink and eat on someone else's check, get around smartly in someone else's cab, and didn't consider it reprehensible not to pay the cabman. He had changed very little: previously he became angry when he was laughed at, now he became only a little embarrassed when they threw or led him out.

The only one who changed was Marysya. She had a new insight, a most frightening insight. She became disenchanted with her brother. For some reason she saw that he had nothing in common with an unrecognized, misunderstood person, but that he was simply an extremely ordinary person, like most, and even worse. . . . She stopped believing in his unrequited love. Terrible insight! Sitting for hours at the window and looking aimlessly at the street, she pictured the face of her brother and made an effort to see in it something fine, trying not to be disappointed, but could see nothing in this colorless face besides an empty man! A rotter! Along with this face, across her imagination flashed the faces of his comrades, the guests, old womanish well-wishers, suitors, and the tearful face of the old princess, dulled by misfortune—and depression squeezed Marysya's poor heart.

How trivial, colorless, and dull; how stupid, boring, and slothful was life with these relatives, these loved ones, but insignificant people!

Her heart was wrung by melancholy and her soul was gripped by a terrible, heretical wish. . . . There were times when she passionately wanted to leave, but where to? There were, she understood, places where people lived who did not tremble at the thought of poverty, did not carouse, worked, did not spend their days with dim-witted old people and idiotic drunkards. . . . And in Marysya's imagination only one decent, wise face stood out sharply; on this face she saw intelligence, enormous knowledge, and fatigue. It was impossible for her to forget it. She envisaged him every day and in the happiest of circumstances, precisely when he was working or appeared to be working.

Dr. Toporkov drove by the Preeklonski home every day in his plush sleigh with the bear rugs and fat coachman. He had many patients. He made his calls from early morning 'til late evening, and succeeded in a day to cover all the main and side streets. He sat in the sleigh as in the armchair, with an air of importance, holding his head and shoulders erect, looking straight ahead, neither right nor left. Nothing could be seen from behind the deep collar of his bear-fur coat but his gold-rimmed glasses, but for Marysya this was enough. It seemed to her that through his glasses, from the eyes of this beneficent human being, shone cold, proud, scornful rays.

"This individual has the right to be scornful!" she thought. "He's wise! What a luxurious sleigh, what magnificent horses! And this was a former serf! What enormous strength of character to be born a lackey and to make yourself, as he did, unapproachable!"

Only Marysya remembered the doctor. The others began to forget him and soon would have forgotten him entirely if he had not reminded them of himself. He reminded them too painfully.

The day after Christmas, in the afternoon when the Preeklonskis were at home, the doorbell rang gently. Nikifor opened the door.

"Is the dear old princess at . . .ho-m-e?" an old womanish voice was heard from the entry, and, not waiting for an answer, a little old hag slipped into the drawing room. "Greetings, dear princess, your honor . . . patroness! Pray, how are you?"

"What is it you want?" asked the old princess, looking with curiosity at the old hag. Yegoryshka laughed up his sleeve. It seemed to him that the hag's head looked like an overripe melon with its stem sticking up.

"Don't you know me, little mother? Is it possible you don't recognize me? Have you forgotten Prokorova? I delivered the little prince!"

The hag crept up to Yegoryshka and quickly kissed his shirt front and his hand.

"I don't understand," angrily muttered Yegoryshka, wiping his hand on his jacket. "That old devil, Nikifor, allows every kind of tr—"

"What do you want?" repeated the old princess, and she caught a whiff of the strong odor of lamp oil from the old hag.

The old hag sat herself down in an armchair and after a long pause, grinning and being coquettish (matchmakers always insinuate), revealed that the old princess had a product and she, the old hag, had a buyer. Marysya blushed. Yegoryshka snorted and, being curious, went up to the old hag.

"Strange," said the old princess. "Does that mean that you've come to make a match? Congratulations, Marie, you have a suitor! Who is it? Do we know him?"

The old hag puffed and panted, took from inside her bodice a red chintz kerchief. Untying the corners so that it could be laid flat, she threw it on the table, and along with a thimble, a photograph fell out.

They all turned up their noses: from the red kerchief that had yellow flowers on it came a strong tobacco odor.

The old princess picked up the photo and languidly brought it up to her eyes.

"A handsome man, little mother!" commented the matchmaker in order to brighten the aspects. "He's rich, well-born. . . . Wonderful person, steadfast . . ."

The old princess reddened and handed the photo to Marysya. She grew pale.

"Strange," said the old princess. "If the doctor chooses to, then, I propose, he could come himself. . . . A mediator is the least thing needed here! . . . An educated person, and supposing . . . he did send you? He, himself?"

"Himself. . . . You have already pleased him when ill. . . . You are a good family."

Suddenly, Marysya let out a cry, took the photo, and ran headlong from the room.

"Strange," continued the old princess. "Amazing. . . . I don't even know what to say to you. . . . I didn't expect this at all from the doctor. Why bother you? He could have come himself. . . . It's even insulting. . . . Who does he take us for? We're not some kind of merchants. . . . Even merchants don't operate this way any more."

"Queer bird!" Yegoryshka muttered in an undertone with a scornful look at the old hag's head.

This retired hussar would have given a great deal if he would have been permitted at least once to "snap his fingers" over this little head! He disliked old hags, like a big dog dislikes cats, and he was transformed completely by a doglike delight when he saw a head that resembled a melon.

"Well, what of it, little mother?" said the matchmaker, sighing. "Even though he is not of princely birth, I can say that, little mother-princess. . . . It's true you are our benefactors. Oh, sins, sins! So he's not of noble blood? But he's educated, rich, and the masters have showered him with luxuries, heavenly tzarina. . . . If you wish that he came, please . . . I will propose it. Why shouldn't he come? He can come. . . ."

And, taking hold of the old princess's shoulders, the old hag pulled her closer and whispered in her ear:

"Sixty-thousand is asked. . . . A well-known business! A wife is a wife and money is money. You know that yourself. . . . 'I,' he said, 'will not accept a wife without money, because she must have at my home all kinds of conveniences. . . . It is necessary for her to have her own capital. . . .' "

The old princess flushed and, rustling with her heavy clothes, got up from her armchair.

"Take it upon yourself to tell the doctor that we are extremely surprised," she said. "Hurt. . . . It is not possible for us to go about it in this way. I cannot say more to you. . . . Why are you so quiet, Georges? Well, she is leaving. . . . You needn't be patient any longer!"

After the matchmaker left, the old princess grasped her head and fell on the divan and groaned:

"What we have come to!" she wailed. "My God! Some kind of a doctor, trash, former servant, makes us a proposal! Honorable! . . . Honorable! Ha! Ha! Tell me what kind of nobility! Sends a matchmaker! If only your father were here! He wouldn't let him get away with this! Vulgar fool! Boor!"

But it wasn't all that insulting to the old princess that a plebeian, a commoner, wanted to marry her daughter as that she was asked for sixty thousand and didn't have it. She took offense at the slightest hint at her poverty. She lamented 'til late in the evening and at night awoke twice in order to have a good cry.

On no one did the visit of the matchmaker have a greater effect than on Marysya. The poor girl became feverish. All her limbs shook, she fell upon her bed, hid her fervent head under the pillow, and began, to the extent her strength allowed, to try to answer the question:

"Is this really true?"

The question was puzzling. Marysya herself did not know how to answer it. It evoked in her amazement, confusion, and a secret joy, which for some reason she was ashamed to acknowledge and which she wanted to hide even from herself.

"Is it really so?! Oh, Toporkov. . . . It cannot be! It can't be so! The old hag must have gotten it garbled!"

At the same time, dreams, the sweetest, most cherished, magical dreams which make one lose one's breath and warm the head, were buried in her brain and possessed her small person with an inexpressible delight. He, Toporkov, wanted to make her his wife, and he was so grand, handsome, and clever! He dedicated his life to all humanity and . . . rode around in such luxurious sleighs!

"Is it really so?"

"I could love him!" decided Marysya toward evening. "Oh, I'm willing! I am free of any kind of prejudices and would go to the end of the earth with this freed serf! If only Mother would say the word—and I would leave her! I am willing!"

Other questions, secondary and tertiary, she had somehow to resolve. There were enough of them! Why a matchmaker? Why and when did *he* come to love *her*? Why didn't he come himself to declare his love? How was she to approach these and other questions? She was thunderstruck, astonished . . . happy—this was sufficient for her.

"I'm willing!" she whispered, attempting in her imagination to picture *his* face with the gold-rimmed glasses, through which peered wise, steady, tired eyes. "Let him come! I am willing!"

And while in this manner Marysya tossed in her bed and felt with all her being how happiness consumed her, the matchmaker was going around to the merchants' houses and with a liberal hand distributed photographs of the doctor. She went from one wealthy home to another, seeking to find a "noble" buyer for a "product" which she could recommend. Toporkov had not sent her especially to the Preeklonskis. He sent her "wherever she wished." As to the marriage itself, which he felt was necessary, he was indifferent: he had made only one decision—not where the matchmaker would go. He needed . . . sixty thousand. Sixty thousand, no less! The house which he was intending to buy would not be sold to him for less than this sum. There was no place to borrow this amount, and there could be no agreement to pay it over time. He had only one possibility left: to marry for money, and this he did. As for Marysya, she was really not at all guilty of being part of his wishes to allow himself to be tied by Hymen's bonds.

At one o'clock that night, Yegoryshka came quietly into Marysya's bedroom. Marysya was already undressed and was trying to fall asleep. She was exhausted by her unexpected happiness: she wanted to somehow calm the incessant beating of her heart, which it seemed to her could be heard throughout the house. In every wrinkle of Yegoryshka's face there sat a thousand secrets. He softly coughed, looked at Marysya significantly, and, as if he wanted to inform her about something terribly important and secret, sat at her feet and leaned toward her ear.

"Do you know what I have to tell you, Masha?" he began quietly. "I will tell you candidly. . . . From my point of view, that . . . really, because it's for your happiness. Are you sleeping? I'm saying this for your happiness. . . . Marry this . . . this Toporkov! Don't hesitate, but go ahead, yes and . . . that'll do! He's a man of many talents . . . and he's rich. That he comes from the lower classes is unimportant. Don't give a damn!"

Marysya closed her eyes tightly. She was ashamed. At the same time, it was very pleasing that her brother sympathized with Toporkov.

"Because he's rich! At least you'll never be hungry. Whatever prince or count you're going to wait for, you'll die from hunger for something fine. . . . We don't have a kopeck! Phewt! Blank! Are you sleeping? Yes? Silence—is that a sign of agreement?"

Marysya smiled. Yegoryshka laughed a little and for the first time in his life he gave her hand a big kiss.

"Marry him. . . . He is an educated man. It will be so good for us! The old lady will stop complaining!"

And Yegoryshka became lost in dreams. Having dreamed, he shook his head and said:

"There's only one thing I don't understand. . . . Why the hell did he send a matchmaker? There's something wrong. . . . He's not the kind of person who would send a matchmaker."

"That's true," thought Marysya, and for some reason sighed. "There's something wrong here. . . . It's stupid to send a matchmaker. That's right, what does that mean?"

Yegoryshka, usually not very observant, at this time did comment:

"However, he may find it a little difficult. He's busy all day long. He's constantly rushing to the sick like one possessed."

Marysya was content, but not for long. Yegoryshka was silent for a bit, and then said:

"But it's still incomprehensible to me: he directed this witch to say that the dowry had to be no less than sixty thousand. Did you hear? 'Otherwise,' she said, 'it's no go.' "

Marysya suddenly opened her eyes, trembled all over, quickly rose, and sat, forgetting even to cover her shoulders. Her eyes flashed and her cheeks flared up.

"Did the old hag say that?" she said, taking hold of Yegoryshka's hand. "Tell her, that's a lie! People like that, that is, like him . . . would not say that. He and . . . money? Ha-ha! Such baseness can only be suspected by those who do not know how proud he is, how honorable, not money hungry! Yes! This is a superior person! They do not want to understand him!"

"I think so too," said Yegoryshka. "The old hag lied. It must be she wanted to do a good job for him. She got used to this with the merchants!"

Marysya's little head nodded in agreement and ducked under the pillow. Yegoryshka rose and stretched.

"Mother is raving," he said. "Let's not pay attention to her. So, what does this mean? Agreed? Excellent. Nothing is ruined. Madame Doctor. . . . Ha-ha! Madame Doctor!"

Yegoryshka gave Marysya's pillow a light pat and, very satisfied, left her bedroom. Lying down to sleep, he listed in his head the guests to be invited to the wedding.

"The champagne should come from Aboltykov," he thought, while falling asleep. "The hors d'oeuvres from Korchatov. . . . He has fresh caviar. Well, and the lobsters . . ."

On the next day in the morning, Marysya, simply dressed but attractive and not without thought of being attractive, sat by the window and waited. At eleven o'clock Toporkov drove by but did not stop. After dinner he passed once more with his black horses before the same windows, but not only did not drive up but didn't even glance at the window by which, with a pink ribbon in her hair, Marysya sat.

"He doesn't have time," thought Marysya, admiring him. "He will come on Sunday."

But he didn't come on Sunday. He didn't come in a month, two months, three. . . . He, you must understand, hadn't thought of the Preeklonskis, but Marysya waited and wasted from expectation. . . . Pricks, like the unusually long claws of a kitten, tore at her heart.

"Why doesn't he come?" she asked herself. "Why? Ah . . . I know. . . . He was hurt because . . . why was he hurt? Because Mama was not very polite to the old matchmaker. He now thinks that I cannot love him. . . ."

"An-i-mal!" muttered Yegoryshka, who had for the tenth time gone to Albotykov's and asked to reserve the very best champagne.

After Easter, which was at the end of March, Marysya gave up waiting.

One day Yegoryshka went to see her in her bedroom and, angrily laughing, informed her that her "husband-to-be" had married a merchant's daughter. . . .

"I have the honor to congratulate you! I have the honor! Ha-ha-ha!"

The news was especially brutal for my little heroine.

Her spirits fell and not for just a day, but for months she embodied herself in an irrational gloom and despair. She pulled the pink ribbon out of her hair and hated life. But what prejudiced and dishonest feelings! Marysya even found justification for *his* action. It was not in vain that she read novels where those married and those about to be married spite loved ones, spite—so that they would understand—sting and wound.

"He married this dummy out of spite," thought Marysya. "Oh, how badly we handled it. We were insulting about his offer of marriage! People such as he never forget insults!"

Her cheeks became pale, her lips forgot how to smile, her brain rejected dreaming about the future—Marysya became numb! It seemed to her that with her loss of Toporkov she had lost her purpose in life. What did she now need to live for if her fate remained only with fools, spongers, carousers! She was despondent. She noted nothing, paid no attention to anything, paid no attention to what was said; her boring, colorless life dragged on, such as those of our unmarried women, old and young. . . . She ignored her suitors, of whom she had many, ignored her relatives, her acquaintances. She looked with indifference and apathy upon their poor circumstances. She didn't even care when the bank sold the princely home of the Preeklonskis with all its family history, which for her was just so much baggage; and so it happened that they had to move to new quarters that were modest, cheap, and in lower-class taste. It was a long, troubling sleep not deprived, all the same, of dreams. She dreamed of Toporkov in all his situations: on his sleigh, in his fur coat, without his coat, sitting, importantly striding. Her whole life was wrapped up in dreams.

But the thunder rolled—and the dreams left the blue eyes with flaxen eyelashes. . . . The old princess, not able to overcome the ruin, sickened in the new apartment and died, not leaving the children anything besides a blessing and some clothing. Her death was a terrible blow for the young princess. The dreams left in order to make room for misery.

III

Fall arrived as damp and muddy as the previous year.

Outside, the tearful morning was gray. Dark gray clouds, as if smeared with mud, thickly covered the sky and their low density brought gloom. It seemed the sun did not exist. For a whole week it did not glance once upon the earth, as if it were afraid to soil its rays in the slippery mud. . . .

The raindrops pattered against the windows with an exceptional intensity, the wind wailed in the chimneys and whined like a dog who has lost his master. . . . You could not see a single figure that did not reflect a desperate tedium.

This same desperate tedium was surpassed by the insurmountable misery that shone on Marysya's face this morning. Shuffling along on the slippery mud, my heroine was heading for Dr. Toporkov's. Why was she going to him?

"I am going to be treated!" she thought.

But don't believe her, dear reader! It is not without cause that one can read struggle in her face.

The princess approached Toporkov's house and shyly, with a sinking heart, pulled the doorbell. Within a minute, steps were heard from behind the door. Marysya felt her legs freeze and fold under her. The lock of the door clicked and Marysya saw before her the questioning face of a pretty maid.

"Is the doctor home?"

"Patients are not received today. Tomorrow!" answered the maid and, shivering from the dampness, stepped back. She banged the door in front of Marysya's very nose, shivered, and noisily locked the door.

The princess was confused and languidly dragged herself home. At home awaited her a performance that had already plagued her for a long time. The scene was far from princely.

In the small drawing room on the divan, which was covered in glossy chintz, sat Yegoryshka. He was sitting in the Turkish fashion with his legs tucked under him. Near him on the floor lay his lady-friend, Kaleria Ivanovna. They were both playing "little noses" and were drinking. The prince was drinking beer, his playmate drank

Madeira. The one who won, along with the right to strike the opponent in the nose, received a twenty-kopeck coin. With Kaleria Ivanovna being a woman, there was a slight change in the fine: instead of paying twenty kopecks, she could pay with a kiss. This gave them both indescribable pleasure. They rolled around with laughter, pinched each other, and constantly jumped from their places and chased each other. Yegoryshka was carried away by a foolish rapture when he won. He was thrilled by Kaleria Ivanovna's clowning when she lost and paid him off with a kiss.

Kaleria Ivanovna was a tall and slender brunette with extremely dark eyebrows and bulging goggle-eyes who came to Yegoryshka every day. She came to the Preeklonski's at ten in the morning, had tea, dinner, and supper, and left around one o'clock at night. Yegoryshka swore to his sister that Kaleria Ivanovna was a singer, that she was respectable, and so forth.

"Speak with her!" Yegoryshka insisted to his sister. "She's smart! Passionate!"

Nikifor, in my opinion, was more correct in evaluating Kaleria as a gadabout and referred to her as "Cavalry's Ivanovna." He hated her with all his being and lost control when he had to serve her. He sensed the truth, and the instinct of an old, dedicated servant told him that this woman did not belong with his masters. . . . Kaleria Ivanovna was stupid and vapid, but this did not prevent her from leaving the Preeklonskis with a full stomach, with winnings in her pocket, and convinced that they could not exist without her. She was the wife of a club marker, that's all, but this did not stop her from taking over the Preeklonski home. This contemptible woman even liked to put her feet on the table!

Marysya lived on a pension which she had received after her father's death. The father's pension was larger than the usual general's pension. Marysya's share, however, was small. But even this small amount would have been enough to live decently if Yegoryshka hadn't had so many whims.

He, having no desire and no ability to work, did not want to believe that he was poor and lost his temper if he were asked to moderate his circumstances and possibly cut out some of his excesses.

"Kaleria Ivanovna doesn't like lamb," he told Marysya from time to time. "It's necessary to have roast chicken for her. What the hell! You're trying to be the mistress but you don't know how. Don't have this foolish lamb! We'll starve this woman to death!"

Marysya protested weakly, but in order to avoid unpleasantness bought the chicken.

"Why wasn't there a roast today?" Yegoryshka would storm sometimes.

"Because we had chicken yesterday," answered Marysya.

But Yegoryshka knew nothing about the household accounts and didn't want to know anything. At dinner he insisted on having beer for himself and wine for Kaleria Ivanovna.

"How can you have a decent dinner without wine?" he asked Marysya, shrugging his shoulders and acting amazed at such human stupidity. "Nikifor! Where's the wine? It's your job to see to this! And you, Masha, aren't you ashamed! I'm tempted to take over the managing myself! It's as if you enjoy making me lose patience!"

This was an unrestrained Sybarite! Kaleria Ivanovna soon appeared in his defense.

"Isn't there any wine for the prince?" she asked when setting the table for dinner. "Where is the beer? Someone must go for beer! Princess, give the servant money for beer! Do you have any small change?"

The princess said that there was small change and gave her last. Yegoryshka and Kaleria ate and drank and did not see how watches, rings, and earrings belonging to Marysya, one thing after another, left for the pawnshop, and how her expensive clothing was sold to the secondhand clothes dealers.

They did not see or hear with what creaking and muttering old Nikifor opened his trunk when Marysya borrowed money from him for the next day's dinner. These evil and stupid people, the prince and his mistress, did not consider it any of their business!

On the following day at ten o'clock in the morning, Marysya headed for Toporkov's. The door was opened by the same pretty maid. Conducting the princess into the entrance and helping her off with her coat, the maid sighed and said:

"Do you know, Miss, that the doctor will take no less than five rubles a visit? You know this?"

"Why is she telling me this?" thought Marysya. "What effrontery! He, poor man, does not know that he has such an impertinent servant!"

At the same time, Marysya felt her heart miss a beat: she had only three rubles, but he would not chase her away for two rubles.

From the entry Marysya went into the reception room where there already sat many patients. Most of those craving to be treated were, as to be expected, ladies. They took up all the furniture in the reception room, were spread out in groups, and were chatting. The talk was very lively and covered everything and everybody: the weather, their ailments, the doctor, children. . . . They spoke loudly and laughed as if they were at home. Some, while waiting their turn, were knitting and embroidering. There were no people simply or poorly dressed in the reception room. Toporkov received patients in the neighboring room. They entered as their turn came. They entered with pale faces, serious, trembling slightly, and came out flushed, perspiring, as if they were coming out of the confessional, as if having shed some kind of back-breaking load, and made happy. Toporkov gave each patient no more than ten minutes. It must have been that the ailments were not serious.

"This all looks like charlatanism!" Marysya would have thought if she had not been immersed in her own thoughts.

Marysya was the last to enter the office. Entering this office, which was overflowing with books that had German and French titles inscribed on their bindings, she shook as a chicken shakes when it has been plunged in cold water. *He* stood in the middle of the room, leaning his left arm on the desk.

"How handsome he is!" flashed through his patient's head before anything else.

Toporkov had never been painted, and he really did not know anything about painting, but the poses which he sometimes assumed materialized somehow as especially grand. The pose, in which Marysya found him, reminded one of those magnificent models from which artists paint great generals. Near his hand, which was on the desk, was a pile of five- and ten-ruble notes that had just been received from patients. Also lying there in what appeared to be a specific order were instruments, clippers, tubes—none she could at all understand, extremely "scientific" to Marysya. The office also, with its luxurious furniture all matching, completed the glamorous picture. Marysya closed the door behind her and stopped. . . . Toporkov motioned to an armchair. My heroine quietly went toward the armchair and sat down. Toporkov moved elegantly and sat down in another armchair across from her, and set his questioning eyes upon Marysya's face.

"He doesn't recognize me!" thought Marysya. "Otherwise he would not be silent. . . . My God, why is he silent? How shall I begin?"

"Well?" Toporkov asked in a low voice.

"I have a cough," whispered Marysya, and, as if to support her words, she coughed twice.

"For how long?"

"It has been for two months now. . . . At night it is worse."

"Hm. . . . Do you have a temperature?"

"No, it seems I don't. . . ."

"It appears that you have been a patient of mine? What was your illness previously?"

"Pneumonia."

"Hm. . . . Yes, I recall. . . . You, if I'm correct, are Preeklonskaya?"

"Yes. . . . My brother was also ill at the same time."

"You will take this powder . . . before bedtime . . . avoid being chilled. . . ."

Toporkov quickly wrote a prescription, arose, and assumed his former pose. Marysya also rose.

"Nothing more?"

"Nothing."

Toporkov stared at her. He looked at her and at the door. He was short of time and was waiting for her to leave. And she stood and looked at him, feasted her eyes, and waited for him to say something. How fine he was! A moment of silence passed. Finally, she roused herself, observed on his lips a yawn and in his eyes expectation, handed him the three-ruble note, and turned toward the door. The doctor threw the money on the desk and closed the door after her.

On the way home from the doctor, Marysya was furious with herself.

"Why didn't I speak to him? Why? I was a coward, that's what! It all turned out so stupidly. . . . Simply upset myself. Why did I hold those revolting rubles in my hands, as if to show them off? Money—such a delicate matter. . . . Lord preserve us! It can be insulting to a person! Payment should be made unobtrusively. Well, why did I keep silent? . . . He would have informed me, enlightened me. . . . It would be obvious why he sent a matchmaker. . . ."

Arriving at home, Marysya lay on her bed and hid her head under the pillow, as she always did when she was aroused. But this did not succeed in calming her. Yegoryshka came into her room and began to pace, his boots stomping and squeaking.

His face was inscrutable. . . .

"What's up with you?" asked Marysya.

"A-a-a . . . I thought that you were sleeping. I didn't want to disturb you. I want to tell you about something . . . very pleasant. Kaleria Ivanovna wants to live with us. I invited her."

"That's impossible! *C'est impossible!* Whom did you ask?"

"Why isn't it possible? She's very pleasing. . . . She'll help you manage the household. We can give her the corner room."

"*Maman* died in the corner room! That's impossible!"

Marysya rose and trembled as if she had been pierced by something. Red blotches appeared on her cheeks.

"That's impossible! You'll kill me, Georges, if you insist on living with this woman! Darling, Georges, it's not necessary! It's not necessary! My dear! I beg you!"

"Well, what is it about her you don't like? I don't understand! A peasant woman acts like a peasant woman. She's smart, lots of fun."

"I don't like her. . . ."

"Well, I love her. I love this woman and want her to live with me!"

Marysya cried. Her face became distorted by despair. . . .

"I will die if she comes to live here. . . ."

Yegoryshka whistled something under his nose and, strutting a little, left Marysya's room. He returned in a minute.

"Lend me a ruble," he said.

Marysya gave him the ruble. She felt it was desirable to smooth the incensed Yegoryshka with something. He now had a fierce battle with himself: his love for Kaleria was clashing with his sense of duty!

In the evening Kaleria came to the young princess.

"Why don't you like me?" asked Kaleria, embracing the princess. "You know this makes me unhappy!"

Marysya released herself from the embrace and said:

"Not for anything could I like you!"

She paid dearly for this remark! Kaleria was settled within a week in the room where the *maman* had died, and, before anything else, found it necessary to take revenge for this declaration. The revenge she chose was exceedingly coarse.

"Why are you putting on airs?" she asked the princess at every dinner. "You're so poor you shouldn't put on airs, but bow to the well-off people. If I had known that you were so impoverished, I wouldn't have come here to live. Why did I come to love your brother?" she added, sighing.

Reproaches, hints, and smirks ended in laughter at Marysya's poverty. Yegoryshka thought nothing of this ridiculing. He considered himself bound to Kaleria and was resigned. The idiotic laugh of the billiard marker's wife and Yegoryshka's mistress poisoned Marysya.

Marysya spent whole evenings in the kitchen and, helpless, weak, indecisive, she shed tears on Nikifor's wide palms. Nikifor sniveled along with her and gnawed away at Marysya's wounds with recollections of the past.

"God will punish them!" he comforted her. "You mustn't cry."

In the winter Marysya went to Toporkov again.

When she entered his office, he was sitting in an armchair, as previously, handsome and grand. This time his face exhibited extreme exhaustion. . . . His eyes blinked like those of a person who had not been allowed to sleep. He, looking at Marysya, nodded toward an armchair opposite his. She sat down.

"His face is pained," thought Marysya, looking at him. "He must be very unhappy with his merchant wife!"

They were silent for a minute. Oh, with what pleasure she would have given him her life! She would lead him a life such as could not even be read about in any of the French and German writers.

"A cough," she whispered.

The doctor looked kindly at her.

"Hm. . . . Do you have a fever?"

"Yes, in the evenings. . . ."

"Do you perspire at night?"

"Yes. . . ."

"Undress. . . ."

"In what way?"

Toporkov, impatiently with a gesture, pointed to his own chest. Marysya, blushing, slowly unbuttoned her shirtwaist.

"Undress. Quickly, please!" said Toporkov and picked up his little hammer.

Marysya took one arm out of the sleeve. Toporkov went quickly toward her and, in the blink of an eye, with a practiced hand took her gown down to her waist.

"Unbutton your chemise!" he ordered and, not waiting for Marysya to do this herself and to the great terror of his patient, took to tapping her chest with the little hammer. . . .

"Keep your arms down. Don't meddle. . . . I won't eat you," muttered Toporkov, and she flushed and passionately wished that the earth would swallow her.

After having tapped, Toporkov began to listen. The sound of the apex of the left lung appeared extremely dull. Clearly heard was the sharp wheezing and hard breathing.

"Get dressed," said Toporkov, and he began to ply her with questions: was the apartment decent, what kind of life did she lead, and so forth.

"You need to go to Samara," he said, and gave her a complete lecture on how she should live. "When you are there you'll drink *kymis.** I'm through. You are free to go."

---

*fermented mare's milk

Marysya haphazardly fastened her buttons, awkwardly gave him five rubles, hesitated a little, and left the scientist's office.

"He gave me a whole half-hour," she thought on her way home, "and I kept quiet! Kept quiet! Why didn't I say anything to him?"

As she walked home she did not think of Samara but of Dr. Toporkov. Why did she need to go to Samara? There, it was true, would be no Kaleria Ivanovna, but then there would be no Toporkov!

Forget about it, this Samara! As she walked she was annoyed and at the same time elated: *he* recognized her as a patient, and now she could go to him without excuses as much as she felt, at least every week! His office was so attractive, so cozy! Especially attractive was the divan, which stood at the rear of the office. She wanted to sit on this divan with him and converse about a variety of differences, to complain, to advise him not to charge his patients so much. From the rich, of course, you can and must charge a lot, but for poor patients some concessions should be made.

"He doesn't understand the way things are; he can't distinguish between the poor and the rich," thought Marysya. "I will teach him!"

This time, at home, a gratuitous exhibition awaited her. Yegoryshka had thrown himself in a hysterical fit upon the couch. He wailed, cursed himself, shook as if in a fever. Tears streamed down his drunken face.

"Kaleria has left!" he lamented. "She hasn't slept here for two nights! She's angry!"

But Yegoryshka's wails were unnecessary. Kaleria came in the evening, forgave him, and took him with her to a club.

Yegoryshka's decadence was reaching an apogee. . . . Marysya's pension was too small for him, and he began to "work." He borrowed money from household servants, cheated at cards, stole money and things from Marysya. Once, while walking alongside Marysya, he filched two rubles from her pocket, which she had saved in order to buy herself boots. He kept one ruble for himself and with the other one bought some pears for Kaleria. His acquaintances abandoned him. The former visitors to the Preeklonski home, friends of Marysya, called him a "shining swindler" to his face. Even the "girls" at the Chateau de Fleurs looked at him with disbelief and laughed at him when he got money from some unsuspecting new acquaintance whom he had invited to have supper with him.

Marysya saw and perceived this apogee of debauchery. . . .

Kaleria's impudence was also reaching a peak.

"Keep out of my clothing, please," Marysya said to her once.

"I'm not harming your clothing," answered Kaleria. "If you consider me a thief, then . . . if you wish . . . I'll leave."

Yegoryshka, swearing at his sister, spent a whole week throwing himself at the feet of Kaleria, begging her not to leave.

But this kind of existence could not go on indefinitely. Every tale has an ending, and so this novelette ended too.

Lent arrived and with it came days that were harbingers of spring. The days became longer, melting snow streamed from the roofs, from the fields came fresh breezes that made you feel spring coming when you breathed in the air. . . .

On one of these Lenten evenings Nikifor was sitting by Marysya's bed. Yegoryshka and Kaleria were not at home.

"I'm feverish, Nikifor," said Marysya.

Nikifor sniveled and gnawed away at her wounds with memories of the past. . . . He spoke of the late prince, of the old princess, their life. . . . He described the woods where the late prince had hunted, the fields over which he had galloped after rabbits, and of Sevastapol. The late prince was wounded at Sevastapol. Marysya loved especially the descriptions of the country estates that were sold five years ago to pay off debts.

"From the terrace you could see . . . the beginning of spring. My God! You couldn't take your eyes off God's world. The forest was still dark, but from there it was as if it were blazing from sheer delight! The stream was high, deep. . . . Your little mother, when she was young, wanted to catch fish with a fishing rod. . . . She would stand by the water for whole days. . . . We loved to stay out-side. . . . Nature!"

Nikifor became hoarse from recounting all this. Marysya listened and would not let him leave. On the face of the old lackey she saw all that which he told about her father, her mother, of the country estate. She listened, peered at his face, and she wanted to live, to be happy, to catch fish in the same river just as her mother had. . . . The river, the fields along the river, and behind the fields in the distance, the woods seemed blue, and over all this the sun was tenderly shining and warming. . . . To live was good!

"Darling, Nikifor," uttered Marysya, grasping his dry hand, "sweet one . . . lend me five rubles tomorrow . . . for the last time. . . . Is it possible?"

"It's possible. . . . I have just five rubles. Take it, it's nothing. . . ."

"I'll give it back, darling. It's a loan."

On the following day in the morning, Marysya got dressed in her best dress, tied her hair with a pink ribbon, and went to Toporkov. Before leaving home, she looked in the mirror a dozen times. A new maid met her at the entrance to Toporkov.

"Do you know?" asked the new maid of Marysya, while helping her out of her coat. "The doctor takes no less than five rubles for his services. . . ."

This time the waiting room was packed with patients. All the furniture was occupied. One man even sat on the piano. The reception of patients began at ten o'clock. At twelve o'clock the doctor had to perform an operation and resumed seeing patients at two o'clock. It was already four o'clock when it was Marysya's turn.

Not having had tea, exhausted from waiting, tremulous from fever and emotional excess, she was not even conscious of how she got to the armchair opposite the doctor. Her head seemed hollow, her mouth was dry, and her vision was hazy. This haziness allowed her to see only glimpses. . . . *His* head appeared for a moment, for a moment his hands, the hammer. . . .

"Did you go to Samara?" the doctor asked her. "Why didn't you go?"

She did not answer. He tapped her chest and listened. The dullness on the left side had taken over almost the whole lung. A dullness could be heard in the top of the right lung.

"You needn't go to Samara. Don't go," said Toporkov.

And Marysya dimly saw something that looked like compassion in his immobile, serious face.

"I will not go," she whispered.

"Tell your parents that you are not allowed to go out. Refrain from eating fatty, overcooked food. . . ."

Toporkov started to give advice, got carried away, and gave a whole lecture.

She sat, heard nothing, and through the haze looked at his moving lips. It seemed to her that he was talking too long. He finally became quiet, rose, and, waiting for her to leave, stared at her.

She did not leave. . . . She liked sitting in this fine armchair and she was afraid of going home to Kaleria.

"I'm finished," said the doctor. "You are free to leave."

She turned her face toward him and regarded him.

"Don't make me leave!" the doctor could have read in her eyes if he were only a minor analyst of physiological communication.

Her eyes filled with tears; her hands weakly dropped down the sides of the armchair.

"I love you, doctor!" she whispered.

And a red glow, such as follows a powerful fire in the soul, spread over her face and neck.

"I love you!" she whispered once more, and her head swayed twice, weakly sank, and her forehead rested on the desk.

And the doctor? The doctor blushed for the first time during all the years of his practice. His eyes blinked, as a boy's does when he is forced to his knees. Not once had he ever heard such words and in such a way from a patient! Not from a single woman! Had he ever heard such?

His heart became troubled and began to race. . . . In his confusion he had a fit of coughing.

"Meekolasha!" was heard from the neighboring room, and at the half-opened door the two rosy cheeks of his "merchant" wife appeared.

The doctor made use of this call and quickly walked out of the office. He was glad to take advantage of anything in order to get away from this awkward situation.

When he returned ten minutes later, Marysya was lying on the divan. She was lying on her back with her face turned up. One hand, along with a strand of hair, was hanging limply to the floor. Marysya was unconscious. Toporkov, flushed and with a furiously beating heart, went quietly to her and unbuttoned her shirtwaist. He unbuttoned one button and, not even noting this himself, ripped her shirtwaist. Out of all the flounces, the openings, and ins and outs of her dress, on to the divan fell his prescriptions, his cards, both visiting and photographic. . . .

The doctor sprinkled some water on her face. . . . She opened her eyes, rose upon her elbow, and, looking at the doctor, pondered. She was asking: Where am I?

"I love you!" she moaned, recognizing the doctor.

And her eyes, full of love and pleading, stared at him. She stared like a wounded young animal.

"What can I do?" he asked, not knowing what to do. . . . He asked with a voice unknown to Marysya, uneven, indistinct, but gentle, almost loving. . . .

Her elbow collapsed and her head sank on to the divan, but her eyes continued to stare at him. . . .

He stood before her, saw the pleading, and felt himself in a terrible situation. His heart beat rapidly, and in his head whirled something unusual, unrecognized. . . . Thousands of uninvited memories filled his feverish head. Where did these memories come from? They were resurrected by these loving and pleading eyes.

He recalled his early childhood and the cleaning of the nobility's samovars. After the samovars and the slaps flashed the memories of the benefactors, benefactresses in their heavy gowns, and spiritual teachers who sent him away for being "cheeky." After the spiritual teachers with their rods and the gruel with sand came the seminary. At the seminary was Latin, hunger, dreams, reading, and a love affair with the daughter of the father-housekeeper. He recalled how, in spite of the wishes of his benefactors, he fled the seminary to go to the university. He fled without a coin in his pocket in worn-out boots. How much charm there was in this escape! At the university was hunger and cold for the sake of being able to do scientific work. . . . A difficult road!

Finally, he had conquered; with his own head he pierced the tunnel of life, passed through this tunnel, and . . . so what? He knew his work superbly, worked hard, was ready to work day and night. . . .

Toporkov glanced sideways at the five- and ten-ruble notes that were piled on his desk, recalled the gentry from whom he had just taken this money, and flushed. . . . Was it really only for the five-ruble notes and the gentry that he worked so diligently? Yes, only for these. . . .

And under the pressure of these recollections, his magnificent body shrank, the proud bearing disappeared, and his smooth face wrinkled.

"What can I do?" he whispered once more, looking into Marysya's eyes.

He became ashamed before these eyes.

And what if she asks: What have you done and what have you achieved during all of your practice?

Five-ruble notes and ten-ruble notes and nothing more! The education, life, peace—all was given up for them. And they gave him this library, an elegant desk, horses, all that which in one word is called comfort.

Toporkov recalled his "ideals" at the seminary and his dreams at the university, and these armchairs and divan covered with expensive velvet, the floor covered by a thick rug, these wall lamps, the three-hundred-ruble clock appeared to him as terribly mired in filth!

He went before Marysya and gathered her up in his arms out of this filth upon which she was lying.

"Don't lie here!" he said and moved away from the divan.

And, as if in thanks, a cascade of marvelous flaxen hair fell onto his chest. Near his gold-rimmed glasses shone someone else's eyes. And what eyes! Such that one cannot resist wanting to touch them with one's fingertips!

"Give me some tea!" she whispered.

*   *   *

On the following day Toporkov sat with her in a first-class compartment. He was taking her to the south of France. Strange man! He knew there was no hope of recovery, knew this exceedingly well, like his five fingers, but he took her. . . . During the whole trip he kept tapping, listening, asking. He did not want to believe what his medical knowledge told him, and with all his strength tried to tap out and hear from her chest at least a little hope!

Money, which even yesterday he had avidly hoarded, he poured out in huge sums on this trip.

He would now have given all he had if one lung of this girl did not give out these cursed wheezes! They both desired so much to live! The sun rose for them and they anticipated the day. . . . But the sun did not save them from the darkness and . . . it is too late for flowers to bloom in the fall.

Princess Marysya died, having lived only three days in southern France.

Toporkov, after his return from France, lived as before. As before, he treated the gentry and stashed away five-ruble notes. However, it can be noted that there was a change in him. When speaking with women, he did not look at them directly but into space. . . . For some reason it became excruciating for him when he looked at a woman's face. . . .

Yegoryshka is alive and well. He has gotten rid of Kaleria and now lives in Toporkov's house. The doctor took him into his home and dotes upon him. Yegoryshka's chin reminds him of Marysya's chin, and because of this he allows Yegoryshka to squander his five-ruble notes.

Yegoryshka is very content.

1882

In the Hospice for the Terminally Ill and the Aged

Every Saturday evening, the school girl Sasha Yenyakina, a small, scruffy-looking girl in torn boots, goes with her mother to the E—sky Hospice for the Terminally Ill and the Aged. Her grandfather, Parfeney Savich, a retired lieutenant of the Guards, lives there. In the grandfather's room it is close and smells of lamp oil. On the walls hang some ugly pictures; they had been cut out of the magazine *Nymphs*: bathers; nymphs basking in the sunlight; a man with a top hat tilted back, looking through a chink in a wall at a naked woman, and so forth. There were cobwebs in the corners, crumbs and fish scales on the table. . . . And the old man is also not good to look at. He is old and bent over and is messy with his tobacco. His eyes are rheumy and his toothless mouth gapes constantly. When Sasha and her mother come in, the grandfather smiles, and his smile looks like a big wrinkle.

"Now, what?" asks the grandfather, approaching Sasha. "What's your father doing?"

Sasha doesn't answer. Her mother begins to cry softly.

"Does he still play the piano in taverns? That's true. . . . All this because of disobedience, of arrogance. . . . He married your mother and . . . the fool left. . . . Yes. . . . An aristocrat, son of a well-born father, and he married a 'nothing,' married this one—an actress, Seryozha's daughter. . . . Seryozha was a clarinetist who cleaned the stables. . . . Howl, howl, little mother! I speak the truth. . . . You were a slut, and still are a slut!"

Sasha, looking at her mother, Seryozha's daughter and an actress, also begins to cry. A difficult, weird pause ensues. . . . An old man with a wooden leg brings in a small samovar made of red copper. Parfeney Savich puts in a pinch of some kind of strange, very bulky, and very gray tea, and brews it.

"Drink!" he exclaims, filling three big cups. "Drink, actress!"

The guests pick up the cups. . . . The tea is nasty, gives off a mouldy odor, and it is impossible to drink it: the grandfather is insulted. After the tea, Parfeney Savich puts the granddaughter on his knee, and, looking at her with tearful affection, begins to fondle her. . . .

"You are the granddaughter of a renowned family. . . . Don't forget it. . . . Our blood is not that of some kind of actors. . . . Don't look at my poverty or that your father bangs on the piano in taverns. Your father, because he is wild and arrogant, and I, because of poverty, live in ignominy, but we were important. . . . Ask around who I was! You'll be amazed!"

And the grandfather, stroking Sasha's little head with his bony hand, continues:

"In our whole province there were only three important people: Count Yegor Grigorich, the governor, and I. We were the leaders and the most important. . . . I, granddaughter, was not wealthy. . . . All I had was some lousy land—about 13,500 acres and 600 dead souls—and nothing else worthwhile. I didn't have an in with the colonels, nor an important relative. I wasn't a writer, nor any kind of a Raphael, nor a philosopher. . . . A human being, in a word, only a human being. But for all this—listen, granddaughter!—I didn't take my hat off to anyone. The governor called me Vasey, I shook hands with the Reverend Bishop, and Count Egor Grigorich was my best friend. And because of this I knew how to live in an enlightened way in the European style."

After this long introduction, the grandfather told about his past way of life. . . . He spoke for a long time with passion.

"I made fools of the peasant women and forced them to get on their knees in order to make them writhe," he muttered among other things. "When the peasant woman writhes, the *muzhiks* laugh. . . . The *muzhiks* laugh, and you would laugh too, and it's lots of fun for you. . . . For those who could read, I had another punishment, not so rough. They had to learn by heart the accounts book or I would order them to climb onto the roof and read aloud from *Youria Miloslavski* and to read it so that I could hear it inside in my rooms. . . . If the spiritual punishment was not performed, then the physical was used. . . ."

Telling about this discipline without which, in his words, "a man is like theory without practice," he notes that punishment is necessary to counteract rewards.

"For very significant deeds, as, for example, catching a thief, I paid well: I married old men with young girls, I saw that young men weren't recruited for the army, and other such things."

In his day, he, the grandfather, enjoyed himself as "no one now enjoys himself."

"There were sixty musicians and singers at my place, despite the meagerness of my means. The conductor of the musicians was a Jew, and of the singers—an unfrocked deacon. The Jew was a great musician. . . . The devil can't play like he, this cursed one, played. This rogue could draw out of the double bass such vibratos, we would say, as a Rubenstein or a Beethoven, that couldn't be gotten out of a violin. He studied music abroad, was greedy for all the instruments, and mastered them all. He had only one liability: he smelled of rotten fish, and this shortcoming made him lose some of his privileges. On holidays, for this reason, he had to be placed behind a screen. . . . The unfrocked deacon too was not a fool. He knew his music and how to conduct. He was so strict that even I was amazed. He achieved whatever he pursued. The basso sometimes sang descant, and a woman with a deep voice sang with the bassos. . . . He was a master, this brigand. . . . He looked important, dignified. . . . But, he was a heavy drinker, and you know, granddaughter, it's like this. . . . It's bad for some but useful for others. The singer had to drink because the vodka thickened his voice. . . . I paid the Jew a hundred rubles a year, but to the defrocked deacon I didn't pay anything. . . . He lived in my house and had one meal, so he got his payment in kind: groats, meat, salt, girls, wood, and so forth. Life for him at my house was comfortable, though sometimes I threw him out. . . . I recall when once I was corrupted by him and by Seryozha, her father, your mother's father, and . . ."

Sasha suddenly jumped off his knee, and pressed close to her mother, who was pale as a sheet and was trembling slightly. . . .

"Mama, let's go home. . . . I feel terrible!"

The grandfather comes toward the granddaughter, but she turns away from him and, quivering, presses even more firmly against her mother.

"She must have a headache," says the mother with an apologetic voice. "It's time for her to go to bed. . . . Farewell. . . ."

Before leaving, Sasha's mother goes up to the grandfather and, blushing, whispers something into his ear.

"No, I will not give you anything!" barks the grandfather, frowning and mumbling. "I won't give a kopeck! Let her father get money for her boots at the taverns—and I won't give a kopeck. . . . I'm not going to pamper you! I'm generous with you, but from you, other than cheeky letters, there's nothing to be seen. You know that your dear husband sent me a letter the other day. . . . 'I would rather,' he writes, 'roam from tavern to tavern than to grovel for some crumbs, than to lower myself before Plyoushkin. . . .' Ah! That's what he writes to his father!"

"But you must forgive him," pleads Sasha's mother. "He is so unhappy, so high-strung. . . ."

She pleads for a long time. Finally, the grandfather angrily spits, opens up his small chest, screens it with his whole body, takes from it a yellowed, greatly wrinkled piece of paper currency. . . . The woman takes the currency with two fingers and, as if afraid to be soiled by it, quickly shoves it into her pocket. . . . Within minutes she and her little daughter quickly walk through the dark gates of the hospice.

"Mama, don't take me again to grandfather!" Sasha says tremulously. "He's terrible."

"That's impossible, Sasha. . . . We have to go there. . . . If we don't go there, we will starve. . . . Your father has no source of income. He is ill and . . . he drinks."

"Why does he drink, Mama?"

"He is unhappy, and drinks because of this. . . . Look here, Sasha, don't tell him that we went to grandfather. . . . He will get angry and then will cough a great deal. . . . He is proud and does not like us to plead. . . . You won't tell him, will you?"

1884

He and She

They lead the life of nomads. They award a few months only to Paris, while they are stingy with the time spent in Berlin, Vienna, Naples, Madrid, St. Petersburg, and other capital cities. They feel at home in Paris; for them Paris—is their residence. The rest of Europe—is boring, dominated by muddle-headed provincialism that you only observe through the lowered shades of the Grand Hotel or from the stage. They are not old, but they have already succeeded in having been two or three times in all the European capitals. They are bored with Europe, and they have begun to talk about going to America, and they will continue to talk about it until they are convinced that her remarkable voice was waning and was not worth displaying in both hemispheres.

It is difficult to see them. It is impossible to see them on the streets because they drive around in carriages: drive, when it is dark—in the evenings and at night. They sleep until dinnertime. They usually awake in a bad mood and receive no one. They receive visitors only sometimes, at an indefinite time, backstage, or at supper.

She can be seen on posters which are for sale. On the posters she is a beauty, but in reality she's never been a beauty. Don't believe the posters: she's ugly. The majority see her on the stage. But on the stage she is transformed beyond recognition. She is powdered, rouged; Indian ink and wigs cover her own face like a mask. It is the same at recitals.

When she is Margarita, she, a twenty-seven-year-old—wrinkled, sluggish, with a nose covered by freckles—appears elegant and as a good-looking seventeen-year-old girl. She resembles herself the least when she is on the stage.

If you really want to see them, get the right to be present at the dinners which are given in her honor, and which she herself gives sometime before leaving one capital city for another. You can get to the dinner by invitation only. . . . At these are the reviewers, the local singers, directors and conductors, the opera buffs and the connoisseurs with their slick bald pates that always attach themselves to the theater, and the toadies, thanks to their gold, silver, and alliances. These dinners are not dull for an observant person—they are interesting. . . . It pays to join them for a couple of meals.

The renowned (among the diners there are many of these) eat and talk. They appear uninhibited: the neck leans in one direction, the head in another, the elbows—on the table. The old ones even pick their teeth.

The journalists have chairs closest to hers. They are all a little drunk and conduct themselves free and easy, as if they had already known her for a hundred years. If they took just one infinitely small step further, it would be familiarity. They loudly crack jokes, drink, interrupt each other (at the same time remembering to say "pardon!"), propose pompous toasts, and, it appears, are not afraid to act like fools; some of them, in a gentlemanly way, tumble across the corner of the table and kiss her hands.

After having paid attention to the reviewers, they instruct the dilettantes and the connoisseurs. The dilettantes and the connoisseurs keep quiet. They are envious of the journalists, smile patronizingly, and drink only red wine, which at these dinners is exceptionally fine.

She, the tzarina of these dinners, is dressed simply, but terribly expensively. A large diamond on her throat glitters from under her lace collar. On each arm—a huge, unembellished bracelet. Her hairdo is as wild and as loose as can be imagined: the ladies love it, the men do not like it. Her face is bright and lights on every diner with her widest smile. She knows how to include everyone at once in her smile, kindly nodding her head; the nod reaches all the diners. Take a look at her face and you will see that she is surrounded by friends only, and toward these friends she entertains the most tender feelings. Toward the end of the dinner she gives someone her picture; on the back she writes the name of the happy recipient and her own autograph. She speaks, of course, in French, but as the dinner concludes she speaks in other languages. Her French and German are laughable, but even her mistakes sound charming. In general, she is so charming that you forget for a long time that she is—ugly.

And he? Oh, *le mari d'elle** sits about five seats away from her, drinks a great deal, eats a great deal, keeps silent, makes little balls from his bread, and reads the labels on the bottles. When you look at him, you sense that he has nothing to do, is tedious, lazy, and bored. . . .

He is fair-haired with a bald patch, which is spreading over his head. Women, wine, sleepless nights, and roaming over the wide world have caused furrows to cover his face and leave deep wrinkles. He is only thirty-five, not more, but looks much older. His face looks as if it had been soaked in vinegar. His eyes are attractive, but apathetic. . . . At one time he wasn't, but now he is ugly. His legs are bowed, his hands are swarthy, his neck hairy. Thanks to these bent legs and unique gait, for this reason, he is poked fun at in Europe as a "rocking perambulator." When he wears tails he reminds one of a wet jackdaw with a dry tail. The diners ignore him. He reciprocates in the same vein.

Drop in on a dinner, look at them, at this married couple, keep an eye on them, and tell me what bound and what binds these two people.

Having observed them, you will answer (it is roughly understood) in this way:

She is a famous singer; he is only the husband of a famous singer or, if you use the expression from behind the scenes, "the husband of his wife." She earns up to eighty thousand a year in Russian money, and he doesn't work; consequently, he has time to be her servant. She needs a cashier and a person who can manage the affairs with the business men, the contracts, and negotiations.

---

*"her husband"

... She has knowledge only of the applause of the public, and as for the box office receipts, she does not stoop to make this prosaic side her responsibility. It follows, therefore, that she needs him as a parasite, as a servant. . . . She would get rid of him if she knew how to manage her affairs herself. He, on the other hand, receives from her a very good salary (she hasn't the slightest notion about the value of money!), and as sure as two times two equals four, he steals from her as do the maids, squanders her money, carouses recklessly, maybe even squirreling some away for a rainy day—and he is content with his status, like a worm buried in a good apple. He would leave her if it weren't for the money.

That's what everyone thinks and says, who observes them during the dinners. They think and talk that way because they don't have the possibility of penetrating more deeply than external appearance. They look upon her as the diva. They keep away from him as a pygmy who is covered by a froglike slime; and at the same time this European diva is bound to this little frog in an enviable, noble marriage.

This is what he writes:

"They ask me, why do I love this shrew? It is true, this woman doesn't deserve love. She also doesn't deserve hatred. What she deserves is to be ignored, given no attention to her existence. In order to love her, you either have to be me, or mad, or both.

"She is not beautiful. When I married her, she was ugly, now and long ago. She has no forehead; in the place of eyebrows over her eyes are two barely noticeable lines; in the place of eyes she has two deep slits. From these slits nothing shines: neither intelligence, nor desire, nor passion. Her nose—is like a potato. Her mouth is small, pretty, and therefore her teeth are ghastly. She doesn't have breasts or a waistline. She smooths over the last defect, however, with her devilish knowledge of how to artfully and in the most natural way to tighten a corset. She is short and stout. She is entirely fat and flabby. Her whole body has shortcomings and—that which I consider the most important—the complete absence of femininity. A pale skin and weak muscles I don't consider feminine, and in this respect I differ with the opinion of others. She is not a lady, nor a well-born woman, but a shopkeeper with crude manners: she walks flapping her arms; when she sits, she crosses her legs, rocks back and forth with her entire body; when she is lying down, she raises her legs, and so forth.

"She is untidy. Especially characteristic of this are her suitcases. Her clean underwear is mixed with the dirty, cuffs with slippers and my boots, new corsets with those that are no longer useful. We never receive guests because our rooms are constantly a filthy mess. Ah, what else can be told? Look at her when she awakes at noon and lazily slips out from under the covers and you won't recognize the woman with the voice of a nightingale. . . . Uncombed, her hair full of knots, with sleepy, swollen eyes, in a nightgown with torn shoulders, barefooted, squinting, shrouded by the previous night's tobacco smoke—does she look like a nightingale?

"She drinks like a hussar, whenever it suits her and whatever she likes. She's been drinking for a long time. If she didn't drink, she'd be better than Patti, or in any case, just as good. She has drunk up half of her career and soon will drink up the other half. The lousy Germans taught her to drink beer, and now, before she lies down to sleep, she drinks two or three bottles. If she'd stop drinking, her stomach catarrh would disappear.

"She's ignorant, so why do student audiences sometimes invite her to their concerts?

"She loves publicity. Publicity costs us several thousand francs a year. I despise publicity with all my heart. No matter how much this stupid publicity costs, it will always be worth less than her voice. My wife loves to have her head stroked and does not like to be told the truth if it does not sound like praise. She finds the purchased Judas kiss more pleasant than the gratuitous criticism. She is completely unaware of her own quality!

"She is smart, but she lacks education. Her brains have long ago lost their flexibility; they have been covered with fat and sleep.

"She is capricious, changeable, doesn't have a single firm conviction. Yesterday she said that money is rubbish, that there is no essence in it, but today, she will give concerts in four places because she has come to the conviction that nothing is more important than money. Tomorrow she will say that which she said yesterday. She doesn't recognize nationality, she has no political heroes, doesn't prefer any newspaper, or has any favorite authors.

"She is rich, but doesn't give to the poor. Besides, she often underpays the milliners and dressmakers. She has no heart.

"This woman has been spoiled a thousand times over!

"Take a look at this shrew when she's made up, her hair slicked down, corseted, moving toward the footlights in order to compete with the nightingales and the larks meeting the sunrise in May. How great the dignity and the charm in this swanlike bearing! Take a good look and you will, I implore you, be attentive. From the moment she lifts her hands and opens her mouth, her slits turn into large eyes and fill up with sparkles and passion. Nowhere else will you find such marvelous eyes. When she, my wife, begins to sing, when the first trills run through the atmosphere, when I begin to feel that under the influence of these marvelous sounds my agitated soul calms down, then glance at my face—and the secret of my love will be revealed to you.

" 'It's true isn't it, that she's magnificent?' I ask my neighbors.

"They say: 'Yes,' but that's not enough for me. I want to annihilate anyone who could think that this extraordinary woman is not my wife. I forget everything that went on previously and I live only in the present.

"Take a look; what an actress! How much deep thought has been given to every movement! She understands everything: love and hate and the human soul. . . . No wonder the theater shakes from applause.

"After the last act, pale, worn out, having in one evening lived through a lifetime, I usher her out of the theater. I'm also pale and exhausted. We get into a carriage and ride to the hotel. In the hotel, she, silent, doesn't undress, but throws herself on the bed. I, silent, sit on the edge of the bed and kiss her hand. On this evening she does not chase me away. We do sleep in the same bed together, sleep 'til morning and awake in order to tell each other to go to hell and . . .

"Do you know there's yet another time when I love her? When

she attends balls or dinners. And here I love the inimitable actress. Really, what an actress you must be in order to outwit and overcome your natural self, as she can. . . . I can't recognize her at these stupid dinners. . . . From a plucked duck she makes a peacock. . . ."

This description is written in a drunken, barely legible handwriting. It is written in German and is speckled with spelling mistakes.

Here is what she writes:

"You ask me, do I love this fellow? Yes, sometimes. . . . Why? God knows. . . .

"It is true he is ugly and not congenial. People like he are born without the right to or the ability for reciprocal love. Such people as he can only buy love, it is not given to them as a gift. Judge for yourself.

"He's dead drunk night and day. His hands shake and that is very repulsive. When he is drunk, he grumbles and is impertinent. He even hits me. When he is sober, he lies down on anything that's around and sulks.

"He is eternally shabbily dressed even though he has more than enough money for clothes. Half of what I earn slips away, who knows where, through his hands.

"There's no way to control him. The unlucky artists have terribly expensive cashiers. The husbands receive half the receipts for their work.

"He doesn't spend money on women, I know that. He despises women.

"He is a wastrel. I have never seen him do anything. He drinks, eats, sleeps—and that's it.

"He never graduated from anything. He was expelled for insolence from the university in the first year.

"He is not a gentleman, but worst of all, he is a German.

"I don't like the German gentry. For every hundred Germans, ninety-nine are idiots and one is a genius. I learned this last from a German prince disguised as a Frenchman.

"He smokes a revolting tobacco.

"But he has his good sides. He loves my noble art more than I do. If before going on the stage I announce that I am sick and cannot sing, that is to say I'm being capricious, he struts around like death is facing him and clenches his fists.

"He is not a coward and is not afraid of the public. I like that in people more than anything else. I'll tell you about a small episode in my life. It happened in Paris about a year after I had left the conservatory. I was still very young then and was learning how to drink. I was partying every evening as much as my young endurance permitted. I was, of course, partying with friends. At one of these wild parties, when I was chug-a-lugging with these experienced drinkers, the table was approached by an unattractive and unknown young lad who, staring into my eyes, asked:

" 'Why are you drinking?'

"We all howled with laughter. My young lad didn't flinch.

"The second question was even more cheeky and was straight from the heart.

" 'Why are you laughing? These scoundrels, who are making a drunkard of you with wine now, won't give you a penny when you lose your voice from drink and become a beggar!'

"What audacity! My associates became noisy. I sat this young lad down beside me, and ordered wine for him. It became apparent that this champion of sobriety was a great drinker.

"*À propos* why I call him a young lad, it's only because he had such a small mustache.

"For his boldness I paid him by marrying him.

"His avoidance of speech is even greater. The most he will say is one word. He speaks this word with a hoarse voice, with a quaver in his throat, and with a convulsive face. This word comes out when he is sitting among people, at a dinner, at a ball. . . . When someone (it makes no difference who it is) speaks a falsehood, he raises his head and, looking at nothing, without embarrassment exclaims:

" 'Untrue!'

"That is his favorite word. What kind of a woman will protest against the one who exclaims this with a gleam in his eyes? I love this word, I love the gleam, and the spasm on the face. Not everyone knows how to exclaim this excellent, bold word, but my husband emits it all the time and everywhere. I love him sometime, and this 'sometime' as much as I can recall, coincides with the sounding off of this fine word. However, God only knows why I love him. I'm a poor psychologist, and in this instance, it seems, one broaches a psychological question. . . ."

This description was written in French in a beautiful, almost masculine, handwriting. You will not find a single grammatical error in it.

1882